White Heat

White Heat

JILL SHALVIS

New York Boston

Copyright © 2004 by Jill Shalvis
Excerpt from *Blue Flame* copyright © 2004 by Jill Shalvis
Excerpt from *It Had to Be You* copyright © 2013 by Jill Shalvis
Cover design by Melody Cassen, cover photograph © Rjlerich/Dreamstime.
Cover copyright © 2013 by Hachette Book Group, Inc.

Forever Yours
Hachette Book Group
237 Park Avenue, New York, NY 10017
www.hachettebookgroup.com
www.twitter.com/foreverromance

First e-book and print on demand editions: March 2013

Forever Yours is an imprint of Grand Central Publishing.
The Forever Yours name and logo are trademarks of Hachette Book Group, Inc.

The publisher is not responsible for websites (or their content) that are not owned by the publisher.

The Hachette Speakers Bureau provides a wide range of authors for speaking events. To find out more, go to www.hachettespeakersbureau.com or call (866) 376-6591.

ISBN 978-1-4555-2964-3 (e-book edition)
ISBN 978-1-4555-4755-5 (print on demand edition)

To Paul and Colleen Wilford, for all the time and invaluable help, I thank you both from the bottom of my heart.

Dear Readers,

I have a thing for firefighters. I always have. There's just something about a guy who's willing to put his life on the line for others, isn't there? The job itself suggests being strong of mind and body and is innately masculine. (With apologies to the women firefighters out there, you're all beautiful!).

Years ago, I wrote three romances featuring firefighter heroes. The books have been out of print for a long time now and never made it to the digital age. My wonderful publisher has taken them out of obscurity and is reissuing them as ebooks.

WHITE HEAT, BLUE FLAME, and SEEING RED are not connected books, so they can be read in any order. Keep in mind they were written a long time ago and are not from this smart phone/digital age. But one thing they do have in common with my more recent books is a sexy, hot hero and a happily ever after.

Hope you enjoy!
Best wishes,

White Heat

Prologue

The surf raged against the rocks on the shore with a violence that, oddly enough, soothed his soul. Seagulls dipped and glided in the fading light, in and out of the faint fingers of fog kissing the Pacific Ocean.

If he squinted, that fog could be smoke. If he cocked his head and listened, the calls of the seagulls could be cries of anguish and disbelief.

So Griffin Moore didn't squint, didn't listen. He just sat on a rock, arms resting on his bent legs, watching the sun slowly sink toward the horizon. Behind him the hills of San Diego stood out against a darkening sky. To his right, lights flickered as commuters made their way home on the 5 South, to their families, friends. Lovers.

Griffin waited for the wave of pain over that. After all, not that long ago, on another coast entirely, one of those cars might have been his as he headed toward his own life. And he'd had a great one. Warm family, lifelong friends—

Ah, there came a twinge now. Yeah, he'd had it all. Interesting that the thought didn't come with the stabbing pain it used to.

He ran his fingers through the sand at his sides as he thought about that—

"Southern California instead of Southern Carolina," someone drawled. "Who'd have thought?"

The unbearably familiar voice went right through him as at his side appeared a pair of scuffed tennis shoes he'd have recognized anywhere. Griffin kept his gaze on the pounding waves and realized why he felt such little pain—he was numb. Blessedly numb. "I asked you not to come."

"Yeah." His younger brother toed a rock loose from the sand, then bent and picked it up. Studying it, he said, "But when have I ever done anything you've asked of me?"

"Brody—"

"Save it." Brody hurled the rock into the spraying surf with an anger that matched the sea. Then he hunkered at Griffin's side, his voice softer now, only his eyes reflecting the swirling emotions that ate at both of them. "You're my brother, Grif. I miss you. I—"

"Don't say you're worried about me."

"I'm worried about you—"

"Damn it." Griffin surged to his feet, shoved his fingers in his hair, and turned so that he wouldn't have to see that worry for himself.

But even with his back to the only person who'd managed to find him in all this time, the sweet numbness that had taken him so many months to achieve dissolved faster than the salty ocean spray on the breeze. "Go away."

"Can't do that."

There was no missing all that was there in Brody's voice: fear, sorrow, need.

Too bad. At twenty-eight and thirty-two years old, they were grown men now. Plenty old enough for separate lives.

But that wasn't exactly fair, and Griffin knew it. They'd been close as far as brothers went; closer still as friends and confidantes. Close enough to live in the same town, hang with the same crowd. Close enough for Griffin to have spent plenty of years of his own worrying about Brody's lack of drive, lack of ambition.

The fact that the black-sheep son now worried about the golden one didn't escape him; it was just that he didn't care. *Couldn't* care. "I want to be left alone," he finally said.

"Yeah, I think I got that. But I have a job for you."

Griffin stared at the man who looked so like him. Same sunstreaked brown hair. Same blue eyes. Same long, lean build. He let out a raw laugh. "A job. That's pretty funny."

"Really? Why?"

"Because unless you've made some great transformation in the past year…" Griffin reached for a rock, too, and chucked it into the sea. "Jobs give you hives, remember?"

"I remember everything. And did I say I had a job for *me?*" Brody let out a mock shudder. "Let's not go overboard, here. I have one for *you.*"

"Doing what? Counting clouds as they go by? Because that's all I'm interested in at the moment." Griffin took another rock, a flat one, and tried his skills at skipping it. It bounced over the water one, two… five times. That's what sitting on a beach all day did for him, it built great rock-skipping skills. Good to know the time hadn't been wasted.

Brody watched the bottom of the sun butt up against the edge of the horizon. Then he picked up another rock. "There's this mountain range in Mexico, near the northwest corner of Copper Canyon." His rock sank after three bounces. "Alpine forests, cold stream canyons, amazing fly-fishing—"

"You've been spending Dad's money fly-fishing in Mexico again?"

"And down there, this wildland fire has taken root in the hills."

Griffin's half smile froze. So did his body, poised to skim another rock.

"It's threatening this village, you see, and yes, I know about it from a fly-fishing trip I just took not too far from there. Because of the big drought this year, there are so many bigger fires in Mexico burning that this one is small potatoes. What makes it worse, their firefighters have antiquated equipment, no agency backup, nothing. They really need a team leader for this one—"

Griffin's gut tightened as any lingering happy little numbness vanished. "No."

"Come on, Grif. They need someone with experience. You know all too well this fire-fighting shit is dangerous. People die. They need someone who's been out there, someone capable of organizing a crew—"

"No." That was all in his past. Maybe he *used* to organize crews, and maybe he used to be quite good at it. But his hotshot teams had worked together for years, and lived and breathed as a unit.

They weren't talking about teams here, not in rural Mexico. They were talking farmers, ranchers, whoever they could get, trying to save their land and their homes. No training, no experience.

No, thank you.

"They're in trouble," Brody said with rare seriousness. "Real trouble. There's no insurance, no money, nowhere to evacuate to if it comes to that. Are you hearing me? If San Puebla burns, these people are left out there in the wilderness with nowhere to go." He picked up another rock. "Tell me that as a former member—make that a *leader*—of an elite hotshot crew with fifteen years of experience that you just don't give a shit. Look me in the eyes and say it."

Griffin looked him right in the eyes. His dead heart didn't flinch. "I don't give a shit."

With a barely contained anger, Brody let the rock go. It skimmed the rushing water six times. He brushed his hands clean and shoved them in his pockets. "You never used to be able to lie to my face before that last fire that wrecked you."

"It didn't wreck me. I lived, remember?"

"Yeah, I remember. I just wasn't sure *you* did."

"Twelve others didn't," Griffin said hoarsely. The men who had died were like brothers to him.

"Yeah," Brody said quietly over the sound of the pounding surf. Darkness had fallen now, hiding Griffin's face, but Brody could hear the sorrow in his brother's voice. "And it was tragic as hell. *Tragic,* Grif. But it's time to stop putting your life on hold while you grieve. You've got to think about starting to move on."

Move on. Sure, that's what people did. But he couldn't. He didn't know how. "I don't want to talk about this."

"I know, but guess what?" Brody's smile was grim. "We're not only talking about it, you're going to Mexico to help fight that fire. You're getting back on the roller coaster of life, so to speak."

"Hell no."

"Oh, you're going," his brother repeated with utter conviction. "If I have to make you."

"*Make* me?" A low laugh escaped Griffin at that. He had to hand it to his brother. He hadn't laughed in all this time, but somehow Brody had made him do it. "At six foot two, I have two inches on you."

"So?" Brody sized him up with an eagle eye. "For almost a year now, you've lived hard with slim rations, I can see it all over you."

"Who cares?"

"You've lost weight, man. I bet we weigh the same now. I can take you." He lifted a brow to accompany that cocky statement.

Griffin let out a breath, feeling a little weak as memories flooded him…Sean, Paul, gone. Greg, too—God, he still couldn't take thinking about them.…

"I brought your gear."

Griffin shook his head. If he'd been going to fight fires again, he'd do it right here in the country he'd adopted all this past year. Hell, he'd even been offered a job with the San Diego Fire Department, twice, but it didn't matter.

He wasn't going to fight fires again. "Brody…what is this really about?"

"You. Me. Mom and Dad. I don't know, pick one. Maybe I'm tired of waiting for you to stop wasting your life away, watching you let one terrible twist of fate ruin your life."

"I keep telling you, it didn't ruin *my* life. *I'm* still alive."

"Yeah? Can you say any of their names yet?"

Unable to believe his nerve, Griffin stared at him. "Go to hell."

"How about Greg," Brody said softly in the night. "Your best friend for twenty years. Can you call his wife and shoot the breeze with her yet?"

"You're an asshole."

"Yeah." Brody's face was grim. "Now here's how this is going to work. You're going to Mexico. You're going to remember how to be a forest firefighter because that's who you are, not some beach bum. You're going if I have to force you myself." His voice softened. "Please, Grif. Do this. Remember how to live."

"I'm not ready."

Brody simulated the sound of a game show buzzer. "Wrong answer."

"Don't be ridiculous. I'm not going anywhere."

"Here's ridiculous. You go—or I tell Mom, and Dad, and all the friends you still have left and have so pathetically neglected in all this time, where you are. I'll bring them out here and let them see you. Hound you. *Feel sorry for you.*"

Griffin's stomach twisted. He turned in a slow circle, sandwiched between the sea and the green hills. "I don't care."

"Oh, yeah, you do."

He let out a disparaging sound. "You've never been particularly inspired about anything before. Why now? Why me?"

Brody studied the waves, lit by a few early stars and the city behind them. "You know, I'd have liked to lay around on this beach with you and just watch the clouds form—and believe me, I'd have come if you'd invited me even once—which you didn't. So now I'm forced into motivational mode." A long, martyr-packed sigh shuddered out of him. "You'd better get packed. You're outta here at the crack of dawn."

"I haven't said I'd do this."

"No, but you will."

"Brody—"

"You're going because you'll do anything to avoid talking to the people you left behind. Am I right, or am I right?"

"I'm talking to *you*, aren't I?" Frustration welled through Griffin. He didn't want to do this; he didn't want to do anything. "This is asinine. I can't…I can't even think about…"

"I know," Brody said very gently. "I *know*. I also know the most social you've been in the past year is to ask the cashier to supersize your fries with your burger, but that's going to change. It has to. What happened wasn't your fault. Stop acting like it was." With a quick salute, he began walking away—leaving Griffin all alone, as he'd chosen to be all this time.

It was all about choices, Griffin thought. Even now, he could choose to remain in solitude.

But for how long?

Once upon a time, he and Brody had shared everything—the good, the bad, and the ugly. And he knew, as a matter of Moore pride, neither of them had ever backed off a dare, or made an idle threat.

Griffin had just witnessed Brody's determination firsthand, and he knew his brother well. Brody would have Mom out here on the first flight. If necessary, Phyllis Moore would walk the two thousand miles if she had to. She'd hover, she'd boss, she'd talk his ear off. She'd hug him tight, she'd offer such love—

No. God, no.

He wouldn't be able to take it, he just wouldn't. Just the thought of her, of his dad, of any of the friends he doubted he still had clogged his throat.

He could run. Maybe the Bahamas this time, though he'd miss San Diego, which had been an easy place to be lost in.

Idly he studied his brother's retreating back. Brody's shoulders were stiff with purpose, his stride sure and unwavering and filled with determination.

Nope, the Bahamas weren't far enough away. Nowhere was.

"*Shit.*" He picked up one last rock. Skipped it into the ocean. Resigned himself to facing his future.

Whatever that was.

1

To Lyndie Anderson, nothing beat being in the cockpit. With the wind beneath her wings and her Cessna's tank full to the brim, the rest of the world fell away and ceased to exist.

Not that the world noticed. She could fall off the planet itself and not a ripple would be felt.

She liked it that way.

No ties, her grandfather had always told her. *Ties held one down. Ties hampered a person's freedom.*

Lyndie wouldn't know if that was true or not, as the last of her own personal ties—her grandfather, a staunch lifer in the military—was gone now.

Kick ass.

That had been his motto, his mantra. He'd taught it to her on her first day of kindergarten, when she'd stood before her military elementary school, quaking in her boots.

He'd loved nothing more than to have her repeat it back to him. At five years old, she'd stared out of the corner of her eye at the school, where she could see other little girls dressed in their pretty dresses and shiny shoes and ribbons. They all danced their way through the front door with nary a look back at their misty-gazed mothers, while the camouflage-clad Lyndie had suddenly wanted to cling to the man no one else had ever dared to cling to.

"Kick ass," she'd repeated to him softly.

"What?" Her grandfather had carved a hand around his ear and frowned. "Can't hear that pansy whisper. Speak up, girl."

"Kick ass, *sir*!" She'd lifted her chin and saluted, aware of the mothers looking her way, no doubt horrified at the rough and tough–looking little girl with the nasty language.

Her own social status had been cemented that long-ago day, but her grandfather had tossed his head back and roared with gruff laughter, as if it had been their own private joke.

And it had been. She'd lost her parents two years before that in a car accident, and by kindergarten her memory of them had faded. Few had dared interfere with her grandfather, and as a result, there hadn't been much softness in her childhood. That had been fine with Lyndie, who wouldn't have recognized softness anyway.

They'd moved from base to base, and after her grandfather had whipped each of those bases into shape, they'd take off for the next. She couldn't remember how many schools she'd attended, having lost track at the count of fifteen before graduating and gravitating toward a similar nomadic lifestyle as a pilot for hire. But she could remember how many different planes she'd flown. She could remember each and every one of them, with her grandfather riding shotgun, teaching her everything he knew.

Those planes had been her real home, and over the years she'd honed her skills, flying whatever she could get her hands on and loving it. When her grandfather died and his nest egg had come to her, she'd upgraded her old beater Cessna 172 to a six-seater 206, which some liked to say was nothing but a big old station wagon with wings.

She loved her *Station Air* as she fondly referred to it. The big thing sure came in handy. Now, at twenty-eight, she worked for an international charity organization out of San Diego called Hope International. She was paid to fly volunteering experts into regions desperate for their aid. Doctors, dentists, engineers, financial experts…she'd flown so many she'd lost track.

She was flying one such expert now, a U.S. forest firefighter this time, to a small but remote wildland fire in the Barranca del Cobre, an area in northwestern Mexico.

Thanks to her job, she'd spent a lot of time in this particular mountainous region. Surprisingly enough, she'd fallen for the wide, open, undiscovered beauty, and had made it her mission to fly south as often as possible, ensuring that each and every one of the myriad of hidden villages received dental and health care, or whatever they needed. Not a small job.

But right now one of her favorites, an especially isolated village named San Puebla, needed help with a slash-and-burn ranch fire. Due to limited water sources and remoteness, the flames had escaped control. Compounding the problem was the severity of the drought this year, and the fact that wildfires had become a nationwide crisis.

More than seventy Mexicans had lost their lives in this season alone in the deployment of airplanes, helicopters, and firefighters. In southeastern Mexico, 250 Mexican firefighters currently were hard at work, along with 550 military personnel and 2,400 volunteers, all battling the out of control fires still burning. Guatemala and Honduras were threatened by similar situations. The San Puebla fire was considered insignificant in comparison.

No doubt, they desperately needed help. She had some of that help on its way. The man in her Cessna had been a firefighter in South Carolina, and had the skills necessary to organize a big crew.

And a big crew was needed. Just a few days ago the fire had been at twenty acres, but it'd escalated since, blooming over three hundred acres now, threatening the village.

"Kick ass," she said to herself, with a grim smile for the man who was no longer around to see her do exactly that.

"We almost there?"

This from her passenger. Firefighter Griffin Moore had gotten on board casually enough, without a glance at her, though she'd glanced at him. She always glanced at a good-looking man; it was a sheer feminine reaction of healthy hormones.

But in the last few moments, since the change in altitude from San Diego as they climbed over the Barranca del Cobre, sailing through majestic peaks dangerous and remote enough to swallow them up if they wanted to, he'd begun to exhibit signs of nerves.

"We're about sixty miles out," she said of the just over five-hundred-mile flight.

"Bumpy ride."

His voice was low, gravelly. As if he didn't use it often. And since he spoke to the window, she wasn't clear on whether he was making an idle observation or complaining.

At least he hadn't hit on her. It happened, and every time it did, it both surprised and amused her. Most of the time she was so wrapped up in her work she actually forgot she was female. But then some guy, usually a gorgeous one—she'd never understood why the better-looking ones always turned out to be jerks—figured her for a captive audience. Not that she had anything against men in general. Actually, she enjoyed men very much, she just liked to do her own picking. And she *was* picky.

Bottom line, her life was flying. And unlike Sam, her boss at

Hope International—a man who appreciated the finer, more delicate dance of getting women into his bed—*she* didn't consider the experts she flew prospective lovers.

When a passenger wouldn't take no for an answer, she had no problem explaining the basics. One, she was a black belt. And two, she wasn't afraid to open the passenger door—in the middle of a flight—to assist an annoying passenger off the plane.

That threat alone usually warded off any further advances.

But this man hadn't so much as spared her a glance. He hadn't even spoken until now. "There's always turbulence right here," she explained, trying to be a good hostess. "And to tell you the truth, it's going to get a little worse."

He lost his tan.

"Need a bag?" Damn it, she'd just cleaned out the back yesterday. "Let me know."

Oh, *now* he looked at her. Right at her with icy blue eyes and a voice turned hardened steel. Except for a sensual mouth, the rest of his face might have been carved from stone. "I'm not going to be sick in your plane."

How many times had she heard that from some cocky expert, usually a know-it-all surgeon pressed into doing charity work by his hospital, only to spend the rest of the day cleaning up the back of her plane?

Once again, she eyeballed her forest firefighter, who was dressed in the dark green Nomex pants of his profession, with a darker green T-shirt tucked in. Broad shoulders and long legs, both of which made fitting into the compact seats a challenge. Light brown hair clipped short. His big hands gripped the armrests. Not good. Not good at all. "You sure you're okay?"

He had a quietly sober face, expression unyielding, gaze unflinchingly direct. "Just get me there."

A charmer. But since she never bothered to be charming either, that didn't bother her. She looked away from him and glanced down at the alpine crests lined with a green ribbon of conifers and small, hidden rivers as far as the eyes could see. Glorious, and a small part of her heart—not usually tied to any land—squeezed.

It squeezed even more when she got over the next peak. Off in the distance, marring the stark blue sky, grew a cloud of smoke that was so much bigger and more threatening than she'd imagined, her throat closed up.

This guy better be good at his job, she thought, and looked him over once again, this time assessing for strength and character. She already knew he hated to fly, which seemed odd. "I'm taking it you're not a smoke jumper."

He had his face plastered to the window, clearly trying to get a better view of the fire, impossible to do with the smoke impeding their visibility. "I didn't drop out of planes, no."

Didn't. Past tense. Odd…"A hotshot, then?"

"Yes."

So he battled his fires from the ground, in fiery, unfathomable conditions requiring strength and stamina, facing mayhem and death at every turn. Still…"You knew you'd have to fly here, right? Maybe you should keep your volunteering closer to home if you don't like to get on a plane."

"Thanks. I'll keep that in mind." His knuckles were white on the armrests. He shifted in the seat and bumped his knees. He was a pretty big guy. Rather mouthwatering, too, if she was being honest, and she usually was. There was a suppleness to all that lean muscle—and a good bit of pure power. It was obvious that physical labor was a part of his lifestyle, weak stomach or not. Interesting.

Taking her eyes off him, she simultaneously turned the control wheel and applied rudder pressure for an eastward banking turn.

He let out a low oath.

"Don't worry," she said. "I could fly this thing upside down and backward and still get us there."

If possible, his grip on the armrest tightened.

"Really," she said. "This is just a barely more challenging approach than most because of the quick change in altitude, but I've done it so many times I could—"

"Yeah. Fly it upside down and backward. Got it."

A smart-ass, too. That bothered her even less than the lack of charm, but because he'd gone an interesting shade of green, she wanted to keep him talking instead of puking. "You do this often? Volunteer?"

"No."

"Yeah, I hear a firefighter's schedule can be pretty hectic. Twenty-four hour shifts, right?"

He lifted a shoulder.

"Well, I hope you're braced for that because you're going to hit the ground running down there. There are people in danger of losing everything. And believe me, they don't have much to begin with."

With another noncommittal grunt, Griffin pressed closer to the window so she could no longer see even his profile, but she had no problem getting the message.

Conversation over.

Fine. She'd only been trying to help him forget to lose his lunch in her clean plane. Instead, she'd concentrate now on getting them there. Time was of the essence this time around. Beneath them lay Copper Canyon, a breathtaking network of more than twenty canyons covering 20,000 square miles. Four times the size of the Grand Canyon, the place was a natural wonder. Lost in there, in the foothills of the Sierra Madre Occidental, lay San Puebla. The village had once been a miner's jackpot but was now too remote and isolated for anything or anyone but the most rugged of ranchers. The thought of them losing what little they had frightened her. She could only hope this man had what it would take to direct the crew, who would likely be a bunch of ranchers and a few military laborers sent in by train, all with little to no fire training.

She dipped the plane into a low valley, her breath catching at the vast beauty of the forest, the undiscovered creeks and rivers. The deep gorges and canyons and high vistas were some of the most amazing in the world, unarguably among the most rugged and secluded.

Above her, the sky spread glorious blue for as far as the eye could see—except for the ominous cloud billowing up from the ground. A cloud that began to threaten her visibility as she came in close.

Nearly there now, she stole another peak at her stoic passenger, over six feet of pure heartache. "You okay?"

He took his gaze off the window to send a baleful stare her way.

Right. He still didn't want to talk.

The smoke thickened even more. It'd been a while since her passenger had spoken. There was no sound in the cockpit except the drone of the engine. She squinted a little, as if that could help her see. No matter how many hours she had in the air, flying in conditions like this could mount tension faster than anything, and she mentally prepared for the inevitable difficult landing.

"Can you even see?" he grated out a moment later when visibility had gone down to next to nothing.

Not so much, no. But they were only a few miles out now. She could see the bright glow of the actual blaze. It was a horrifying sight, and she could hardly make out the land beneath, but she knew the layout extremely well. "Don't worry."

He let out a muttered response to that, but he didn't understand. Flying was her life. Some women her age had husbands, or kids.

She had this.

Up here she controlled her destiny; up here she was free as a bird, and just as content in all this wide open space, no matter what the challenge. This would be a difficult and unwelcome challenge, but she wasn't in over her head—yet. She made a sharp bank to the right to accommodate the stunning landscape beneath her—and for one quick moment, visibility deserted her entirely. Nothing but dark, thick, choking gray smoke in every direction. She blinked rapidly but didn't see even a crack in the smoke. She let out a long breath and carefully checked her instruments, decreasing their altitude.

"We're going down?"

One way or another, but, concentrating on her instruments—all she had at the moment—she didn't answer. Still no visibility. She dropped them even lower in a last-minute attempt on her part to clear the smoke. "Damn."

"What?"

"The wind's picked up to thirty knots."

"Too high?"

Well twenty would have been mildly challenging, forty would have been deadly. "Hopefully we'll miss any crosswinds, so really, it could be worse." Again she had to adjust their altitude, this time going higher to miss the craggy, sharp mountain she knew was there even if she couldn't see it. The rocky turbulence threw them around for a moment but she fought for control and maintained it, barely. Even *her* stomach pitched.

Only a few more minutes.

Another rough drop but her hands and eyes remained steady, as did her heart, though her palms had grown damp.

Behind her she heard the slap of a sweaty hand on an armrest. Heard the low, muttered curse.

In her mirror, their eyes locked and held. "We're okay," she said.

"Don't waste your breath coddling me, just get us there."

She dropped altitude again.

At the abrupt shift, she heard another sharp intake of breath. She took one herself, then let it out slowly, using all her strength to guide them in.

Blind. "Hang on." Thrusting the throttle forward, she executed a sharp climb to miss the crest that was leaping with flames, banking sharply to the right, swinging back around for another shot at the landing.

And again lost all visibility.

"Pull up again," he said. "Take your time."

She glanced down at her gauges. "No can do."

"Why the hell not?"

"Not enough fuel."

Their eyes locked. A trickle of sweat ran down his temple. Her own skin was damp. "Hang on," she said again, and with another drastic maneuver brought them back around, slightly to the west this time, and over fire-free land. "Ready?"

"Shit." He closed his eyes. Then opened them with a grim determination that took her by surprise. "Ready."

Ready. And she took them directly into the remote, dizzying, dangerous, and definitely rough-around-the-edges Mexican mountains, flames and smoke and all.

2

The timbered peaks had vanished under the smoke, and Griffin felt his own heart rate accelerate to a pace it hadn't reached in quite some time as they descended for their landing. Then suddenly they flew in beneath the smoke and could see again, and he took in the heavily grown hills, the bushy plain—and the flames in them.

They came down into a valley, over a low running river and a bridge that looked as if it'd been around for centuries, and then they hit with a hard bump that sent Griffin's stomach plunging. They bounced up once, twice, then skidded unevenly over the rough dirt road that looked as if it was going to end before they could stop.

Leaving them to plunge down an embankment of which he couldn't see the bottom.

Lyndie shoved the throttle forward and stomped on the foot pedals, and Griffin gritted his teeth, stomping his own feet into the floor as if he could help stop the plane.

When they finally stopped—mere feet from the end of the runway—he closed his eyes, trying to regain his equilibrium. For a long moment, he sat there after the engine powered down, concentrating on breathing. He'd been told, by just about everyone he knew, that post-traumatic syndrome could and would take place in many forms.

That had pissed him off then, and the thought of it pissed him off now. He wasn't suffering from post-traumatic syndrome. He'd *lived,* damn it, and that had been good enough for him.

His pilot stared worriedly into his face. She'd managed to somehow do the impossible, flying on pure skill and talent, keeping them alive, and instead of taking a moment to breathe herself, she was staring at him with concern. "Okay?" she asked, and put a hand on his knee.

"Yeah."

She didn't take her hand off his knee. "Take a moment."

"I don't need one." He took off his seat belt with unsteady hands out in the middle of an on-fire nowhere, and he had to shake his head. Just flying had nearly undone him along with the butt-squeaker of a small craft that had shimmied and shuddered like a toy.

How the hell was he supposed to fight that fire out there waiting for him? "That was some flying."

"Thanks."

Easy confidence. Something he'd lost. God, this had really been a stupid move. His palms were damp, his heart still threatening to burst right out of his chest. He'd been in some tough spots before, the toughest, but after months of doing nothing more than watching time pass on the beach, clearly he'd lost his edge.

No, scratch that. He'd lost his edge on a mountain in Idaho nearly a year ago....

Her fingers, still on his knee, squeezed gently. He put his hand over hers and looked into her eyes. She wasn't beautiful by any means, and yet her eyes could devastate a man at close range. "I'm okay."

She stared at him for a long moment, then nodded and backed up.

Standing, he came face-to-face with her for the first time. Lyndie Anderson had fiery auburn hair sticking straight up from the aviator sunglasses she'd shoved to the top of her head. The rest of her hair was hacked to her chin as if she'd taken the scissors to it herself. With her temperament, she probably had. Her eyes were sharp green, void of makeup, and narrowed on him as if he were a bug on her windshield. She wore dark blue trousers and a white blouse that could have used an iron, on a tough, lean body he had no doubt could kick some serious butt. And she hardly came to his shoulder.

Had he thought she wasn't beautiful? At the moment, with her hero-worthy flight still fresh in his mind, she was the most beautiful woman he'd ever seen.

She thrust her chin in the air. "What are you looking at?"

"You." For some reason, he couldn't take his eyes off her. She was interesting—arresting—he had to admit. "You're tiny."

"I'm stronger than I look."

Together they moved toward the door, but she pushed ahead of him, throwing a shoulder against it, muscling it open before he could lean in and help her.

It creaked open as if the movement was painful.

"At least the thing got us here," he muttered.

"Thing?"

"Nicer word than a trap."

"*Trap?*" With a lithe easiness, she jumped to the ground and patted the plane. "Don't listen to him, baby," she crooned. "You're a beauty, and solid to boot."

"You...talk to your plane."

"Yep."

Shaking his head, he grabbed his two duffels; the firefighter's red bag, which held all his personal stuff, and his backpack with the IA gear. Inside the initial attack pack was everything a wildland or forest firefighter might need out in the field, and everything he'd hoped he wouldn't ever need again.

He eyed the sharp, jagged mountain peaks to the north—what he could see of them, anyway, through the smoke—noting all the heavy vegetation with dread. It was late August now. He knew they'd experienced an incredibly wet winter, followed by no precipitation since. With all the new, thick, heavy growth, things were as bad as they could get.

"Let's go." She nodded toward the two metal buildings a few hundred yards away that looked more like an old movie set than a real airport. "It's an abandoned silver mine," she said to his unspoken question. "But it's got the only good solid road around that's both the right length and straight. Perfect makeshift airstrip. Add in a couple of hangars, and one lone gasoline tanker that comes with a guy named Julio who'll only fill 'er up if you tip him in booze, and you've got yourself an airport."

"Right."

She lifted a shoulder. "Hey, it works. So..." She sized him up from toe to forehead, somehow making him want to stand up taller. "You didn't need a bag to toss your cookies after all."

"I'm stronger than I look," he responded, mocking her own words to him.

She smiled, apparently unapologetic for her bluntness, which was oddly both refreshing and a little startling. "You still look a little green, but strong enough," she decided. "You'll need that strength, with the job ahead of you."

As if his stomach wasn't wobbly enough, it did another somersault. It'd been so long. A year.

A lifetime.

And it would have been longer if Brody hadn't interfered.

The thought of his brother, probably at this very moment lounging on the beach, grinning at bikini babes and chuckling over what he'd done, made Griffin grit his teeth. "Let's just get this over with. Take me to the fire."

"Oh, no. My job was to get you here." Turning to an old weathered guy in beat-up coveralls and a cap low over his eyes, she nodded when he pointed to the gas tanker. *"Gracias,"* she said, and handed him a brown bag that no doubt held the required booze.

Julio, apparently.

"Good luck, Ace," she said to Griffin over her shoulder as she headed back to her plane.

"Wait." He stared at her, stunned. "You're leaving?" He didn't like her, mostly because she'd provided the means to get him here, but she was also his only tie down here.

"Don't worry. Tom Farrell will be here any minute to pick you up."

She'd told him not to worry a few times now. He hated those words. "Tom?"

"The postmaster." She cocked her head. "In fact, I hear him coming now."

"What? Where?"

"Shh." She listened some more. "Yep, that's his Jeep. For your sake, I hope he got the brakes fixed."

Two seconds later, a Jeep roared right onto the "tarmac," and skidded to a stop a few feet from the plane. There were no windows, no fenders, no top, and what might have once been a cherry red paint job had long ago faded and rusted down to the metal.

"Hey, Tom." Griffin's pixie pilot smiled, transforming her face. "You washed this heap, I see."

"Nah." Tom hopped out. Fiftyish, he had a tough, rangy body, long blond-gray hair pulled back in a leather strap, and deep brown eyes. "I drove through the *rio* yesterday. Just long enough to spruce it up some." He stuffed his hands in his front jean pockets. His tanned Caucasian face crinkled into a welcoming smile.

"Tom came from North Dakota," Lyndie explained to Griffin. "In case you're wondering why he's as white as I am. He showed up here in the seventies to fish, fell in love with a local, and never left."

"True, true," Tom said, thrusting his hand out to Griffin. "And you're the help we need so desperately."

"Yes, and you're…the postmaster."

Tom gave Lyndie a long, wry look. "You never get tired of messing with the guys' heads, do you? I bet you took the long way in, too."

"Who, me?"

Tom shook his head, still pumping Griffin's hand. "I'm mostly the sheriff now, but also I deliver the mail. When we get it. Don't worry, son. You're not dreaming, you're really here."

Not so much of a comfort, actually.

"How bad is it really?" Lyndie asked Tom, who sighed.

"Bad."

"Well, keep me posted." His pilot, the little she-devil, gave them both a wave and started backing away. "Later." She tossed a look Griffin's way. "You go play hero, now. I'll be back for you at the end of your shift. Sunday night."

That wasn't a comfort either.

"Yeah…uh, Lyndie?" Tom took off his hat and scratched his head. "Nina's sort of in a mood again."

Lyndie stared at him, than laughed a little and shook her head. "Nope. I'm not translating for you all weekend. I haven't had a day off all damn year. Sam gave me this weekend, and I've got a date with a long nap and a pleasure joyride wherever I feel like winging to."

"So who's going to translate for your hotshot here?"

"He's not *my* hotshot, he's yours."

"Now, Lyndie—"

"No." She pointed at him. "Don't you 'now Lyndie' me. Sam pays Nina to do it, and you know it."

"Who's Nina?"

Both Tom and Lyndie looked at Griffin as if they'd forgotten he existed.

"My daughter," Tom finally answered. "She's uh, rather head-strong."

"Code for stubborn and selfish." Lyndie let out a sound of annoyance. "She's a native with flawless English who translates for our volunteers in return for cash. When she's in the mood, that is."

"Yes, she's a hothead, that one." Tom lifted his hands in the helpless gesture of someone who'd created a monster and now didn't know what to do with her. "Stay, Lyndie. Please? You yourself said you had time off, and how better to spend it if not in a place you know and love, a place now in danger if the wind doesn't cooperate and our men don't get that fire under control?"

"Yes, but—"

"But you hate to be social, I know. I know—"

"I don't hate to be social," Lyndie said through her teeth, which Griffin thought was interesting.

She didn't want to help any more than he did. After the plane had landed, she'd put her hand on him to soothe. The urge to return the favor shocked him.

"Then you won't mind helping us out," Tom said smoothly.

Lyndie put her hands on her hips and glared at Tom, who pretended not to notice.

"Into the Jeep, now," he said to no one in particular, putting a hand on Lyndie's back and trying to push her toward the vehicle.

"I can't stay," she insisted, notably less forcefully this time. "I have..."

"Yes?" Tom smiled sweetly, his warm eyes guileless. "You have something more important?"

Lyndie stared at him, then suddenly her shoulders sagged. "No. Damn it. Of course not."

"There you are," Tom opened the beat-up door and patted her arm. "You know it's okay to admit you have a home here," he said gently.

"I do not."

"You *feel* at home here," Tom said.

"My home is the sky—which I should be up in right now, thank you very much."

"Whatever you say, Lyn."

She let out a low, unintelligible reply that sounded like a growl.

Griffin had never known a woman who could snarl so convincingly, as if she might launch herself at the source of her aggravation. He wondered if he touched her now if she'd snap at him. He put a hand on her shoulder.

Whipping around to face him, she stared at him.

Unbelievably, he nearly smiled.

"It's all settled then." Tom nodded approvingly. "I'll make sure your plane is properly tied down and cared for, and that Rosa knows you'll be staying for the weekend. Get in now, darlin.'"

And to Griffin's amazement, the strong-headed, temperamental, free-spirited Lyndie merely sighed and climbed up into the waiting Jeep.

In the front seat, naturally.

Leaving the back to him.

3

Why had he touched her back there? Lyndie couldn't figure it out so she stopped trying and looked around. They made their way toward the fire on a narrow, rutted road that wound around the hills in a meandering fashion. If they could get there as a crow flew, they'd have arrived in two minutes flat, but the roads here in the Barranca del Cobre were few and far between. Just outside the airport, they crossed a set of railroad tracks that nearly rattled the teeth out of Lyndie's head.

"That's where the train comes through," Tom explained to Griffin. "Which is the only way to travel this area. It's not really safe any other way. Too many deep, dark canyons where one can fall to their death; too many wild animals, including hungry bears. Too many damn places to get lost and never get found again."

Griffin didn't look happy at that knowledge.

After the tracks came a creek. They used the one and only rickety old bridge to cross, which Lyndie tried not to think too much about as it creaked and groaned with their weight. She glanced back at Griffin to see how he took it, but he just sat there, immobile, face utterly unreadable.

Halfway across, the Jeep stalled. "Damn," Tom said.

The bridge swung with their weight and Lyndie gulped. "Tom."

"On it." He tried to restart the temperamental Jeep while they all hung there in the balance on the wobbly bridge with the fire ravaging the hills around them.

The Jeep didn't turn over.

The bridge shuddered.

"Just give it a sec," Tom said calmly, and cranked the engine again. Finally it turned over, and they began to move.

And still no reaction at all from Griffin.

So he wasn't easy to ruffle, she thought, with just a little bit of admiration. She appreciated that in a volunteer. In anyone.

The road widened a bit after that, crossing through the low-lying hills beneath the hot day, the sun trying to beat down on them through the thick smoke. Breathing became a challenge as they came into San Puebla. The sandstone and brick facades of the buildings lined well-traveled narrow cobblestone streets, concealing courtyards, some empty and deserted, some lush with bougainvillea that had been lovingly tended to for centuries. The city's beautiful and unique architecture reflected a Moorish influence brought by seventeenth-century architects from Andalucia in southern Spain.

There was a gas station and tire shop next to an eighteenth-century cathedral. A farmers' market next to a cantina that had once been home to a Spanish run-away prince. And an undeniable peaceful, timeless feel to it all, if one didn't count the ominous cloud of smoke overhanging it, threatening, growing...

Lyndie's heart leapt at being back here, she couldn't deny that. Nor could she deny the lump in her throat at the overhang of smoke and the terrible stench of the fire so close that the sky seemed to glow.

She glanced over at Tom. He seemed tense, too, but when he caught her looking at him he reached over and squeezed her hand. "It'll be okay now."

She hadn't been looking for reassurance, but she'd take it. The choking air, the way the smoke seemed like a live, breathing thing, scared her to death, and she didn't scare easily. "This is bad," she whispered.

"Yeah." Tom let out a heartfelt sigh. "It's all bad. The record high temps, the rainfall at less than one tenth the norm…" He shrugged his shoulders. "Mexico's lost an area the size of Rhode Island in this season alone."

Lyndie's heart clenched. She didn't want San Puebla to be just another statistic.

And still their stoic firefighter didn't say a word.

They passed through town, and it seemed as if they headed directly into hell as they climbed the hills, totally engulfed by flames. The smoke swirled around them, thicker and then thicker still, billowing so high in the sky they could see nothing else.

Tom's radio squawked.

He pulled over because, as Lyndie knew, attempting to manage the narrow, curvy road and a radio at the same time was bad news, and he'd gone through four Jeeps in his career to prove it.

While he fumbled for his radio, she turned and eyed their passenger. Griffin Moore looked over the rough road, the cliff on one side, a drop-off on the other. In front of them lay mountainous terrain so rough and unfriendly that few humans had dared to venture.

Now that they were out of the plane Griffin looked even leaner than before, the lines of his face more stark. He'd pulled out a pair of sunglasses from somewhere, which covered his blue eyes just enough that she couldn't get a feel for what he was thinking. Not that it took a genius to make a guess.

There was a hauntedness in those eyes, she'd seen it in the brief moment before he'd covered them. He didn't want to be here.

Not her problem; he'd volunteered. Maybe he'd gotten himself in hot water with his captain or someone, and had been forced to put in the time, but it didn't matter, he was here.

What was wrong with people anyway? What was the big deal about volunteering, giving some time, helping others? Hell, she was no saint, and she did it.

But still she sensed it was much more than mere reluctance to help…

"You're staring at me," he said, not moving his head. "You have something to say?"

Slowly she shook her head. "Nope."

"Sure? Because you're thinking loud enough to give me a headache."

"I'm thinking you look like you'd rather be having a root canal without drugs than be here."

"And you'd be right."

She opened her mouth to say something to that, but Tom said, *"Ahorita voy,"* into his radio, and that got her attention. "You'll be right where?" she demanded.

He set the radio down and gave her a long look.

"More good news, I take it?" she said.

"Well." He scratched his head, which had Lyndie's heart sinking because he was thinking, and thinking hard. Never a good sign. "You're going to have to take over for a bit. I've got a bar fight to break up." He unhooked the strap across his lap, as the shoulder part of the seat belt had long ago disintegrated. "It's been a whole week since I've had me a good bar fight."

Lyndie rolled her eyes. "Try to keep all your teeth this time."

"Hey, I haven't lost a tooth in a fight in years." Tom got out.

Griffin remained quiet, but his grim expression said it all. He was no more thrilled at being left alone with Lyndie than she was.

"I'll walk back," Tom said. "You get our hero here where he needs to go."

Griffin stirred at that, shifted in his seat, which Lyndie found interesting. A reluctant hero? Not many men would fit that bill, and damn if that didn't pique her interest where she didn't want to be piqued.

"It's half a mile," she pointed out to Tom, who wasn't exactly known for his interest in exercise. "You always say the walk from your desk to your filing cabinet is too long."

"Yeah, but it'll give them a good chance to beat the shit out of each other. By the time I get there, they'll be too tired to resist arrest."

"And you'll be in time to get your afternoon nap in."

"Not today." His smile faded as he gestured to the smoke. "I'm coming back. Stay safe, you hear?" With a fond pat on her head, he nodded to Griffin. "See you soon. You stay safe, too." And he began walking.

"How are you going to get out to the fire?" she called after him.

Tom stopped on the dusty road.

"Do you have a tractor?"

Lyndie turned in surprise to Griffin, who kept his eyes on Tom. "Do you?" he asked.

"I could probably get my hands on one."

"A tractor can get anywhere and clear a path," Griffin said, using more words than he had all day. "That'll work for fire lines, or even an emergency road exit, if we need it."

"Consider it done, then." Tom saluted, then he was gone.

Lyndie climbed over the stick shift and into the driver's seat, grumbling at the condition of the seat belt. While she clipped herself in, Griffin put a big, tanned hand down on the console between the seats and hopped from the back to the passenger seat she'd just vacated. He slid his long legs in first, then rested his broad shoulders back, tilting his face up to look at the marred sky before glancing at her. "Better," he said.

She jammed the shifter into first gear and hit the gas. She had to give him credit, he didn't react, not other than reaching for the seat belt as the acceleration pressed them both back. He settled in, one elbow resting on the passenger door, his face inscrutable. In charge of his world.

She liked to be in charge, too, so she supposed she could appreciate that. She certainly appreciated having the view of his nicely built, long, leanly muscled body to look at. Not that she'd ever do more than look. Unlike her boss, Sam, she rarely mixed business and pleasure.

The road took a sharp turn and arched up toward a series of ranches, and then beyond them the sharp, ragged peaks. The road was narrow, pitted, and frankly, quite dangerous. With the sheer cliff on one side, the drop-off on the other, it was impossible to tell yet how far the fire had raged.

The smoke around them thickened along with the choking, clinging scent of the fire. The hills above them, between the village and the alpine mountains beyond, were nearly invisible, and what wasn't invisible glowed with flame. Lyndie squinted into the smoke as she drove, desperately wishing she could reach out and shove it all aside. Her lungs grew tight, an unfortunately familiar feeling. She patted the inhaler in her pocket, knowing she'd need it before this was through.

"What's the problem?"

Griffin Moore had a way of looking at her that made her feel as if he could read her mind. Too bad she never allowed a man close enough to do such a thing. "No problem."

He knew that wasn't the truth, she could tell, he just wasn't going to pursue it right now. "We're nearly there," he said.

She nodded to the ashes raining down over them. "Yeah."

His nod was tight, his mouth growing grimmer by the minute. Odd, as she'd have figured as a firefighter, he'd get more excited the closer they'd gotten to the front.

Because she'd been staring at him, she hit a deep rut, and nearly tipped them over. Applying the brakes didn't help as they didn't give right away. "Sorry," she gasped when they finally stopped. She began again, slowly. "The road's a little rough."

"In the States this would barely qualify as a fire road."

"Yeah." There weren't many "fire roads" in this part of Mexico; there weren't a lot of roads, period, but there were plenty of little known places where people might want to disappear. The Barranca del Cobre was one of those places. As the road all but disappeared, she said a silent thanks for the way the Jeep could get over just about anything, including all the rocks and branches blocking their way. Of course the shocks were nothing to write home about, and she thought the fillings in her teeth might just rattle right out of her head, but she had to get him there before this thing got worse.

"How many men are out here?"

"I'm not sure." She maneuvered around a fallen tree and ended up on her two side wheels for a terminally long second. She was going to need a bottle of aspirin after this drive.

"Do you know how many acres have burned?"

"I know nothing, I'm sorry. I fly in a doctor every two weeks, alternating a dentist in every once in a while to get the locals some desperately needed health care, that's all." Which she did for other places too, wherever Sam sent her, but San Puebla was her favorite, and when she'd heard about the fire late last night, she'd insisted on flying in their "specialist" herself. "I also fly in supplies and highfalutin fishermen willing to pay the locals for the hot spots, people guaranteed to drop their money in the bar. This fire thing is new for me."

"Who's in charge?"

"We've never had a fire out this way, so I have no idea, though I imagine no one. You'll be lucky to have the proper equipment, much less enough people. The only reason *you're* here is because you volunteered through Hope International, and because you supposedly have some experience directing a fire crew—"

"I didn't."

"What?"

"I didn't volunteer. My brother gave them my name."

She risked taking her eyes off the road again to stare into his tense, rugged features—and because she did, they hit a deep pothole blindsided.

As she went airborne, Griffin gripped the dash with his right hand and thrust his left arm across her body while swearing impressively. With only the lap belt for protection, Lyndie slammed into the hard sinew of his forearm, wincing in anticipation of breaking his limb between her body and the steering wheel, but thankfully he was rock solid and held her back against the seat. No steering wheel involved.

Without his arm squashing into her breasts, holding her back as the shoulder harness would have if there'd been one, she might

have been hit face-first into the steering wheel herself. Arms
tight, she held on to it for dear life and gritted her teeth, calling
herself every kind of fool until he dropped his arm away from her.
"Thank you," she said from between her teeth, trying not to notice her asthma was kicking in right on schedule.

"Maybe I should drive," he said.

"I'm fine." Stewing, she drove in silence for a moment through
the smoke, the flames in plain view now on their left. She hated
to stew, but unfortunately, she was good at it. Then they came
around a turn and into view of a ranch, and Griffin let out a low
curse. Lyndie's breath caught, too.

The fields were on fire. Directly behind the hilly fields was the
first higher peak. Because it was entirely engulfed in smoke, she
couldn't see how far up the flames had raged, but she had no
problem seeing the ten-foot walls of flames on their left, at road-
side.

"Careful here," Griffin said grimly, eyeing the hot flames so
close. "A sudden sharp blast of wind will take them right over the
top of us."

Terrific. Resisting the urge to duck, she drove on. She knew
from Tom that the "fire central" was back here, behind this ranch,
somewhere amidst all the flames, so she turned at the crossroad
and hoped she could find it. "This is one of those days where I
think a desk job wouldn't be so bad."

Her passenger let out a choked sound that might have been a
laugh, which had her risking a glance at him. "People who volunteer don't show up all the time," she said. "Why did you?"

"It doesn't matter."

He was right, it didn't, not at the moment. All that mattered
was that he'd come, experience and all, to help get this wildfire
under control. She knew he would do his best or die trying, be-

cause whether she liked him or not, he'd once been a hotshot. Helping others was ingrained.

Or so she hoped.

A hot wind was a constant now, and the thick ash and smoke combined to block out the sun but trapped the heat. Her chest tightened uncomfortably. The situation seemed far more desperate than she had imagined.

She eyed the way the scorching wind fueled the flames. "I guess the weather is pretty crucial here. You have one of those fancy little weather kits on you?"

No response from the firefighter, so she dared another quick peek. Ah, hell, he didn't look so good again.

Well, he could get sick all he wanted now, this wasn't her Jeep. It was no less than Tom deserved for sticking her here with him alone.

But in that moment, she lost a good amount of her confidence in him, and in their combined ability to be any help at all.

4

Lyndie navigated the narrow rutted driveway that wound past the charred ranch house and barn, around the base of a low hill. She knew from Tom that no one had died here last night when the house had gone down, but it was a devastating loss for the family.

She made the last turn and stopped the Jeep in a natural clearing where they had a clear view down to San Puebla. They had a long afternoon and evening ahead of them, keeping the flames from making this last leap down the hill to town.

There were a handful of guys sprawled out on the ground in an already burned-out area. A few appeared to be napping, some just sitting quietly or eating army rations, all with dirty faces and clothing, looking hot and exhausted.

Lyndie turned off the Jeep and got out. "Let's go, Ace."

Griffin didn't move.

She bent down and retied her boots, but when she straightened, squinting in the gusty, hot wind, her skin tight and feeling sunburned from the heat of the flames, Griffin still sat in the Jeep. "It's going to be hard to work from there," she said.

With a face that might as well have been carved from granite, he got out of the Jeep. Head tipped back, he studied the sky, or what there was to see of it. Then he turned into the wind, his T-shirt plastered to his chest. "Weather sucks."

"It's what we've got."

He looked at her, still pale. "It's extremely dangerous."

"I imagine it is." Something was going on here, something she didn't quite get—other than that he didn't want to do this. She got that part loud and clear.

But why? "Look, you seem...sick. Maybe I should radio Tom—"

"No." Reaching into his pack, he pulled out a Nomex fire-fighter's shirt. It was yellow and long-sleeved, and he shrugged into it, covering up what she had to admit was a drool-inducing chest and strong shoulders. He buttoned up, and when she lifted her gaze up to his, his was lit with the knowledge that she'd been looking him over. Unashamed, she lifted her chin, but instead of saying a word, he simply started walking toward the men, two of whom she recognized.

Jose ran a horse ranch on the other side of San Puebla with his family, and Hector worked at the farmers' market in town. They introduced her to the others, all of whom worked in or around Copper Canyon and did indeed have some limited fire experience.

She spoke in Spanish, in which she was fluent, introducing them to Griffin. That they were ecstatic over his help didn't need translation.

"There's no real leader here," she explained to Griffin after she got the terrifying scoop. "Jose says that as a result, there's been little progress in containing it. It's got three ranches in its grip right now, and the hill behind us. If it goes north, it claims the peaks, and he says they'll never catch it. If it goes south, it makes its way right through the town. At the moment it's poised to do both."

Griffin didn't respond to her words, he just stood there, shoulders tense, hands fisted at his side, staring into the fire. The scorching heat and gagging smoke were insufferable; the sound of the flames licking at the vegetation fairly petrifying. "Griffin?"

There were beads of sweat on his forehead, and he was breathing shallowly, and her annoyance at him became something else entirely, and the most unsettling urgency to touch him again nearly overcame her. "Hey." She put her hand on his arm. "You okay?"

He jerked his head toward her, and the stark pain in his eyes grabbed her by the throat. "Griffin?" She kept her hand on his arm, not positive he wasn't going to keel over on her right where he stood. Medically, that wouldn't be a problem—she was trained in the basics, but this wasn't about the basics. This guy had a problem, and she didn't know what it was.

There'd been little softness in her life, and therefore, little coddling. She didn't need or miss it, but neither did she know how to give it. And yet she had to try to help him, it was that simple. Maybe it was the utter desolation in his stance, or the way he stood there rigid as stone, but she lifted her other hand to him as well, holding both his arms.

The men around them shifted uneasily. *"Que pasa?"*

She had no idea what was the matter, but she smiled over her shoulder at them. It'd been a long day, she told them. A rough flight.

As she said this, Griffin backed away from her, then…turned and walked away.

After sending the men an apologetic smile, she followed Griffin in silence back to the Jeep—the growth crunching beneath their feet, the heat of the fire beating at their backs—and when he got in the passenger seat, she stared at him in disbelief.

Griffin felt the stare but he didn't return it, he couldn't. Not with the nightmare rolling in his head, showing him in vivid Technicolor the last time he'd stood before a fire. Over and over again he'd replayed the scene, always in slow motion, of course, so as not to miss one agonized second of all that he'd lost.

God, once upon a time he'd loved this life, he'd thrived on it; the rush to get the fire under control, working as a team against the awesome force of Mother Nature.

Now all he could hear were the screams. Smell the burning flesh. Suffer the heat blasting him, scorching him.

He remembered watching Greg go down, remembered hearing the helicopter coming, knowing it was useless...

A moment ago, he'd stood with Lyndie and the others, all looking at him, waiting for him to take charge, and he...couldn't. His heart had been pumping—was still pumping—so fast and hard it was a miracle it didn't burst right out of his chest, and though he was sweating through his clothes, he shivered.

He heard Lyndie say his name as she got behind the wheel of the Jeep but he shook his head harshly. It'd been inhumanly hot that day, too, the winds vicious, with gusts over fifty mph. Humidity at twenty percent, dropping suddenly to less than ten.

No doubt, the weather had destroyed them—combined, of course, with miscalculation and human error, and there'd been plenty of that.

As a result, twelve people had died, twelve people he'd loved dearly. He didn't know if he would ever be able to forget, but he did know one thing. He shouldn't have come here, should never have allowed Brody to get him into this, into letting people depend on him.

He couldn't be depended on, not ever again.

Next to him, Lyndie still watched him with those luminous drown-in-me eyes. "Well, hell," she finally said, and shoved the Jeep into reverse to turn around in the clearing. She got them halfway back down the flaming road before she spoke. "You going to be sick?"

"No."

"Sure? Because I can stop." She sent him a quick glance of concern.

She felt sorry for him.

Jesus, he really had to get it together. But thinking it and doing it were apparently two different things. He started with breathing, counting each and every inhale and exhale. *One. Two—*

"You're okay?"

"Do I look okay?"

"Actually, you look like death warmed over."

Three. It was ironic, really. All his adult life he'd been with quiet, unassuming women. And yet here he was, inexplicably attracted to this brass, blunt, upfront one who probably wouldn't recognize quiet and unassuming if it bit her on the ass.

A shame he'd given up women for now. He was simply too screwed up for anything but solitude. *Four. Five...*

The ride back felt every bit as bone-jarring as it had been coming, and his teeth rattled in his head. Maybe it rattled his thoughts, too, because though he'd fallen apart back there, suddenly leaving seemed wrong. "Pull over."

"Right." She kept going.

"Pull over."

She risked another glance at him, then slammed on her brakes right in the middle of the narrow, pitted road, as pulling over wasn't really an option unless they wanted to either barbeque themselves or fall off the cliff.

Instead of stopping, they slid for a heart-stopping moment.

Six. Seven…

The Jeep rocked to a stop.

"Go back," he said into the silence.

She slowly shook her head. "No can do. I have to take you home and find someone else. You obviously have some serious shit to deal with. On your own time."

Message clear. She was going to come back here. She'd been flying all day, but she was going to repeat it all in order to see this through. Her dedication was humiliating and shaming, and just the kick in the ass he needed. "Go back," he said again.

Again, she just looked at him as if he was crazy, and in truth, he was. He wasn't going to reach her with words, he didn't deserve to. But he wasn't going back home. Just as she had in her plane, he reached out and put a hand on her knee. "Do it, or I'll walk back to that fire."

She stared down at his hand on her, then looked into his face.

"I'm doing this," he said softly.

The wind rippled, the ash continued to rain over them. The eerie silence except for the ominous crackling of the fire made him feel like he was starring in a bad horror flick. He squeezed gently on her leg, feeling the strength quivering within her. "Please, Lyndie."

She let out a sigh, and rolled her eyes. "Fine, if you want to make a fool out of yourself. *Again.*" She knocked his hand off her knee, then shoved the Jeep into reverse, and with a startling skill and ease, hit the gas, driving *backward* up the curving, narrow dirt road until she came to a spot in the road where she could turn around without toasting them. She did this so fast his head spun as he ate their dust.

Grimly, she worked the stick into first gear and took off again, heading forward now, getting them to the clearing in the same heart-stopping manner she flew her plane. For a minute she sat there, short fiery hair blowing about her like a halo, eyes flashing with determination and more grit than he'd seen in a good long time. She was strong and brave, and amazing.

Griffin would have liked to match her determination and grit, pound for pound, to be as brave and strong as she. Even sweating, shaking just a little, heart still racing, he wanted that.

But he'd left all his courage and strength on a different mountain, in a different country entirely. He'd left his heart there, too.

She turned off the engine. "Before we try again, you want to tell me what's going on?"

No. No, he didn't. He didn't want to tell her he'd lost everything, that he didn't know how to get it back, or if he even wanted to. "I'm fine."

"Uh huh."

"I am."

She stared at him for a long moment, her green, green eyes revealing nothing but her impatience to do this. "Play it however you have to, Ace." She leaned in close enough that he could smell her, some complicated combination of plain soap and one hundred percent woman. "Just play it. You hear me?"

Up close and personal, he could see her eyes weren't just green, but a deep jade, and so clear and fathomless he could have dived into them. Her bangs were just a little too long, and impatiently she pushed them out of her way just before she stabbed him hard in the chest with her finger, reminding him that while she might have been something to look at, while she might have unbelievable passion and strength, she was also rough and gruff and pushing him in a way he didn't want to be pushed.

"Whatever's going on," she said, "Deal with it on your own time. *Vamanos.*"

Let's go. Grabbing the finger digging into his pec, he pulled her hand down but didn't let it go. Like it or not, she happened to be his only lifeline out here. There'd been a time when he hadn't needed one, but apparently those times were a thing of the past. She was a reluctant lifeline, but a lifeline just the same, and he held on tight. *"Vamanos,"* he repeated softly.

In a move that shocked him, she turned her palm in his so that suddenly they were holding hands. Gently she squeezed, maintaining an eye contact he couldn't tear away from. "Can you really do this?"

In his life, until a year ago anyway, he'd always been the one with all the strength. People looked to him, people leaned on him.

Or they had.

It should have been humiliating, at the very least humbling, to need someone to lean on now, but somehow being humiliated and humbled were the least of his concerns.

Getting through this, getting them all through it, was apparently so deeply ingrained he couldn't ignore it. He looked over his shoulder at the group of men, all of whom had come to a stand when they'd driven back into the clearing. He saw their willingness to do whatever it took. Even as he stood there, the clinging, choking smoke moved in, cloaking the beautiful scenery that they were losing with every passing second. "I can do this," he said.

Please, God, let him be able to do this.

"Then get out of the Jeep." Tugging her hand free, she got out and slammed the door. She gave him one last long look so completely void of any of the brief softness he'd just witnessed, he figured he'd only imagined it.

Then, turning forward, she walked her sweet ass right into the fray.

The air was laced with the burning heat of the flames, with the putrid smoke, tasting thick and acrid in his mouth, stinging his eyes. Just like old times.

Wanting to curse his brother, wanting to curse Lyndie, wanting to curse every damn thing, Griffin got out, too. He reached into the back of the Jeep for his gear, and then with one deep breath full of smoke and remembered horrors, he followed her, right into hell.

5

As Lyndie walked toward the waiting men, she wondered what Griffin would do. Would he freeze again? She hoped not, as she really had no idea what to do with that.

But his long legs quickly caught up with her much shorter ones, striding along at her side. When they reached the men again, he dropped his pack, put his hands on his hips, and drew a deep, ragged breath. "Okay."

God, it looked sober from here. The charred ranch house, the fields and mountains ablaze...terrifying. But Griffin stood there, tall and strong, thankfully, and she had the urge to put her hand on his big, tough shoulder. Since that made no sense, she gave him a long, even look. "What's first?"

He gave her the long, even look right back. "Ask them what the coverage is, and how many people they have?"

Turning, she translated his questions, and the laborers' subsequent answers, which were simple. Incident base had been forced westward, past the ranch's boundaries. Everything else...they didn't know.

The knowledge, or lack of it, didn't hearten Griffin, by the look of him. He dropped to his knees and started pulling things out of his bag. Hard hat, canteen, fire shelter, headlight for the hard hat, radio, extra batteries. He handed her up a radio. "My King," he said. "It's the common name of our standard issue radio. Do they have these?"

She turned to ask, but the men were nodding. They gave her the frequency, and she went to hand it back to Griffin but he shook his head. "You keep it. You'll be the one talking into it." He pulled out a compass, and a...

"Weather kit," he said. He lifted what looked like a torch next, silently questioning the men.

They both nodded. *"Si, si."*

"Okay, they either already have these fuses to help burn lines or they know what it is," he muttered. "That's something."

In return, the men showed them a piece of equipment they had, an agave stalk topped with strips of rubber from inner tubes.

"Fire swatter," Griffin said, nodding. "Good. Are they clearing, too?"

Jose told her people were clearing, but there didn't seem to be much in the way of organization. Lyndie looked at Griffin, silently willing him to fix that.

"Map," Griffin said. "We need to start with a map. I need to drive around as much of the perimeter of the fire as I can to see what we're dealing with." He shouldered his pack and started walking back toward the Jeep. "Keys?"

Apparently, he'd not only found his sea legs, but was as naturally bossy as...well, as herself.

His shoulders were stiff with impatience, his body long and lean in his dark green regulation firefighter pants that seemed made for him, moving with quick determination.

So he'd put away whatever his problems were in order to deal with this situation the way it needed to be dealt with. She was glad of that, and for a moment she just watched him, because damn, there was something incredibly sexy about a man in his element, especially when that element was saving something important, like this land. It left her unsettled, and a little confused.

"Let's go." Griffin opened the driver's side door of the Jeep, wriggling his fingers for the keys.

She liked to drive, and debated arguing with him, but he stood there so unexpectedly authoritative, she actually dropped the keys into his hand and stalked around to the other side. "If you damage it, you tell Tom."

"Damage it?" He eyed the beat-up old Jeep. "You've got to be kidding me. A bomb couldn't damage this heap." He hopped in, shot her a long look. "You're coming?"

"Of course."

"Then hang on." His smile was bleak but resolute. "It's going to be a bumpy ride."

He wasn't kidding. Face intent, his hands handling the Jeep in a sure, confident way up the narrow trail in the lowest gear it had, he handled the northbound road better than she could have.

Not that she'd admit it.

The trees were tight together now, the growth beneath thick and dry. A tinderbox. In the open Jeep she felt like a sitting duck.

The wind whipped their faces hard, and a flying ember landed at her feet. "Stomp on it," he demanded, reaching out to air-swat away another flying ember from near her face. "Damn it, you're not dressed for this!"

In the air she'd been in her element. Not here, not now, and she hugged herself, looking over when he touched her shoulder. "I'm okay."

"Stay that way," he said, and in less than two minutes they

came to the end of the road. It was another clearing, with two old military trucks, each with a large tank in the back. Beyond them, beyond the clearing, the low bush surrounding the area was completely ablaze. The flames seemed small and manageable, but she knew that it was deceiving, especially since the flames danced in the trees just beyond the bush, vanishing over the top of the hill.

There were men here, working at the two trucks, laying out hoses and creating firebreaks with rakes, machetes, their bare hands…whatever they had. Lyndie translated the introductions, and here they found Sergio, a local rancher with limited fire experience. He was running the show the best he could, though he seemed a little baffled by the whole thing, and the fact that a slash-and-burn ranch fire had grown so out of control.

In rapid-fire Spanish, along with lots of hand gestures, Sergio told them they had six men on the two fire trucks. They had about thirty more clearing fire lines at various points on the perimeter, but the fire just kept jumping them. They'd lost three ranches to date, and were about to abandon this clearing for fear of being surrounded by the flames.

Sergio didn't know what more to do, and couldn't hand this over to Griffin fast enough.

On all of their faces was worry and fear. These strong, resilient people didn't fear often, but they were afraid now, afraid for their homeland.

It seeped into Lyndie's bones, as well. Homeland. Not a term she personally grasped, not with the nomadic way she'd grown up, changing addresses like others changed hats. In her own travels, and even before that with her grandfather, she'd seen just about every corner of the planet. In all that time, she'd loved many, many places, but had always been fine leaving them when the time came. She was good at leaving, real good. Almost as good as how she never attached to anything.

Other than her plane, that is. Now, that beautiful hunk of steel, she was quite attached to.

Maybe that's why this place scared her to the bone. Like San Diego—a place that had a part of her heart only because she felt close to her parents there, this place felt like a good fit.

Even if she didn't know what to do with that fit.

"Ask him if he has a map," Griffin said.

She turned to Sergio. *"Tienes una mapa?"*

He pulled a piece of paper from his pocket, smoothing it out, revealing a crude drawing of the landscape, and a line of fire, which even Lyndie could see had been drawn before the flames had moved to nearly on top of them.

"Christ." Griffin took a deep breath and looked at the men working hard to clear a fire path. "It's not wide enough." He shook his head. "And there's not enough of them." He took in the mountain above them, thick with dried out vegetation, then went through his pack and pulled out a palm held digital unit.

"What do we do?" Lyndie asked.

He looked up. "We?"

"I'm your translator, remember?"

"The reluctant translator."

"But I'm here."

He eyed her with an expression that might have been admiration. "Okay, *we* then. Without air support, and without a way for the Jeep to go any farther, I'm hiking the rest of the perimeter, or at least going high enough to see how much is burning. While up there, I can create a good map on this." He lifted out his palm-held digital device. "It's got a GPS and an onscreen map, though it would help if someone had a computer I could download to so that all the men could see, too."

"Maybe we can come up with one tonight."

"Okay." He glanced at the fire lines being cleared, his face tight and unhappy. "Tell them the lines need to be wider. At least three to five feet. They should use their fuses, too, burning the vegetation between them and the fire, getting down to good black."

"Good black?"

"Completely scraping the earth clean of needles, branches, everything, to rob the fire of fuel. Do they have any other gear?"

"Like...what?"

"Fire shelters. Or, as we call them in the field, Shake and Bakes."

She blinked, waited for him to smile, but apparently he wasn't kidding. "Sounds macabre."

"It's meant to be. Getting caught by a fire and needing to deploy a fire shelter means you're out of hope."

She turned to the men and asked about additional equipment. But other than hard hats and gloves, they were out of luck. She told them about creating wider fire lines, then turned back to Griffin. "Let's start hiking."

"Again with the 'let's,'" he murmured, and snagged her arm when she would have started walking. It wasn't the first time he'd touched her, he seemed to do that a lot. In other times, she hadn't had any reaction other than wanting to make sure he was okay, or wanting to be okay herself.

Now she waited for one of two reactions: either the urge to slug him, or the letting loose of a smile that would later lead them to the bedroom.

But this time her reaction came from somewhere far deeper

than either simple anger or simple lust, and that confusion settled over her again.

"This is going to be damn hard, hot work," he said, his eyes dark and on hers. "Not to mention dangerous as hell."

"So?"

"So I'm used to it. You're not. You don't have to be."

He was worried about her. That probably shouldn't have moved her, or deepened the confusion. "I've been in worse situations, believe me. I can put in the time. Tom is expecting me to."

"I'm in charge here now, Lyndie, and—"

She laughed good and hard over that. "A few minutes ago you were ready to throw up on your boots, Ace, so don't talk about who's in charge here. You want to see the perimeters? Great, let's go. I'd fly you, but as we discovered on the way in here, we'd have no visibility anyway. So…lead the way."

He stared her down for a long moment, but when she didn't budge, he shrugged, then donned his pack. "Have Sergio radio us when Tom gets here with the tractor and latest weather report."

"Fine." She translated the request, then followed him.

It was rough going. They didn't waste energy talking, but kept to the perimeter of the fire, climbing upward as they went. With the sun blocked, the day looked like dusk, adding even more spookiness to it.

In excellent shape, she shouldn't have had a problem, but she was in tennis shoes, not boots, and the smoke was getting to her. The going was steep, and almost overwhelmingly dusty. Slippery beneath her rubber soles. She climbed, extremely aware of her rough breathing, of the man at her side, and maybe it was that awareness that made her slip and fall hard to her knees. "Damn it."

An arm slipped around her waist, lifted her up. Snug to Griffin's side, she blinked at him. "I'm fine."

"Your knees okay?"

"I just said I was fine."

Running a hand down her thigh to the new hole in her pants, he pulled the material aside to reveal a bloody knee. "I have a first aid kit in my pack."

Since his touch eased her pain, she scoffed. "This doesn't even warrant a Band-Aid."

With a shake of his head, he lifted his hands from her in a surrendering gesture.

They moved on, with Lyndie's knees screaming in protest. But she figured she'd fall off a cliff before admitting such a thing. The man hadn't been kidding; it was hard, hot work, made more time consuming by the fact he was creating a map as they went. At five foot three, she had trouble keeping up with his long stride and had to really kick it in gear to keep him in sight, and that annoyed her. She'd slacked off with her running lately. She decided she'd have to add a mile to her regimen. Already her lungs felt like she had a vise on them from inhaling the bad air.

They kept going, up the next hill, the whole time keeping the fire at their right. She was stunned and dismayed at the extent of it, and startled at how she now felt like she had a knife between her ribs. "This has to be bad for us."

"Yeah." But he wasn't even breathing hard. "You okay?"

Hell if she'd say otherwise. "Why wouldn't I be?"

"I don't know, maybe because your knees are bleeding. Maybe because the flames are licking at us no matter how fast we move ahead of them. Maybe because it's hot and smoky, and we're climbing hard and fast, and you're breathing pretty hard?"

Damn it. She was not. "Are *you* fine?"

"Yes."

"Well then, I am, too."

When he gave her only a long glance, she sighed. "You just worry about yourself, Ace."

And yet he still looked her over, slowly, from head to toe, as if he had to check for himself. "Okay," he finally agreed. "You're fine." His eyes were back on her now, but with an awareness in them that seemed strange and different from the usual sexual spark, because he clearly felt a reluctance to feel that spark.

Well, *that* was mutual, she thought grimly, with little satisfaction. She didn't want any sparks either.

They came to the base of a craggily steep-looking, unwelcoming mountain. The flames were still uncomfortably close to their right, steadily eating their way north and southbound. Fire central was also south of them about a mile or so she figured, but they still couldn't see the end of the northbound flames.

How much farther could this thing go?

Griffin craned his neck. "Up."

She sucked in air, which she couldn't get enough of into her asthma-tortured lungs. The sky was red, the heat unbearable, with the smoke so thick she wanted to part the curtains to see. "Right behind you."

Nodding, he turned and began to climb. She whipped out her inhaler, hating the weakness, taking as deep a breath as she could. Holding, counting, she kept her eyes on Griffin's back in front of her.

He kept going.

Kick ass, she told herself, and feeling slightly better, she pocketed the inhaler and followed him.

* * *

Griffin glanced at the sun, then back at his compass. They stood just east of the fire, surrounded by towering pines lining the mountain in a blanket of dark green. Deep gorges, high rock-lined peaks…Lyndie had told him there were villages scattered extremely sparsely throughout this region, most of them completely self-contained and so isolated people were born, bred, and died all within the same few square miles.

Amazing country. "We still have a few hours left before nightfall," he said, still unable to believe how primitive a fight this was going to be. No air support. No smoke jumpers. No hotshot team. Hell, what was he saying? He didn't even have a *trained* crew. They weren't that far from the States, but they might as well have been on another planet.

Or another century.

Lyndie had matched him pace for pace, assuring him the pilot was in better than just decent shape, though he had already seen that just by looking at her tight, compact yet curvy body. He'd never met anyone like her, which didn't explain why his eyes kept getting drawn back to her time and time again. He was worried about her, as he would have been with anyone without training, and yet somehow it went deeper.

"What does your weather kit say?" she asked.

"Sometimes you have to go by instincts." Something he hadn't done on that long-ago day in Idaho, something he'd regret for the rest of his life.

She put her hands on her hips, breathing hard but evenly enough. "Well, what do your instincts say, then?"

That they were screwed. The fire had taken root in the dry timber, going both north and southward, eating up everything in its path, and they still hadn't gotten to the end of it. "They say we have a lot of work ahead of us, but everything will be okay."

She stared at him for a beat. "Now say that again without the bullshit factor."

She was right, he'd automatically added in words of comfort to ease her mind. He was used to coddling the women in his life but it felt startlingly refreshing not to have it expected of him, even if he still wanted to tuck her away somewhere, safe and sound, and far away from this fire. "All right. We're in trouble."

Her gaze somber but calm, she nodded. "Tell me."

She could have no idea how amazing it was not to have to be careful with her. She wasn't fragile; hell, she was stronger than he was. He gestured with his head southward, down the hill toward the direction of town. "That's where we should be concentrating our efforts. To save the village from the flames."

"Right. But..."

"But the fire is racing uphill, as it always will, toward the wild, open wilderness. We need to get ahead of it. But we don't have enough men or resources to divide our efforts."

Lyndie drew in a shaky, shuddery breath. "Yeah. We're in trouble—hey." She cocked her head. "Hear that?"

He did. *Running water.* Wishing for a little luck had seemed too much to hope for, especially since he had no luck left and hadn't for some time, but he heard what he heard. "Come on."

"Coming on."

Her echoing words had been uttered innocently enough, but for some reason his mind played with them, turning them into something else. Coming on. *Coming...* He had to be crazy to have any brain power left for sexual thoughts, especially given that he'd not felt anything in that department for a year, but when he looked at her, she looked at him right back.

Unwavering, direct.

He was so not prepared for that. For her.

"The *rio*," she said. "It's low right now—"

"It's still music to my ears." He scrambled through the bush, with her right behind him, until they came to it. It was definitely a river, low-running, yes, but falling north to south from the peak above, running parallel to where they stood, then eventually falling again, down another rocky cliff, to the ranches and town below. "My God..."

"What?"

"A natural firebreak." He let out a rare smile before adding some of the coordinates on his GPS. "So. We've got a river bisecting a canyon, and a hard rock hill above us, both of which are good, very good." He slipped his unit back into his pocket and wriggled his fingers. "We're going to cross. Give me your hand."

"Why?"

"So I can help you."

She laughed. "I can manage."

No doubt she could, so he lifted his hands in surrender and let her pick her way unaided over the rocks and branches through the water.

He'd known what he was going to be doing today, and he'd dressed appropriately in boots. Lyndie hadn't. She'd counted on flying him in, and then leaving again, hence the tennis shoes, which hadn't been too much of a problem until now, as they began some serious climbing. Another concern he'd had all along...her blouse, the sleeves of which she'd shoved up past her elbows. He'd asked her twice to pull down her sleeves, but she hadn't. He stopped. "We're not going on until you pull down your sleeves and put on the gloves Sergio gave you. I have an extra shirt, too—"

She shot him one of her patented quelling looks, one he was quite sure sent everyone in her path shaking in their boots. But he had far too many other things going on to allow her to scare him.

Hell, his very life at the moment was terrifying enough. "Just do it, Lyndie."

She tipped her head up to the sky, sighed, then looked at him again. "You always so bossy?"

He thought about that. "Yes."

She studied him for a long time, then lowered her sleeves. "I am, too."

"Is that right?"

"Yeah. So watch it."

He would. He watched it and her as they continued to hike along the perimeter of the fire, with him occasionally making notes, sometimes coming close enough to the flames to feel the heat of it on their exposed skin, sometimes able to stay so far back it was hard to believe the mountainside was burning at all. They had no trail to speak of through the bush for another half of a mile.

Then suddenly they came to a rock cliff—miraculously, the northern tip of the fire. Griffin eyed the rock. Not so high, maybe forty feet, it had a jutting point, and he figured he could get an excellent view from up there. The burning was behind them now, to the south and west. "I'll be able to see everything from up there."

Lyndie craned her neck, too. "Right." She glanced behind her at the bush. They couldn't see the flames, but they could hear them, crackling and popping, accompanied by the whistling wind coming through so eerily and the faux darkness of the day.

Uneasiness flickered over her face, the first sign maybe she wasn't quite as tough as she wanted him to believe. "Stick with me," he said, and pulled her by the hand close to his side.

"Yeah." With her free hand, she rubbed her chest as if her

lungs ached. His certainly did. "I'll be so close you'll be wondering if I'm attached."

They began their climb. She scrambled up the rock beside him, their shoulders brushing, their legs brushing. He had the inane thought that she smelled…soft. A bundle of contradictions, this woman who was hustling up the rock cliff as if she did it every day, stumbling here and there but still meeting him inch for inch.

The climb wasn't novice. Rocks interspaced with dry, rough, scratchy vegetation that clung to their arms and legs and exposed faces as they went up.

And up.

"Here." He pointed out her toe hold when she kept slipping. He reached down for her ankle to put her foot in the right place.

Her gaze flew to his, surprise there, as if she wasn't used to being helped.

He took his hand off her ankle and put it around her wrist. "Reach here—"

"I've got it." She turned her head away to survey the climb, tickling his nose with her hair.

"Hold here—"

"Really," she said tightly. "I've got it."

He looked into her face as they hung there, some thirty feet above ground. "You've got some trust issues, don't you."

Hanging there by her own sheer will, she frowned at him, her chest rising and falling. "I don't need to trust you. I'm just here to translate."

"Yeah." He sidled even closer on the rock they clung to. Beneath them and to the west were the flames. Above them, more rock. She was at his right, and at *her* right the cliff jutted out in a peak, though they couldn't see the other side. "So you've mentioned a hundred times or so," he said, thinking they needed to stay away from that jutting edge, where the rock and sand would be uneven, and therefore dangerous to be hanging from.

She squinted at him. "What does that mean, so I've mentioned?"

"It means you want me to think you're only here because you have to be. Well, I don't buy it."

"Thank you, Dr. Griffin. Should we examine *your* head now?"

"I'm just trying to make sure you don't fall, Lyndie."

"I won't."

Not if sheer will counted for anything. But this wasn't about sheer will, it was about the elements, and the exhaustion on her face. He was responsible for her out here, and hell if he'd lose another single person on his watch. Ever.

She shifted sideways, away from him, and around the jutting edge.

Just where they shouldn't go. "Lyndie—"

"Hey," she called back. "There's better rocks over here on this side, and softer—"

"No—wait." He reached out to grab her but she scooted out of his way, and around the corner faster than he expected.

"Shit," he muttered, going after her. "Slow down, damn it—"

But she wasn't listening, and had gone completely around the jutting edge so that he couldn't see her until he followed.

Right onto the unstable hill. *Christ.* "Lyndie, stop. It's unstable, you're going to—"

Her body slipped a little, and she gasped.

Fall. Heart in his throat, he scrambled farther along the slippery hillside to catch her, and felt the difference in the hold immediately.

From their weight and movement, several rocks loosened,

both above and behind him, and hundreds of little pebbles pelted them, falling to the ground below.

Lyndie took a hit on her shoulder and winced, just as he took a heavy hit on his chest. "Lyndie—" He reached for her, but before he connected, she let out a little *oof*, and lost her hold.

He snagged her by the wrist, barely. "Don't move." His other hand clung to a rock he could feel was about to give way, and his heart slammed against his ribs. "Lyndie, listen to me," he said urgently, eyeing the more gradual slope beneath them on this side of the rock. Thank God. "I'm going to let go of you."

She choked out a response that he didn't catch.

Probably a good thing.

"It's okay," he said as calmly as he could. "There's more sand here, and more of a slope than a sheer drop. You'll slide," he said into her wide eyes.

At the last fire he'd fought, in that hellish event that he relived every night, he'd looked into Greg's eyes and yelled "run." Griffin had, and it hadn't been until it'd been far too late that he'd realized Greg had momentarily frozen in shock. A terminal mistake.

No freezing, and no hysterics for this woman, she simply braced herself and let out a tight nod.

But he couldn't let go, he just couldn't do it. He looked into her amazing green eyes for a long moment, longer than he should have, and she jerked her head again, impatiently this time.

He got the message—she knew what she had to do, she trusted what he'd decided they had to do.

She *did* trust him. Hell of a time to realize the burden of that. One last time, he looked into her eyes.

And then let go of her.

He let go of his own perilous hold, as well, following her down, desperately trying to make sure he didn't kick or fall into her.

Dirt went up his nose. He heard her cry out as he hit his hip on a rock. A branch raked across his face.

And still he slid.

He could smell the smoke, it choked the air out of his lungs. More dirt deposited itself in every part of his body. He could feel the heat in the ground, but it was the sound of a sudden and viciously hot wind that got him as they slid, because behind it came the ominous crackling of the actual flames.

They were sliding to the west of where they'd climbed up, and by the sound and feel of it, right into the fire.

"Lyndie!" he yelled, but he heard nothing but his own whoosh of air as it left his lungs.

And he figured he knew right then.

In all the fires he'd worked on, he hadn't died.

All through last year when he was so grief stricken, he hadn't died, not even when he'd wanted to.

And yet now, out in the middle of nowhere, with only an oddly thorny, oddly irresistible woman at his side, he was going to.

6

Lyndie's graceless slide was broken by a nice bush. Unfortunately her weight was no match for said nice bush, and she plowed right through it, fell through the air again, bashing her knee, and also her ribs, and what seemed like a lifetime later, landed with a splash.

With a gasping breath—an extremely *tight* gasping breath because her lungs had tightened and dried like a Shrinky Dink—she sat in a running river, the body of which was maybe thirty feet wide and currently swirling up to her belly button. Behind her was the sharp, craggy rock and sand they'd just slid down.

On the other side of the river, blowing straight at her along with the harsh wind, was a wall of fire. Mesmerized, horrified, she stared at it.

Then, from behind her came a splash. She jerked out of her shock to remember Griffin had fallen, too, and had landed a few feet away.

Turning in the water, she set her eyes on the only steady point in a crazy, dangerous world.

"Lyndie." As drenched and dirty in his Nomex flame-resistant clothing as he was, he came to his knees, then hauled her up to hers, as well, his expression tense and tight with what she realized was fear. For her. "You all right?" he demanded, and when she just stared at him, he added a little shake. "*Lyndie*. Are you all right?"

Sure. Unless she counted the yearning for the safety of his arms. But she didn't need anyone's arms, warm or strong or otherwise. She never had. She had no idea then, why she shook her head no in answer to his question. "I don't think so, no."

"God." He hauled her into the arms she'd wanted around her. "I'm sorry."

She could feel the pounding of his heart, the bite of his wet fingers spread wide on her back. It didn't feel like anything but the protective hug of a man she could count on, who'd be there if she needed him.

Like now. Horrifying herself, she let out a sound that might have been a pathetic whimper.

He pulled back, only to run his hands over her body. "What's hurt?"

Actually, she had no idea. If she was relying on a man she didn't even know for comfort, when she never relied on anyone, then no doubt, she'd hit her head. She glanced down at herself. Two arms, two legs…everything seemed to be in focus and all in one piece, but before she could answer, he'd put his hands on her face, tilting it up to his.

"Lyndie." His voice was hoarse, rough. His clothes clung to his every hard inch. The yellow shirt delineated the fact that he was made up of corded muscle, without an inch of excess. Something she already knew, now that she'd been plastered against him. He had a scrape over his chin and another on his throat, both bleeding lightly, and yet he never took his eyes off her. "Talk to me."

Because he looked so serious, and because she was quite re-lieved to find herself in one piece, she let out a strangled sound that was half laugh, half cry. "I'm…good."

He didn't look convinced. His finger gently stroked her jaw, and the growing swelling there from where a rock had glanced her.

"Superficial stuff," she whispered. "Really." For a moment, a very brief moment, she felt like putting her mouth to his cuts and bruises to kiss them all better, and with another man she might have, but she retained her sanity. Griffin Moore—sexy, brooding, haunted—was not a man to mess with. "Guess what…we lived."

He blinked once, slow as an owl. "Yeah."

Because she was still just a bit in shock, she splashed him, and then because he looked so surprised, she did it again. "Feel that? *Alive.*"

Another slow blink, and then the hands that he'd put on her face tightened, just a little. His expression was fierce, so fierce, but before she could soothe him, he'd leaned in, sinking his fingers in the tangled mess of her hair.

She could feel the heat of his breath against her face, and then her own shockingly needy response.

"We're okay," he murmured.

"Right." Against her brain's command, her body struggled to get even closer to his. "We're okay."

He stared down into her face, specifically at her mouth, which she nervously wet with her tongue, making him groan, and then in the next breath, his mouth hungrily covered hers.

Just one quick, hard kiss. She had the time to think he tasted like sun and incredibly yummy man, but then it was over before she could even fully register it.

He stared at her, still close enough to bring his mouth back to hers without effort if he chose to, which to her disappointment, he didn't.

"What was that?" she asked, breath heaving even more now.

"A good, hard fall."

"No, after that."

"You were in shock."

"Was not. You put your lips on mine."

"I kissed you." His gaze dropped to her mouth again. Speculation and something else flickered in his expression. It was the something else that got to her.

"It was a confirmation of your statement," he said. "We're alive."

As a rule, most men were intimidated by her, and if they weren't, well, then they usually weren't interested. In all the kissing she'd experienced in her life, she'd have to say, she'd started most of it.

She hadn't started this.

Or had she? She'd have liked to hit rewind and relive it.

A few times.

Griffin took in the flaming vegetation so close, and shook his head in surprise. "It does feel good to be alive. I'd forgotten how good."

She felt herself leaning toward him, drawn by an energy she couldn't seem to resist.

"It's okay," he whispered, misunderstanding her reason for wanting to be close. "We're both really okay." He stood, and pulled her up as well. Both of his hands came up to once again cradle her face, his big, warm hands amazingly gentle.

"Yeah." But still she leaned in, craving the next kiss as she craved...air. This time he didn't disappoint, his mouth covered hers, deepening the connection, using his entire body, his tongue, and this time it wasn't a kiss driven by fear and desperation, but one of warmth and affection. And then, need. Hunger.

When it was over, she slowly pulled back. Licked her lips to enjoy every last taste. Then turned toward the fire.

Griffin shook his head as if to clear it, drew in a ragged breath, and also eyed the burning bush only a few feet away. "I'd have done anything to keep you from having to fall like that—"

"I'm fine." Even if her breathing hadn't slowed or eased, and the problem wasn't so much a sexual reaction to a delicious kiss, but asthma-related.

"What you are," he said, "is tough as hell. And for what it's worth, it's pretty damn inspiring." He touched her again, just a brief stroke of his finger over her jaw. "At a time when I needed inspiring. I owe you for that."

"What you owe me is to get control of this fire." Never comfortable with compliments, she tried to turn away, but he stopped her.

Purposely she looked down at his hands on her, then up into his face, giving him a look that had singed the hair off plenty of men.

And yet he didn't scare off. "I know," he said. "You want to get on with it, but Lyndie, you *are* amazing. You're amazing to me."

"Look, I don't know what to do with words like that, okay? Or the way I liked your kiss but don't want to like you."

He let out a sound that might have been a laugh. "Make that two of us." Once again he turned to the flames licking at the brush lining the river. Most had burned black by now, but there was still plenty left for the fire to eat up. "Let's go upriver, I still need to see above the fire, see how far west it goes. Then back to the men and set a plan in motion."

"Right." She took as deep a breath as she could—which wasn't much—fortifying herself for another trek. "Up the river."

She started trudging through the water, but Griffin stopped her with a hand to her elbow.

Slowly she looked up at him.

"Thanks for not letting me quit," he said quietly, shocked by how much it meant.

She tried to shrug him off. "I didn't do much. You just have a misguided sense of heroism."

He blinked. "What?"

"You have a 'save the world' complex, Ace." She patted his arm. "It's actually quite annoying."

He narrowed his eyes. "Is it, now?"

"Yeah." Looking quite smug for someone with dirt on her nose and a ripped blouse, she splashed her way down the river, breathing heavily, clearly assuming he'd follow. When he didn't, she turned and cocked a brow at him.

He cocked a brow right back. "Would it be showing my…misguided sense of heroism, if I pointed out that you're going the wrong way? I want to go *up*-stream."

She stopped and looked around, at the fire, the cliff, then both up and down the river before rolling her eyes at herself. Muttering beneath her breath, she whirled and splashed her way back to him, passing him, ignoring his soft laugh.

Then, oddly enough, she slowed down and let him pass her. But because this wasn't a woman to give up the lead, he paused. "What's the matter?"

"Nothing." She still splashed along, but was clearly lagging, and still breathing heavily, too heavily he realized now for a woman in incredible athletic shape.

"What is it?" he pressed.

"I said nothing." But she slid her hand into her pocket, and then her other pocket, and then went utterly still. "No." She slapped her back pockets now, then looked at him, making him realize he'd not really seen her afraid.

Until now.

"Lyndie?"

Again she slapped her pockets, then whirled in a circle, looking around her. Her breathing had gone from ragged to wildly out of control.

And his heart sank. He moved back to her, grabbed her arm. "What is it? Asthma?"

"Yes," she wheezed.

"*Christ.*" He looked at her helplessly. "Why didn't you say something?"

"No need. At least not until now." She tipped her head back and eyed the slide of rocks they'd just tumbled down. Her chest rose and fell with her shallow little breaths, the clenching of her fist over her shirt telling him how bad it was. "I lost my inhaler."

"Where?"

"Before the fall, I think. On the trail."

"Okay." Finally, something he could do without her beating him to the punch, and he was a man used to the doing. Shrugging out of his pack, he set it on a rock big enough to keep it out of the water. He pulled out a bandana.

"What are you doing?"

"Going back for it."

"No! Griffin, the fire—"

"I'm going. God, Lyndie, the smoke must have damn near killed you. Wrap this around your face."

Without waiting for her to do it, he came up behind her and placed it around her mouth and nose before tying it at the back of her head. Then he pushed her down to a rock. Surrounded by the swirling water, with the rocks to her back, she'd be safe. "Stay here."

"Griffin—"

"I'll hurry." Her breathing was so erratic it terrified him. "Stay as still as you can."

"No." She tried to hold him back. "You'll be in danger, the flames have moved by now—"

Hands on his arms, he sat her down again. "Shh. It'll be okay." Bending close, he looked into her eyes, hating the way she struggled for every breath. "You'll be okay," he said, and when she nodded, he backed away, praying it was the truth.

* * *

Lyndie lay back against the rock and studied the fire-ravaged sky as she carefully and painfully drew in each breath, none of which were deep enough to satisfy her lungs.

He'd gone back. He'd gone straight into the fire.

For her.

The thought of him retracing their steps, facing the flames straight on, all because of her, really got to her. Closing her eyes, she concentrated on breathing, one gulp at a time, instead of picturing all the things that could happen to him.

She had no idea how long she sat, eyes closed, desperately doing her best to survive on the shallow breaths, working even harder not to hear the fire ravishing the woods around her, when two hands closed over her shoulders.

Gasping, she opened her eyes and locked gazes with Griffin. One eye was a little swollen, probably from their earlier fall, and the cut above it had bled a thin line down the side of his face. She reached out to touch it, but he caught her hand, and put her inhaler into it.

She stared down at it.

"Damn it, what are you waiting for?" He lifted it to her mouth. "Use it, you're practically blue."

She used it, staring at him as she did. He didn't take his hands off her, or his eyes. And only when she'd pulled the inhaler away from her face did he appear to relax slightly.

"No one has ever done such a thing for me," she whispered when she could.

"There's a first time for everything."

She stared at him, fighting the real and frightening urge to cry. She never cried. "Right."

He pulled her to her feet, took the inhaler from her hands and put it firmly into her pocket. "Keep track of that, now."

"I will."

"Let's move. You okay?"

"I am now."

Griffin eyed her closely, trying to decide for himself whether that was true or not. "We can slow down."

"I don't need you to slow down."

"Lyndie, I'm not suggesting you're weak because you have asthma."

"Good, because I'm not." Again, she started trudging through the water, banked on one side by the rock, the other by burning mountainside.

"You always get testy when someone tries to help you?"

She didn't bother to answer, and Griffin wondered if that was because what she'd said could possibly be true.

No one ever helped her.

The thought tugged at him. He came up alongside her, reaching out to take her arm, just to steady her, to try to control her pace a little so that she didn't have to breathe too hard, but she actually smacked his hand away.

"Okay," he said, lifting his hands. "You've got it."

"Yeah." She passed him again, slamming her feet down into the river hard enough to be sure to splash him with her every step.

After at least a quarter of a mile, she finally looked at him. "Thanks," she said simply.

And for some reason, he felt like he'd been given a gift.

* * *

On the way back, they found some of Sergio's men on the east side, furiously digging a firebreak, trying to block the flames from racing down the short canyon…and onto another ranch. They were doing a good job, and with Lyndie translating, Griffin showed them how to widen their lines, and how to use the fuses to burn the vegetation between the lines they were digging and the fire, to rob it of fuel.

By Griffin's estimate, they had one side of the fire blocked in by the river, another side partially blocked in by the rock. But it still left a lot of retaining to do, and a lot of the fire left to its own devices. He glanced at the tired, wet, dirty, incredible woman at his side. "You hanging in?"

Her eyes said it all.

"Right," he said on a rough laugh. "Don't ask you how you're doing. Got it."

"Hey, you're no easier than me to be with, Ace."

Didn't he know it.

They made their way back to the water trucks, where the men were taking a late food break. Tom had arrived with the tractor, and had taken it, along with a group of men, as far south as the fire raged, clearing fire lines to try to keep the flames from jumping down to town.

With Lyndie translating, Griffin arranged some of the men around his small handheld screen, showing them how they'd use the river as one firebreak, the rock cliff as another, but that to protect the town, they were going to have to watch the south, unprotected side like a hawk, clearing effective firebreaks that couldn't be jumped. He sent some of them down to assist Tom, and the rest up to help the eastern efforts to save the ranch in danger.

Which left only the north tip free, a huge problem, but one they couldn't yet face without more manpower.

At dark, with the fire at their backs, and thirty men going at it with all their might, using the tractor, their shovels, the fuses to burn the vegetation between the rock and the river, desperate to keep San Puebla safe, they were forced to call it a day.

7

Most of the men dispersed into the darkness. A few would stay behind, near the perimeters of the flames with radios, but little more could be done until daylight.

Lyndie could see that Griffin didn't like it as he stood there watching most of the men go. He'd been appalled at their second-rate equipment, saddened and anxious over the men out here without the proper training and tools, and stressed about leading this fight.

"How can it be this bad?" he murmured, taking a moment to lean on the shovel he'd been wielding. "It's just not right. We're killing ourselves to save the village and the ranches, and because we're shorthanded, the north end of the fire is making its way into those mountains."

Lyndie had watched him work the land all day, the long, lean lines of his body moving with easy strength as he cleared fuel from the path of the fire, never giving up. Over and over again he'd stressed safety to everyone around him, making sure no one got hurt.

What had he done and seen in his experiences as a firefighter that had made him the man he was? Undoubtedly, he'd been molded by each experience, as she had by her flying, and she wanted to know more. The wanting made her incredibly wary. She'd always prided herself on her independence, on her no-strings-attached way of life. She lived as she wanted, when and where she wanted, and had no one to account to. When she needed a man, she got herself one.

And then went on her merry way.

More than once she'd been told, *accused,* of being far too much like a man. She'd never taken that as an insult. She didn't understand why she should. Sure, maybe a part of her would have liked to have Griffin on a sexual level. He was here for two days tops. A hot bout of mutually satisfying sex would have been perfect to ease the fear and danger and tension.

Except for two things.

One, they wouldn't have time to do anything but breathe and fight the fire. And two…he was just different enough, just complex enough, to complicate things.

She hated complications in her sex life.

And yet she couldn't deny certain things lingered on her mind, things she'd never spent time lingering over before. His hands, for one. They were big and work-roughened and warm. She knew this because as they'd hiked, he kept putting them on her, helping her, guiding her…which made this all his fault, really. If he'd just have kept them to himself, she wouldn't be wondering anything right now.

And then there'd been the kissing. She really couldn't stop thinking about that.

Also his fault.

But the way he'd risked himself for her, going back to get her inhaler…"Food and sleep," she decided out loud. That's all she needed.

"I have a tent and some rations," he said. "I'll just—"

"You can't work two days and nights straight. Come on," she coaxed. "I'll even let you drive back."

That got him. He liked being in charge. The Jeep had been moved twice during the day to keep it safe. They got into it as full darkness hit, the headlights vanishing into the thick smoke as they started back.

The ride felt even more spine-chilling at night. Without a moon or stars, the landscape was utterly invisible, the only sight being the terrifying glow of the earth burning and the reflection in the smoke hanging overhead. It was like a bad dream, an out of focus one, and Lyndie found herself blinking over and over again to try to clear her vision. "I don't want them to lose it all," she whispered.

"They won't."

She glanced over at his profile, lit only by the Jeep's instruments. "That's quite a promise."

"Just determination."

Their headlights wavered, muffled by the rising dust from the Jeep's tires and smoke. He drove with the same fierceness she did, working the steering wheel and gearshift with tense arms. "You were…incredible out there today."

He glanced at her. "I was just doing my job. But you…"

"What?"

"*You* were incredible."

They hit a rut hard. She gripped the dash and tried not to let his praise get to her. "You're right. It's much nicer to drive."

"Yeah." He reached out and squeezed her leg. "You really doing okay?"

"Why wouldn't I be?"

"Don't go all bristly on me, I just—" He took them around a hairpin turn, the two headlights bobbing up and down. "I just meant your asthma."

"I'm okay." If she took only shallow breaths.

He shook his head. "Why am I asking? You sure as hell won't tell me anything."

"Turn right."

"I remember the way back. Have you always been domineering and bossy?"

Since the day her grandfather had come and gotten her after her parents' accident, barking orders to mask his grief, in turn showing her how to do the same. "Yep."

"Is all your family this way?"

"Turn right again."

"I'll take that as a yes." He turned. The lights of San Puebla appeared ahead in the night. Above them, from where they'd just come, glowed the fire.

Not nearly far enough away to suit her.

"Where to?" he asked.

"Your weekend accommodations." The cobblestone streets rattled their brains, the sweet, quaint, small buildings reminding her of why they'd nearly killed themselves today. "And I should tell you now," she warned of the place that had unexpectedly captured her heart five years earlier. "The Rio Vista Inn is not quite a five-star."

"And here I was, looking forward to a facial and pedicure, along with caviar and a good Sex on the Beach."

She blinked.

He glanced at her innocently. "The drink."

"Oh. Right." Sex on the Beach was a drink, some complicated mixed drink. But he really shouldn't say the word "sex" in that voice of his—it made her insides do funny things. "I knew that."

He didn't laugh, but did smile, and damn if now her hormones didn't stand up and tap dance.

"How much farther?"

She pointed. "Until the end of the road."

"There's hardly a road now. How did you find this place the first time?"

"Long story."

"We happen to have lots of time."

She lifted a shoulder. "I had plane trouble a few years ago."

"Plane trouble? I'm almost afraid to ask, but what in your world specifies 'plane trouble'?"

"I had to make an interesting landing out here, which I thought was the middle of nowhere. Turns out I was right. Turns out I also like it out here in the middle of nowhere. Watch out for that pig in the middle of the road."

"You, Lyndie Anderson, are a fascinating woman." He did indeed slow down, moving carefully around the pig, who held its ground in the dark and stared at them, its eyes glowing in their headlights as they passed. "An 'interesting' landing? What does that mean exactly? You had to crash land? Save your passengers single-handedly? Walk through the woods barefoot for days? Rebuild your plane with parts you built yourself?"

"Who do you think I am, MacGyver?" But she was smiling, damn it. God, she so didn't want to do this, share stories, share herself. It would make things worse in two days when she dumped him back in San Diego and they went their own merry way. "I don't like to talk about myself."

"Well, I'm with you there. I was just wondering what ruffled you. I know it's not hairy Jeep rides, or falling off a cliff, or running from a wall of fire."

What ruffled her? Tall, rugged, rangy men with expressively haunted eyes and a heartbreaking smile, and a tendency toward unusual courage and a save-the-world soul, all while facing some mysterious nightmare. That's what ruffled her. "Nothing gets me," she finally said, and he let out another of those tummy-quivering low laughs.

They were silent for a moment, the comfortable kind of silence, which in turn made her *un*comfortable. She stared at the glowing hill, beyond which were the flames. She could still hear them, smell them. "So you really just usually camp out when you're fighting fires?"

"Yes."

"Have you done this...recently?"

"Fishing, Lyndie? For personal information? Because that goes both ways."

Yes. Yes, it did. "I'm just asking you about your work. Nothing personal."

"My work?" His face in shadow, he gave nothing away. "It's been about a year, but apparently nothing changes. As you learned today, it's dirty. It's hard work, and a good amount of the time, boring as hell. You're either struggling against time and the elements, taking orders from a headquarters that can be miles away and clueless, or waiting for the trucks to refill. Or if you're lucky, sleeping in pure exhaustion."

"If you don't like it, why do you do it?"

He jerked his head toward her, and in his eyes was pure surprise. "I do like it. I love it."

"You know what?" she said on a laugh. "You're crazier than I am."

"Laugh if you want. Fighting fire is what I do, it's who I am."

"Then why doesn't it make you happy?"

"It used to." He downshifted for a sharp turn. "It used to be my entire life. I'd go from fire to fire—Colorado, Utah, Idaho, California, Wyoming…you name the state, and if they had a wilderness, I'd been there."

"Been. Past tense."

His long fingers tightened on the wheel. "I told you, I haven't fought a fire in almost a year now."

"Why?"

"Now that question definitely leaves the realm of work-related topics and dips into personal."

Right. And she of all people valued privacy, not wanting to be probed at by a sharp stick. But that was when *she* was the one wanting to avoid something.

He came to a stop at the base of a hill. Above it came the nerve-racking glow from the fire.

"Right is a loop back to downtown. Left is suburbia, Mexican style. You'll find Tom's place that way, five places down. We need to get him his Jeep back."

The first two casas were little more than one-room cabins, though the yards were tended to, and pride of ownership was clearly an issue. "That one turns into a wild place at dusk," she said pointing to the third place, a slightly bigger bungalow. "The owner's a woman who was born here. She has seventeen brothers and sisters, most of whom are within a few square miles. She raised them, and charges them every night for drinks, then kicks them out when they start to fight. And that house—" she pointed to the fourth, "that's Tom's. His daughter Nina lives there, too, and she runs a cantina out of the back courtyard. It's a popular place for locals. And here's the fifth." They pulled into the lot. "This is where you're staying tonight."

Griffin took in the classic Spanish style dwelling that to Lyndie's critical eye could use some work. Still, the comfortably cozy inn with its low flower-lined windows, the cream walls built of all natural materials including lots of Mexican stone, had stolen her heart. She knew there were spots that needed patching, that the yard needed help as well as the courtyard the inn had been built around, but the Old World charm drew her, soothed her like few other places had, and inside she'd found her own personal haven.

Griffin parked near two other trucks and two unidentifiable cars. Dust rose up, choking them. He looked at the hanging sign that read RIO VISTA INN. "Not quite the Hilton," he noted with a smile.

Inexplicably, she felt her defenses rise. "Look, it's real life, all right? Maybe the rooms are small, and maybe half of them don't even lock. You might even see the occasional large and unwelcome roach. But the food is spectacular and the ambience genuine. The owner is saving up her cash to remodel. You just go on inside and let them take care of you."

He blinked, clearly surprised at her passion. "I was just kidding, Lyndie."

She sighed. "Yeah."

"Who's the owner?"

Oh, no. He didn't want to share himself with her, and neither did she. "Ownership is a rather odd issue," she finally said. "But it's open to any weary traveler, which you certainly are."

They both looked at the inn, at the stucco that needed patching again, at the brick in the arches that were the color of dirt, thanks to the latest dust storm. Due to the drought, the plants out front, the ones that got direct sunlight all day long, had long ago begun to wilt.

But there were lights on inside, and she could already smell dinner—real food, not fast food—that would fill their empty bellies. Far better than any fancy hotel.

Griffin got out of the Jeep and grabbed his gear. "Hey, as long as there's running water…" he said with a teasing grin she ignored because he had a way of wearing her down, of turning her defenses into something else entirely. "Running *hot* water," he added. "I'd do just about anything for a shower."

"A bath is closer to what you'll be getting." She eyed him beneath the lights coming from the inn. He'd do "anything" for a shower? He really shouldn't have told her that. "What do you hear?"

He cocked his head and listened. "Water."

"You're quick, Ace."

She moved toward the sound, which led them to the side of the inn. There was a small creek running there, around back, disappearing into the vast, dark wilderness beyond. Above them the moon struggled to light their way through the smoke, as around them, oblivious to the wildfire raging not too far from this very spot, insects hummed and a coyote howled off in the distance.

The banks of the creek were mossy and thick, the trees hanging over the water creating a private little haven. "Don't tell me," Griffin said, looking dejected. "*This* is my bath?"

"Okay I won't tell you." Oh yes, she definitely had replaced her defensiveness with something else. *Mischievousness.* "I also won't tell you that the soap is hanging from the vee of those two branches to your right."

He eyed the hanging soap, then looked down at his filthy body. "I suppose I need to clean up before going in."

She lifted a negligent shoulder. "I suppose."

Dropping his bag, he looked her over. "Do you bathe in here, too?"

"When it suits me." She didn't mention that she'd only done so once, in the thick heat of summer, and she'd been giving Rosa's dog a bath with Nina. They'd gotten a nice tan that day, too.

But for a good, hot shower, nope, she'd go inside and use the communal bathroom.

Which had perfectly fine running hot water.

Griffin was still looking at the water. She imagined that creek—snow melt—was still pretty darned chilly for this time of year.

He lifted his head. "I don't suppose it suits you to bathe in here now…"

At the look of unexpected heat in his eyes, the one that sped up her heart rate for no good reason except that he looked like wicked fun standing there with a challenging gleam in his eyes, she bit her lip and slowly shook her head.

"Yeah. Thought not." He kicked off his shoes. Lifted his hands and began to unbutton his shirt. "How is it I got more dirty than you did?"

Oh, she was plenty dirty, and she'd have her shower.

Hot.

Private.

And inside.

But at the moment it was her thoughts that were the dirtiest. Leaning back against a nice, comfy tree, she crossed her arms, confident she'd come out on top of this situation, that she'd gotten the best of him, because surely he wouldn't really strip down, not right in front of her—

He shrugged out of his Nomex shirt.

Shucked off the T-shirt beneath, and tossed both aside.

Oh boy. "Um—"

His hands went to his pants.

8

As Griffin tossed off his clothes, he was unsure which he needed most—to be clear of the dirt and grime that clung to him, or a nice bed to crash in.

Make that food. Lots of it. Someone had once figured a firefighter needed seven thousand calories a day, and he'd always thought that a huge exaggeration. But he decided he could consume twice that now. Burgers and fries. A steak. An entire chicken…His mouth watered with the fantasy, knowing the reality was going to be far, far different.

Then he looked up and caught Lyndie's expression as she watched him strip, which immediately put a different spin on his mood.

Her gaze was caught on his chest, his stomach…everywhere, as if she couldn't help herself, but his body had been just a shell for so long it felt like a shock to have someone be interested in it.

He adjusted quickly, and his hunger for sustenance turned in a distinctly different direction, only, just as with everything else he'd faced earlier in the day, he didn't know what to do with it all. Yes, he'd kissed her, and yes, all that aloneness in the wilderness had combined into one ball of heat in his gut and also lower, but he didn't plan to act on it.

Not while facing all he had to face here, because the sorry truth was, he had nothing, nothing left at all to offer a woman.

Not even sex.

So he turned his back on her and shucked off his pants, leaving him in just his shorts. That was the best show she was going to get.

The night was so full of noises—the wind, crickets, the cry of something mysterious—that he hesitated, wondering if there were mountain cats or bears he should be worried about. It was hard to believe that just on the other side of the timbered hill raged an out of control wildfire.

But he had the cold, hard memory of the day to prove it, and the grime that went along with it. With a deep breath, he stepped into the creek. *Holy sh—*

"Cold?" Lyndie asked sweetly.

Only freezing. "Just right." He reached for the soap, scrubbing away at both the dirt and memories. The water went up only to mid-thigh at its deepest point, but modesty had gone out the window years ago in his crowded apartment in college, and even more so out in the wildlands for weeks at a time with a coed crew. The night remained unseasonably warm despite the wind rushing over his body like long fingers, reminding him of what Lyndie had said earlier.

He was alive. So very alive.

Dipping in the water to rinse off, he straightened, and faced Lyndie, who stood smug and contrarily beautiful at the edge of the creek. In the meager light from the inn behind her, her eyes…danced? Hmm. The night suddenly took a different spin. "What are you up to, Lyndie Anderson?"

Five feet three inches of pure trouble, she shook her head. "Nothing."

Right. Nothing. She made him want to run like hell, she made him want to laugh.

Scary combination.

"Better?" Again she used that sweet voice, and he had no doubt. In some way he'd just been had. Ah, but he should have warned her not to mess with the master. "You know you have a little dirt spot…" Waggling his fingers, he gestured to her face.

"I do not."

"You do."

Eyeing him suspiciously, she bent, scooped up some water, and scrubbed at her jaw.

"Not quite," he said seriously, and pointed at her chin. "There."

Again she bent, scooped more water, scrubbed.

He made his way out of the creek, splashing with each step. "Nope, it's still there. Here—" Cupping his hand full of water, he brought it up and tipped it over her head.

Droplets rained down her cheeks and nose, into her eyes, which she opened and stabbed him with. "Thank you."

"Don't mention it." Smiling to himself, he bent to his bag for a clean pair of jeans and a shirt. No towel, but being dirty had been far worse than being wet. He shoved his legs into the pants. "I suppose you—" But his words stuttered to a halt because she was looking him over again, a long, frank gaze sliding down his wet body—a body that suddenly enjoyed remembering what it felt like to react to a woman. "Lyndie." Against his better judgment, he stepped closer. "What's going on?"

"I'm…not sure."

"You think being tired is making us both so…"

Her breath caught, and it wasn't asthma, not this time. "So...what?"

Unbearably attracted? *Aroused?* He stared down at her mouth, which was only fair because she'd been staring at his. But while his body was able, his mind was not, and he took a big mental step back. "Nothing."

He took a real step back as well. Disappointment flashed over her features, but she remained silent, for which he was grateful because he couldn't possibly explain why, when he had a beautiful woman standing here, clearly wanting him, that he couldn't give her what she wanted. But he had no idea how to explain the fact he didn't know his mind when it came to feeling again. Bottom line, he couldn't trust his emotions, and she shouldn't either.

He pulled on a fresh T-shirt, buttoned up his Levi's, and, unable to resist, he smiled and gestured to the creek. "Your turn."

But she'd clearly sensed his withdrawal, and with a little laugh, she backed up, too. "Oh, no. I don't bathe with an audience." She whirled on her heels and started toward the inn. "Let's go, Ace. I owe you a meal."

"What you owe me is the same strip show you just got."

She stumbled for a step but caught herself. And then kept walking as if he hadn't spoken.

But her ears glowed red in the moonlight.

* * *

Lyndie walked up the stone tiles, under the archway of the inn, extremely aware of the silent, incredibly sexy Griffin behind her. She couldn't remember ever having a nearly naked man this close without also being nearly naked, and she wasn't happy about the experience.

Little lights lined the aged stone pathway, and a scattering of pine trees swayed lightly in the night breeze. The ground crunched dry and brittle beneath their feet. So different from San Diego, or any other place she'd ever been for that matter.

She opened the front door and would have entered, but Griffin stopped her with a hand on her wrist. She looked at his hand, big and tanned on hers, then up into his eyes, which were filled with heat and frustration, which made no sense for a man who'd backed off first.

Then his free hand came up, his finger stroking a gentle line over her cheekbone.

"More dirt?" she asked, a little confused at all the conflicting things he stirred up within her.

"No dirt."

Then why the hell was he looking at her like that? "I thought you were hungry."

"Oh, I'm hungry," he assured her.

"No." She let out a little laugh. "Hell, no. You had your shot, Ace." She slapped his hand away. *"Vamanos."* Heat racing now, damn him, she entered the reception room, her tennis shoes squeaking on the tile floor. She took in the beautiful aged stone fireplace, the lovely but starting to crumble brick archways leading from room to room, the soft chenille fabrics covering some of the furniture—which she knew needed replacing—and felt her heart sigh. But other than what she could have been doing on the bank of the creek with the man behind her, she had only one thing on her mind: *food.*

"God, something smells heavenly."

She wondered if he knew what his low, husky voice did to a woman who was already thinking about sex far too much today.

Apparently oblivious, he turned hopefully toward the hallway from which came an admittedly delicious scent.

Thank you, Rosa. Just as she thought it, the tall, curvy, dark-skinned woman appeared, wearing a multilayered skirt and matching bright, floral blouse snug to her full figure. Her jet-black hair—carefully dyed every month to cover the gray—was, as always, piled on top of her head. Her birth certificate said she was fifty-five, but Rosa scoffed at that, preferring instead to be thirty-nine.

She had an incredibly large family, all of whom had migrated out of San Puebla to Encinitas, California, years ago. Rosa spent every winter there with them, and as a result was fluent in English, though she still swore only in her native tongue—and often. Her greatest joy was bossing everyone around her, twisting them around her finger. That, combined with her gift of getting people to do whatever she wanted, made Rosa the powerhouse of San Puebla.

Lyndie didn't know how it worked exactly, but even she jumped when Rosa said to do so. She hadn't grown up with a mother figure, or even a grandmother figure, and yet somehow Rosa and her loving, unbendable demands were law.

"*You.*" Rosa smiled, grabbed Lyndie's face, and kissed each cheek as she spoke in flawless but heavily accented English. "You stayed. If I was older than my thirty-nine years, you would be the daughter of my heart. Now get out of my sight and shower, you are filthy. I will have food waiting."

Lyndie's mouth started to water at the thought. "I have to eat first."

"Wait," Griffin said. "You have a shower here?"

With a wince, Lyndie turned to face him. Oddly enough, he looked more amused than mad, and also just a little bit challenging, and she realized that when it came to getting the best of this man, she just might have bitten off more than she could chew.

"Of course we have a shower." Rosa turned to Griffin. "You are our hero, *si*? You, I have to hug and kiss." Never stingy when it came to affection, she grabbed his face as she had Lyndie's, and noisily kissed both cheeks, chirping at him the entire time, telling him how happy she was to meet him, how grateful that he'd come, how much she looked forward to fattening up his skinny butt—

Suddenly she went still. She sniffed at him, and then put her hands on her hips. "Why this boy smell like my Tallulah's soap?"

Her "Tallulah" was her precious, ridiculous poodle that one of her grandkids had given her last year, but Lyndie's mind was still on Griffin's "skinny butt," because she'd seen it, in nothing but wet, clinging shorts, and didn't think it was so skinny at all. Granted there wasn't an ounce of fat on him, but what he had was solid as a rock, and extremely…nice. But as for why he smelled like the soap they used on Tallulah…"Well…"

The poodle in question burst into the room with the momentum of a rocket ship. Barking fiercely, she launched herself toward Griffin, but once she reached him, she stopped short so fast her back end nearly tumbled over her front end. Without warning, she collapsed to her back, exposing her belly to be scratched.

Tallulah, it turned out, was fond of men who smelled just like her.

Lyndie might have laughed at the look on Griffin's face, but Rosa was hugging them both again. "You spend all day out there? *Dios mio,* such hard workers." Her eyes locked on Griffin. "Tom didn't mention how pretty you are."

Griffin appeared baffled by Rosa's quick subject change, but Lyndie bit her lip. "Yes, he is rather pretty, isn't he?" She smiled when he let out a low growl from his throat for her ears only. "And he's hungry. What do you have to take care of that?"

"Much. *Venga*," Rosa demanded, and gestured them both down the aged stucco hallway, which was lined with large, cool, smooth tiles and potted plants to cover up all the cracks, of which there were many. "Sure you don't want to clean up first?" she asked Lyndie.

"Soon as I eat. I'm starving."

The kitchen was a large, homey room. Pots and pans hung from the low stucco ceilings, and on the big scarred wooden table in the center sat enough food to feed a small army. Rosa pushed Griffin into a chair, then started loading meat, beans, rice, and freshly made tortillas on a plate. Only when it was heaping did she hand it to him. "Eat."

Then she turned to Lyndie and repeated the entire process. "It's spicy tonight," she warned, and stroked a strand of hair from Lyndie's forehead. "Spicy enough to clear out your lungs. You're having trouble today, no?"

"I'm fine."

"Yes, you are," Rosa soothed, then ruined the effect by rolling her eyes at Griffin. "Pigheaded fine."

Griffin laughed.

Rosa beamed at him. "You agree?"

"Oh, I most definitely agree," he said, and took a big bite. He moaned—a sound that scraped at her nipples for some reason—then ate as he appeared to do everything else: with intense concentration. She already knew he worked like that, he talked like that...and he most definitely kissed like that.

Lyndie couldn't help but wonder what else he did like that.

He kept shoveling in the food, stopping only to lick a dab of rice off his thumb with a small sucking sound that pulled at any erogenous zones that hadn't already stood at attention. When he finally slowed down some, he shot her a challenging smile. "So, on this pigheaded thing," he said.

"Ah, yes." Rosa smiled. "She can't really help it. She thinks she knows everything."

"She also thinks she's funny." Griffin smiled at Lyndie, and the slight wickedness in it made her nervous. "She neglected to tell me the creek wasn't the only moving water here."

Rosa lifted her brow so high it vanished into her hair. "Most interesting."

"I think so." He shoveled in some more food, clearly savoring every bite.

If he moaned again, Lyndie figured she'd groan right back. "Oh, for God's sake, I was just teasing you." She lifted her chin to add authority to the claim. "And before I knew it, you'd taken off all your clothes. Far be it from me to stop you."

"Far be it," he said dryly.

"You…teased him." Rosa clearly found this fascinating.

"I do have a sense of humor, you know."

"Uh huh." Rosa put her tongue in her cheek. "Of course you do."

Lyndie drew in a deep, irritated breath and ate some more.

"I've got your rooms all ready," Rosa said. "Oh, and as for re-doing that upstairs bathroom this summer—"

"Your plans are your plans," Lyndie said.

"But I wanted to go over—"

"You're in charge, Rosa." She tried to add a "not now" look to her words. "You don't need me."

Rosa frowned. "You bump your head? What do you mean my plans are my plans, this is your—"

"Rosa. Pantry. *Now.*" Brushing off her hands, Lyndie got up and headed into the pantry ahead of her, and directly to the second refrigerator there, where she knew she'd left—Ah, yes, there was a God. The six-pack of beer with her name on it was still there. She grabbed one, turned around, and ran smack into Rosa.

"What is with you?" Rosa demanded. "You forget to take your vitamin B?"

"I—"

"Listen, *querida,* I just try to tell you, you have paying guests tonight. They're already in for the night. I gave the man room one, and the couple room two."

"Okay." Paying customers were good.

Rosa still had her hands on her hips. "So why you not want Griffin to know you own this place? That you keep us all together out of the goodness of your heart, that you have a soft spot for San Puebla?"

"I keep you here to keep you out of my hair." Lyndie took a long pull of the beer.

"No, you have soft spot."

"Yeah. For your food."

Rosa laughed and hugged her. *"Estas llena de caca."*

Lyndie endured the physical affection—along with Rosa's telling her she was full of shit—with an eye roll. "I just don't need to spout out all my personal business for just anyone, that's all."

"He is not just anyone. He is helping, he is a hero. You don't want him to know you have a soft spot, for my food or otherwise. Admit it."

"Lyndie Anderson has no soft spots."

Rosa crossed her arms, the universal stance for irked mother figure. "Do you know what I think?"

"If I say yes, will you stop talking?"

"I think you just will not admit that this is home." Rosa's smile was warm, and smug. "You know what I know about you?"

"Christ, another question. That you drive me crazy?"

"That you're always the nastiest to those you care about." Rosa patted her cheek. "It is an especially lovable trait of yours."

Lyndie glanced out into the kitchen. Griffin was still eating as if he hadn't been fed in a week. "If you're talking about the bath in the creek," she said, watching him enjoying his food, "he had it coming."

"You care about him."

"Sure. He's going to help stop the fire."

"You care about him as a man."

"Don't be ridiculous, I've only known him one day."

"A day, a year, it does not matter when it comes to matters of the heart."

"Rosa." Lyndie laughed. "Maybe we should switch back to Spanish, your English is starting to fail you." Grabbing a second beer, she walked back into the kitchen and plopped the bottle down in front of Griffin, who looked up at her warily.

"It's not poisoned," she promised, then smiled. "In fact, consider it a peace offering. You know, for the whole creek thing."

He took a long pull of the beer, then slowly shook his head in regret. "I don't think so."

For some reason, the silky words caused her belly to quiver. "You don't think so what?"

Tipping his head back, he took another long drink, then set the beer down and licked his lower lip.

Another odd quiver.

"We're not even," he said softly. "Not yet."

Oh, boy. "You know what? I'm tired. I'm going to bed. If you want an escort to your room, she's leaving now."

He laughed and got up. "So pleasant and agreeable. So positively sweet."

"Didn't tell you? Sweet is my middle name." She led him back down the arched hallway, through the open reception area, to another hallway, down which there were five rooms that Rosa rented out as often as she could, which it turned out wasn't that often way out here.

But tonight the first two were taken. Beyond that on the right was the one communal bathroom. And then the last three bedrooms. One for Rosa, one for herself, and one for Griffin.

She stopped in front of the bathroom, pushed open the door. Watched him as he registered the perfectly in-order shower.

He didn't say a word, just slowly craned his neck and looked at her.

As he did, an unusual sound came from behind the second bedroom door behind them. An undeniable moan, low and rough and sensual. Eyes wide, they both turned and looked at the closed door, just as another soft, pleasure-filled feminine cry filled the air.

And then the answering male groan.

"You know what else this place has besides a communal bathroom with a perfectly operational shower?" Griffin asked softly. He leaned toward her, and when he spoke, his lips brushed the sensitive patch of skin just beneath her ear, making her shiver. "Thin walls."

"*Dios mio!*" the woman cried out. "*Otra vez...*"

Again, she was begging. Oh, God. Lyndie stared at the wood, images floating in her mind, and she didn't know what to do. For once she didn't know what to do. She glanced at Griffin, wondering what could possibly be going on in his head.

His eyes were dark, and the look he gave her seared the hair right off her arms, tweaking the hot spots in her body yet again, a good many of which she'd forgotten she even had.

Until today anyway.

"It's funny how just a sound can make you ache," Griffin said silkily, his eyes never leaving hers.

Oh, man, am I waaaay out of my league. "I don't know what you're talking about."

He lifted a brow. "Is that right?" He stepped close. Too close. He was in her space. "I feel a challenge to prove just how a sound can make you ache."

"N-no need."

"Want to try me?" he asked very softly.

"Well, I—"

His mouth came down on hers, cutting off her words, her thoughts. He kissed her for a long, long moment before lifting his head. Now his lips were just a whisper from hers, close but not touching, and she stared at them, willing him to do it again. *Needing* him to do it again.

When he didn't she grabbed his shirt and closed the gap, doing it herself, opening her mouth to his, and suddenly the twin moans from behind the closed door weren't the only ones in the inn.

When they broke apart this time, she staggered back a step, staring into Griffin's slumberous eyes as she let out a shaky laugh. It was that or beg, and she never begged. "I'm still dirty, Ace."

"You wouldn't be, if you'd joined me in the creek."

"Your room is the last on the left."

"Is that good night, then?"

Just beneath the casual banter was something far too real to play with, and she knew he knew it, too. "Yes," she whispered, and the same sense of relief flickered through his eyes as well.

With a nod, he turned and started down the hall in his soft, faded Levi's and worn polo shirt. His hair was still a bit wet from the creek. He looked so good walking away from her that she actually reached for him, but luckily her arms weren't long enough.

Behind her, the sighs and moans were still coming.

In her own bed, there'd be no such sounds.

Damn it. "Griffin."

He went still.

"I lied," she whispered to his broad shoulders. "I ache. Kissing you made it worse."

He let out a long breath. She knew because his shoulders sagged, just a little, and then he turned to face her. Coming back with his loose-legged stride, he lifted a hand to stroke her jaw. "Lyndie." He closed his eyes, then opened them on hers. "When we're just playing, teasing…that I can handle. I can handle it because I know if I tried to take you right now, you'd probably run."

No. No, she wouldn't. She would reach for him right back, screw pride. She'd let him do whatever he wanted to her if only to assuage this ache he'd placed between her legs, behind her ribs. But hell if she'd admit that. "Yeah. I'd run."

"It's freeing to know it. It's freeing to understand this is all just a game, a temporary distraction from why I'm really here, because if it's not…" He touched her arm, ran his fingers up to her shoulder, then slowly shook his head, letting his hand fall from her. "Then I can't do this. I…can't."

"Why?" she heard herself ask, then wanted to crawl in a hole. Or do as she'd promised and run. "No, I take that back, I don't want to know why—"

He put his fingers over her mouth. "When I want, Lyndie, I tend to want for the long haul. Do you know what I mean?"

"Yeah." She paled, she could feel it. Long haul. Two bad words in her book.

He nodded grimly. "I can see you're not the long haul type."

"No."

"Then you want to do as you said, Lyndie, and run. Because I'm screwed up, but not so much so that I wouldn't risk my heart, and enjoy very much teaching you how to risk yours."

Her stomach dropped and quivered at the same time, and not having a glib answer or any retaliation for that at all, she did as he'd suggested and ran.

* * *

Lyndie ended up using the creek that night after all, with only the occasional cry of a coyote or the hoot of an owl for company. It was quiet and dark, and the water felt cold, which worked.

Griffin's words echoed in her head…the ones about being willing to teach her to risk her heart. That was the last thing she wanted or needed.

But God, she was lonely.

It'd been a long time since she'd felt this way, maybe since her school days, a time when her grandfather had usually been busy with his work late into the night, regretfully leaving her alone more often than not. Back then she hadn't had anyone to turn to for company, not even a pet. Pets required a stable home life, something they hadn't had.

She'd gotten used to that, having only herself, and rarely even gave it a thought anymore.

But she was thinking now. She splashed in the water and thought of Griffin. By his own admission he was screwed up. She didn't know his past, only that he'd clearly faced something hor-rific, tragic. A loss.

And yet he'd have been willing to risk all again and be with her tonight.

She'd faced losses in her life, too. And she wasn't willing to risk her heart again, no matter how good a teacher he was.

She didn't like what that said about her, but there was no deny-ing it. Griffin scared her. He was different, and while that was an attraction, it also required a good amount of distance. It would have to be a mental distance, of course, but she was good at that, real good.

9

Nina Farrell sat on the edge of the creek and waited for Lyndie to finish her late night bath. She didn't think it strange that her friend had stripped down in the creek, she'd done it a few times herself. No, what she thought strange was that Lyndie was still up at...she checked her fancy watch, the one she'd pined for until Lyndie had given it to her last Christmas, looking so elegant and American on her wrist...past midnight.

Interesting.

Everyone knew Lyndie couldn't handle late nights, that instead she preferred to jump out of bed at the crack of dawn, ready to work, of course.

It was all about work with Lyndie, but despite the tough personal ethics, Nina still loved her.

Even if work was the bane of *Nina's* existence.

Sure, she was the beloved daughter of Tom Farrell, a man everyone in town respected despite his white skin and terrible fly-fishing skills. And sure, she had a relatively easy job compared to many women her age in rural Mexico. She ran a cantina that her great aunt Lupe had started. The hours suited her, the people she met suited her, the pay suited her.

She just hated being twenty-three and feeling as if her entire life had already been written in stone. She lived in a place out of step with the rest of the world, which meant getting married, having too many babies, and working like a dog until she'd lost all her teeth and was a burden on the very kids she'd given her life to.

No, thank you. She didn't want that life, she wanted her own. And it wasn't that she didn't love kids. She did. She just wanted to teach them, not necessarily have them. She wanted to do that in the States, the land of do-whatever-suits-you. She wanted everything her half-American blood was entitled to: the language, the music, the movies, the everything. She loved it all so much she'd demanded that her father teach her English years ago, and prided herself on her fluency.

If only she could read it as well as she spoke it, she'd be home free.

With all her heart, she'd wanted to go to college in the States, but five years ago when she'd graduated high school, she'd taken one look into her father's hopeful, expecting eyes, and had known the truth. He wouldn't let her go.

Normally, that wouldn't have stopped her, but she didn't have any ties except right here in San Puebla, and back then, her young, naive eighteen-year-old heart had chosen.

Incorrectly.

She'd regretted it ever since and Nina didn't live well with regrets. She wanted to go to the States and stay, and she would. Somehow.

Her own dark arms gleamed in the moonlight, mocking her. She was only half American, and didn't even look that, but she didn't care. God, to live in a city that had more than a handful of people she'd known forever, with a chance to make a difference, and not because of whose daughter she was, or how many drinks she could mix a night.

It wasn't as if she was looking to forget her mother's heritage, not at all. After all, she planned to teach Spanish. There were kids there she could help, she just knew it.

"Lyndie," she said softly as her friend came out of the water.

No jumping in fright for Lyndie, nope the woman was far too tough for that. She merely reached for the towel she'd set over a branch and wrapped it around her lithe body. Tossing back her short hair, which was lit like fire beneath the meager moonlight, she sighed as she faced Nina. "Why am I not surprised to see you up this late? Who did you go out with tonight?"

"Hey, I don't always go out. I long ago went through all the guys around here." Nina sighed dramatically. "I am ready for new waters, Lyndie. Very ready."

"You always have been." Drying off, Lyndie sank next to Nina on the edge of the creek.

Around them the smoke clogged out much of the night. The insects hummed. The water rushed over the rocks, the only other sound. Nina wanted to hear cars, trucks, planes. Honking, hollering…She wanted big city noises as her lullaby.

"So what's up?" Lyndie combed her hair with her fingers. "You're looking for me in the middle of the night, you're up to something."

"It's only midnight."

"Which is the middle of the night," Lyndie pointed out in her rational voice, making Nina laugh.

"Okay, yes, I am up to something," she admitted. She took a deep breath and looked at her friend—her escape route. "I want to go back to the States with you. I want to move to there and—"

"*What?* Why?"

"To go to college."

"It's cheaper here."

"I do not want cheaper. I want American."

Lyndie stared at her. "You can't just up and leave Mexico."

"Why not?" Nina leapt up to expel some of her energy. God, would no one see? "Because I have a cantina to tend to? Because I have a future all planned out and already rotting? Because I am not allowed to have hopes and dreams like you, and then follow them through to reality? I speak the language as well as anyone there. I am half American, *more* than half if you count my great aunt's first cousin on her mother's side, who married a guy in Bakersfield and—"

"Nina." Lyndie shook her head. "You're young, and sometimes—"

"Don't give me that crap about being too young. You're not that much older than I am. You just feel older because your life is your own and you live it how you want to." She shoved her fingers through her long hair and turned in a slow, frustrated circle. "Oh, Lyndie, don't you see? You've done what you want, when you want. You've seen the world, and you've never, not once, let anyone or anything hold you back."

Lyndie stared at her for a long moment. "Yes, but we've had very different experiences."

"Maybe I just want some experiences."

"Nina..." With a disparaging sound, she lifted her hand. "Your entire life is here."

"But my heart is not." Kneeling at Lyndie's side, she took her friend's hands and pressed them within her own, close to her beating heart. "I want this," she whispered. "I want this so much.

Take me with you. Please? I'll get a job, I'll support myself, I'll—"

"What about Tom?"

"He'll get used to the idea."

"You haven't told him."

"No."

"Nina, you have to tell him—"

"Not yet. He'll try to stop me."

"Nina." She pressed her fingers to her eyes. "I can't. I can't do that to him, I can't help you run away without a word, without—"

"Fine." Nina stood again, feeling her chest tighten, her eyes brighten with the tears she would absolutely not shed. "I'll find another way. On my own."

"Nina—"

But Nina wasn't in the mood to hear empty platitudes, she was in a hell-raising mood. And lucky for her, the night had just begun.

* * *

Lyndie woke to the scent of fresh tortillas and the sound of Tallulah's collar jangling, and sat straight up in bed.

It was still dark. Her clock glowed five o'clock. Rosa's dog had pushed open the door that never locked and now sat on the floor by her bed, waiting expectantly to be rewarded for such adorable behavior.

"Go away." Lyndie stretched and groaned. Every muscle ached, and then some. The long night hadn't helped. She'd heard Griffin get up every few hours. The last time, near four a.m., she'd gotten up also, and had found him whispering with Tom at the front door.

Tom had the radio, checking in with the men on the status of the fire, and then relaying that info to their firefighter.

Griffin's dedication and concern had tightened her chest, and she didn't know why. Didn't want to know why.

Still on the floor by her bed, panting sweetly, Tallulah added a little whine for attention.

"Oh, all right." Leaning over, she reached out to pet her. With a blissful grunt, Tallulah lay on her back, exposing her pathetic hairless pink belly, which Lyndie now couldn't reach. And she wasn't getting out of bed to pet a dog.

She wanted to lie back and pull the covers over her eyes. Normally she popped right up in the mornings, but last night had been a long one, and she glared at the paper-thin walls, through which she'd also listened to that amorous couple go at it for hours—and they had been particularly amorous, and arduous.

It hadn't relieved any of her inner tension, that was for sure. "Damn it." She sat up. On the nightstand was a note from Rosa: EAT.

That it was in English, not Spanish, made Lyndie shake her head. Rosa wanted to make sure she got it.

She did. But for once, it wasn't food on her mind, but the fire, and the long day ahead.

She got out of bed, tripped over Tallulah, then ended up squatting down to pet her for a moment. Then she grabbed a towel and headed down the hall to the bathroom.

In the Rio Vista Inn, there wasn't any sense in locking the bathroom. There were two toilet stalls and two showers, and no such thing as privacy.

Tossing aside the big T-shirt she'd worn to bed, she hung up her towel right outside one of the two showers, which were nothing more than a long tiled wall and two shorter tile walls no higher than her collarbone, jutting out to create the two different stalls. A plastic curtain could be pulled across the back, creating the fourth wall. Hopping into the shower, she yanked the curtain closed, dunked her head beneath the hot spray, and wondered what Rosa had left her to eat.

Something good, of that she had no doubt. Something with eggs and peppers and beans and lots and lots of fat.

Her mouth started to water.

Rosa always spoiled her rotten when she came, they all did. She kept her eyes closed as she shampooed and conditioned. What was it about being here, with these people, that got to her? Why did they matter so much when all her life what had mattered had been seeing everything and everywhere and never staying in one place? "And why here," she murmured as she rinsed her conditioner out. "Why am I growing roots *here*?"

"Roots…where are they, coming out your feet?"

Her eyes flew open at that low, already extremely familiar voice. Sure enough, standing there amidst the rising steam of her shower, looking quite pleased with himself, was one hotshot fire-fighter Griffin Moore.

Far too at ease, he leaned back against the door and let out a slow smile. "Maybe I should just come in closer and take a peek at those roots."

Her heart had kicked into gear at just the sound of him, but she managed to sound bored. "Sure. Come on in and get a closer peek. In fact, peek all you want, Mr. All-Talk-And-No-Go."

An eyebrow lifted as he studied her. He wore another pair of wildland firefighter trousers and a plain white T-shirt with a fire-fighter logo over his left pec. And a nice pec it was. Either he'd gotten more sleep than she had in spite of checking on the fire, or he managed to hide it well.

She lifted one eyebrow right back at him, then nearly swallowed her tongue when he pushed away from the wood and started walking toward her.

"Hey!" She lifted a soapy arm and pointed it at him. "You're not supposed to take that dare."

"If you knew me a little better, you'd know I take all dares."

"Great time for you to open up and tell me such a thing." He was still walking toward her, with his long legs and tough, rangy body, and determined, intense expression. His eyes glittered with intent, and suddenly she couldn't breathe. Exactly what kind of intent did he have, and why-oh-why did it make her body hum? "Okay, stop!" She wanted to wince at how shaky she sounded, how breathless. "Stop right there, Ace."

Halfway between the door and the shower, and only about two feet from her, he did.

The air seemed to crackle around them, as it had on several occasions now. Griffin smiled, just a little one, with a good amount of wickedness in it as the steam swirled around his head. "What's the matter?" he asked softly.

"I didn't expect you to really have the *cajones* to come in closer for a peek," she had to admit. "Not after last night at the creek."

"Surprise."

"I hate surprises." She knew he couldn't see anything, at least not yet, but her entire body was doing the strangest thing in reaction to his invasion.

It was melting. Nipples tight, thighs quivering, stomach dancing, the whole deal. Apparently, it'd been too long. "Okay, show's over. You can get out now."

"Funny thing about bathing around here. No privacy. Take, for example, when I was taking *my* bath." He said this in a perfectly reasonable tone, as if they were discussing what they were having for breakfast instead of her very naked body. "In fact, you goaded me into that water, and then never took your eyes off me."

Yeah, but he'd been something to look at. It was what had led her to the cold creek only a little while later, needing the cool air and water to soothe her unwelcome aching and yearning. "In case you haven't noticed the difference between last night and today," she said. "I'm completely bare-ass naked here."

"If you expect *that* to work as a deterrent…" He let out a soft little laugh that was so incredibly sexy to her. "Think again."

The water began to cool, a warning she knew all too well. She had less than one minute to get rinsed off and out before it went cold. "*Why* are you in here?" she asked desperately.

"To brush my teeth." He brandished a toothbrush and a tube of toothpaste. With that wicked smile still firmly in place, he sauntered on over to the sink, which put him only a foot from her.

She hugged up close to the tile wall of the shower and glared at him.

"Oh, don't worry. I can't see anything you don't want me to see," he said all friendly-like, and turning away from her, flipped on the water.

Her water went a surge warmer, only a surge, warning her she was really on borrowed time. "I wouldn't swallow any of that," she warned him when he bent over the sink.

"Don't worry." His words were a little garbled because of the toothbrush in his mouth. "I have a stomach of iron." He rinsed and lifted his head, and met her gaze in the reflection of the steaming mirror in front of him.

The water cooled even more.

Lyndie hugged the tile and ignored it while she watched him. She had no idea what was so sexy about him brushing his teeth. She considered herself good at reading people. The gift had come from her grandfather, who claimed he could tell the strength of a person's soul by the look in their eyes.

Lyndie had no doubt of the strength of Griffin's soul. He was here. No matter the reason, he was here volunteering his time, his very life, so far from home. She'd seen more of his character yesterday when he'd automatically, instinctively, taken over at every turn, wanting to ensure her safety, and everyone else's, as well.

And then there'd been last night. He could have gone for it, dug into what she'd have been willing to give, but he hadn't. And that fascinated her. Scared her, too, in a way she didn't fully understand.

He finished rinsing and met her gaze in the mirror. "What's going through that head of yours?" he asked.

"I'm just standing here wondering how it is I'm even here this weekend."

He turned off the sink. "Hmmm."

"I had it off, you know. All I had to do was drop you." She lifted a shoulder. "Drop you and go. Those were my instructions. Then I was free to fly back to San Diego."

"And yet you stayed."

"And yet I stayed," she agreed, and crossed her arms on the edge of the tile so that she could rest her chin on her hands as the water beat down on her.

Cold water. And she didn't care. "I stayed when it went against the grain."

"Why was it against the grain to help a village you love?"

She didn't know. She wanted everything to be black and white, and in her world she did her best to make it so. Griffin, like San Puebla, wasn't black or white, but a terrifying mix that she couldn't put her finger on. "Helping isn't against the grain," she said. "Staying is."

He set down his toothbrush and turned to face her, and though he could have tried to get an eyeful, he kept his baby blues right on hers. "Why's that?"

"I'm an Army brat. We never slowed down enough to settle in anywhere, much less fall in love with a place. But here..." She shrugged. "I've settled a little, and that's scary."

"Why?"

"Because once you care, you can get hurt."

His voice was suddenly, terrifyingly gentle. "Did someone hurt you, Lyndie?"

"Not on purpose, no. But...people eventually go away." Since that was a shocking admission, she turned away to face the water. "And I have no idea why I just told you that."

"Because the water has gone cold and you're freezing your brain, but of course you're too stubborn to admit such a thing." He reached in, his arm brushing her shoulder and back as he cranked the handle and turned off the water.

The sudden silence seemed deafening.

As he retrieved his arm, she craned her neck to meet his gaze. She felt surrounded by him and yet he barely touched her.

Oh boy, oh boy. Pulling her towel over the tile wall, she wrapped it around herself, making sure everything was covered on the body that felt startlingly, shockingly, wide awake and ready to play.

Then and only then, did she yank back the curtain and step out of the shower, standing before him, water streaming down her limbs from her hair.

His cocky, naughty smile was long gone.

She was fairly certain she herself couldn't have smiled to save her life.

His voice sounded hoarse. "Lyndie—"

"I need to ask," she whispered into the steamy room. "What *your* demons are that made you face that fire yesterday, when you didn't want to, and what will make you face it again today."

For a long moment he didn't so much as breathe, then he slowly shook his head. "It's complicated." Reaching out, he ran a finger over her wet jaw. This time when he smiled it was a heart-breakingly sad one. "Very complicated."

10

As dawn burned red and orange in the sky, lighting the forest, the rock formations, the overhang of smoke, Nina walked in the front door of the small but well tended casa she shared with her father—just as he was leaving.

Tom scratched his head and studied his precious only daughter. "I got your note. What do you mean you want to go home with Lyndie? Lyndie *is* home."

"No, this is just a stop for her." They stood in the open tiled hallway her great, great uncle had laid himself. The walls were stucco from two centuries back, lined with shelves that collected dust like a showcase. She looked around her and made a sound of disgust. "There's so much damn dust in these damn mountains that it's permanently seeded in my pores."

"There's dust in other cities, Nina. And even in the States."

"Yes, well, it's probably a cleaner dust. And this isn't Lyndie's home. She loves us, very much, but San Puebla isn't her home."

"She's home here," Tom insisted, because he wanted it to be so. He wanted everyone to be as happy here as he was. "She owns the place next door, now, doesn't she?"

"Yes, because otherwise Rosa would have gone belly-up. But you and I both know Lyndie's true home is the air. Her home is wherever the fancy strikes her." She sighed. "Do you have any idea how the freedom of that draws me?"

Tom felt his stomach slide to his toes. "You don't want to live like that." *Please, don't let her want to live like that.*

"Papa, I've told you before, I don't want to live here. You don't listen."

God help him, he'd ignored it, thinking she'd outgrow the need to go. But she'd never sounded so determined before, never.

To the bones, she was her mother's daughter, with pure willpower running through her forceful, proud veins. Maria had been his heart, his soul, from the moment he'd set foot in these rugged, isolated hills. Actually, at first it'd been delirium, as he'd come through on a fishing trip, and had collapsed from a terrible flu.

Maria had taken care of him, babied him, spoiled him for days, and by the time he recovered, he'd fallen hard. Thank God it'd been mutual. He'd gladly stayed, loving the wide, open spaces, the pace of life, the feel that time had stood still. They'd married, spent a few blissful years so in love it almost hurt to look at each other. Then in one tragic heartbeat, she'd given him his precious daughter and lost her own life.

Even now, the memory grabbed him by the throat and threatened to choke him. He'd stood in that hospital holding the newborn Nina, unable to accept what the doctor told him. He'd gained a baby, and lost his wife.

Over the years he'd come to terms with the loss, and even though he still missed Maria terribly, he had Nina.

And now she was going to leave him, too.

"Don't look at me like that," she whispered. "You make my

heart hurt. Papa, you are my family, you are my everything, but I…I need more."

"What? What is it you need? Just tell me."

"That's just it! I don't know, not until I get out there and do some living." She cupped his face, kissed both his cheeks. "You came here on a whim when you were younger than I am right now. Your parents didn't stop you. Your friends didn't stop you. Now let me do the same."

"My folks are gone now. There's no one for you there."

"I don't care. There was no one for you here, either."

"Your mother."

"But you didn't know that when you first landed here."

He stared at her for a long moment, wondering how to reach her, how to make her happy. "You don't know what the States are like, *querida*," he said desperately. "It's too dangerous for a beautiful young woman alone on the streets—"

"I'm not going to be on the mean bad streets of Los Angeles or New York. I'm going to be in sunny, beach-town San Diego, at least at first."

"Nina." God, how to reach her? "I'm sorry you're unhappy. I hate that you are, but this will pass. Your home is here, your job is here, and translating—"

"No. Papa, please, listen to me. I'm not trying to disconnect from you, or even forget my culture. I'm still going to love you. This is just something I have to do. Lyndie is going back to San Diego either tonight or tomorrow, you know she is. I want to go, too. I want to be more American than holding a piece of paper. I want to live it. Like you did."

"Don't be silly. I'm a Mexican now."

She looked at his white skin, his pale, pale hair, his freckles, and laughed.

"In *spirit*," he said. "I'm Mexican in spirit, which is all that matters. Your mother was Mexican. That makes you full-blooded."

"No. I'm half American. I speak flawless English, you yourself saw to that. I want to go to college there."

"You said you didn't want to go to college. I tried to send you—"

"Mexico City doesn't interest me. I've told you, you don't want to listen."

"Because I love it here, I feel close to your mother here. I can no more leave here than I can forget her, and it terrifies me that you can."

"I just want to see the rest of the world."

Tom sagged a little, stared at the tall, beautiful, headstrong daughter he loved with all his heart. "You look so much like her. I want you to be happy, like she was."

"You want me to be happy here. But I can't be." She took his hands, kissed them. "I'm glad I look like her, Papa. She was beautiful." She rubbed her cheek over his knuckles. "But I can't be happy here, not like she was. Please understand."

"No."

She looked into his eyes. "Then I'm sorry for you."

"You're not going."

"I love you, Papa."

Tom watched her walk away from him, and right out of the room, and wondered how much longer he could put her off before he had to let her go. Let his only baby go.

* * *

Griffin sat outside under a still dark, fire-ravaged sky after Lyndie's shower, concentrating on breathing and breathing only. If he

didn't, he might wonder at the way he'd reacted to a woman after all this time, a woman unlike any other he'd ever met. What
was it about her that made him want to feel again? Maybe he was
tired of feeling raw and wounded. Maybe deep down he wanted
more, and was willing to fight for it.

Because that was a difficult thought, he switched gears, thinking about the day ahead, about having to be out there dealing
with the fire.

His stomach dropped. His gear was at his feet, he was ready to
go. As ready as he got, anyway. He figured Lyndie wasn't the type
to linger over hair or makeup or whatever other mysteries women
engaged themselves in every morning. She'd be in a hurry to get
back up the hill and see what was happening.

He should be in a hurry as well, but he couldn't deny that he
wished he was sitting on a beach in San Diego, with his biggest
concern being the rising tide.

The porch of the inn was wide and cool, and he leaned back
against a post. Once upon a time he'd loved this early hour.

Now he typically slept it away.

Tallulah wandered out of the woods toward him, her little
legs slowly carrying her. She whined, and when she finally came
close enough, he could see why. She was sporting a two-inch gash
alongside her nose, just beneath her left eye.

"What did you put your nose into, dog?"

Looking pathetic, she sat at his feet and whined again.

With a sigh, he went into his pack for his first aid kit. "Come
here, then."

Trustingly, she moved closer and a drop of blood fell at his
feet. "Poor baby," he said, and scooped her into his lap to clean
her up, which she let him do with only an occasional whimper.

He'd just set her back down again when his open backpack

rang. Odd, as he didn't have a cell phone. He went through the red bag he'd have sworn he'd searched thoroughly by now, and pulled a cell out of an inside pocket.

His brother's. He lifted a shoulder at Tallulah, who looked as surprised as he, and punched the answer button. "Hello?"

"You okay?" Brody asked.

"This is a new low, even for you, planting your cell phone on me."

His brother laughed softly. "I was wondering if you'd even know what a ringing phone sounded like, seeing as you've been avoiding one for a year now."

"Don't you have something more important to do? Say, take a nap? Or maybe find a lake to toss a line into?"

"Nah. I've got plenty of time for both later. So..." All humor disappeared from Brody's voice. "How's it going? I didn't sleep last night worrying about you, wondering if I'd pushed you too far too fast."

"Well, you did. I hope that keeps you up tonight, too. Make that every night."

"Damn, Grif... It's that bad?"

"What do you think?"

"I'm sorry. God, I'm so sorry."

"Yeah. That helps a lot."

"I just thought if I tossed you in, you'd swim, you know? I didn't know what else to do."

Chest uncomfortably tight at the anguish in his brother's voice, Griffin squeezed his eyes closed and pinched the bridge of his nose. "Look, I was perfectly happy sitting on that beach—"

"Alone."

"I didn't need this—"

"Yes, you did. You needed that kick in the ass."

"It feels like a kick in the heart."

"Look, we've been through all this. Just promise me you'll use the phone, okay? Call Mom and Dad—"

"I've got to go." Griffin clicked off and resisted the urge to toss the thing into the bush. He purposely blanked his mind, petting Tallulah, listening to the birds…and he managed, too, until unbidden came the lovely image of Lyndie and how she'd looked in the shower, all wet and shiny and alluring.

That worked, too.

Hard to believe that in all this time, another woman hadn't turned his head, not once. And yet Lyndie turned his head plenty. Hell, she turned him completely around. Almost as scary as what he had to do today.

Fight a fire.

He'd dreamed last night; long, haunting, terrifying dreams, reliving everything that had happened a year ago, and had woken breathless, with the names of the fallen on his lips and tears on his cheeks.

And he had to go back to that hell today. Now he had Brody's words in his head as well.

Call Mom and Dad…

Damn it. He hadn't spoken to them in so long…too long.

He'd lost his way back.

Brody wanted to help him. The surprise of that—of his wild, irresponsible baby brother coming through for him instead of the other way around—would have been far more potent if he wasn't here in this very spot facing his nightmares because of Brody.

He hadn't called home, and there was great shame in that, but he knew the pain of hearing his parents' voices would break him. They'd want to talk about what had happened, and he just couldn't go there, not even for them. Couldn't relive the incident that had led to so many deaths, not unlike the fire he had to face today—

Footsteps sounded behind him. The denim-covered legs that appeared in his peripheral were tight and toned. "Well, look at that, you're so eager you're waiting outside for me." Lyndie came down the stairs so that she stood right in front of him. "Or maybe you just want to get it over with?"

Her hair was still damp, the fiery auburn strands cut in those short chunky layers that framed her small heart-shaped face. She smelled like strawberries today.

He loved strawberries. "Take your pick."

"The latter," she decided. "You definitely have the look of a man who needs out of here."

The front door slammed again. Rosa came out on the porch wearing a gauzy skirt and blouse as bright as yesterday's, and carried a tinfoil-covered plate. "You," she said, and jerked her chin at Griffin. "You are in trouble with me."

He craned his neck to look around, but nope, she had to be talking to him.

"You did not eat." She thrust out the plate, which he took rather than see it tip into his lap. Then, standing right in front of him, she put her hands on her hips and waited.

He glanced at Lyndie, who only lifted a shoulder. "She's the boss," she said. "I'd do what she says."

"I'm sorry, but I'm not that hungry—"

"Tallulah!" Rosa had caught sight of her dog, and dropped to her knees in the dirt, opening her arms. "*Mi querida,* what happened to you?" She touched the white bandage beneath the dog's eye.

"I think she put her nose where it didn't belong," he said. "I cleaned it up so it wouldn't get infected."

Rosa kissed Tallulah, then looked at Griffin. "You are a doctor?"

"Paramedic training, that's all."

"And a true hero." Rosa gave him a big hug, and Tallulah—still in her arms—licked his face from chin to forehead. "*Heroe mio.* No way are you going to work all day long without a good solid base." Rosa pointed to the plate. "That is a good solid base, I cook it myself."

"Thank you—"

"So eat. And you—" Rosa pointed at Lyndie, whose strawberried lips went from smug to surprise. "I double load that plate. Sit your pretty little butt down next to him and dig in."

Lyndie shook her head. "I grabbed a few tortillas off the counter. We have to go."

"It's not quite six. You're early enough, the sun just barely coming up."

Lyndie opened her mouth, probably to give another argument, but Rosa merely pointed her finger to the spot next to Griffin. With a roll of the eyes, Lyndie sat.

He opened the foil. Eggs, beans, fresh tortillas…the delicious scent wafted up and tickled his nose, coaxing his stomach to rumble hopefully. "Rosa, you're amazing."

Lyndie let out a snort but scooted her "pretty little butt" closer and grabbed a chorizo, a spicy Mexican sausage.

The door slammed again, and out came Tom, who eyed the plate with interest.

"Don't even think about it," Rosa said and held him back. "I just fed you."

Tom patted his flat belly. "Can never get enough of your cooking, Rosa."

Rosa patted his flat belly too, and smiled fondly. "Is that right?"

Tom smiled at her for a long moment, then turned to Lyndie. "You be careful up there today with your asthma, you hear me?"

"I'm always careful."

Tom jutted his chin toward Griffin. "You watch her, you keep her safe."

Griffin felt each of those words of responsibility like individual gunshots to his gut. "I will."

"I'm not Griffin's responsibility," Lyndie said. "He's mine."

Griffin snorted. "I take care of myself—"

"Uh huh." She grabbed another chorizo, the last one, and he stared at the plate in regret because though he hadn't thought himself hungry, it turned out he was.

Her eyes on his, Lyndie fed it to him, her finger touching his lips, making him stare at her as all sorts of interesting reactions occurred within his body.

Tom watched all this and chuckled. "You can take care of each other," he decided, looking pleased as he once again turned his charm on Rosa. "So are you going to make some of that magical, soul-enriching coffee this morning?"

Still holding Tallulah, she gave him a sideways glance. "Are you trying to charm me because you are too lazy to make your own coffee?"

"Why…is it working?" Reaching out, he pet the dog, who panted happily.

"Not so much."

"No? Ouch, then."

Rosa let out a slow, indulgent smile. "You silly man." She touched his jaw. "You know I always have coffee for you."

Tom's return smile was slow and sweet. He started back in the house, then glanced at Griffin. "Oh, and I located another tractor for you. It'll be up there sometime this morning, after I make the rounds. I'll come up, too, and lend a hand, or whatever it is I can do to help."

"Bring the latest weather report."

"Will do." He turned back to Rosa, smiled into her eyes. "You take care of yourself."

"I always do."

And then he was gone. Rosa went inside, too, leaving Griffin with Lyndie. Alone.

Not a state that he felt comfortable with. "Let's do this," he said, and drew in a deep, fortifying breath.

11

You okay?" Lyndie stared down at Griffin.

He looked down at the food on the plate and his stomach turned. "As okay as I'll get." He had the most inexplicable urge to tug her back down next to him, slide his arms around her and hold on as dawn continued its rise. Always, he'd loved a woman's touch.

Until this last year, when he'd felt dead inside.

Now he was slowly coming back to life, thanks to Brody's meddling, and also thanks to his body's reaction to this woman. She was hot, sexy, smart, tough, independent...the whole package.

Truth was, he was slowly getting used to the idea of being alive when his friends weren't, and painful as that felt, he couldn't deny it. He looked into Lyndie's eyes. Strong and sure and courageous as anyone he'd ever met, she wasn't anything like anyone he'd ever been with.

And yet, right at this moment, it was Lyndie he wanted, with all his heart.

Her arm and thigh brushed his. Her hair, still damp and spiky in that cut that should have been too masculine but instead seemed so soft and feminine he wanted to sink his fingers into it.

The wanting became an ache, a physical ache…to touch her, kiss her, to have her touch him back, kiss him back…to obliterate anything else churning inside him.

She was so close he could see himself reflected in her green eyes. He could lean in if he wanted, and rub his jaw to hers. He could put his mouth right on the corner of those strawberry glossed lips and start in, nibbling to his heart's content.

As if suddenly just a little nervous, she tossed the keys to the Jeep up and down in her hand. "You ready or what?"

Was he?

Loaded question if he'd ever heard one. Was he ready to be far, far away? Oh, yeah.

Was he ready to nibble off that distracting gloss? A double resounding oh, yeah. Ready to get in that Jeep and go to the fire? Hell, no.

But neither was he ready to admit it, so he set the plate aside and got to his feet, snatching the keys from her in midair as he did.

"Hey!"

With a little smile on his lips, he headed toward the Jeep, the ground crunching beneath his feet, pretending they didn't feel like two leaden weights. Already the day was warm moving toward hot, which wasn't going to help them any. He started the engine, revved it until Lyndie planted herself in the passenger seat. She'd barely shut the door before he hit the gas.

He was sure she made a comment as her spine hit the back of the seat. He saw her lips moving, but the tires spinning kept him from hearing her.

No doubt, that was just as well.

She waited until they were out of the driveway and on the road. "So today you're in a hurry. Interesting."

"A hurry to get it over with. If you'd moved any slower getting in, I'd have left without you."

A laugh choked out of her as she clicked in her seat belt. "Well, I suppose I'd feel the same way. Not sure I'd have admitted it to you though."

"Yeah, you would have. You're the most brutally honest person I've ever met."

"Is that right?" She leaned back, made herself far more comfortable than he could have if he'd been the passenger. "Yeah, I guess I am. I'd sure have told you what was freaking me out by now."

"I'm not freaking out."

"Uh huh." Completely relaxed, she stretched out, hair whipping in the wind. "Whatever you say, Ace."

He decided he liked her quiet best. Real quiet. "I'm not freaking out," he repeated.

"So you said."

They drove in silence through the town, squinting through the smoke and falling ash, over rough cobblestone streets and past centuries-old architecture.

Griffin had checked the weather meticulously before he'd left the house, with Rosa helping translate the radio news. The high today was going to be ninety, with forty percent humidity. Not great—rain would be the only great thing in this situation—but it wasn't so bad either. Physically, he was as ready as he could be, which wasn't saying much.

Mentally…he had no idea. And suddenly he did need to tell someone, to confide in what he'd faced last year, what he was still facing. And not just anyone, but Lyndie. He wanted her to know everything. "Lyndie."

She had her right arm resting on the door as they began the climb above town, fingers tapping to some tune only she could hear. Her hair blew wildly around her face in the wind. She'd been watching the landscape go by, and when he said her name, her fingers stopped tapping.

"About that freaking-out thing..."

She turned her head to face him.

Shifting into a lower gear for the hill, Griffin concentrated on the road for a moment, which was lined on one side with a rock wall, the other a sheer drop-off back to town the hard way. "The last time I fought a fire..." He drew in a deep breath and kept driving. "It all went bad."

Everything about her softened. "How bad?"

"Pretty damn bad. People got hurt. People...died—"

"Look out!" she cried, just as a coyote darted out in front of them, followed by another. "Don't hit them!"

He hit the brakes, hoping like hell the coyotes moved in time because he wasn't willing to die for this.

They turned sideways, and began a slide.

Teeth gritted tight, Griffin eyed the jutting rocks on their left, the sheer drop-off on their right. Some choice, but he'd take the jutting rocks over a fall off the cliff any day.

They spun toward the cliff.

Lyndie gripped the dash for all she was worth and remained utterly silent as the coyotes leapt toward the jutting rocks, vanishing out of sight.

The Jeep continued to slip toward a definite messy outcome.

"Griffin—"

Yeah, he knew, he saw. Desperately he worked the wheel, steering into the slide, letting off the brakes, and finally, *finally*, the Jeep responded to the gentler touch, swerving away from the drop-off, toward the rocks, before slowly righting itself.

Then they came to a dead stop, facing forward as if nothing had happened. Silence reigned. Slowly the dust settled; not a coyote in sight.

Griffin let out a long breath, then looked over at Lyndie. "That was fun." When she didn't say a word, just gripped the dashboard for all she was worth, he frowned. "You okay?"

"Dandy."

He studied her frozen posture for a moment as his heart began to settle. "Because heaven forbid you admit something scared you, right?"

"Plenty of things scare me. Your driving, for one."

"You're the one who said not to hit them."

"Well you shouldn't listen to me!"

He stared at her, then laughed. "You're not going to admit to being ruffled, are you? How about if we'd gone over the cliff, would you have admitted it then?"

"Just because I maintain my cool, doesn't mean I don't ever get ruffled. I get ruffled. I get plenty ruffled."

"Well, let me know when, because that I'd like to see." He shoved the Jeep back into first gear and started again, slower now.

"Griffin—"

"Not now," he said, scanning the road for more animal life as they moved over the first hill and into the burning landscape. He knew what she wanted, to talk about the Idaho fire he'd started to tell her about. "Apparently I can't multitask. I'm incapable of driving and angsting at the same time." And he drove on. Right into the heart of this fire, the one place on earth he didn't want to be.

12

They made the rest of the drive into the harsh smoke and falling ash in silence. The flames flickered on either side of them now. The air was hot; Lyndie's mood somber. She was sure Griffin felt just as somber.

Despite the coyote incident, he had one hand sure and easy on the wheel, the other on the gearshift, and used both with a confidence and skill she could admire.

Given how distraught he'd been yesterday, he seemed to be holding up just fine now as they drove into the fire. That is if she didn't acknowledge the way his jaw kept bunching, or how his tan seemed faded the closer they got. But then again, she already knew he was tough, and a true survivor.

She imagined his training had had a good deal to do with that, and his character, as well. He was a save-the-world sort of guy…which meant his terrible losses, the ones he'd started to tell her about, would have been taken doubly as hard.

She'd known he'd dealt with something big, something horrific in his past, but she hadn't imagined the truth, that people had died, *his* people. The raw emotion she'd glimpsed in his eyes when he'd said that would have brought her to her knees if she'd been standing.

Is that what made him so serious? So intense? Is that what made him fight the attraction between them, what made him want to push her away at every turn? In that case, on a much different scale, she supposed she understood. She'd lost people in her life, too.

They were nearly there, surrounded by fire when her cell phone vibrated in her pocket. *Sam.* "Yes," she said when she answered. "I'm still on the clock. *Your* clock."

"So you did stay to translate." There was a smile in Sam Logan's voice. There was always a smile in Sam's voice.

"Nina wasn't up for it." She squinted into the smoke. "If I hadn't stayed, your man here would have been pretty much stuck."

"And so you jumped right in. You keep trying to tell me this is just a job for you, Lyndie, and you know what? I don't buy it."

"It's the bottom line. Don't forget, you're paying me by the hour while I'm here dreaming of a fun, easy flight to Catalina, and I'm not as cheap as Nina."

He laughed. "Bill me."

"I always do, Sam, I always do."

"Yeah, just come back in one piece."

She knew Sam Logan ran Hope International on pure adrenaline and love. He paid his pilots, but the various experts they flew all volunteered their time and went unpaid. Sam felt they made enough money on their own time, and mostly, he was right.

What he wasn't quite right about, however, was that while *his* heart might be big enough for the entire world, not everyone felt the same excitement for their job as he did.

Because for some, like Lyndie, this was just a job.

Yes, she got to help people, and that made her feel good, but she also got to fly for a living, and pretty much picked when and where she went.

Not many had that freedom, and she was grateful, but at the moment, she was also just a little resentful at having to stay when she'd wanted, needed, to be alone. Resentful at all the feelings that surfaced when she thought about possibly losing San Puebla, or the feelings that Griffin seemed to cause within her.

"Take good care of that firefighter, too," Sam said. "Maybe we can get him back sometime."

Lyndie glanced at Griffin. His body was tense, his expression growing more and more unnerved as they pulled off the main road. The fire had progressed even farther toward town than she'd imagined.

Would this weekend help him forget...or remember? "I don't know about a repeat on this one, Sam."

"Hey, once they get a taste of the philanthropist lifestyle, they love it. We don't have anyone as skilled as he in what he does. You can talk him into it."

Griffin turned his head toward her.

She met his eyes and thought...no one talked this man into anything he didn't want to do.

And yet his brother had. "Prepare yourself for a very large bill from me. Bye, Sam." She disconnected while he was still chuckling.

"Your boss?"

She shoved her hair out of her face, only to have it fly right back in it. "He wants me to talk you into doing this again sometime."

The sound that escaped him might have been a laugh, or a tortured groan.

"That's what I thought," she said.

"Hey, you're no more thrilled to be here than I am."

"I just wanted some alone time."

"You like that? Being alone?"

It was what she was used to. "Doesn't everyone?"

He considered that. "It's new for me. But being alone right now would be better than…"

"Being here?"

"Yeah."

She'd gotten that loud and clear from him, so why it felt just a little bit hurtful to hear made no sense at all. The engine roared up the road, as did a sudden wind, and the noise of that and of the fire seemed as loud as thunder.

Griffin parked next to the water trucks and tossed her a bandana. "Tie it over your mouth." He turned off the engine. "You have your inhaler?"

"And a spare."

They got out of the Jeep, with Griffin looking more and more distant as they moved toward a group of men who had just gotten there themselves. They all greeted each other somberly, and Griffin pulled out his PDA, bringing up the screen of the map. He pointed to the lines he'd drawn in yesterday, indicating the fire's perimeter.

Two men came forward, and pointed to where they were now, indicating how much the fire had grown.

Griffin let out a long breath, then made adjustments to the map accordingly. He looked at his weather kit, then started talking. He talked slowly and clearly, and always waited for Lyndie to translate before moving on to the next point in his plan of action.

And he did have a plan of action, one that he'd clearly thought out meticulously and precisely.

"As yesterday, we'll use the river as one line of defense," he said pointing to the water line. "The sheer rock wall as a second. But we'll have to start digging new lines, from here." He pointed to the area just south of them, above the town. "The fire is strong here."

Everyone nodded. They understood.

"Long, hot, hard day," he said quietly to Lyndie. "I had Tom load the back of the Jeep with gallons of drinking water, along with more shovels and gear. He's also hunting up more men. Now that they know what I need, we can make do if you want to go back."

"Go back?"

"Seriously, Lyndie. This is incredibly exhausting work. Almost all of it will be manual labor clearing lines. You don't want to do that again."

She hadn't met many men as tough and rugged as this man, who was also gallant. Why that felt like a plus, she had no idea. She didn't want a tough and rugged and gallant man in her life.

She didn't want *any* man in her life, at least not for more than a night, maybe two. And she especially didn't want one who thought he knew what was best for her. "How do you know what I want?"

He stared at her, let his broad shoulders sag as he let out a long breath. "This is not a good time to go all stubborn on me."

"Because you know best?"

A gust of wind hit them, plastering his shirt to his torso, emphasizing hard muscle. He was big, solid, and quickly becoming far too familiar. She pulled him around the side of the first truck, away from the eyes of the others. "Look, I know this is just some misguided sense of responsibility. You're afraid I'm going to get hurt."

"Hell, yeah, I'm afraid you're going to get hurt." He gently touched a bruise on her jaw, courtesy of their fall from yesterday. "I'm afraid you're going to get *dead*. Can't you just listen to me and go the hell away?"

She was pretty much a stranger to him, and yet he cared, deeply. Not many felt that way about a person they didn't know, but he did. Another plus about him, if she'd been counting pluses. She hadn't.

She'd been counting minuses and she would continue to do so. One, he was pigheaded. Two, he was single-minded to the point of making her blood boil, and three—the biggest minus of all—he apparently wasn't capable of mindless sex. Damn him.

Then, totally disarming all her thoughts, he gripped one of her hips in his hand. The other cupped her face, stroking her skin with his thumb, the look in his eyes haunting and melting all at once. "Please, Lyndie. Go back."

She covered his hand with her own. She understood he needed her to go, but she couldn't. "I'm sorry."

He stared at her, then dropped his hands from her. "You're not going to listen to me."

"No. But hopefully you'll listen to me, because I'm only going to have this out with you once. I'm not going back. I'm not going anywhere but up that hill with a shovel in my hand."

"You aren't trained."

"And neither are more than half the men waiting for you to help them fight this fire. You know that from yesterday, I'm here, I'm staying. So…" She gave him her toughest smile. "Lead the way, boss. Let's do this."

Turning his head, he studied the trail they were going to take, the men waiting for him to lead, and closed his eyes for a moment. Then he opened them, kissed her once, hard, and nodded grimly. "Just stay safe."

"I intend to."

"Okay. Let's do this."

No reason to point out that he looked as if he'd rather face an execution squad, and when he didn't move, she merely gently nudged him along to face the day ahead.

* * *

Brody sat in the living room in South Carolina, where once upon a time he'd leapt from couch to couch like a wild puppy, where he'd kissed his first girl at age thirteen and had gotten caught by his grinning brother…where he'd told his parents one year ago that Griffin was gone and no one knew where.

He let out a careful breath and smiled, because, after all, today he had good news. "I found him."

A gasp shuddered out of his mother, and she reached blindly for his father's hand, clenching it tight. "You found—" her voice broke. "My Griffin?"

"The one and only." His parents sat side by side, Phyllis and Ray Moore, his father in his "retired" clothes of stiff jeans and a cardigan sweater his mother had probably insisted he wear, his mother in her fashionable Capri pants and carefully ironed blouse.

They'd always looked so happy to him, so absolutely in charge of their own world. So much so it had always seemed impossible for him to even attempt to replicate it.

So he hadn't. He hadn't even tried. If asked, he would have said he hadn't found his calling, but he was working on it—on the couch with his eyes closed.

But that had been before Griffin's life began to unravel, and for once, his brother hadn't been able to pull things back together.

For Brody, turning his back on Griffin's troubles would have been expected. Easy.

And wrong.

Apparently he did indeed have a conscience. Damn it.

"Son, tell us." His father stroked his mother's hand, the one that held his so tight his skin had gone white.

"How is he? *Where* is he?" Tears swam in his mother's eyes. "When is he coming home?"

He had to do this right—he, the son who'd majored in kidding around, the class clown, the guy who'd never successfully created a single relationship worth having except for the one he had with Griffin. "I can't tell you where he is. I promised I wouldn't."

"Oh, Brody—"

"But I'm in touch with him. He's okay."

He hoped. God, he hoped. He was flying back to San Diego in a few hours, he wanted to be there when Griffin got back late tonight or the next morning. Not that Griffin would want him there.

"Can't you tell us anything? What he's been doing? Why he's stayed away so long...*something*, Brody," his mother whispered. *"Please."*

He looked at them, his parents who'd aged in the past year more than in any other time in their lives. "I don't really know what he's been doing all this time," he said. "Just existing, I suppose. But I managed to talk him into—" He let out a mirthless laugh. "I bullied him, actually, into volunteering for Hope International. It's a charity organization that sends out volunteers to assist in whatever their specialty is."

His mother gasped again, her hand to her chest. "And he went on a fire?"

"He did, he went out on a wildfire in Mexico. I want to be there when he gets back."

"Oh, my God." His mother got up, drew him up also, and hugged him tight. "Oh, Brody. You're such a wonderful brother."

Brody let her squeeze him while he squeezed his eyes tight. He wasn't a wonderful brother, he'd never been a wonderful brother. That had been Griffin.

But letting her think so felt…really good. "I'll talk to him, try to get him to call you."

"I love you, Brody."

He knew that. He did. But for the first time he wanted to live up to that love.

Much later, before he left his parents' house for the airport, still basking in that nice, warm, "wonderful brother" glow, he called his own cell phone.

He got the voice message, which had been changed.

"Brody," Griffin's voice said. "Don't even think about leaving me a message and asking how I'm doing, because I'm going to tell you. Remember that time when you climbed that tree out front of Aunt Gail's house? You slipped and fell, but a branch caught you on the way down, leaving you hanging there, upside down, bleeding and screaming for an hour before anyone rescued you. Remember that, Brody? Remember that feeling? *That's* how I'm doing. I'm hanging in. Literally. Now go away. Go far, far away."

"I'm sorry," Brody said regretfully. "No cando."

* * *

Griffin leaned on his shovel and swiped sweat off his forehead with his arm. Three times this morning alone the increasing winds had forced him to call the crew back and redirect. The only saving grace had been the river and the rock. All they had to do was use them effectively and pray the weather cooperated. If that happened, they just might get this thing contained.

The tractors were barely able to handle the mountainside, but they put them to work anyway, dragging thick, heavy railroad ties behind each machine, which effectively cleared the dead pine needles and small branches and made a damn good firebreak.

He himself had been scraping dead and extremely flammable growth for hours now, and his stomach was still bouncing around. At the moment they had the fire at their backs and were working on setting the flames back on themselves, hoping to trap the hot monster.

A hot, hard gust of wind hit him, and then another, which made his heart sink. The weather report Tom had brought had been for a steady barometer and low winds.

And yet that's not what it felt like. If they weren't careful, the fire was going to jump this latest firebreak as well, and head south, right into town, never mind what the northward climb up the mountain would do.

Griffin lifted his head from his work, immediately searching out and finding Lyndie, only about ten yards away, digging hard.

She still wore the bandana around her mouth. It was filthy. *She* was filthy, sticky, damp with perspiration, and looked every bit as exhausted as he felt, and yet her arms never slowed as she worked as hard as any man out there. He thought she was the most beautiful woman he'd ever seen.

And then suddenly, vibrantly, the wind shifted and the fire reacted accordingly; jumping, writhing, and just like that, he was hit.

Not by the heat, which was intense.

Not by the flames themselves, which were hot enough to make him feel sunburned.

No, what doubled him over was a sudden, menacing, unstoppable panic.

13

He couldn't breathe. He couldn't think. Unreasonable and in-sidious, twisting inside him, Griffin actually grabbed at his throat as if that could help him drag air into his lungs.

He was back in Idaho. Staring helplessly at the crew that hadn't made it to the other side of the firebreak as the flames flew through the air on the current from hot, harsh winds. The heavy winds without moisture had been like gasoline on a lit match.

Too late for fire shelters, too late for anything, in a blink of an eye, he'd watched, horrified, as they'd all perished.

"Griffin." Suddenly, Lyndie stood right in front of him. She'd tossed aside her shovel, she'd tossed aside his, and held his arms in her hands, standing on tiptoe to look right into his face.

"The wind shifted," he said hoarsely.

"Yes." Her fingers dug into his arms, the only sign of her distress. "The wind shifted. What do we do?"

The best safety lies in fear. Who'd said that, he wondered inanely, Shakespeare? Because nothing had ever been truer.

"Griffin, tell me what to tell them."

He looked into her face, which was cool and calm, only her

eyes filled with worry and apprehension, and hell if he was going to screw up now and lose her, too. "We retreat." As he knew all too painfully, a change of even the smallest magnitude meant the difference between escape and entrapment.

He didn't intend for anyone to get trapped. He took her arm, needing to hold on to something, someone, oddly relieved that it was her. Behind them, he felt the heat wall that always ran just ahead of the fire, and his heart kicked into an even higher gear. "Come. Hurry."

Lyndie nodded and yelled over her shoulder, *"Ven por aca, apurarse,"* and the men did exactly that, running with them eastward.

"Faster," he said to Lyndie, still holding her arm. He thrust his radio at her. "Tell them all to move now."

She translated into the radio, and they scrambled up the path that only yesterday they'd used to map the perimeters, the fire now nipping at their heals.

At higher ground, safe for the moment, they began all over again, digging, clearing, more digging.

* * *

Several hours later, Griffin climbed a little higher to see what was happening. And when he did, he had to admit, despite the unpredictable wind, things were steady.

A hand settled on his shoulder. "We've made excellent progress, right?"

Lyndie's soft voice penetrated the protective shell he'd donned like the rest of his gear, the one to protect him emotionally, but her touch slayed both it and him. He didn't know how it was she could do that—make him feel, make him ache, but she did. She made him want to be a whole man again, she made him want so many things, and his throat was so tight when he turned to her that he didn't trust his voice so he simply nodded.

Shockingly enough, they *had* made excellent progress. They'd nearly made back the time they'd lost this morning. East and west movement were covered, fully contained. Northbound, the fire had made little headway, appearing to be trapped by the rocks, and southward, toward town, they were frantically working ahead of the flames and, unbelievably, were actually close there as well.

They stood together like that for a long moment. Lyndie sighed and pushed her hair out of her face, her fingers leaving a long streak of dirt across her cheek and jaw, which joined several streaks already there. Looking at her, he couldn't believe how badly he'd lost it, and how she'd managed to break through with just her voice and a touch.

"I really think we're good," she said.

"Yeah." He couldn't look away from her. "We're good."

But she frowned, and grabbed his hand, which was bloody. "Where the hell are your gloves?" Pulling them out of his own back pocket, she waved them in front of his face. "Hello, earth to Griffin, come in Griffin."

A grim smile touched his lips. How was it that this rough and tumble woman drew him? "You're quite the cuddler, aren't you."

Lyndie resisted the urge to smile. "If you want a cuddle, go find your mom." But because she couldn't help it, she lifted his palm to her cheek, something inside her reacting to that simple connection. She wondered if he felt it, too. Or was he drowning in all the emotion he faced? "I know today is hard for you," she said softly. "And that you're upset and sick with it—"

His thumb skimmed over her jaw. "I'm not sick."

"Griffin."

"Do I look sick to you right now, Lyndie?"

She looked him over. Now his eyes were glittering, but not with fear or panic. Before she could mention that, he'd put his free hand on her hip, backing her to a tree. Blocking her from view with his broad shoulders, he looked down at her with an expression that took her breath.

"Maybe you should take my temperature," he suggested.

Oh, my.

"Here, let me help you." He covered her mouth with his. He kissed her hard, sucking her tongue into his mouth, and only when she was breathless and letting out pathetically needy little whimpers did he pull back.

Breathing as hard as she was, he held on to her. "Do I feel sick to you?" he asked again.

She put her hand to her pounding heart. "You feel…hot." My God, she thought, did he feel hot.

"Hot." He nodded. "Yeah, that sounds about right."

At her hip, the radio squawked, and never taking his eyes off her, he removed it from its clip and lifted it to her lips.

"*Si,*" she said, then listened. Sergio spoke, saying they had a group of about twenty men at the southwestern tip of the fire, the closest point to town, and they'd managed to contain that end. Hugging her radio, she looked up at Griffin and felt her eyes go moist. "We've got it."

After nearly six hundred acres and vicious winds fighting them every step of the way, they were finally one-hundred-percent fully contained.

He stared at her. "Sure?"

Gripping his shirt, she tugged him close. "Sure." And then she did as he'd done... she kissed him, hard and hot as the fire around them.

* * *

At the end of the day, with dusk approaching faster than their exhaustion, another crew came to relieve them. They'd traveled from Mexico City and were going to patrol and mop up, making sure the contained fire didn't jump any more lines while it burned itself out, an event they figured would take another three days at least.

The mood was light and relieved. Griffin drove back, and Lyndie let him because she was so tired she could hardly keep her eyes open. Down the hill they went as darkness fell, the shadows and bumpy road hypnotizing as she fought to stay awake.

"Close 'em," Griffin said over the roar of the engine and the wind. "I'll be on coyote watch."

She relaxed back against the seat, drifting along on thoughts of a hot shower and a soft bed—only to jerk awake, holding on for dear life when they hit a rut. But she couldn't have flown out of the Jeep, she was hooked in by the seat belt, and also by Griffin's arm, which he held out in front of her over every bump they hit.

"Relax," he said. "I've got you."

I've got you.

She closed her eyes, tried to picture herself flying home tonight, which was their plan. By tomorrow morning she'd be wherever she wanted, doing whatever she wanted, when she wanted. Which meant she'd be alone.

I've got you.

Funny thing, but no matter how she tried, she just couldn't get past those three little words and what they meant. Why was it that with this man, she could let her guard down? For once, she didn't have to have everything covered at all times...

She awoke with a start when someone touched her hip. Sitting straight up, she bashed her head into—

Griffin's.

"Ouch," he said, and unhooked her seat belt before rubbing his head.

She could see him in the dark now—they were parked. The lights of the inn twinkled in the background, as did the scents of Rosa's delicious dinner. Lyndie's body's clock was all screwed up but she knew she could have only been out a few minutes.

Rubbing her head where she'd bumped it into Griffin's, she looked into his face. "I can't believe I fell that hard."

"A fifteen-hour day like the one we just had would get to anyone." He took her hand and pulled her out of the Jeep, slipping an arm around her.

"I'm not that tired," she said, but didn't smack his hands away like she might have anyone else. Instead, she leaned into him, surprising them both when she set her head on his shoulder. Just for a moment, she told herself, letting out a little sigh of pleasure when he pulled her closer. Just for a moment...

"Hey." This was accompanied by a gentle shake. "Let's get you some food."

"Right." She blinked, startled to find herself at the front door, still in his arms. And strong nice arms they were.

Inside Tallulah barked with sheer happiness at the sight of them until their ears felt like they were going to pop off, and Rosa yelled at her to be quiet. Rosa kept hugging her "heroes," tsking and clucking over them, stuffing them with food until Lynide couldn't move. She glanced over at Griffin, who was smiling and making small talk, but the tension was still there around his mouth and in his eyes, and she knew he wanted to be home. Pushing away from the table, she smiled. "Okay, let's hit it."

"No, no you should stay until tomorrow," Rosa protested. "Rest."

"I got a catnap on the way back here. That's all I needed."

Rosa rolled her eyes. "How you do that, sleep in pieces, I will never understand. Fine, go. Go wherever the wind blows you, eventually you will come back."

"I think I'm on the schedule for a fly-in next week."

"We'll take what we can get until you admit this is your home."

"My home is the sky. I've told you that."

"And I've told you," Rosa said calmly, taking their plates away, "That your heart can have more than one home."

"My heart doesn't need a home."

"Of course your heart needs a home." Rosa made a soft sound of disgust. "Every heart needs a home."

Uncomfortable, Lyndie glanced at Griffin. He sat watching her, eyes inscrutable.

What was he thinking? And why did she care? Throwing up her arms, she stood. "I'm out of here, Ace. If you want a ride, it's now or never."

Striding down the hall, she headed out the front door and ran smack into Nina.

The young woman crossed her arms and held her ground. "I suppose you're sneaking out of here without me."

"We already discussed this," Lyndie said, trying to go around her but she wouldn't move. "Don't be mad."

"I *am* mad," she said in her heavily accented English. "You could take me. It would be no skin off your ear."

"You mean nose. It'd be no skin off my nose."

"Whatever."

Lyndie sighed. "I told you why I can't take you to the States."

"Yes. You care more about my father than me. And after five years of being friends."

"Nina—"

"If your next sentence does not start and end with 'yes, I will take you' then don't bother."

Lyndie closed her mouth.

And Nina turned away.

"Nina—"

Nina lifted her hand, shook her head. Fine. Lyndie stepped out into the night, then got behind the steering wheel of Tom's Jeep. She *was* driving tonight. She *was* flying tonight. Alone, except for her one passenger, and she could ignore him if she had to.

And she wouldn't feel guilty for needing to get away from Rosa's knowing eyes. For leaving Nina. She wouldn't.

She was in charge of her own destiny, and no one else's. The freedom of that had always been thrilling, driving her. She understood Nina's wish to be as free, but that was for her to work out with Tom.

Where the hell was Griffin?

She started the engine. Revved it a few times. "Come on, Ace," she muttered, and wished the Jeep had a horn that worked so she could blare it.

Finally the front door opened, and he sauntered out. "You'd think you were late for a date," he said, when he finally got close enough.

"Maybe I am."

He tossed his two bags in the back and eyed her. "You're too ornery to have a date waiting for you."

"Just get in."

"You really up to flying home?"

"You'd rather stick around here until morning?"

As an answer, he slid his long body into the passenger seat. She put the Jeep into gear but he settled a hand on hers. "Lyndie."

She let out another sigh. "I'm fine."

He just looked at her.

"I am. I really can sleep in little increments, it's a gift from my grandfather." She softened her voice as he held eye contact. "I just want out, too, you know?"

"Yeah." His gaze traveled over her face, settled on her lips. "I know."

14

Before heading to the airport, they picked up Tom so he'd be able to drive the Jeep home, and the three of them rode off into the night in comfortable silence.

At the airstrip, Tom got out, took a long inhale. "Smoke's down already." He came around and took Lyndie's hands. His wizened face creased into an easy smile, his long ponytail of silver hair gleaming in the moonlight. "Thank you."

"For what? Using up all the gas in your Jeep?"

"For lots of things. For not taking Nina."

She knew how much Tom still loved this old village as if he'd been born here, knew how he thought everyone loved it as much as he. "I didn't want her to run away from here because she's getting antsy," she said. "I wanted her to work it out with you."

"She's going to stay."

"Tom." She shook her head, cupped his jaw. "We all know, *you're* meant to be here. You love the slower, laid-back lifestyle, the isolation, the wilderness…but it's not for everyone. There's not much available to Nina. She's young, she wants to get out, she wants excitement, she wants to spread her wings."

"I just want her to spread those wings close to me."

"Yeah, well, she has other ideas, and my not taking her isn't going to stop her."

"What could she possibly want that's not right here?" he asked, baffled, lifting his hand, gesturing around him in the dark night to the mountains, the quaint town they couldn't see...everything.

Lyndie lifted a shoulder. "She might not know until she finds it. You had to go find it, remember?"

Tom let out a sad smile. "You know, she said the same damn thing. And I'm still not ready to hear it." Turning away, he reached into the back of the Jeep to help Griffin with his bags.

Lyndie left them there to go see to her plane. She'd paid Julio to fuel her up and watch over her favorite piece of steel on earth. She'd added his favorite bottle of booze to guarantee he'd done just that.

He must have liked the booze, because he'd also washed the plane until the white wings gleamed. "Hey, baby." She patted the bottom of the wing as she opened the door. She didn't like that the plane hadn't been locked up, and would mention it to Julio, but since there wasn't anyone around who could pilot it out of here anyway, she supposed there wasn't much to worry about.

She climbed in and looked with pleasure at the clean floor, the shiny windows. At the pilot's seat...and the small ball of fluff curled up there.

"You take."

Lyndie turned and found Julio looking at her from beneath his low cap. In his dark, dark bloodshot eyes was an expectant expression. She laughed, at both the expectation and the way he insisted on using broken English simply because he liked the language. "No. No way. Even if I had more booze for you, I'm not taking a damn cat."

He got the gist of that statement whether he understood every word or not. No was no in both their languages. So was the emphatic shake of her head that she added.

Julio merely lifted a shoulder and walked slowly away, vanishing into the night.

Without taking the kitten.

"Hey!" she called out to him. "Come back here, I can't just take this flea-ball—"

"Mew."

She let out a long breath and stared at the thing. It was all white except for a black spot on its nose and one ear. Well, not white exactly, more like the color of a white T-shirt freshly washed with a dark sock."Shoo."

The kitten blinked the bluest eyes she'd ever seen—with the exception of one Griffin Moore—and didn't budge.

"Shoo," she repeated, and added a little wave of her hand.

The tiny kitten hunched into the farthest corner of the seat, looking terrified even as it hissed at her.

Ah, hell. "Look, I'm not the bad guy here. I just don't take stowaways."

Griffin climbed aboard. "What's this? Yours?"

"Nope." Hands on her hips, she stared at the kitten, who was beginning to resemble a pain in her ass. "I've got to give this thing back to Julio before we go."

"He just left in the oldest truck on the planet."

"Then Tom can take it—" Scooping up the kitten, she jumped out of the plane and strode toward the Jeep. Tom was leaning against it, and when he saw her, he straightened.

"Lyndie, have I told you that you were a godsend this weekend?"

"I was. And now you owe me. I need you to take this kitten—"

"Whoa—" Tom lifted both his hands and flattened himself against the Jeep. "Allergic. Deathly allergic."

"You are kidding me."

He sneezed dramatically, then three more times in quick succession.

"Okay, okay," she muttered, pulling the kitten back against her. "Damn it."

Tom sneezed once more, then slid into his Jeep. "Sorry. See you next week, with that dentist for the kids, right?"

"Right." She stared down at the kitten.

The kitten with the laser beam eyes stared right back.

Tom roared off into the night, and she sighed. "I don't like cats."

The kitten showed her tiny teeth and hissed again. For added measure, the little thing displayed its brand-spanking-new and needlelike claws, right before she dug them into Lyndie's chest.

"Hey!" She tried to pry the thing loose but the kitten had quite a grip on her tank top and didn't appear to have any inclination to let go. She pulled harder, and beneath her fingers, she could feel the ribs of the kitten, which went a long way toward squelching her urge to toss it into the air. "You're starving," she said, and felt her heart sink.

"You're not going to leave it here, are you?"

She stared into those light blue feline eyes and then turned to look into another pair of blue eyes, these filled with complicated human emotions she didn't know what to do with. "But how can I just take it?"

"I don't know." Griffin stroked the kitten beneath its chin. "But it's going to be interesting to watch you decide, either way."

"What does that mean?"

"It means you, Lyndie Anderson, have a little commitment issue."

"Don't be ridiculous."

He looked amused. "Are you telling me you're not reserved to an extreme? That you don't like to pretend you have no one in your life, when in fact you're close to—and loved—by several people that I know of?"

Rolling her eyes, Lyndie brushed past Griffin and got into the plane. She set the kitten down on a seat, and was hissed at again for her trouble. "Okay, listen up," she told it. "I'm the boss here. Rip those seats with your claws and you're Dead Kitty Walking."

"That's so adorable," Griffin said. "You're bonding already."

"Shut up."

With a grin, he brushed against her back as he came closer. For a beat he settled his big hands on her shoulders, his mouth at her ear. "I love it when you sweet talk."

At his touch, she shivered, but kept staring at the cat. "It's half starving, you know."

"Yes."

"It's just begging to be eaten by some nosy coyote the moment I take off."

"If you were going to leave it here, yes."

"*Fine.*" She tossed up her hands. "It can come. But don't tell Nina, she'll be even more pissed I said no to her and yes to this fleabag."

"Ah. Too many strings on your heart." He nodded. "That's what you're worried about. You might have to talk, laugh, have a good time, even…open up."

"I laugh plenty, not that it's any of your business. And I don't know what you're griping about, I'm taking you, aren't I?"

"You're getting paid to take me."

She stared at him. "You make it sound so…so missionary."

"No, you do that all on your own."

His eyes were fathomless now, revealing nothing, and that he could do that at all made her mad, made her want to reach him, want to know what he was thinking. "Yes, this is my job. Some of us don't have the luxury of not working for an entire year," she said.

Turning away at that, he scooped up the kitten she'd dumped. "We'd better go."

Right. She started to pass him but he was holding the silly little kitten against his big body, stroking it until the thing had closed its eyes in ecstasy, and she couldn't take her eyes off him.

"What?" he asked.

"I didn't say anything."

"You're thinking something."

Yeah, she was thinking. She was thinking a lot of things, starting with the fact that he did something to her insides.

In fact, he turned her inside out.

Deciding that was a bad thing, she plopped into her seat, slammed on her headphones and sent him a cool glance. "I was thinking this is where I come on and say 'have a nice flight.'"

"It is going to be nice, isn't it?"

At the slight unease in his voice, she smiled grimly. "Nervous?"

"When you smile like that, hell yeah. Who taught you to fly?"

"My grandfather. Air Force lifer. He taught me everything I know."

"Is that why you're such a softie?"

Her smile widened. "You know it. I'm a living example of what happens when a girl gets raised by a tough officer."

He didn't smile back. "What happened to the rest of your family, Lyndie?"

She shrugged. "My parents died when I was four. My grandfather took me on. And flying was how we bonded. Do check your seat belt. It's going to be a bumpy ride."

"Lyndie—"

"Just going over procedure."

"You're trying to avoid talking serious."

"Yep."

"All right." He looked at her for a long moment. "How about we forget procedure and I come over there and kiss you stupid?"

She laughed. *"What?"*

"Yeah, you're always really nice to me after I kiss you stupid."

"You have *never* kissed me stupid."

He lifted a brow.

"You haven't."

"Is that a dare?"

"No." *God, no.* "Look, Ace, no one…kisses me like that."

"No one?"

"No one."

She ignored his knowing expression and began her takeoff. Always she'd been able to clear her mind, but now she found herself thinking about what he'd just said. About how good his mouth was, how he could indeed render her idiotic with just a kiss.

Damn him.

"Lyndie—"

"No. I don't want to talk about it." Shifting in her seat a little, the silent sexual current between them making her itchy, she told herself it was all in her imagination.

She told herself that every time she glimpsed at him during the flight; every time he sent her one of those Griffin Moore looks, making her itch all over again.

15

They landed in San Diego. A lineman helped Lyndie tie the plane down, and he did so with a sweet, eager, pathetic smile that made Griffin want to tell the poor guy not to waste his time.

Lyndie Anderson was immune to such things. Hell, she was barely human.

Only he knew that wasn't true. He'd seen firsthand how much she did for others, he'd felt her melt in his arms. She *was* human, extremely human...and extremely tough.

Had it been losing her family so young? Being raised by her apparently equally tough grandfather? For all that Griffin had lost last year, he had a solid foundation of love. He knew about friendships and family and trusting people.

Lyndie, apparently, did not.

He could try to give her some of that, could be her friend, let her trust him. It wouldn't be a hardship, he liked her, very much. Affection would be easy, so would a physical relationship...maybe it could even grown to more, far more.

But he didn't trust his own emotions at the moment. He didn't know if his feelings for her were real, or if he was just waking up after a year of emotional shutdown. He knew he wanted her physically. God, he wanted her physically.

But that was lust. Lust wasn't close to love…And no matter how he spun it, did he really want to coax her out of her shell, coax her into opening her heart to him, into starting something serious until he knew what was in his own heart?

He couldn't, it was too unfair.

He followed her through customs, the airport too noisy and chaotic to talk, not that Lyndie looked in a mood to talk by the fact that she didn't look at him and walked so fast he could hardly keep up with her.

When he got outside, Brody was there waiting for him, hands in his pockets, hair blowing in the middle of the night breeze. Griffin sighed as Brody asked, "How was the flight?"

He still had butterflies in his stomach from the landing, which he suspected Lyndie had taken so roughly just to see him turn green. She seemed to like him green.

It was the only time she was nice to him, though nice as it pertained to Lyndie was a relative term. He turned to glance back for a glimpse of her at the exact same moment she came outside with a cat carrier she'd gotten in customs. She brushed past him. "See ya, Ace."

See ya? He'd waited for her, and she was just going to…walk away?

Since she kept moving, he assumed so.

Curious at the odd light in his brother's eyes as he stood there on the sidewalk outside the terminal, Brody moved closer. "Hey. You okay?"

Griffin growled some sort of unintelligible answer as he watched a woman—a hot, curvy little thing in a leather bomber jacket and short fiery auburn hair—stalk away.

"Who's that?" Brody asked with interest.

"My pilot." Griffin's voice suggested sheer frustration and bafflement—common emotions when it came to women in Brody's opinion.

She might have kept walking if Griffin hadn't surged forward, snagging her arm to hold her still, leaning in to say something Brody couldn't quite catch.

The woman pulled free, and then stalked off as if Griffin had made her so mad she could hardly contain herself.

Brody understood the sentiment, he'd been there, done that with him himself many times, but still…very interesting.

Silent and brooding, Griffin came back to Brody's side.

Oh, yes, *very* interesting, Brody decided. Before coming here, he'd snooped around in the small house his brother had rented all year, and had discovered not a single personal tie. Not a phone number of a friend, or any evidence that Griffin had contact with anyone.

And yet something had jolted him back to the land of the living the past few days. Despite the deafening silence, there was a spark of life in his brother's eyes. Granted, it was temper, but a spark was a spark, and Brody would take what he could get. "Your pilot?"

"Yeah."

"She's hot."

"No. Yes. Damn it, *no.*"

"Do I need to reteach you *everything*?"

Griffin growled, and Brody laughed. Then he reached out for his brother. "God, it's good to see you." Knowing full well he risked being strangled, he hugged him.

Griffin endured it for a moment, then pushed away and started walking—in the opposite direction as the hot pilot had gone.

With a grin, Brody followed. "So, you had a good time?"

"Where did you park?"

"I bet she was able to take your mind off getting back on the job, right?"

"Brody, tell me which way to go or I'm going to call a cab."

"Hey, I'm just making small talk here."

"Screw small talk. Get me the hell out of here."

Yep, definitely back amongst the living, which could hurt like hell, he had to admit. "Does she kiss as hot as she looks?"

Fists clenched, Griffin whirled around, and Brody laughed, joy filling him. "You're really back. Christ, I missed you."

"I was only gone for two days."

"I missed you for a year. A whole damn year. Tell me you're not going to vanish on me again. On us again."

Griffin started into the night lit by the lights and sounds of traffic, jaw clenched. "I don't know what the hell I'm going to do…" He let out a breath and looked him in the eye. "But I won't vanish again."

Brody's throat went tight with relief, and he nodded. To give them both a moment, they watched the pretty pilot cross the street, heading toward the parking lot. "Don't you want to thank her?"

"For what? Driving me crazy for two days?"

"For bringing that life to your eyes. What else did she bring life to?"

"Brody?"

"Yeah?"

"Shut up."

Brody laughed. Oh yeah, it was good to have him back.

* * *

Riiiiiip.

At the sound, Lyndie woke and sat straight up. "What the hell—"

She blinked the room into view. Small bedroom, plain with white walls, white comforter, pine wood floor. The sound of waves crashing and the scent of salty air came in the open windows.

She was home in Del Mar, in Sam's guesthouse, which she rented for a song. She'd been back for two full days, so this shouldn't have surprised her, but sometimes she traveled around so much she forgot where she was when she woke up.

It was barely seven in the morning, but apparently the breeze had made the curtains flutter, which in turn had turned the kitten into a wild thing, as he was currently swinging from them.

Hence the ripping sound as his claws tore into the material.

"Damn it." Surging to her feet, she tried to liberate him, but was rewarded with a long hiss as the little ears went flat back against his head.

"Feeling's mutual, tough guy." She lifted him up, looking him in the eye. "Rule number one, no noise before eight a.m. Rule number two, no swinging from the curtains, they're not even mine."

She deposited him on the floor. "Rule three, *stay out of trouble.*"

Made for trouble, the kitten went scampering off. She should have left him in the cat carrier the airport had forced her to purchase to transport the animal. She looked around her. There were piles of clothes here and there that she hadn't had time to take care of. She tended to run into Target and just buy more underwear rather than actually do laundry. As for other personal effects, she hadn't collected anything of her own for the place in all the time she'd been here. Because of that, there wasn't much else for the kitten to destroy, which actually wasn't a comfort.

When had this place gotten so sterile?

But she already knew the answer to that. Every single place she'd ever lived in had been sterile, starting with the military houses she'd inhabited with her grandfather. She'd gotten real good at keeping only what she could easily pack into a suitcase when it was time to go.

Oh well, all that mattered now was that she had a few days to herself. She could clean out her refrigerator. Scratch that, it was already empty. Hmm... She could call Sam and see if he'd give her an extra shift, but she'd already made a big deal about having a few days off, so that was no good.

She could... hell, she could count ceiling tiles if she wanted, but a better idea came to her. She'd go lie on the beach and watch the waves. That should take up an hour. Maybe she'd even swim, and use up some of this restless energy she couldn't seem to shake. Tugging off the T-shirt she'd slept in, she pulled on her bathing suit, grabbed a towel, and headed for the door, stopping only when she realized she was being watched.

The kitten from hell lay on the floor, chewing a perfectly good leather flat, watching her from those laser blue eyes.

"Hey," she said. "Those are mine!"

"Mew."

"I'll 'mew' you." Grabbing the ruined shoe from between his paws, she waggled it in his face. "This is a direct violation of the rules."

Unconcerned, he lifted a paw and began to wash his face.

"Fine." Giving up, she tossed down her shoe. "But I'm outta here."

At that, he stopped licking himself and looked at her.

"Don't even try to give me that look. I'll be right back. Don't destroy a thing while I'm gone, you hear me?"

The spawn of Satan merely yawned.

Stepping outside, she slammed her door closed. She turned away from the big house—Sam's—which had 10,000 square feet of fancy rooms and fancy things that always made her feel like a bull in a china shop—and headed toward the beach. Del Mar was one of those awe-inspiring places where people spent far too much money on their houses in order to have this incredible view of blue, blue ocean and a sky so bright she needed her sunglasses to look at it.

The other night haunted her, she could admit out here in the early day as she walked the pebbly path to the sand, with the fog kissing the beach. She didn't like the way she and Griffin had parted, but she couldn't figure out why it mattered. She'd told herself she had her own life to worry about.

And yet today, her own life seemed...empty.

The way she'd lived had been her own choice. She could have made changes along the way, but she hadn't. Now she was alone on the beach as she'd wanted, and that worked too. No one to care about, no one to lose.

With a restless sigh, she sat and hugged her knees to her chest.

"Wow, look at that, you *can* relax." Sam's long legs appeared at her side. "Should take a picture of this," he said. "No, wait, scratch the picture." Hunkering at her side, he smiled into her face. "Because you're the only person I know who can kick back while wearing such a fierce frown." He sprawled his lanky body on the sand next to her and stretched out. "Oh, yeah, this is good. Should have been a beach bum."

With his shoulder-length, sun-streaked blond hair and a rangy build suggesting he was ten years younger than his thirty-five, he'd have made a good one. Plus she'd seen him surf after a long day in his office. He looked perfectly at home in the waves. Actually, he always looked at home.

A feat she'd never managed. But then again she hadn't been born bored, with a silver spoon in her mouth and more family than she knew what to do with.

Sam hadn't had many bumpy roads in his life, but he was one of those startlingly well adjusted people who just wanted to give back. And he did, in spades. He gave everything to Hope International, and all he asked for in return was the occasional hour to surf when the conditions suited him.

She wished her life could be so simple.

"What is it?" He cocked his head. "What's making you so sad?"

"I'm not."

"Well you're something." He nudged her shoulder with his. "You've been something ever since you came back from Mexico two days ago. What happened down there, anyway?"

"Nothing."

"Uh huh." He eyed her. "That was the most defensive nothing I've ever heard. Did you have a problem with the volunteer you flew down?"

She stared at the waves. They were good today, four- to six-footers.

"The firefighter...Griffin Moore, right?"

A picture of Griffin crossed Lyndie's vision: tall, gorgeous, and tortured. "I remember his name."

Sam cupped his hand to her jaw and made her look at him. "He try something?"

"You know I have no problem punching their lights out if it comes to that."

"Did it?"

"No."

Sam relaxed marginally but he was still watching her. "I had you scheduled to take a dentist down to San Puebla, but he canceled until next week. Now I've got you scheduled to fly a pediatrician and an optometrist to Baja tomorrow. Then you've got another trip back to San Puebla."

"With supplies?"

"Some. The fire's still contained, but there's problems with the weather. They're expecting trouble tomorrow when the winds are due to kick up."

She knew this. She'd called Tom every day to check. "Fine."

"Same guy is going down. He's called several times checking on the status of the fire. When he found out they needed help with the suppression, he said he'd go back."

She stared at the waves. So Griffin had offered to go back. Which meant she'd be seeing him again. No big deal, really. Maybe they'd shared a little more of themselves than they'd intended, but that was to be expected given the situation they'd found themselves in. Whenever adrenaline, adventure, and danger got all mixed up together, things got accelerated.

And things *had* gotten accelerated.

But they were adults. They could handle it.

God, she hoped they could handle it.

Sam was still looking at her. "Are you going to tell me what's going on?"

"It's not in my job description."

"Screw the job description, Lyndie. I thought we were friends."

Not having many, she valued the few she had managed, by sheer good luck, to cultivate. "We are."

"Friends tell."

Lyndie sighed. "Fine. I kissed him."

He stared at her with his dark, dark brown eyes. And then he laughed. "You did not."

"I did." She winced. "Look, we got caught up in this whole situation, okay? The fire was hot and dangerous and far too close. We were alone, together, afraid..."

"Ah. The danger thing." He nodded. "I know."

"You know?"

"Hey, I flew for five years before I hired you."

"Right." She sighed.

"That bad?"

No, *that good.* "I really don't want to talk about this, and I sure as hell don't want to see him again."

"No problem." Joking aside now, he touched her arm. "I'll get someone else to fly him."

"No," she said too quickly, far too quickly, and Sam slowly lifted a brow. "I'll do it, it'll be fine."

"You just said you didn't want to see him again—"

"I also said I'd do it." Surging to her feet, she dropped her towel and headed toward the waves. She needed a hard, fast swim.

"Maybe I should come along on this one," Sam said, appearing at her side as she walked to the water. "Just to make sure you don't do something stupid."

"Like what?" she asked, annoyed now. She never did anything stupid.

Except kiss Griffin. That had been really stupid. Wonderful, hot...but really, *really* stupid.

Sam dove into the water ahead of her, and then resurfaced, tossing back his hair as he turned to face her. "Like actually let yourself feel for someone."

She opened her mouth, then slowly closed it, because what could she say? He'd nailed it on the head.

She rarely let herself feel for anyone.

She *never* let herself feel for anyone. Things were better that way; cleaner, easier. Safer.

Sam splashed her. "Am I right?"

She offered him her middle finger, then dove in the next wave and came up near him. "And just so you know, I feel for plenty of people."

"Really? Name two."

"You."

"*Two.*"

"Okay, you and…"

"Yeah? Me and…who?"

"And everyone in San Puebla." Pleased, she ticked them off on her fingers. "Tom, Nina, Rosa…"

"Oooh. Four whole people."

With a frown, she dove into another wave, and when she came up, Sam was bodysurfing next to her. "You know, I changed my mind, it's only three people," she informed his cocky grin. "Tom, Nina, and Rosa."

Sam laughed and shook his head at her, spraying saltwater in her face before he went for the next swell, his long sleek body taking the water like he'd been born for it.

She went for it, too, and prided herself on the fact she rode the wave better than he did. She liked to be the best, it made her world right for that one moment, and she came up with a smile.

"That's such a classic Lyndie move," he said.

"What is? Looking better than you out here?"

"Pretending you don't give a shit when you know you do."

"I give a shit. The waves are perfect."

"That's not what I'm talking about. I'm talking about people."

"Oh." She patted his cheek with her wet fingers. "Don't worry. I give a shit about you, too. A little, anyway."

"You know what, baby?" He floated on his back, arms spread wide. "Someday you'll admit you want me. You know you do."

She laughed good and hard over that one, then splashed him. "I'm not getting in line for a piece of you. I don't compete for a man. Ever."

"Too bad. You don't know what you're missing." He dove under again, but when he came up, Lyndie was waiting.

"I care about people," she said, unable to let it go. "I just don't always feel like wearing my heart on my sleeve, that's all."

"Hey, we all have our little quirks. Some are more stupid than others."

With a sigh, she dove back into the water. She sure wouldn't be wearing her heart on her sleeve in a few days' time, when she picked up Griffin. Even if she had wondered how he'd fared after his first fire in a year; wondered if he'd had any trouble thinking about it.

Wondered if he thought of her, or even cared.

16

Two days later, Lyndie readied for takeoff. Sunset had always been her favorite time of day, but this evening she didn't take the time to enjoy it as she moved around her plane.

The fire in San Puebla had jumped the lines again. This afternoon it had taken out another ranch. Two ranchers had suffered serious smoke inhalation and were on a train to the closest hospital.

She flipped through the preflight papers on her clipboard, not really seeing any of it. What she saw, out of the corner of her eye, was Griffin striding toward her, wearing soft, faded jeans and a white T-shirt she knew would have a firefighter logo over his left pec. It offset his tan, telling her that whatever he'd been doing all week, it'd involved the sun.

There were other people milling around as well, but only Griffin stepped close, blocking her view of anything or anyone but him. Slowly she lifted her gaze from his long, tough body to his face.

He pushed his sunglasses up on his head. "So we're doing this again."

"Define *this*."

A hint of a smile touched his mouth, though in his eyes she saw the tension. "I didn't know it would be you."

So he probably also didn't know what had happened in San Puebla today, about the fire jumping the lines, the loss of both another ranch and his hard-earned containment. He wouldn't take it easily. "Would you like a different pilot?" she asked.

He looked startled at that. "No. God." He scrubbed a hand over his face. "Listen. I wanted to tell you I'm sorry for the way I acted Sunday night."

She began to walk past him. "Forget it, I wasn't any peach either."

He stopped her with a hand to hers. "I can't forget it. I didn't even thank you—"

"There was nothing to thank me for."

"Are you kidding? You were there for me every time I began to fall apart."

"I said forget it." She pulled her hand free. "People fall apart on me all the time. It's because of where I take them, which is usually a world beyond what they know, and the things we see and do—"

He took her hand again, looked into her eyes. "So you kiss all your passengers?"

Uh... "No." She squeezed her eyes shut to the memories reflected in his. "Griffin, I don't want to do this now. I *can't* do this now. Let's just...start over, okay?"

"Lyndie—"

"Please."

He hesitated, as if he wanted to say more, but finally nodded. With one last long look that might have melted her if she'd been a melting sort of woman, he moved past her and got on board.

She watched him go, then rolled her eyes at herself for watching, and followed him, only to run smack into him when he stopped short. Pulling her hands back quickly from where they'd landed on his back, she opened her mouth to ask him to use brake lights next time.

Then she saw what he was looking at.

The kitten sat curled up on one of the seats, fast asleep, looking deceivingly adorable, for something that had destroyed her house in a matter of a short week.

Within the close confines of the plane, Griffin turned, shooting her a knowing look that also had quite a bit of heat in it. "You kept him."

They were close enough to kiss, not that she was noticing. "No one else wanted him."

"So you're not attached at all. It's just another humanitarian gesture on your part."

"Except he's not human," she quipped. "I guess that makes it an animaltarian gesture."

But he refused to let her joke her way out of this. "You're looking me in the eyes and telling me you're not attached," he pressed.

Nope, not attached. And not even under the threat of death would she admit that she liked how Lucifer's little kitty bowls looked on her bare kitchen floor, or that she didn't mind sharing her bathroom with his litter box.

In fact, the thing had slept on her feet the past two nights, pouncing her well before dawn, attacking her if she so much as twitched in her sleep…reminding her with his every move that she wasn't entirely alone. "That's what I'm saying."

"Liar," he chided softly, and tugged on her hand until she stepped so close their toes touched. "Why can't you just admit you're attached to something?"

"Look, the thing eats more than he's worth."

"The thing? You haven't even named it?"

"Sure. I call him Lucifer. Especially when he's hanging off my curtains, swinging back and forth and hissing at me."

Griffin scooped the little guy up against his chest and stroked him beneath his chin.

Lucifer mewled softly as he woke up and began to purr.

Purr!

Lyndie bit back her growl but couldn't take her eyes off the sight of Griffin nuzzling the kitten, completely oblivious to the fact that he was coming off like a marshmallow. "Put the devil down and get ready for takeoff."

Still cradling the cat, he let out one of those slow, sure smiles that had an annoying effect on her pulse. "If you're so unhappy with him, why don't you let me take him off your hands for you?"

"That won't be necessary."

"It's the least I can do."

Lyndie looked down at Lucifer, who was practically drooling in bliss and rapture, and felt her heart crack just a little, tiny bit. She couldn't believe it, but somehow she'd actually grown fond of the little idiot. "I said I'd keep him."

Lifting his free hand from Lucifer, Griffin stroked a strand of hair off her cheek. "Tough to the end, aren't you," he whispered. "Why is that?"

"I'm just…independent."

"Have you really never let yourself lean on another person, ever?"

"Haven't needed to, not since my grandfather died."

"So you have it all covered, all by yourself."

"Yep."

He slowly shook his head. "Everyone needs something else once in a while. There's no shame in that."

"You want me to lean on you? Really?"

He stared at her, torn between saying "Hell, yes" and backing away for fear of hurting her because he still had no idea where the hell his head was at. "I'm attracted to you," he said quietly. "You know I am. But I don't trust my feelings yet."

"Yeah? Well that makes two of us."

"But I can say I *want* to trust my feelings." He shot her a wry grin when she just looked at him. "I take it you can't say the same."

"No. And don't think I don't see the irony. You're willing to risk and I'm not. But leaning on you isn't in my plans, Griffin."

"What is?"

"I've been wondering that myself." Her gaze met and held his, and she licked her lips in a nervous gesture that made him groan.

"God, Lyndie." He touched her face, moved even closer. "I—"

But another man stepped on board right then, one who looked shockingly like the man already standing there. Not quite as tall, and a little beefier, he shared Griffin's see-all light blue eyes, sun-kissed light brown hair, and rugged facial features.

At the sight of him, Griffin dropped his hand from Lyndie's face and sighed.

"I've got great timing, huh?" the man said with a grin.

Griffin set the kitten down on a seat. "Lyndie, meet my brother. Brody's gotten himself invited to come along by promising Sam a whole plate of donated supplies. He thinks I need a keeper."

"Nah." Brody shook Lyndie's hand with a charming smile. "What he really needs is a personality transplant."

Lyndie, whose heart was still leaping from the almost-kiss with Griffin, found herself smiling. "I think I like you already."

"You like him but not me?" Griffin said in disbelief.

"He's quick," Lyndie said to Brody.

"That's my Grif, quick as lightning," Brody agreed. "Mom always said it's because she didn't eat enough protein when she was pregnant with him. So really, it's not his fault."

Lyndie smiled, and it was a real one. "Are you really coming along?"

"Is that all right? I thought I could volunteer as well."

"Are you trained?"

"Nah. Grif here, he's the overachiever in the family. I'm not equipped for such tremendous dedication." He toed Griffin's bag at their feet. "His pack alone must weigh eighty pounds. That's a lot of carrying."

Lyndie glanced at Griffin, who wore a perfectly inscrutable look on his face.

"Actually, I'm skilled differently than my brother," Brody said easily, and picked a seat. "In a little bit of everything."

"You mean in a little bit of nothing." Griffin sank to a seat as well. "He majored in napping."

"And that's a fine skill, I might point out," Brody said.

Oh, this was going to be very interesting, Lyndie decided. "You have any reason why leaving the country would be illegal?" she asked Brody.

"Not at the moment. Sam said it would be no problem."

Lyndie checked her pager, and indeed she had a text message from Sam, approving Brody. "Well, then. Buckle up, boys, we're in for a bumpy ride."

Brody looked excited.

Griffin groaned.

And oddly enough, Lyndie found herself feeling alive—extremely, beautifully, vibrantly alive.

* * *

The weather for the flight behaved itself, and the night sky opened up in front of them, with mid to high humidity and little to no winds.

Perfect, for both flying and for the fire. But as if he'd read her mind, Griffin shook his head, "We won't be so lucky in San Puebla."

Lyndie glanced over at him. The cat was sprawled upside down in his lap, exposing his scrawny little body and full tummy for scratching, which had caused him to fall in a deep sleep. "It could happen," she said. She was not going to comment on her silly little kitten and how at home it was in his hands. "And if it stays like this for a few days, we could get back to one hundred percent containment, no problem, right?"

"Get back to?" He tensed. "I thought it *was* contained."

"The wind kicked up and the flames jumped the fire lines. It took out another ranch."

"Jesus." He looked devastated. "Anyone hurt?"

She didn't want to tell him. "Two ranch hands suffered serious smoke inhalation, they're on their way to the hospital."

Silent, he stared out the window for a long moment, looking at nothing really, since night had fallen and they were flying over high desert. A muscle in his jaw bunched with whatever dark thought he was having.

And she had that urge to soothe again. "But if the weather stays this good tomorrow..."

He broke off her words with a slow shake of his head, only

his eyes revealing that he knew far too much about such things. "That's where people go wrong. They gauge the weather too soon, or from too far away. Then they get content, or worse, confident. Trust me. The fire creates its own weather. At the very least, we'll have winds, low humidity, high temps—"

"Ever the eternal optimist," Brody said.

"It's just the nature of the fire, not *my* nature," Griffin protested, and after that, they flew in silence for a while. Brody brought out a deck of cards and tried to coax his brother into a game.

But Griffin wasn't in a gaming mood.

"If you stay too intense for too long, Grif, you're going to get wrinkles. Didn't you ever listen to Mom?"

"I did. I'm just surprised to find out that *you* did."

"Yeah, I always was the one in trouble, wasn't I?" Clearly trying to lighten the mood, Brody grinned at Lyndie. "My mother said 'You're the death of me' so many times I thought that was my name."

Lyndie found his grin contagious. "You two look alike, but you're not."

"That's because I got all the good traits," Brody said.

"If you call sleeping through life a good trait," Griffin offered.

"Not this past year, I haven't been sleeping through life."

"Really?" Griffin arched a brow. "What have you been up to? Besides fly-fishing, that is."

"I've been taking care of Mom and Dad, for one. And keeping up with all the friends you deserted. In fact, big brother, I've been doing all the things you should have been doing but haven't, not since you vanished on us."

Griffin turned to the window.

"Yeah, I can see you're glad you asked." The laughter and teasing had left Brody's face. Serious, he looked even more like Griffin.

"You…vanished?" Lyndie asked Griffin.

"I don't want to talk about it."

His rough, low voice took her aback.

"Of course you don't," Brody said. "Because if you don't you can continue to dwell." He looked at Lyndie. "There was a wildland fire in Idaho last summer. It was terrible, you probably heard about it on the news."

"I should have never let you on this plane," Griffin muttered.

"I heard about that fire." Lyndie remembered she'd thought how courageous and amazing the people were who fought fires like that.

"Twelve died." Brody sighed. "Twelve wildland firefighters."

Griffin, still turned to the window, closed his eyes.

"Grif was on that fire," Brody went on. "In fact, he was in charge of one of the ground crews. They were his friends. One of them, Greg, had been his best friend since kindergarten."

"God damn it," Griffin said.

"You've got to be able to hear it out loud, man. It's time." Brody's voice softened as he finished his story. "Afterwards, he up and walked away from all of us: me, my parents, his friends—including Greg's wife, whom he was also close friends with. Moved across the country and sat on a beach in San Diego. Moping. Sulking—"

"Brody—"

"Quiet, Grif. I'm telling a story."

"My story."

"Yes, well, it's an important one and should be told." Brody leaned back, put his hands behind his head, and sighed. "So I had no choice. I got motivated. I tracked him down, told him it was time to move on. Time to stop blaming himself when it wasn't his fault. I got his ass in gear."

Lyndie flew in silence for a moment as any remnant of temper at Griffin drained away.

Neither brother spoke. There was nothing to say, no possible way to make anything better for Griffin. He'd lost twelve of his crew—*My God, and his best friend*—and just thinking it made her heart stutter at the magnitude of his loss.

So much about him suddenly made sense. "Griffin…"

"Don't," he said, still looking out the window. "Don't say anything. Unless it's how to open an escape hatch so I can dump Brody out."

"See?" Brody's smile was a bit grim. "Brotherly love at its finest." But he put his hand on Griffin's shoulder and squeezed, his worry and love reflected only in his eyes. "I'm proud of you, you big idiot. I'm so damn proud of you."

"What for?"

"For being here. For trying again. For doing what you do so well it's always made me want to be a better man."

At that, Griffin looked at him. "What the hell are you talking about?"

"You give back," Brody said quietly. "You put yourself out there. You always do, Grif, and it's awe-inspiring, if you want the truth."

"Look, all I'm doing is avoiding you calling in the troops."

"You're that afraid of Mom? Come on, after all you've faced?"

Griffin stared at him for a long moment, and Lyndie's heart cracked yet again at all that was going on behind those amazing eyes. "I didn't want to be here," he finally said.

"I know."

"And you forced it."

"I know."

Griffin sighed, then let out a tight laugh. "You do realize I'm going to be your supervisor out there, right?"

"Yeah. But you'll go easy on me."

"Sure I will."

Brody blinked. "You'll have me handing out drinking water, making sure everyone has snacks to eat, or something like that, right?"

"Something like that. Don't you worry about a thing."

"Yeah. Thanks. I won't worry about a thing."

Lyndie concentrated on flying, and evening out the tightness in her throat. Soon enough, she took them into their final descent through the dark and smoky atmosphere, the flying as difficult as last time with the limited visibility. But she was prepared for that, and it was nothing she couldn't handle, marveling instead at the depth of love between the two men, despite all they'd been through.

Would she have had a brother or sister if her parents had lived? Would she have done anything, *anything,* if her sibling needed her, including putting her life on hold to make sure he or she got back on with hers?

As she had no blood connections left, the wondering seemed vain and silly, and certainly irrelevant, and she put it out of her mind.

But she couldn't put what she'd learned about Griffin out of her mind as easily, and found herself in the position of wanting to soothe him, heal him. Touch him. She wanted to pull him close and never let him go.

As terrifyingly complicated, and as terrifyingly simple, as that.

17

They got to San Puebla late. Once at the inn, Griffin went to bed, leaving Brody with an entire evening in front of him and nothing to do.

His favorite kind of evening. He'd been through Copper Canyon only once before, on the fly-fishing trip when he'd heard of San Puebla and their fire, but he'd not gotten this close to the village itself.

He already knew he loved Mexico. The weather was always good and the fishing even better. Plus the people here lived on their schedule, meaning things got done in their own good time—his favorite part about the place.

At the moment, his stomach was full from Rosa's cooking, and he stood right outside the small inn where they would sleep tonight, staring down at a running creek so full of fish swimming by the pale, smoke-filled moonlight he could have reached out and grabbed one.

Now *here* was a place where a man could take a decent breather, a place where he could forget any stresses and just kick back. Life was for nothing if not kicking back.

Unfortunately with every breath, he inhaled thick smoke, but Griffin would fix that, he was confident.

"*Maldita sea.*"

Knowing a little bit of Spanish, Brody lifted his brow at the oath let out in a musical female voice. Turning, he could barely make out the outline of someone sitting against a tree, their feet in the water. Taking a step closer, he saw it was Nina, Tom's beautiful daughter. He'd gotten a nice eyeful of her at dinner, and had enjoyed her wild spirit.

Long hair tumbling down the middle of her back, she wore the same bright red sundress she'd worn at the table, and he spent a moment to marvel that she'd packed her curves into such a snug fit. Not that he'd been complaining. Lord, no. He liked nothing better than to look at a gorgeous woman over a mouth-watering dinner.

At the moment, she was concentrating down at the pages of an opened book, her lips moving as she read, and also as she swore, quite impressively.

"Now, darlin', if that book is annoying you," he said, "just toss it aside."

Her head jerked up. Her lips stopped moving.

He leaned back against a tree to enjoy the sight of her. "Life's too short to spend it reading a story you don't like."

Slowly, she set down the book and laid her almond-shaped dark, dark eyes on him. "What are you doing out here?"

Pushing away from the tree, he came closer and looked into the water rushing over rocks and sand. "Love that sound," he murmured. "Don't you?"

"I…" She let go of her aggression and let out a low laugh. "I don't even hear it anymore."

"Well, that's just a sorry shame, if you ask me. What were you reading?"

"Nothing."

"Nothing always make you swear?"

She sighed. *"Princess Diaries."*

"Princess Diaries."

"It's the original American version. I'm…" She gave him a long don't-you-dare-laugh look. "Teaching myself to read English."

He stared at her. "But…that's amazing. You speak it so fluently I just assumed you could read it as well."

Her lush bottom lip pushed out just a little. "No. Not so good. I learned to speak it by ear, not formally." She eyed him from beneath lowered lashes. "You read English?"

Of course he did, not that he gave much thought to it. "Yes"

Nina stretched out a little, arching back, thrusting up her pretty breasts in the moonlight before giving him another sidelong look to make sure he was watching.

He most definitely was.

She patted the spot next to her.

And because he was a male, and apparently a very weak one at that, he sat.

"If I read out loud," she purred, "you could tell me all the words I do not know."

"I could," he agreed, smiling when she made sure her thigh, hip, and breast were snug to his side. She settled the open book half on her lap and half on his. Serious now, she bent her dark head over the pages and flipped her flashlight back on.

"Why *Princess Diaries?*"

"Lyndie brought it for me. She likes to call me a princess because…" With a low, sexy laugh, she shifted a little, closer, snugger to his body, which was beginning to enjoy the attention—a lot. "Because let's face it, I *am* a princess. No use denying the truth, no?"

Brody laughed a little huskily, enjoying having such a beautiful, interesting woman come on to him. "No use."

"Are you like your brother, Brody Moore?"

"What do you mean?"

With one finger, she lightly touched his heart. "Do you give and give, until there's nothing left?" Her smile was sad when he looked at her in surprise. "I can feel people," she said. "And in your brother, I feel an emptiness."

"That's not from helping others. That's from loss. Big loss."

She nodded. "I've lost, too. But life is too short to dwell on it. Life is too short to do anything but what you want." She ran her fingers up his throat, around the back of his neck, sinking them into his hair and tugging, just a little, so they were that much closer.

Only a breath away, he looked down at her mouth. "My brother would give his last breath to anyone who needed it," he said softly. "I'm…far more selfish than that."

He thought she'd back away at his brutal honesty. Instead she brought her other hand up, cupped his jaw. "Then you're like me. You do what it takes, whatever it takes, to do as you please."

"Yes—"

Which was the last word he got out before she closed her mouth over his.

* * *

Griffin slept like the dead and woke with a start, already aware of one most unusual fact: He hadn't dreamed.

He sat straight up, scrubbing his hands over his face as the covers fell away from him, racking his brain for remnants of the lingering nightmares, because surely he'd had them. He always had them.

Nothing.

In amazement, he dropped his hands from his face and blinked Lyndie into view. She stood at the foot of his bed wearing jeans and a T-shirt with a smiley face on it.

"Are you wearing that so you don't have to smile?" he asked.

"You know me so well." But she just stood there, watching him.

"Uh…good morning?"

"Did you dream about them?"

"Who?"

Her voice was full of compassion, so unexpected it bowled him over. "Your crew, your friends. Greg."

His voice was rough from sleep and the emotion that came with thinking about Greg. "I…usually do."

"You lost so much."

"Yes. But last night…" He shook his head, baffled. "I didn't dream about any of that, no." *I dreamt of you,* came the startling realization. He'd dreamt of Lyndie in his arms in the river by moonlight, her soft-skinned, tough but curvy body writhing against his.

A direct hit to his usual brooding memories, and yet he didn't flinch as he might have only a week ago. He'd spent the last year mourning the loss of his friends, men like brothers to him, men who had fought fires with him, men who had sweat and cried and laughed with him. He'd been miserable for so long, and overwhelmed by the sense of loss. Their memory was firmly entrenched in his mind, but suddenly there was room for something else.

The wanting of this strong, amazing, beautiful woman.

"I'm sorry," she whispered. "I'm so sorry."

"Brody shouldn't have told you."

"I don't think he told me all of it."

"No."

She looked at him, clearly waiting, and he shook his head. "I don't talk about it, Lyndie."

"Ever?"

"Ever. I wish you didn't know."

"I'm glad I do. It helps…" She bit her lower lip, looked away, then met his gaze again. "That first night, by the creek. Do you remember?"

"When I took a bath in the creek for your amusement? I remember," he said dryly.

"I…wanted you. I wanted you hard and fast and quick, and then I wanted you to go away. That's…that's how I like it."

He let out a surprised laugh at her admission. Her honesty never failed to startle him. He loved that about her. Comparisons were wrong, he knew that, but he'd always had to drag the feelings and thoughts out of the women in his life. Lyndie could have no idea how refreshing it was not to have to do that.

"But you didn't want me that way," Lyndie told him. "When you want, you said, you want for the long haul."

"I remember that, too." His voice seemed serrated and hoarse now, which could no longer be blamed on the early morning.

"You have a family you're close to, you have friends from kindergarten." She looked baffled by that. "You're the long haul type of guy."

"Yeah."

"I'm not."

He sighed. "Lyndie."

"I'm not saying it's any easier to take," she said. "That I threw myself at you and you backed off." Her mouth twisted in a wry smile. "But at least now I can understand it. I can understand you. I'm so sorry for what you went through, Griffin. I know people say those words when they don't really know what they're talking about, but I do."

"I doubt you feel like you have twelve lives on your head."

"You shouldn't feel that way either—"

"Don't tell me how to feel." As soon as he said the words, he regretted them, and lifted a hand when she would have spoken. "No, I'm sorry. Look, clearly I'm unfit for human company."

A little "mew" sounded then, and Lucifer took a flying leap at the bed. He missed by a good foot and ended up clinging to the side of the mattress, his razor sharp claws digging into the blankets as he gazed at them helplessly.

Unable to do anything else, Griffin helped the kitten the rest of the way up.

"That damn cat." Belying her words, Lyndie reached out and stroked Lucifer beneath his chin. "I told you I lost my parents. I was four," she said quietly. "And later, when I was older, I lost my grandfather, too. He was all I had left." Her eyes clouded over when she met his gaze. "I know loss. I might not know it to the same degree as you—"

"Loss is loss," he said gruffly, his throat tight. "And I shouldn't have implied otherwise. Lyndie, you being so nice and understanding right now is making me feel like slime."

"Well, Slime, it's time to rise and shine." She offered him a hand.

He stared at her. Here was one of the strongest women he'd ever met, a woman without need or want of softness or compassion for herself, and she was trying to give some softness to him.

"And you're right about one thing," she whispered. "Loss *is* loss. I'm sorry you find yourself here, having to face it all over again."

"I'm not sorry I'm here, not if I can help." He'd taken her hand, but now let it go. "Okay. I'm going to get out of this bed now."

"Good."

"I'm not wearing much. Actually, I'm not wearing anything. Fair warning."

Her gaze ran down his bare chest, then to the part of him the blanket covered. No blushing for this woman, just frank interest.

He might have laughed, if his body wasn't responding to that unmistakable hunger in her eyes, a body that hadn't worked for him in that way in a year. "Lyndie—"

"Right." Whirling, she headed toward the door. She could feel her face get hot, which was new, and she glanced over her shoulder. "I'll just meet you out—" She broke off because he'd moved fast. He'd already kicked off his covers, put his bare feet to the floor, and stood.

Gloriously naked.

He didn't run for cover, or leap back into bed. Nope, he just stood there, looking rumpled, brain-cell destroyingly delectable, and just a little confused. "I thought you were leaving."

"Right. Leaving." Her feet didn't move. But her eyes did, all over him, she couldn't seem to help herself. Good God, he was beautiful.

The man actually took a step toward her. "We keep dancing around this, don't we."

"D-dancing?"

"You wanting me, me wanting you…"

"You didn't want me."

"Oh, I did. I just didn't want a quickie. But if you keep looking at me like that, I just might change my mind."

Her gaze flew off his fascinating…parts…and up to his face. "You're going to sleep with me?" Oh, God, was that her voice, all hopeful and needy?

"I wasn't actually thinking about *sleep*."

She felt her body react to that. Her skin tightened, her nipples went happy, thighs all quivering, the whole works.

Damn, it had been far too long.

But his first instincts, the ones that had him warning her about the long haul thing, were good. And needed to be respected. With a sigh for what might have been—and what might have been promised to be so fantastic her body heated up yet another notch—she took one last good look. She just couldn't help herself.

And then slowly backed to the door.

"You running scared?" he asked.

He didn't mean it, she knew that. She'd only pushed him into reacting for the moment. She fumbled for the handle, turned to face the wood.

"I guess you're all talk, then," he said. "Isn't that what you once accused me of?"

Damn it. She could only be so strong for the two of them. "I'll show you all talk," she promised, and whipped around. Then gasped, because he was much closer than she remembered.

"Is that right?" he asked silkily.

"Damn right." She gulped as she took in his amazing body. "When there's not eighty-something men depending on you." Summoning up all her willpower, much of which had deserted her, she turned again—God, he was impressive—and ran out the door.

She escaped into the kitchen for lack of a better place to go, and she ended up standing there, a little overwhelmed by what had just transpired, fanning her hot face, her body on the highest of high alerts.

"*Que pasa, querida?*"

So lost in her own world, Lyndie nearly jumped right out of her own skin at Rosa's voice. "What? Nothing." She stopped fanning her face and strove for looking casual. "Nothing's up with me."

"Uh huh." Rosa gently shoved Tallulah out from underfoot and handed Lyndie a plate loaded to overfilling with *heuvos rancheros.* She eyed Lyndie from head to toe and then back again. "You look like you were just visited by Santa Claus."

"No." Lyndie started shoveling in food, a little bowled over by one fact—Griffin really *did* want her. She'd just seen the most magnificent proof of that bouncing in the morning air.

High on the rush of that, she grinned. And had to fan herself all over again. "Not Santa Claus." Her grin spread. "But something just as good."

18

Ten minutes later, still off balance, Lyndie glanced out the window of the kitchen as she set her plate in the sink. She worried about the thickness of the smoke and how close the fire might be. Rosa had just left to check on a guest and, thinking she was alone, Lyndie turned to go outside to a barely new day.

And ran right into Griffin.

His hands came up to steady her. "Ready?"

"Yeah." She tried to keep her gaze on his instead of on the body she now kept picturing naked. "Are you?"

He looked over her shoulder and out the window, to where the Jeep was parked. Brody was out there already, as was Tom. "I hated coming back," he admitted. "I hate that there's a need for me to be here, but…" He drew in a deep breath, shook his head. "But living again, having something to do other than mope and brood…that's been an interesting—if painful—process."

"I'm sorry, Griffin."

He lifted a shoulder, eyeing the smoky sky. "Tom told me they've lost control three or four times, the worst being yesterday. We have some work ahead of us to save the other ranches."

"Tom's grateful you're back, and..."

"And...?"

"And...so am I."

Griffin looked into her lovely eyes, which she normally kept free of emotion. They weren't so free of emotion now, nor had they been a few minutes ago in his bedroom. "I don't want your gratitude."

"What is it you what?"

She'd used her fingers as a comb again, and hadn't bothered with any of the usual feminine vices except that her lips once more smelled like strawberries. He thought he could nibble at them for a good long time and never get tired of doing so, but that was a dark and dangerous thought process so he concentrated on the truth.

She still wasn't looking for anything more than a quick scratch to their obvious itch.

And he still couldn't fathom having her once, and then walking away. "I just want to get this over with."

"Then let's do it."

"Yeah." He could have stepped back when she moved past him and out the door, instead he stepped closer.

She eyed him with a question, an expression that turned into something else completely when he put a hand on her hip. "Be safe today," he murmured.

"I always am—"

"No, don't give me that automatic response crap you give everyone else. *Be safe*," he whispered again, his mouth so close to her ear he couldn't help but let his lips touch the sensitive flesh just beneath.

Her eyes fluttered shut. "I'll...try."

"Yeah." God, just the taste of her sweet skin..."Try real hard."

Insanely, he had to have more, so he dragged his mouth down over her jaw, to the very corner of her mouth.

"Griffin—" Impatient as always, she slid her fingers into his hair and lined them up better, giving him that taste of strawberry gloss and woman he'd been dying for. Heaven, wet, hot, glorious heaven—until footsteps came into the kitchen.

Lyndie pulled back first, that's how gone he was, and he slowly blinked Rosa into focus.

The woman smiled. "Don't you two have something else to do first?"

* * *

When Lyndie got outside, Tom, Griffin, Brody, and three other neighboring ranchers were all climbing into the Jeep to get to the fire.

Lips still humming, Lyndie looked at all of them, trying to figure out how to get in without sitting on someone's lap. "Maybe we should take another car."

"There's nothing else," Tom said. "A caravan of three other vehicles just left. Hop in, you know it's practically around the corner now."

Yes, but…hmm. She glanced at Griffin, who'd taken the front seat. Lyndie could tell he wasn't thrilled about all of them risking their lives, but hell, his entire crew was risking themselves, as he knew all too well.

Then Nina sauntered out of the house wearing clothes so unlike herself, Lyndie blinked. "You actually own a pair of pants?"

"Look closer."

Lyndie did, then scowled. "Hey, those are *my* clothes."

"Yes, and thank you." Nina danced around in a little circle

wearing a pair of Lyndie's favorite jeans and a long-sleeved chambray button-up, looking like a pinup girl playing dress up. "Good on me, yes?"

Better than on Lyndie's much leaner body, but now wasn't the time to lament the fact she'd never been overly feminine and wasn't likely to get that way anytime soon.

Nina sauntered up close to the Jeep and smiled at Brody in the backseat. "Guess I'll have to sit on someone. You don't mind sharing your seat, do you, cowboy?" she asked.

"Are you kidding?" Brody opened his arms. "Come on in, baby."

She hopped over the door and right into Brody's lap as if the spot had been made for her. Brody caught her, barely, looking like he'd won the lottery as his hands got quite comfortable with his load.

"Thanks for spending time with me last night," Nina purred in his ear.

Tom whipped around and glared, not at Nina, but right into Brody's eyes, suddenly looking far more like a sheriff who means business than a hapless, go-lucky fly fisherman.

Brody immediately straightened, lifting his hands, managing a small smile at the woman in his lap. "Teaching you to read English was...my pleasure."

"Then you can teach me more tonight," she said.

Once again, Brody glanced at Tom, who was now giving him the evil eye in the rearview mirror. "You having fun, boy?" the sheriff asked.

"No. No, sir."

"See to it that you don't."

When he started the engine, Brody let out a long breath, halted short when Nina leaned in and bit his ear.

"Nina—" Holding his hands at his sides, Brody closed his eyes, tilting his head to give her better access, but dutifully keeping his fingers to himself.

Lyndie rolled her eyes at Nina's antics, then looked at the man sitting shotgun, the man who was eyeing her right back.

"You getting in?" he asked.

"Yeah," she said, wondering where she was supposed to do that. She sure as hell wasn't going to give everyone a show like Nina just had.

"Come on then," he said, all business except for that glint in his eyes while he waited her out.

And waited.

"Damn it. Scoot over."

"Seat's pretty small." He patted his legs. "But I've got plenty of room right here."

Did he, now. Opening the door, she climbed in over him and sat, wriggling her butt until he was forced to scoot over on the seat. "See?" she said triumphantly. "We both fit."

"Uh huh." He'd had to lift his arm to give her room, and as a result, it draped across the back of her shoulders. Tom hit the gas, and Griffin's other hand, braced on the dash, left her feeling surrounded by him—and just a little bit breathless.

"Funny, for two people who want some distance from each other," he said in her ear, "We never quite manage it."

"Yeah. Funny." Turning away, she gasped as they left town and began their climb. She'd seen the land from the air last night, but the dark and smoke had hindered her view. She was shocked at how much had burned.

"Yeah, it's bad. We've got that north and southwest end to block in again." Tom pointed to the closest mountain peak, where Griffin had climbed that first day to get a good look at the perimeter. The flames had nearly claimed it. "We get them and things are good, right, Griffin?"

"Right." But he eyed that peak with misgiving.

Fire headquarters had been moved far east of where it'd been because of the flames. Again, Lyndie was horrified at how much was gone. "My God..."

Griffin looked equally grim as they got out and gathered around the two water trucks.

There were three guys at each tank laying out hoses. They'd just come in from the river where they'd filled up the tanks. One of them had a GPS unit and a computer inside the truck, running on batteries to show them the map onscreen.

"EBay," he said in heavily accented English and smiled. *"Buena, si?"*

"Yes, very good." Griffin studied the map, then pulled out his palm-held and brought up the earlier map, updating it to the current fire lines. Then he dove right in, reassessing what had been done over the last week, what still needed to be done.

Lyndie watched him run the men with a natural leadership and a genuine caring about the efforts that took her mind off the hot, grinding work. She saw that it was easier for him this time, but not by much, not missing the sick look in his eyes as they walked some of the perimeter, taking in the total of five completely destroyed ranches. She saw him go pale when she translated the news that three more men had suffered smoke inhalation last night, and were being taken out of here. And she saw him continually search her out as if checking to make sure she was okay.

Each time he did, something happened to her deep inside, something she didn't really understand, but they concentrated on the borders of the fire, which should have remained contained and hadn't. This took a lot longer at the nearly 1,500 burning acres now than it had at 300 last week.

Hours went by, and Lyndie spent much of the second half of the day alone because Griffin kept moving around from small crew to small crew, making his way around the edges, looking for true containment, a state that kept eluding them.

Her arms ached, and so did her lungs. She figured she could stand in a hot shower for a week, go to sleep for two, and maybe even eat Rosa's entire refrigerator, and not necessarily in that order. Sagging just a little, she leaned on a large rake she'd been dragging over the dead pine needles near the northwest end of the fire lines, just above three more ranches, which she kept looking at just to reassure herself they were there in one piece. She also kept searching out Griffin, for the same reason.

"He's strong," Brody said quietly, coming up beside her. Griffin was scaling the rock north of them, and just north of the fire, as well.

Lyndie turned to look at Brody, then back at Griffin as his long, lean body easily made the climb. "Hell, yes, he's strong."

"I wasn't sure if this would make or break him."

"If that Idaho fire didn't break him," she said. "I don't think anything could."

Far, far above them, Griffin stopped to check his GPS, then began climbing again. "And if it means anything," she said to Brody. "I think you're an amazing brother."

His eyes never left Griffin. "It means a lot."

Lyndie smiled and went back to watching Griffin. She wanted to be with him up there, even though she knew she'd have slowed him down, because her asthma was really getting to her today. Still, she wanted to be with him in a way that was new and fairly terrifying. So she purposely buried herself in the physical work so that she couldn't possibly think. She shoveled and raked, used her inhaler, and then shoveled some more.

It worked, and much, much later, hours after their lunch break and more hard work, she looked up in surprise when two arms snaked around her from behind.

"We're contained," Griffin said, the victory in his voice as he twirled her around and around. "Tell them as long as the wind stays calm, we've got the son of a bitch."

She started to smile, but his mouth came down on hers in a hard-earned celebratory kiss.

* * *

At dusk, they fell out of the Jeep at the Rio Vista Inn, an exhausted, filthy, hungry bunch, parting ways as everyone stumbled on their own various routes home.

Brody stood there for a moment in the pitch-dark night, as tired as everyone else, but unable to get over all they'd accomplished today. He couldn't remember the last time he'd been part of a team like this, or the last time he'd worked so hard.

Maybe he'd never worked so hard. Ever.

Not an easy admission even to himself, surrounded as he was by people who worked that hard all the time, including a woman he'd known all of one day and couldn't get enough of.

He looked at her now. Nina looked right back, her eyes soft, sexy. Sweet. She waited until her father went inside his house. Then, managing to look cool and pretty despite being out in the fire all day, she put a hand on Brody's chest and leaned in. "Tonight?" she whispered.

He turned his head and watched Tom's front door shut. It had the sound of his own coffin shutting, and yet the promise in her voice drew him in like nothing else.

"We could sit in the courtyard," she said. "And read just like last night…"

Though they both knew that hadn't been all they'd done last night.

"I know I can get a good job in the States if you show me just a little bit more," she added softly.

"You underestimate yourself, you're already reading English—"

"Are you worried I'll keep you up too late? Work you too hard?" There was such a promise in her gaze, it took his breath. "Don't worry, big guy. I'll tuck you in if that's what you want."

"What I want," he said, shocked to realize the truth, "is to just be with you."

A slow smile curved her mouth, and she hugged him tight, pressing in closer, sighing when he wrapped his arms around her body. "You're such a good man, Brody Moore. A good teacher, too."

Closing his eyes, he held on. A good man? A good teacher? Hell, he might be educated, he might have his degree and be capable of teaching, true, but he'd never bothered. Too much work, too much time…

And if he was facing truths here, then he had to face this one—he'd been quite lazy with his life, and quite content with that. "I'm not the man you think I am."

"No?" Her smile was softhearted. "You haven't traveled five hundred miles to see that Griffin is okay while he fights this fire for us? You haven't lent your own hand to the cause when you could have stayed in the village all day and let the others do it? You haven't spent your valuable sleeping time helping me learn

English?" She leaned in close, put her mouth to his ear. "You haven't made love to me beneath the night sky and showed me a heaven I didn't know existed?"

"Nina..." He cupped her face and looked deep into her eyes, letting out a helpless groan as he saw the emotion reflected there. "I'm different at home. I don't work very hard, I don't. I just skate by, and...and people let me."

"It's your sexy smile."

"I mean it. Until very recently I was a shitty brother, and I wouldn't have wanted to see you again after we—"

"Shh." She put her fingers to his lips. "I don't know that man you describe. I know the man I'm standing in front of, the man who is going to help me read better English, and then who is going to drive me wild for the rest of the night, because we are good together. Now." She let out a breath, smiled. "Any questions?"

He removed her fingers from his mouth and smiled back, his chest loosening with relief, with arousal, with other things too, things that suddenly no longer scared him. "No questions."

Her smile caught his breath, his heart. "Good."

* * *

Too keyed up to go to sleep, Griffin left Brody outside with Nina and went in the inn. He got halfway to the kitchen when he realized there was one thing he wanted more than food.

Lyndie.

He walked back down the hallway, but no Lyndie in the front room, the courtyard, anywhere. He checked her room, which was empty of all fiery-haired women.

And also empty of wild kittens.

What had she done with Lucifer? And how, after the day

they'd had, did she have the energy to be anywhere but in that bed?

Exiting again, out the back door of the inn this time, he heard her voice in the darkness and moved forward. He found her sitting by the creek, Lucifer in her lap batting at her chin with his paw.

"Cool it," she said to the cat, who did his best to climb up her body. "Did you really think I wasn't coming back for you?" She let out a soft laugh over the sound of the rushing water. "Would have served you right, you obnoxious little fleabag."

"Mew."

"Yeah, yeah." She stroked the little back and Lucifer arched with pleasure. "Look, I'm not going to ditch you or anything, but honestly, I'm not a good bet."

Surprised, Griffin stopped short. She thought she wasn't a good bet? She, with the strength and bravery of ten men? How could she believe that?

Still not seeing Griffin, she plopped to her back on the creek bank, lifting the kitten up to look into his face. "Look, cat...I'm not that good for you. I'm demanding and pushy, and quite honestly, I'm not even that nice. Seriously," she whispered, "you ought to be running for your life."

The kitten didn't appear concerned, and Lyndie let out a soft laugh that broke Griffin's heart, bringing Lucifer down to her chest. "Why aren't you running?" she asked, rubbing her cheek to his.

Griffin ached to go to her, to prove her wrong about being a bad bet.

But he wasn't a good bet either.

So he steeled himself, not an easy task, and turned and walked away.

19

After getting back from the fire, Tom took a quick shower at his place, then walked his own well-worn path to the inn, entering in the back door, where he stepped directly into the kitchen. As he knew she would be, Rosa was there, directing several of the local women on how to set everything out; "everything" being more dishes and platters of food than Tom could count.

"You nearly ready for all of us?" he asked, smiling when she whipped around, looking unusually harassed.

"Did you tell everyone?" she demanded.

"How come you always answer my question with one of your own?" He touched her on the very tip of her worried nose. "Everyone'll be here, soon as they clean up." He bent to pet Tallulah, who was sitting on his foot, waiting, quivering, for his attention. "For an impromptu fiesta, they'll come out of the woodwork."

"And Nina—"

"She'll be here, too. Her obsession to get to the States has been superseded by her obsession with Griffin's brother. She won't miss a chance to dance with him." Tom wasn't naive; he knew his daughter had an abundantly healthy appetite for men. He just didn't like to think about it, especially because this week she was hungry for the jobless, directionless American, damn it.

"Where's Lyndie?" Rosa asked.

"The girl worked her fingers to the bone today, she has to be exhausted. She can't have gone far."

Rosa's mouth pulled into a concerned frown.

"Don't fret, you know our girl. She'll be drawn in by the scent of food."

That got a smile out of the woman who'd probably been cooking all day. "She deserves a little fiesta, *si*?"

"Impromptu or otherwise," Tom agreed. "You do understand this is going to piss her off when she figures it out. She hates being the center of attention."

"She does so much for us. She needs a life, and since she won't get it for herself, we are going to help her. If she is as exhausted as you say, she won't question all the fuss anyway."

"She's exhausted, yes, but smart as hell—" He broke off when Rosa took his face in her work-roughened hands. "What?"

"You know this fiesta could just as easily be for you, Tom Farrell."

A little stunned at her touch, more than a little stunned at the way he wanted to hold her hands against him so that she could never stop, he blinked at her. "Rosa…"

"*Si?*"

"Don't be alarmed, but…"

"You want to kiss me?"

Unable to speak, he just stared at her.

"Oh, Tom." She let out a soft smile. "How come in all this time, you've never thought of this before?"

He blinked again, slow as an owl. "Thought of what, exactly?"

Her fingers slid into his long hair, restrained by a length of string. Her body shifted just a little bit closer.

His reacted.

"That," she whispered. Her mouth curved sensuously as she pulled away. "Think of it sometime, will you? I'm tired of waiting." Smiling into his surprised face, she turned him around and shooed him out of her kitchen.

* * *

Twenty minutes later, Lyndie stood up from the bank of the creek and picked up the cat. "I'm hungry." And led by her growling stomach, she walked inside the inn. She entered the side door, which led her to the courtyard, then stopped in shocked surprise at the crowd there among the flowers and stone benches. Colorful streamers zigzagged overhead, and there was food everywhere, while Mexican fiesta music blared, courtesy of four men in the corner and their makeshift band.

She recognized them as men she'd seen that day at the fire; she recognized lots of others, too, and was immediately swallowed up by people who wanted to thank her, hug her, talk to her. "What is this?" she asked Rosa, who handed her a drink in exchange for Lucifer. "A celebration for the fire being contained?"

Rosa smiled and kissed Lyndie's right cheek, and then the left. "It's a celebration of life, *querida.*"

Over Rosa's shoulder, Lyndie caught sight of an equally baffled-looking Griffin entering the courtyard. Tom handed him a drink as well, and slapped him on the back.

Griffin took the bottle of beer and smiled at Tom, and then his gaze scanned the room, stopping only when it collided with hers.

Time seemed to stop, and so did her heart. And then he was working his way through the people, still holding her gaze prisoner, stopping right before her. "You do all this?" he asked her.

"Ha! My *querida* here does not know how to boil water." Rosa hugged him. "This is *my* thank you."

"But…the fire isn't out yet."

"It will be. Everyone say how hard you work. Without Lyndie's help, without your help, God only knows what would happen to San Puebla. To our casas. To Lyndie's inn."

Griffin looked at Lyndie. "Your inn?"

Damn it. "Well—"

"She owns this place," Rosa said proudly. "She bought it when the previous owner went to prison three years ago. That man, my boss…horrible, very mean. One day Lyndie came here with a doctor for the kids, and she stay. She like. She save me, she save my job. Sweet, *si*?"

"Very sweet." Griffin's eyes never left Lyndie's. "I thought you said your only home was the sky. That you liked being as free as a bird, no ties, no strings attached."

Rosa beamed. "Oh, no. Lyndie has many ties." She leaned in close, talking in a conspirator's whisper. "She just doesn't like to admit it."

"Hello," Lyndie said, waving. "I'm in the room."

Rosa merely hugged her. "Such a generous boss, you let me do whatever I want."

"Let you—" Lyndie shook her head, and had to laugh. "Like anyone 'lets' you do anything you don't want to do."

Rosa just smiled.

But Griffin hadn't been able to get past this new information. "This place is yours," he repeated. "The Rio Vista Inn is Lyndie Anderson's."

"Yes," Rosa said, tapping her foot to the music, swiveling her hips. "She is so beautiful, inside and out. You think?"

Lyndie set down her drink and shot a wry glance at Rosa. "Okay, you. Stop."

"Stop what?" Rosa lifted her hands in innocence. "I am just standing here."

"Yeah, you're just standing there. I'm on to you." Lyndie pointed a finger at her. "And it's not going to work. Griffin and I are grown-ups. We don't need you interfering in our lives."

"Yes, well, if you would get on with your own life, I would not be forced to interfere."

Lyndie let out a helpless laugh, then looked around her, at the people partying, celebrating, so happy and full of life. "I need some fresh air."

"Fresher than this?" Griffin shook his head. "You're not going to get it until the fire is all the way out."

"Then I need space." She'd made it through the courtyard and out the side door before she realized he followed her.

"Maybe I needed space, too." He leaned against a tree and took a long pull of his beer, watching her over the bottle. He licked a drop off his upper lip, probably without a clue that she'd been yearning to do just that with her tongue.

"So," he said. "This air any fresher than in the courtyard?"

"Rosa's matchmaking."

"Matchmaking. You mean…you and me?"

Lyndie had to laugh at his surprise. "You're not that clueless." She laughed again at his blank expression. "I guess you are. It's ridiculous, right? I mean, the two of us—" She swallowed her words at the heat that came into his eyes. "We…" She drew a breath. "We don't have a chance in hell. Not a single one."

He just looked at her.

"Do we?" she whispered with a horrifyingly needy voice.

"Lyndie—"

"Look, I don't even want a chance," she assured him, her heart pitter-pattering with the first lie she could remember uttering. "All I want is a good night's sleep before tomorrow's action. Night." Whirling, she made her way back into the kitchen and managed to get upstairs and into her bedroom without being interrupted.

Somehow Lucifer followed her. Maybe he thought he was a dog, she didn't know, but he climbed up the blanket to the top of the bed. His eyes glowed like the very devil in the light as he waited to be petted.

"Sorry," she said, anything but. "You should have latched on to someone who cared."

Lucifer blinked, and, feeling like a jerk, she moved closer to pet him. "All right, I care. Damn it. But only a little."

The windows rattled with the laughter and music below, but she figured she was just exhausted enough that nothing could keep her awake. She flopped to the mattress to begin the pity party she didn't want.

As she did, her bedroom door opened, then slammed shut.

Griffin stood there in his dark jeans and dark T-shirt and matching dark expression. "It's not that I don't want a chance," he said grimly. "It's that I don't know how to…I don't—" He shoved his fingers through his hair, looking uncharacteristically flustered and frustrated. "Ah, hell."

She sat up. "Griffin—"

"No, let me say this."

But he stalked to the window and leaned on the sill, dropping his forehead to the glass as he looked out at the night. There wasn't much to see with the low, sliver of a moon nearly covered by the long, drifting fingers of smoke.

But whatever he saw, his broad shoulders seemed to carry the weight of the world. "I lost a lot in that last fire."

"I know." Her entire heart softened. "Griffin, I know." It seemed she could feel her heart cracking in two. How was it possible to want to ease his pain with every fiber of her being?

He closed his eyes, then turned and looked at her. "I lost my nerve."

She got off the bed. "Maybe temporarily. Anyone would have."

"And yet today I managed just fine."

"Because you're adapting."

"I hated it. I felt ashamed at my ability to forget, so much so that I forced myself to remember Idaho just to torture myself. All the way back here tonight, I felt so hollow and destroyed, I just wanted to go far away. Anywhere."

Helpless against the pull of the emotion coming off him in waves, her feet brought her to him.

"I didn't think I'd ever do this again," he said softly. "Fight a fire, or—"

"Or?"

"Look at a woman." He wrapped his fingers around her hips, drawing her close, then buried his face in the crook of her neck. "When I lost my friends, my comrades, in that fire, I thought I'd never want another person in my life again." Destroyed, he lifted his face. "But I'm looking at you, Lyndie."

Her breath caught.

"I want you," he whispered and pulled her flush against him, his hands spread wide on her back as if he needed to touch as much of her as possible. "I tried to ignore it, I tried to fight it, but I can't. I want you so much, I can't do anything else."

Holding his gaze in hers, she backed to the door.

Locked one of the few doors that actually locked in the place.

The click sounded extraordinarily loud in the room, a sound that managed to compete with the music and laughter and talking from below.

There was no need to come forward again to reach for him, he'd never let her out of his grip.

"I want you right back," she said, and then they were kissing, stumbling back against the door for leverage as their hands fought for purchase, their bodies strained against each other, their mouths melded together as one.

20

Like the rest of Lyndie's world, there was nothing simple in their kiss. But for someone who hadn't so much as kissed another woman in a year, Lyndie decided Griffin seemed to remember just fine what to do and how to do it, so much so that her bones seemed to melt away. His fingers tightened against her scalp, holding her still for his plunging kisses.

As if she wanted to be anywhere but right here pressed between a hard wood door and an even harder, fiercely aroused Griffin. She arched even closer and was rewarded with the hoarse sound of his groan.

Freeing his mouth to suck in some air, he buried his face in her hair. "God. I don't even know if I can do this." His arms banded tightly around her, so tightly she could feel him quiver with passion, with fear, with so many things, but she was feeling just as shaky herself.

"It's like getting on a bike," she promised, and bit his throat gently before soothing it with a lick of her tongue.

That ripped another groan from deep in his throat, one that mingled with a reluctant laugh. "Lyndie...I'm serious."

Since she could feel the proof of his wanting pressing into her, she kissed his throat again. "You seem to be quite serious, and also in working order."

"Mechanically, yeah, I can hardly see straight with all the blood loss for parts south. But—"

"No buts." Cupping his face, she smiled at him over her own ache and yearning. "That's all we need here, Griffin, working mechanical parts."

He stared into her eyes, his own filled with so much she couldn't take it.

"This is about the here and now, and needing a release," she said gently. "That's all."

"Lyndie—"

"Kiss me again." She didn't want to hear why this was a bad idea. There were a million reasons why, but what would be a really bad idea would be stopping. Stopping would kill her. Her body hummed, pulsed, high on the adrenaline and yearning. "Kiss me…"

And he did, oh, God, how he did. His tongue, moist and hot and seductively determined, slid into her mouth again, and she met him with the soft whimper of her own acquiescence. By the time they broke apart for air this time, she was panting for more. "This isn't ending with just a kiss, damn it."

"No. *Christ*. I can't believe how much I want you." His voice sounded low, thrillingly rough, making her breath catch at the heat in his shimmering baby blues. "I have to touch you." One big palm stroked up her hip to cup a breast. His thumb rasped over her nipple, already so tight she couldn't contain her little needy gasp.

"Skin to skin." She tugged off her own shirt, leaving her in a white sports bra.

He ran his finger over the plain cotton, then the zipper between her breasts, and smiled. "Practical and pragmatic to the end, aren't you?"

His finger slipped beneath the material and her legs buckled. The small talk, the light, sexy banter, the sheer heat in his eyes was going to kill her. "Always." All she wanted was the end product now, the few seconds of complete oblivion, and he wasn't moving fast enough to suit her. To help, she yanked his shirt out of his jeans, then shoved it up his chest, revealing a wedge of his flat, rippled belly that made her mouth water. "Off," she muttered, and hauled the shirt over his head. "Hurry."

To ensure he did, she reached for the buttons on his Levi's and popped them open one at a time. He was a quick man, and quickly got the hang of the idea of stripping.

He started working on her jeans as well. "This is crazy," he murmured, his mouth dragging hot, wet, openmouthed kisses along her jaw as he unzipped her sports bra.

"Uh huh." She backed him to the bed, shoving Lucifer off, who leapt to the floor and settled on her discarded top. Lyndie pushed Griffin to the mattress, laughing breathlessly when a breath of surprise shuddered out of him. Still, he managed to tug her down with him, gliding his hands up the backs of her thighs, cupping her butt, squeezing as she fell over his chest.

She held him down and bit his chin.

He let out a groan, and shot her an endearingly crooked grin. "Be kind to me."

"Oh, trust me, I plan to be very, *very* kind." She got off the bed long enough to grab a condom out of her bag where she always carried them. Then she climbed back up his long, rugged body and sucked on his earlobe, loving how that seemed to make him melt. Still, he managed to tug off her loosened bra and toss it across the room…

Okay, *now* she was in her comfort zone, and it was a good place to be. Sex. Hot, fast, good. Pushing down her jeans, she scissored her legs, kicking the denim off to the floor, letting out a helpless hum of pleasure when Griffin's hands dragged her up higher so that he could draw a breast into his mouth.

"Oh, my God." She held herself up on arms that shook as he licked, sucked, and nibbled at a nipple until she didn't know if she was coming or going. Settling her legs around his hips, she arched against a most impressive erection and knew exactly where she wanted it to be. Inside her. *Yesterday.* "Now, Griffin. Now."

"Wait. I want to—" He broke off on a gruff moan when she wrapped a fist around him and stroked.

She couldn't help it. Seeing him sprawled out beneath her, hard and tanned and tough, feeling his hot, sleek skin over rigid muscles, his long fingers biting into her hips, hearing the raw sound she coaxed from his throat, all combined to have a blinding, intense need surging through her body.

"Slow down," he begged, slipping a hand between their bodies, cupping her wet heat until she cried out his name, holding on to him for dear life. She didn't want to slow down, not then, and not when he rasped his thumb over her core, taking her to a place where slowing down was utterly impossible.

She opened the condom, helped him put it on. Then she guided him home. She'd barely sunk down on his long, hard length when he growled, rolling her, tucking her beneath him so that he towered over her, his eyes glittering with desire, intent. "So you don't want to take our time." His voice was hoarse and tight. "You have to promise we'll linger on the next round then."

Next round? There wasn't going to be a next round—

But one single powerful stroke put him inside her to the hilt, and they gasped in tandem at the delicious heat as all thoughts scattered from her brain.

"Next time…" He grounded this out, as if he was holding on by a thread. "We take this slow and easy. Deal?"

"No—"

In the middle of a beautifully hard thrust, he went still. She tried to arch up, but his big body held her still. "Deal?" he asked again, softly.

"Fine! Deal! Now do it, damn it."

"Oh, yeah, I will." And he began to move, bending low to whisper naughty nothings in her ear, this wild, earthy, sexy man who'd thought he'd forgotten how to do this. She was lost then, lost in the sound of her name on his lips, lost in the feel of him thrusting into her with his powerful body, lost in the heartbreaking way he held her gaze as they both fell over the edge.

* * *

As usual, Lyndie woke up sprawled facedown, sideways, across the bed, naked and starving. And alone.

Definitely a smart move on Griffin's part to leave, she thought. Waking in each other's arms would have been… Well. She'd never know. And in any case, he might have held her to that lingering Round Two she'd promised him.

Good thing he'd decided against it. Round Two was always overrated.

But waking in his arms?

Even she had to admit, that might just have been perfect. She closed her eyes.

So perfect.

Lifting her head, she glanced at the clock and found Lucifer's questioning eyes instead.

"Mew," he said, and moving daintily across the wildly strewn covers, he came close to lightly bat her on the nose.

So she wasn't alone after all.

She pushed the obnoxious little kitten away, but he only came right back. Settled on her butt. She pushed him away again, and rolled over.

The tenacious kitten came back and sat on her chest this time. He was quite a weight for a little guy, so it was odd that suddenly she felt as if she'd had a weight lifted off. She stared into his feline eyes, that odd little feeling in her chest increasing, blooming, spreading.

"What is it about you?" she whispered, and when he didn't—couldn't—answer, sighed. She had a bad feeling it was affection.

Good thing then that it was nearly dawn, and she had a fire to get to. Never one to sit around wishful thinking, she pushed Lucifer aside and reached for her clothes.

* * *

When they arrived at the fire, Griffin got out of the Jeep and jumped right into the fray. He supervised refilling of the tanks from the river, the laying out of the hoses, the line digging and clearing, everything, and he did it so automatically it left his brain free for other things.

Things such as last night, and the feel of Lyndie under his hands, his mouth, his body.

But obsessing over that meant he didn't have the time to feel sick over fighting this fire, didn't have to relive the horrific memories floating so freely in his head, nothing. He simply worked.

But again, like yesterday, it shamed him that he could have gotten over the Idaho fire at all, that he could move on and be okay, when twelve weren't. So he stood there and brought back the screams, the heat, the vicious wind, the misguided directions and incorrect weather report from base nearly thirty miles away—and only when his heart had filled with pain, did he nod grimly.

Now he could face this fire again.

"Where are we at?"

Griffin turned his head and looked into Lyndie's green eyes. Her easy smile faded at whatever she saw in his. "Hey." She put her hand on him. "You okay?"

"You ever notice how you only touch me when you think I'm falling apart?"

"You're too hardheaded to fall apart," she said, but dropped her hand from his arm. "And what do you call last night? You weren't falling apart then and I touched you plenty."

He sighed. Scrubbed a hand over his face. "We've got the fire trapped between the river, and the rock, and the firebreaks we created. Town is safe enough. But that up above..." He pointed out the cliff above them. "I don't think it's stable. We need to get up above it, fuse all the vegetation between the rock and the flames. That's when we'll have it nailed."

If the weather conditions remained right.

If the crew wasn't too exhausted from the ongoing battle, not to mention last night's fiesta.

If they weren't thinking about something else, like their families, or what they'd had or not had for lunch.

If, if, if...

So many variables, and on a job like this, even one thing off could make or break them.

As he knew all too well.

Oh yeah, *there* was that sharp stab of pain. He hadn't forgotten. Good. He didn't have to force himself to relive it, it was still right there. And though there were still many dangers, this fire would not end in tragedy as his last had. Not if he had breath left in his body. "I'm going to climb up there and see how much growth is beyond that rock. See if you can get Hector and a few others to walk the south, west, and east perimeters to check on them."

"Will do." Lyndie watched him stride away, a funny feeling in the pit of her gut. She had a bad feeling it was fear, which made no sense. This was good. They had this thing under control.

But soon as she contacted Hector, Tom ran up to her, huffing and sweating. "Just got back with more men…on the way up here we caught a weather report…" He bent over his knees and dragged air into his lungs. "Heavy winds forecasted, leading into dry thunderstorms…"

Which meant lightning, and more wind without moisture. *"Damn it."* She glanced at Griffin climbing the mountain directly ahead of her, already reaching for her radio to fill him in, but it squawked first. She brought it up to her ears just in time to hear Sergio say that he was already on the northeastern edge with a crew of fifteen men. Hearing that, she called Griffin. From above, high on the rock, she watched him pick up his radio and turn to look at her.

"Bad news, good news," she said. "Bad first: Tom said dry thunderstorms are on their way. Good news: You have a group of men who made it to the base of that northeastern canyon directly to your right, they're between the river and the wall of rock. They're above the fire. Repeat, they're already above the fire. They have fuses on them, just tell me what to tell them."

She watched him go stiff. And even though she couldn't see his eyes, she knew they were chilled and right on her. "Lyndie," he said. "They're right above the canyon next to me?"

"Yes," she verified.

"Get them out of there."

Next to her, Tom nodded. "Tell him they'll be out of there as soon as they check on the perimeters…"

Lyndie repeated that for Griffin.

"No." His voice sounded hoarse. *Terrified.* "Tell them to get out of there. Tell them now—"

The radio died.

"Griffin?" Lyndie banged the radio against her thigh and tried again. "Griffin?"

Her batteries had died. "Tom—"

"Got it." He slapped his pockets for more batteries, came up empty-handed. "Shit, I gave away my extras earlier."

And Griffin had *her* extras.

She could see him up there, suddenly and furiously on the move, going sideways across the rock now instead of up. He was moving…directly toward the crew she'd just told him about.

She glanced at Tom, who had shielded his eyes and was watching Griffin. "What's he doing?"

"I don't know…it looks like maybe he's trying to get to where the crew is…though that's got to be a difficult climb from there—"

She could see the glint of the hard hats of the crew now, to the right of Griffin and down a bit.

And then below them, the northern front of the fire.

The wind whipped around them suddenly, and though they were a good twenty yards from the flames, and on the other side of the fire line they'd dug, the heat made her skin feel tight. Her eyes, already tortured by the smoke and dust, watered, and her lungs burned. "What's happening?"

"The wind is moving ahead of the thunderstorm."

Whipped by the wind, the smoke thickened.

Griffin disappeared near where the glint of hard hats had been only a moment ago, though now none of them were visible. Coughing, wheezing with the asthma that had never been worse, Lyndie blinked furiously but she could see nothing but flames and smoke, which seemed to blow up right before her very eyes and head northward with shocking speed.

Heading right for where Griffin and the others had disappeared.

"Oh, my God." She ran to one of the men, grabbed his radio and lifted the radio to her mouth. "Griffin! The fire just blew up, it's coming at you! Griffin, can you hear me? *Ven por aca, apurarse*," she shouted, hoping if he couldn't hear her, the men could, and that they would indeed come this way, and hurry.

No answer, just static and the sound of the fire licking at them, crackling, which she imagined was the sound of them all dying. God, she was listening to them die, and with a helpless glance at Tom, she hooked the radio on her belt and began running.

* * *

Griffin heard Lyndie's frantic warning through the radio, just as he jumped down a ten-foot drop to the crew of about fifteen guys, getting ready to work on turning the fire back on itself across the most northern front.

But they hadn't heard the weather change. They didn't know that if the wind started at the bottom of the canyon beneath them, it would whip the fire into a frenzy, creating a vacuum up the ravine, sucking the flames right up and out the cliff rock above them.

Annihilating every one of them in the process.

Just one little mistake, he told himself grimly, his heart pounding hard, he'd known that's all it would take here. In this case, that would be lack of swift communication from the fire central to the last man out in the field, a critical error that would rest on the incident commander's head.

His.

It wouldn't be the first time. In Idaho, the conditions hadn't been that different, despite the fact that fire had been three times the size, their equipment the latest available, the crew all trained.

That fire had stretched out for three weeks, until every last one of them had been exhausted, made worse by the remote conditions. With no neighboring town nearby, they'd all been camping at their base. The food situation had been army rations for the most part. Then there'd been the long hot hours. Everyone's attention span had been low, they'd been sluggish.

A nightmare waiting to happen, and it had.

He wouldn't let history repeat itself. When he leapt down, the crew all looked up in unison, surprised, just as Griffin remembered one important little fact.

He didn't speak Spanish. *"Vamanos ahora,"* he shouted. *Let's go, now* thankfully being some of the only Spanish he knew, and pointed eastward, where they could go parallel across the mountain if they climbed up and over the rock cliff. They stood at the low point in the canyon, with the fire beneath them, looking at the deep gorges and dizzying heights, some of the most scenic views in the world. With one single burst of cold, moistureless wind, the fire would whip right up this point like a funnel.

They'd all perish.

He'd seen it happen. Hell, he'd lived it. "Move!" he shouted, pointing them in the right direction, showing them where he wanted them to go, then jumping back down to make sure every last one of them moved.

Despite the panic and fear, they began the climb out, helping each other, scrambling as fast as they could.

But the fire did exactly as he knew it would, he could feel it, hear it, roaring up the canyon wall in an unbelievable explosion of heat and wicked flame, moving in on them.

There were two men left to climb out, then one. Paco was a rancher, not a firefighter, and doing the best he could to scramble along, but he was clearly exhausted and terrified, and upon closer look, not older than sixteen. His fingers kept slipping on the rock, and Griffin, feeling the wall of fire at his back, hearing Lyndie's frantic cry for him over the radio, saw his life flash before his eyes.

Not his early life, which had been full and happy and good, but the last year, which he'd completely let slip him by. He'd wasted an entire year, and now there were no second chances.

He gave the kid a shove and scrambled along after him, just as the hair on the back of his neck began to singe. At the top, the men waited for direction from Griffin, who felt paralyzed. The incredibly intense heat and wall of fire was coming at them, the smoke so thick and choking, they were all coughing and gasping.

But the only place to go was eastward, where there lay another ravine, this one a twenty-foot drop down.

God damn it, not now, Griffin thought. He wasn't going to die now. Hell, he'd gone through so much, suffered so much, but he'd never planned on dying.

And he didn't plan on it now.

21

The ravine might be a twenty-foot drop but it had one thing going for it—it'd already been ravished by the fire and was down to black. Because he couldn't make himself understood to the men, and because the flames were going to be licking at them in seconds again, he simply showed the men what he expected, and ran.

He came to a stop at the drop-off and pointed. Some went easier than others, but they all went, sliding down the face of the mountain. Griffin waited until each of them had gone before he jumped. It seemed he fell forever before he hit, hard.

The first thing he noticed was the lack of the scorching wall of heat from the fire.

Slowly he raised his head. They were now in an area that had already burned, and while the ground was black and still quite warm, the area couldn't burn twice. Amazingly enough, they were safe.

And alive. "Okay?" he asked the men all around him, all looking as dirty and frightened as he probably did.

"*Sí,*" a few said. Others nodded. They got up and looked

around in the same slow motion, jerky movements he'd seen and recognized so well.

Shock. Relief. Overwhelming relief. Above them and to the east and south the fire ravaged, but they were safe.

"Griffin. *Griffin!*" From the west side, the safe side, Lyndie appeared, chest heaving, skin damp, face white with fright. She stopped short of him and gasped for air. "You're okay." Turning, she took them all in and sagged. "You're all okay."

For some reason, an idiotic grin spread across Griffin's face. "Yeah."

She stared at him; his non-cuddler, kick-ass pilot, wavering slightly on legs that seemed unsteady. And then her eyes filled with tears.

His heart broke in two. "Ah, Lyndie, no. Don't do that."

"I'm not doing anything." Angrily, she swiped at the one tear that fell and shot him a scathing look as she dragged air into her poor, tortured lungs. "I just have smoke in my eyes."

God, she was magnificent. He took the step that separated them and cupped her jaw. "What, no hug? No sobbing, weeping woman throwing herself at me—"

"Bite me." But she lifted her arms and threw them around his neck and squeezed so hard he couldn't breathe. In that moment, breathing was highly overrated anyway.

This, though…this holding a bundle of solid, curvy, teary, sexy-as-hell woman in his arms, this was not overrated at all.

In fact, he dropped his hard hat and held on for a good long time, burying his face in the crook of her neck, which smelled like smoke and Lyndie. Her skin felt soft and cool against his and he figured he could stand here forever, but her breathing was so erratic and raspy, he couldn't stand it. "Lyndie, your medicine—"

"I thought you were—"

"I know. Get out your inhaler, baby."

She just squeezed him even tighter, pressing so close he couldn't tell where he ended and she began. "I couldn't get here fast enough—"

"It's okay—I'm all in one piece, everyone is."

"I'm not falling apart." But neither did she let go.

And neither did he.

* * *

By nightfall, Griffin and two others had indeed managed to get above the fire to verify it had reached the rock cliffs and had nowhere else to go.

It had turned back on itself, and all in all, they'd not lost too much more acreage. The south end of the fire, the one that had come so close to town, had begun to burn out as well, leaving only the higher elevations still hot. With or without cooperating weather now, it'd only be a day or so more before it ran out of fuel entirely.

Lyndie had never felt more satisfaction or relief. She'd had enough of danger and adrenaline and horrifying fear to last her a lifetime. The ride back to the inn was once again a crowded affair. She sat in the Jeep with her inhaler out—she'd needed it too much today—practically in Griffin's lap in the front passenger seat, with everyone around them talking, chattering, excited.

Griffin smiled at something Brody said in the backseat, and she found herself staring into his dirty, exhausted face.

His smile slowly faded, but his eyes warmed.

So did her body. God, she'd died a thousand deaths today when he'd vanished on that mountain. She had no idea how he could have come to mean so much to her in such a short time, she a woman who never took any time at all to know anyone, but she couldn't deny what she felt when she looked at him.

Around them chaos reigned; the engine and the Jeep, the roar of the wind, the laughter of the others...but Griffin reached out and stroked a finger down her cheek, and at the simple touch, everything else faded away. The dark night and its sounds, the roar of the Jeep, the conversation around them, everything, until it was just the two of them.

"You okay?" he asked softly.

Was she okay...This past week had seemed an eternity, a blink of an eye. She'd met this incredible man, this amazing, strong, intelligent man. She'd watched him face his own living nightmare head-on and come through it. She'd laughed with him, cried with him.

Slept with him.

And tonight they'd all eat together, they'd probably talk and laugh some more. She might even sleep with him again—she really hoped she slept with him again—and then, first thing in the morning, she'd fly him back to his world, and then take herself off to hers.

The end of yet another little episode in her life. She had a bunch of episodes, all unconnected, all floating around in her memories now, always coming back to just her.

Just her.

It was what she'd always wanted. Freedom. Independence.

"Lyndie?"

"I'm okay." She managed a smile. "I always am."

* * *

At the inn, Rosa waited with more mountains of food. She didn't have to bully anyone to eat tonight, they were all starving, Lyndie included. She ate, and afterward, before she could vanish to her room, Brody spun her around the courtyard to the Spanish music blaring from the small boom box on the brick wall.

The night was warm and still. Maybe she was hallucinating, or maybe she just wanted it so badly, but the night seemed clearer, more stunningly beautiful than she could remember. The moon cast a glow on the hills around them, and on the beautiful gardens in the courtyard that Rosa loved to slave over.

Unused to such frivolity, she tried to pull away because he was making her dizzy twirling her around. "I'll step on your feet," she warned.

"That's why I wore steel-toed boots, darlin.'" Brody grinned. "Step on me all you want."

She looked into a face so like Griffin's with its quiet strength and see-all eyes, and yet so different. Brody's smile came far easier, with deeper laugh lines, and Lyndie had a feeling the women found this Moore brother much easier to approach. "Why are you dancing with me anyway?"

"What, I can't dance with a beautiful woman?"

"The beautiful woman who wants to dance with you is standing on the edge of the dance floor, dressed to the hilt to grab your attention, shooting me daggers with her flashing eyes."

"Ah. *Nina,*" he said on a very masculine sigh.

"You know her father is armed, right?"

Brody grinned. "He wouldn't really shoot me."

"If you believe that, I've got some swampland up the street for sale." She looked into his eyes and saw something behind the laughter. "Seriously. I wouldn't play with her, fair warning."

Brody's smile faded. "I'm not playing."

That's what she'd been afraid of. "Rumor is you've been playing two nights running."

"Rumor?"

Ooh, the baby brother did have a temper, suddenly it showed in every line of his body. She took pity. "Nina told me herself," she said, and patted his shoulder. "Don't worry, no one is ruining the princess's reputation but the princess herself."

"I care about her," he said, his voice low. "I know that sounds crazy, but I do. Maybe as much as you care about my brother."

She stared at him, unexpected emotion clogging her throat. "Well, then we're both crazy." With that, she tried to turn away from him, but he held her back.

"Lyndie, this is none of my business, but about Griffin—"

"That's right, it isn't any of your business."

"I lost him for an entire year."

She let out her breath. "I know. But he's back now, and he's—"

"Falling for you."

"Don't be ridiculous, he's just trying to get back to the living, he's—"

"Falling for you," he repeated quietly. He leaned in and whispered in her ear. "Are you falling back?"

She stared at him. "He's not over what happened to him last year. He's not ready to fall for anyone."

"Probably not, no."

Each word felt like a stab to her heart, which didn't make any sense.

"But they're gone," he said softly. "They're gone and he isn't. He's learning he's not dead. That his heart can love again—"

"Oh, no." She laughed. "Listen, you're way off base here. We're not in love, we're just…" *Jumping each other's bones.*

Brody laughed. "Yeah. You're just." He twirled her around

again. "You know you're really different from anyone he's ever been with."

She scowled. "So?"

"So…" He looked amused now, damn him. "That's a good thing. You're strong, independent. Tough as hell. I think that's exactly what he needs. Someone to challenge him."

"I'm going to challenge *you* here in a minute. To a nice dunking in the creek."

Brody laughed again. "Hey, I'm not trying to pry. I want him happy again, that's all."

"He's going to be plenty happy once I fly you both back in the morning."

"And what about you?"

"I'll be happy, too."

"You sure?"

"Positive."

Brody stared at her for a long moment, then sighed. "All right." He lifted his hands in surrender. The song ended and he stepped back, a sad smile on his face. "Don't hurt him, Lyndie."

And then she was standing on the dance floor by herself, suddenly and desperately in need of quiet.

Whirling to find a door, she plowed right into Tom.

"Hey," he said. "I was just looking for a pretty dancing partner."

"No way, I—"

He spun her until she was cursing at him and laughing. "That's better," he said. "That's way better. I know there haven't been many reasons to smile down here for the past few weekends—"

"We've almost got it all behind us now."

"Yes," he agreed with a relieved smile. "But in any case, I believe things happen for a reason."

"The fire? You think something good can come out of all that damage and destruction?"

For a moment he didn't say anything, just continued to spin her around the room to the wild, loud music. "Yes," he finally said. "I do. I think the ranchers learned a valuable lesson, one that the U.S. government has been trying to teach them for a long time. Their slash-and-burn methods have to change. I think the town realized how much of a team they are, and how important every single person is. I think Nina learned the world doesn't always revolve around her."

"Did you learn something, too?"

"Nothing I didn't already know. Life is short, Lyndie. Too damn short. Things happen. Bad things." He clipped her lightly on the chin. "So make the most of it. Make the most of every single second." He smiled. "Though given what *you* learned, I probably don't even have to say it."

"Oh, really? And just what is it you think I learned?" Out of the corner of her eye, she saw Griffin enter the courtyard. Immediately he sought her out, and when he found her, she felt her heart stutter just a bit.

Tom touched her nose, his smile widening. "You just smiled genuinely for the first time all evening, did you know that?"

Startled, she looked back at Tom. "I did not."

"You did. And you know what else? It suits you. Do you know yet what you learned down here, Lyndie?"

"What is it about tonight that makes you all think I want or need to hear about my life? I don't need advice, I don't need any lessons attached to what's happened down here. Bottom line, you needed help, and getting you that help is my job. End of story." And if she'd gotten a little action on the side, well then, that was no one's business but her own. "But if you need it spelled out...I learned what a nosy bunch you all are. Now get out of my way, big guy, I need out of here. Badly."

Tom laughed. "You can run, but you can't hide."

"Cut him off," she said to Rosa, who was coming by with a tray of beers.

If Rosa did, Lyndie couldn't have said, because she went out of the inn and into the night, drawing a deep breath of it into her lungs, holding it for a long moment before letting it go slowly.

She should be up in that air right now, flying her ass off, without an important thought in her head.

She shouldn't be standing here by the creek, wondering if Griffin was going to give her another mind-blowing orgasm tonight. She shouldn't be wondering if he was wondering about her.

And she sure as hell shouldn't be wondering if he was going to miss her, even a little. She took a deep breath and reminded herself that here was her peace and calm whenever she needed it, a place that had stolen a chunk of her heart.

It would be enough.

"You needed out, too."

She took her gaze off the sky and eyed the man most on her mind, who stood there, hands in his pockets, his shoulders slightly hunched as he stared off into the night.

"Yeah." She pushed away from the wall, came toward him. "Everyone in there seems to feel so comfortable telling me how to run my life, so I felt comfortable getting the hell out."

"It's funny what people do in the name of love." Griffin lifted a brow when she stopped midstride. "Oh, that's right. You don't like that L-word. It must really overwhelm you to come down here then, with Tom and Nina and Rosa all so crazy about you that they'd do anything for you. Including each of them threatening me with bodily harm if I hurt you."

"What?" She sputtered over that for a moment, then growled, but Griffin cocked his head, studying her with an interest she wasn't sure was a good thing. "Look," she said. "No one hurts me. I make sure of that."

"Right." He nodded agreeably, and walked around her.

She turned in a circle, keeping her face to his. "What does that mean?"

"I know exactly how tough you are. I know you don't let people close enough to even think about hurting you." Reaching out, he stroked a cheek. "And when I first met you, when I first felt that zing of heat between us, I worried about that—I worried about leading you on, hurting you somehow in spite of it."

"Because of what happened in that Idaho fire."

"Because I knew I was no good to a woman, not in the state I was in. In any case, you were so impenetrable, I decided it didn't matter."

Direct hit.

"But then I got to know you."

"You did not," she said. "It's only been a week."

"I got to know you," he repeated gently. "And you know what?"

Seeing that heated, affectionate look in his eyes as he stepped close and put his hands on her hips, she started to shake her head. She didn't want to know, she—

He kissed her, just once, soft and undemanding, but her body flared to life. "You might be fearless," he whispered. "You might be independent, but on the inside you're just as in need of love as the rest of us."

"No—"

He put his finger on her lips, came in even closer. "I know you think you don't need it. I know love's hurt you in the past, that you've suffered losses, too—" When she started to shake her head at that, he cupped her jaw with his other hand to hold her still. "Your parents, your grandfather…"

"Not like you," she whispered past the sudden lump in her throat.

"We've already been there. Loss is loss, remember? But before that Idaho fire, I'd never experienced such tragedy. My life had been easy and good and filled with warmth and love from every corner." He stroked an uneven strand of hair from her eyes. "I had that solid foundation beneath me. I don't think you did."

"I was fine."

"Sure. Fine. All on your own, right?"

"Right."

"Because you don't like to let people in. That way you don't have to lose anyone else."

She went very, very still.

"Anyone would feel that way if they'd had your life," he assured her very quietly. "They would, but Lyndie, you don't have to live like that."

She pulled free. "Says the man who was running out of the party as fast as I was."

He let out a gust of air. "Yeah. My brother—"

"He's trying to rush you along in the life department?"

"Yeah."

"Well, welcome to my world."

"Tom and Nina and Rosa all have your best interests at heart—" He broke off and let out a low laugh when she gave him a long, knowing look. "Okay, fine. I get the message."

"Do you?"

"Yeah. They have your best interests at heart. I suppose in the same damn way Brody does mine."

She smirked. "Doesn't make it any easier to take, though, does it?"

"No."

They fell silent, just looking at each other for a long moment. There was something different in his gaze tonight. Something that snagged her breath. "This is our last night," she whispered.

His eyes heated. "Yeah."

Her nipples hardened. Her skin tingled in anticipation. "So what do you say we blow this Popsicle stand, Ace?"

His eyes heated again, his hands tightened on her, pulling her flush to his body—a body that already knew hers. "What did you have in mind?"

She arched against the interesting bulge behind the buttons on his Levi's. "I'm thinking the same as you."

22

They ended up in Griffin's room, which had a nicer bed and a soft, warm Tallulah on the covers, fast asleep. They kicked her out and put a chair in front of the door in lieu of a functioning lock.

Lyndie tried to draw Griffin down to the mattress immediately, her engines revved and roaring to go, but he held her face and kissed her, turning her away from the bed with his body.

"Standing up?" she murmured, game for that, surprised when he let out a low laugh. Pulling back, she blinked up at him. "What? What's so funny?"

"Are you always in such a hurry?"

She could feel his chest brushing her nipples, his long legs so snug to hers, his impressive erection low on her belly. Hell, yes, she was in a hurry. "I want you," she said simply, and ran her fingers down his body to cup him. "And you want me."

"Oh, yeah." He tipped her face up again, his voice hoarse. "I want you. I just want to take it slow."

"Why?"

"You know..." He kissed her ear, her jaw. "The confusion on

your face is adorable, and bears discussing—" He kissed the tip of her nose, then her chin. "But you taste so good—" And now her mouth for a long, delicious moment, and when he pulled away this time she heard her own little murmur of protest.

He danced his thumb over her wet lower lip. "I just can't believe I'm here. With you. About to kiss and lick every inch of you."

"Our bodies work fairly well together, in case you've forgotten."

"Yes." He watched his hand as it grazed her throat, her collarbone, then a breast, which he lifted and cupped and ran a thumb over a tight, aching nipple until her knees nearly buckled. "Our bodies definitely work fairly well together. I just didn't think mine worked anymore, period."

Lyndie went still, then covered his hand with her own. "Look, *I'm* a little blown away over all this, so I can only imagine how *you're* feeling. I can go—"

"No." He pulled her flush against his body, in an embrace that made her want to burrow in even closer and hold on for dear life. "Don't move."

"I won't." She sank her fingers into his hair. "I'd say I'm sorry for encroaching on all that sexy broodiness you had going, but—"

He kissed her again, nibbling on her lower lip. "But you're not?"

"No." She tugged on his shirt. "What I am sorry about is how many clothes you're wearing. I'm really sorry about that."

"I didn't think you could do it," he said on a sigh, letting her strip him out of his clothes one piece at a time, while she reveled in his hard, athletic body that made her mouth water.

"Didn't think I could do what?" Distracted, her fingers ran

down his chest, over the belly that made her want to kiss every inch of him, down to the current center of her universe, which was hard and heavy and pointing right at her.

"Stay still." With mock disappointment, he bent and grabbed her behind her knees, straightening with her in a fireman's hold, which meant she flopped over his shoulder.

"Hey!" She smacked his bare ass. "Put me down. *What are you doing?*"

He dumped her onto the bed, the expression on his face a mixture of wicked mischief and fierce intent as she bounced. Her heart skipped a beat, then two. "Grif—"

"Shh." He sprawled out beside her, skimming his fingers down her body, thoroughly engrossed in watching his own hand on her. "You said you wouldn't move."

"I didn't mean—"

"I did." Leaning in, he tugged open her blouse while he kissed her ear. When her hands snaked up to touch his bare, sleek chest, he sucked in a breath and shook his head, his voice thick and heavy, filled with dark promises. "You don't seem to be able to follow directions."

"Not very well," she admitted, but he brought his free hand to the side of her face, holding her cheek in his palm, his fingers running through her hair at her temple.

The gesture felt so tender, so raw, she felt the unexpected sting of tears, and when he kissed her softly, then pulled back to say, "You turn me upside down, Lyndie, like no one ever has," a little moan stuck in her throat.

"Upside down," he repeated softly, and swiped at a tear she hadn't even known she'd let loose.

"I haven't the foggiest idea what to do with you," she whispered.

"No?" Holding her gaze, he slowly stripped her out of her clothes. "Good thing I know what to do with you."

"You mean *to* me," she gasped when he stroked her nipple with his tongue.

"Uh huh." He kissed her ribs, dipped into her belly button, then slipped between her legs, his broad shoulders holding her open to him. He ran a finger over her, absorbed the helpless little gasp that escaped her, and said, "Am I driving you crazy?"

She arched up into him, and then he lowered his head, kissing her right...*there.* "Y-yes."

"Good." He did it again, and her every muscle went on quiver alert. "Because you're driving me right off the very edge of sanity." Another mind-blowing stroke of his tongue. "So we're doing this to each other."

That sounded a little too relationship-involved to her, and she surged up to her elbows to tell him so, except he chose that moment to bend his head again to his task, and this time he took it quite seriously. She fell back, sinking her fingers into his hair to hold him in place, which turned out to be unnecessary because he wasn't going anywhere—he promised it in every touch, every kiss, stoking her into one desperate, feverish mass of nerve endings.

When she came, she lost track of all her senses for what might have been an hour, or only a moment, but when she could see again, Griffin towered over her, his big beautiful body poised to take hers. "You back?" he asked.

"I'm not sure....Did you get the license plate of that truck?"

He placed a soft kiss over her temple, his breath fluttering over her hair like a gentle touch. "No truck, Lyndie. Just me."

Just him. God, just him. "Well, then, run me over again, could you?"

His low chuckle sounded in her ear. After that, she lost her train of thought because then he was kissing her mouth, a heavy, intoxicating kiss somehow deeper and more exquisite than anything he'd done to her before. Holding on for dear life, she kissed him back, letting herself fall into the moment, into the unrelenting heat and passion in a way she didn't fully even trust. "Griffin—"

"Don't worry, I still know what to do—" He broke off on a groan when she slid her hand downward and got a grip of him fully aroused.

"I'm glad," she whispered, and held up the condom they'd snagged from her room.

He put it on, then sank inside her wet, willing body to the hilt, their twin moans dancing in the air around them.

"Oh, yeah," he whispered against her mouth as he began to move, began to take them both to the place they desperately needed to go. "I definitely still know what to do."

* * *

At dawn, Nina sat barefoot on the edge of the creek, splashing the water with her toes. She wasn't usually up at this hour. In fact, she wouldn't be up now except her body still hummed from all the things Brody had done to it.

Her heart felt full to bursting.

But her stomach...her stomach was dancing with butterflies in tune to the rushing water.

"Hiya, Princess."

Pasting a confident smile on her face, which had caught her more than her fair share of men in the past, she turned to face a gorgeously rumpled Brody.

He might be just another man…but he was also the first she didn't want to walk away from.

He hunkered at her side. The day was already hot, and he wore dark blue surfer shorts to his knees, with a wild blue Hawaiian shirt for the flight back, and just looking at him made her want to cry.

"Hey." He stroked her cheek when her smile crumpled. "You look so…sad."

She had no idea how to tell him that what had started out as fun had turned to something else entirely.

"Did I hurt you last night?" he whispered.

"No." *Dios Mio.* "It's just that…" She had nothing to lose by telling him. "You're leaving."

He sighed and sat next to her. "Yeah. I'm sorry, Princess."

"If I were really a princess, I could come and go as I please. Like you do."

The water rushing over the rocks was the only sound for a long moment. "And where is it you want to go?"

"The States."

"To do what?"

"Something. Anything." She threw up her hands. "I just want out of here." She closed her eyes. "Wait. That's not quite true. I *do* know what I want. I want to teach there. I dream about it, it's my calling. But my father wants me here." She smiled at him but it didn't meet her eyes. "I love him but I can't live my life for him, Brody."

"Of course not."

"So…you understand? You think I should do as I please?"

Brody looked into her earnest eyes and didn't know what to say. He was leaving any moment now. Typically, leaving was something he did extremely well, and yet this time…

He didn't want to.

"I want to teach kids Spanish in a country that gives so much to most of its population, but forgets others. I want to be a proud American, or half American, anyway. I want to make a difference."

"You don't make a difference here?"

"In a cantina?" Her laugh was harsh. "I want so much more than this. I can make a difference there as a teacher, a true difference to help immigrant children." She went up on her knees, wrapped her arms around his neck. "You helped me forget for a few days, and for that I'm grateful, but now the wanting is back." She looked deeply into his eyes. "And there is more."

"More?" He didn't know why, but his heart started to beat faster.

"I want to be near you."

"To…practice reading?"

She bit her lush lower lip. Watched him with those expressive eyes that heated him from the inside out. "Not exactly."

"What exactly?"

"I want to be with you, Brody." She laid her two small, work-roughened hands on either side of his jaw and looked him right in the eyes, honest and open, daring him to be that way back.

But he wasn't good at the open, honest thing.

In fact, this was usually where he took off running, but oddly enough, his feet weren't so much as twitching. His stomach hadn't even fallen.

His heart raced, though, and it had nothing to do with panic or needing to run.

"I don't mean I want to tie you up," she said.

"You don't mean to tie me down?" He managed a smile. "Because, darlin', you can tie me up anytime."

"You are making a joke and I am being serious." Leaning back, she crossed her arms over her chest. Her lower lip became even fuller and he had the most insane need to nibble at it. "Are you making a joke because I'm scaring you?" she wondered. "Or because *you're* scaring you?"

Wise beyond her years. And dead-on accurate. Okay, hell. Here came his honesty, though it was rusty. "What I feel for you, Nina, terrifies me." In another unusual move for him, he pulled her close, cuddling where he'd never felt the need before. "I'm not exactly known for having these conversations while sober."

"I am not asking for anything from you other than being able to see you again. I like you, Brody. I lust for you, too, but I have lusted for many men. I haven't liked many men."

Again with her honesty, leaving him humbled to the core. "I'm not the kind of guy you bring home to meet Mom and Dad."

"I know."

"I'm also not the kind of guy to go back for seconds."

She smiled sadly. "I know that, too. It's okay—"

"But I would do anything to see you again." He let out a rough laugh. "And if anyone in my world could hear me say that, they'd fall over in shock."

"You are telling me the truth?" She looked breathless, and filled with so much expectation it almost hurt to look at her.

"I am telling you the truth. But sweetheart, I'm leaving. This morning. Any minute. I'll come back when I can, but—"

"But if I was in the States it would be easier."

"Well, of course it would—oof," he said when she flung herself at him. He fell to his back on the damp bank of the creek.

"I *will* see you again." On top of him now, she grinned as her hair fell all around him like a curtain, closing them in together against the rest of the world. "I will see you soon."

The dew seeping in through his shirt, he stared up at her, then hauled her down to him. "God, I hope so—"

His words were halted by Nina's hungry, talented mouth, which she used until he'd forgotten about the dew, until his eyes were crossed and his body hard and aching again. Then, all too soon, she stood, calmly brushing off her clothes.

"Nina—"

"It's time for good-byes," she said, and held out her hand.

Right. It was. He'd never minded a good-bye in his life, but now, his feet felt like leaden weights as he allowed her to pull him around to the front of the inn, where Griffin and Lyndie were talking to Rosa. Tom was in the Jeep already, waiting to take them to the plane.

Brody watched Rosa engulf first Griffin and then Lyndie in a hug. It occurred to him that Griffin looked far better than he had when Brody had laid eyes on him last week for the first time in a year. Then his brother had been lean, haggard, and edgy. He'd filled out slightly now, and had lost much of his hollowed despair.

Lyndie turned from Rosa and nearly walked right into Griffin, who put his hands on her arms, murmuring something softly in her ear.

In response, she tilted her head up and smiled into his eyes, and whether she knew it or not—and Brody suspected she did not—her entire heart shone through.

When Griffin smiled back, still holding her, it too was with everything he had.

Brody didn't think he'd seen Griffin smile this entire weekend, and he sure as hell hadn't seen him smile the weekend before, when he'd blackmailed him into coming here in the first place.

For the first time since then, Brody could see he'd really done the right thing, and it made him almost weak with relief and even hope.

Griffin still had his hands on Lyndie. Things were clearly different between them, and far more…tender.

Obviously, he'd not been the only one getting lucky. And if that was the case, then Griffin was good to go. Brody's job was done.

He could leave now, and not ever look back.

Except for the tug on his heart, and the woman beside him who'd caused it.

23

W hat are you going to do when you get back to San Diego?"

The question from Lyndie startled Griffin. They'd been flying northwest for forty-five minutes, mostly in comfortable silence. She'd look at him every once in a while, searching his expression for a moment, looking for what, exactly, he had no clue, but then she'd smile—a balm on wounds he hadn't even realized he'd had. "I don't know what I'll do when I get back," he said.

"You going home?"

To South Carolina, she meant, and his parents. To the friends Brody insisted he still had. He glanced back at Brody, crashed out on the seat behind him and dead to the world. Griffin still couldn't quite believe that his lazy-bones, laid-back brother had gotten him to a fire. The Brody he knew didn't like to tax himself.

And yet he'd worked his ass off in Mexico this weekend, as hard as any of them. He'd changed a lot in this past year, apparently.

And so had Griffin. "I'm not sure," he admitted.

Lyndie nodded, as if that was a perfectly acceptable answer, when, in fact, it wasn't. If she had family alive, he doubted she'd stay away from them simply because of what they'd make her feel.

"I'd like to see them," he said out loud for the first time, and let out a long breath. He really would like to see them.

"I bet they'd like to see you, too."

"But as for permanent roots…" He shrugged. "I'm fond of San Diego."

"It's a great place, and, funny thing, they have a fire department."

He turned his head toward her, and she smiled. "You're just too good at what you do to walk away, Griffin."

"Actually…I'm done walking away. In every aspect of my life."

Startled, she stared at him for a beat before looking forward again.

Yeah, that means you, he thought, just a little grimly. What the hell. If he was back to doing the whole feeling thing, he might as well face everything head-on at once. Including this woman, and how he felt about her, which was far, far more complicated than he'd ever intended. "And once we're back, Lyndie—"

"No." She swallowed hard. "No promises, okay?"

"You don't even know what I was going to say."

"And I'm going to keep it that way."

Brody yawned loudly and widely as he sat up. "Nice catnap. What did I miss?"

"The pizza and beer," Lyndie said.

"Ah, *man.*"

When Lyndie laughed, Brody rolled his eyes. "Oh, sure, make fun of the sleepy man, but in my dreams it's possible to get beer and pizza up here." He looked at his brother. "You take advantage of my nap?"

"What?"

"Maybe you guys joined the mile high club or something."

Griffin let out a disbelieving laugh. "Just when I think you've grown up—"

Brody grinned. "Yeah, I know. So…did you?"

Griffin threw a magazine at him. "Go back to sleep."

He didn't, but mercifully, he stayed quiet, watching the scenery go by, which left Griffin with several hours of being almost alone with Lyndie. Quiet and reflective as well, they didn't say much.

They didn't have to. Time was nearly up, and they both knew it.

Several hours later, Griffin watched the airport runway in San Diego rise up to meet them as they came in for their landing. Griffin glanced at the still and strangely subdued Brody. "What's up?" Griffin asked him as they taxied toward their terminal.

Brody just lifted a shoulder. Code for I-don't-want-to-talk-about-it. "Well, isn't that something," Griffin muttered.

"Isn't what something?"

"You don't want to talk about what's bothering you and I'm supposed to just leave it be."

"That's right."

"You never let *me* be," Griffin said. "You dragged my sorry ass out of the country."

"You needed it."

"And what is it you need?" Griffin asked.

"Nothing." Pure misery crossed Brody's face. "Maybe a place that serves good drinks and has some good scenery, and I'm not talking a view of the beach." Grabbing his bag, he got off the plane.

Griffin shook his head and pulled out his two bags from the backseats, and also Lyndie's. When he looked up, she was standing there facing him. "Thanks," she said, and reached for hers. "Through customs we go."

And yet neither of them moved. Griffin had the urge to haul her close, but he realized he wasn't looking into the face of the woman whom he'd made love to last night and also this morning. That soft, warm, loving, laughing woman had already left him.

"Thanks for your help with the fire," she said politely.

"Thanks for my help." He repeated her words, even nodded agreeably, feeling anything but agreeable. *"Thanks for my help?"*

"Sam appreciates what you've done, and I—"

"I didn't do it for Sam. Jesus, Lyndie, are we really going to do this? Just ignore everything—"

"I've got to check in."

And unbelievably, she pushed past him and left the plane. He stood there for a long moment, certain they weren't really going to leave it this way, but she didn't come back.

Finally Brody did. He poked his head back in the door. "You coming or what?"

"Yeah. Guess I am." He shouldered his bags, took one last look around, shook his head, and left the plane, too.

Lyndie was just outside, looking over a clipboard. Griffin slowed. "I'll meet you inside," he said to Brody, and stepped toward her.

Distracted, she looked up. "What?"

He could only stare at her. "You can honestly say you expect me to just walk away?"

"Yes."

Oddly deflated, he looked around them at the organized chaos of the airport while Lyndie studied her clipboard. Shaking his head, he started to do as she wanted and walk away, but got only a few feet before he whipped back around. "Damn it, I don't know what to do with you. About you."

"Don't do anything."

"Just ignore the feelings, the emotions?"

Her eyes were a little wide, and more uncertain than he'd ever seen her. "Maybe...maybe I don't have any."

"Is that what you tell yourself?" he asked. "Is that how you do it, live so isolated and on your own? You ignore everything, including what's going on right here, right now?"

Swallowing hard, she lifted her chin and met his gaze. "Well, truthfully, I've never had feelings or emotions such as what's going on right here, right now."

He felt his jaw drop at that, and without another word, she whirled on her heel and walked toward a lineman waiting for her attention.

Shocked, he stood there as she walked away.

* * *

Lyndie walked blindly toward the lineman, a little afraid she'd just walked away from the best thing ever to have happened to her.

"Need fuel?" the lineman asked.

She blinked rapidly to see around the tears making her vision shimmer. "Uh..."

"Because I can fill 'er up for ya."

"Yeah. Sure."

"Need a wash?"

Snapping at the kid would be like kicking a puppy, so she took a deep breath. "What the hell."

"Need a—"

"Just...give me the works, all right? Charge it to Sam's account," she said with grim satisfaction.

She hadn't expected Griffin to need or want a goodbye. Foolish of her, she could see that now. He wasn't the type of man to just walk away from anything, much less someone he cared about.

And she knew he cared about her—it'd been in every kiss, every touch, every single look they'd ever exchanged, even the last one he'd just given her.

A tear hit her cheek. Damn it, that was the *last* one, the very last tear she'd shed. It wasn't as if they'd made any promises to each other. They'd both gone into this with their eyes wide open. They'd sparked immediately, yes, but considering the danger element they'd faced, the adrenaline, the urgency of their situation, not to mention the forced intimacy, they'd been bound to act on those sparks.

But it was over now. Back to reality.

Head down, she hopped back up into her plane. She'd just sit here for a few moments, staring blindly at the controls if she had to, until she had herself under control. She'd sit there and…pet Lucifer, who was on her seat looking deceptively sweet and innocent as he washed his face.

But that wasn't what caught her attention. No, it was the woman sitting next to the kitten. Nina Farrell wore the pair of jeans she'd pilfered from Lyndie, along with a bright red halter top. Her long, thick hair fell around her shoulders as she smiled broadly.

"You…stowed away on me," Lyndie said, surprised, even though she shouldn't have been.

"Sure did." Nina's grin broadened. "You were so preoccupied back in San Puebla, so concerned about saying good-bye to your firefighter that you never—"

"I was not preoccupied. I never fly preoccupied."

"No? So you knew I'd hidden beneath the bags, then?"

"This is against immigration and customs—"

"I have my papers." Her eyes flashed. "I'll pass through no problem, I belong here, too."

"The point is you could have gotten me in trouble, Nina. I need to know what I have on this plane. It's my business to know everything, including potential problems."

Nina's eyes were dark, and spitting with temper. "Is that all I am to you, a potential problem?" She came to her feet and lifted her chin. "Fine, then. Do not you worry about a thing, I am taking my potential problematic self right on out of your way."

"Nina—"

"I belong here. You as a pilot should have no issue with me coming along—"

"As a pilot—and I speak for the entire industry here—we sort of frown on stowaways."

Nina shook her head. "Why are you really so angry? This is my life, not yours."

"I'm angry because you asked me if I'd bring you, and I said no. Call me stubborn, but I hate it when people ask for my permission and then disregard it."

"But why did you say no?" Nina stared into her eyes, which Lyndie knew were still wet. "Too many attachments on your heart?"

"What? Don't be ridiculous." And yet her heart kicked up a notch at the accusation.

"And I suppose it's also ridiculous that you're standing here fighting tears. Is it the 'damn' kitten, Lyndie? Or that damn man you just kicked right out of your life because heaven forbid you let anyone in, really in, that rigid heart of yours."

"Okay, now you're just pissing me off."

"Of course I am. That's because I am in your face telling you what is wrong with you. I'm surprised you're not trying to kill me."

"I'm too tired, that's all."

"I know." Nina's temper faded, and she stroked Lyndie's cheek. "You've worked your ass off. You probably have no idea how much I admire you, how much I am awed by all you do for everyone else."

"Nina—"

"I want to teach," she said softly. "I want to teach kids in this country, kids who might not get a chance to fully understand their culture otherwise. I want to help, too, Lyndie. Don't be mad at me anymore."

Defeated, Lyndie sat down in her pilot's seat. "I'm not. Go through customs, damn it. Meet me out there."

"Thank you." Nina came forward and gave her a hard hug. "You won't regret this particular attachment, I promise."

But she already did. She regretted all the "attachments" she'd collected, every last one, because with each of them came the distinct possibility of getting hurt. It scared her.

She really hated that.

24

Back in San Diego, Griffin did as he had for the past year. He sat on the beach. He walked the hills. Slept.

But after two days he'd had enough, even if he couldn't put his finger on what exactly he'd had enough of. At least not until Brody eyed him over a bowl of cereal he'd mooched for the third morning in a row. "You don't get it, do you?" His brother pointed at him with a spoon dripping milk. "You were never a loner."

"So?"

"So you're done with moping, you're done with brooding. I don't know if you'll ever be done grieving entirely but—"

"How can I be?"

Brody sighed. "You'll never forget, I know that, but seriously, man, it's time to *forgive.*"

"Who?"

"Who do you think? *Yourself.*"

Griffin closed his eyes. He had no trouble dredging up the memory of the tragedy. Hell, he dreamed it nearly every single night for a year.

But not the past two weeks. Nope, those nights had been filled with newer memories: Mexico, and a village of the bravest people he'd ever met. And a woman unlike anyone he'd known before; a woman he couldn't seem to stop thinking about, even if she wanted him to. Just this morning he'd woken, reaching for her because his dreams had been so real.

"It's time to give yourself permission to go on," Brody said. "Because what happened wasn't your fault and you know it."

"Yeah. Logically I know that. I do."

Brody set his spoon down and refilled his bowl to the brim. "Good. Because now that I found you, you're done having breakfast by yourself. Besides, you buy good cereal."

"Maybe what *I'm* done with is you mooching out of my fridge and sleeping on my couch—"

"Which is damned uncomfortable, by the way. You think you could get a futon? I'd sure sleep better—"

"Go home, Brody."

"Funny, that's what I was going to tell you."

"What?"

"Go home, Griffin. You can't just lounge the rest of your life away because you suffered some losses. It's time to move on. *Go home.*"

He stared at his brother. "But I don't know where home is."

"Sure you do. It's wherever makes you happy."

But that was the problem. He really didn't know where that was anymore—and, even worse, he had the feeling it wasn't a "where" at all, but "who."

Given that he'd walked away from anyone who'd ever cared about him—or had let *her* walk away from *him*—he felt pretty damn homeless at the moment.

God, he was tired of missing people. His friends. Greg. His parents.

Lyndie. Shockingly enough, he missed her so much it was a physical ache, and not just of the lust variety. His chest hurt, his mind hurt. How had he done it for an entire year—remained alone and silent? And why did he suddenly need...more?

Maybe because for a couple of weeks now, he'd had it. He'd had a purpose, a job—and been surrounded by people he cared about, and who cared about him in return.

Once again he'd been needed—wanted—and he'd thrived on that despite the guilt that came with it.

"Figure it out yet, Grif?"

He stood up. "I'm going for a run."

Brody shook his head. "So you're still the ambitious one. Well, go for it. See if you can outrun feeling guilty for starting to live again."

"Brody—"

"Hey, no excuses, not for me. Just go."

Griffin tried to do just that. He certainly ran hard enough to exhaust himself, but everything else—his memories, his hopes and dreams—unfortunately, as they had all year, they stuck with him.

When he got back to the small house he'd called his own for a year now, he stood on the deck, still huffing and puffing and sweating. Brody's backpack sat alone on the table, but his brother wasn't in sight.

No one was, and as he stretched his sore muscles, he cursed the very aloneness he'd sought out for so long.

He wondered what Lyndie was doing right now. Flying? Yeah, no doubt. South America this time? Hell, she could be anywhere, with anyone.

For so long he'd not allowed thoughts of anyone else to creep into his existence but now that he'd gone out and been so alive for a few weeks, it'd become impossible to remain in a cocoon.

He'd never forget what he'd lost, never. But the harsh truth remained—they were dead.

And he was not.

Lyndie couldn't be a replacement, but, God knew, he hadn't been looking for one—hadn't been looking for anything, and yet he'd found...something incredibly good, and incredibly special.

From inside Brody's pack on the table, a cell phone rang, the one he'd given back to his brother the night they'd returned. Knowing that it was likely his parents calling, Griffin turned away. He still couldn't talk to them, he didn't know what to say, or how to say it—

The phone rang a second time. He could see his mother tapping her foot the way she did when waiting. For such a warm, loving woman, she had little to no patience, and certainly none for a cell phone.

That's how Griffin knew they really had no idea where he'd gone, or they'd have been here, right here, demanding, bullying, coaxing him along.

The third ring shrilled into the day. His mom would be chewing on her lower lip now, her eyes filled with worry.

Shit. One quick peek at the display had his heart kicking into gear. He'd been right, it was one Mrs. Phyllis Moore, mother extraordinaire.

He stared down at his thumb resting on the answer button, wondering why all of his reasons for avoiding her for so long seemed so stupid now.

The fourth ring started, but his thumb cut it off. With a deep breath, he spoke. "Hello."

A brief, shocked silence. Then his mother's shaky voice, "Griffin? Oh, my God, Griffin, is that you?"

A huge weight seemed to lift off his chest. "Yeah." His voice was gruff as she burst into tears. "It's me, Mom."

* * *

Brody hung out. He did that well. In fact, he'd made quite the hobby out of making sure life came as easy as it could, but nothing seemed to come easy these past two days.

He felt bored with his own company and, even worse, disgusted with himself and his lack of direction. Sitting on Ocean Beach, he stared out at the waves, the tide hitting his toes. The foggy morning had tendrils of long, low clouds skimming over the water and a chill in the air. The ocean pounded the sand in tune to a headache brewing in his head.

A headache. That was what he'd come to, he was actually stressing enough to get a headache.

An older couple walked past him hand in hand, their golden retriever running eagerly ahead of them, a stick in its mouth. They'd probably been together forever, the way his parents had, helping each other along the way, working hard for what they had, nurturing it, loving it.

Brody had never nurtured a soul, except his own.

The sun peeked its way out from behind a cloud, lighting up the ocean, the sand, everything around him. God, it was so beautiful here. Griffin had really found a place worthy of home status to hang out at all year, presumably doing so on his savings.

Brody couldn't have done that. In lieu of his own hard-earned savings, he'd mooched off his wealthy family's trust fund instead, when he was perfectly capable of making his own way.

For the first time in his life, he felt ashamed of himself, sitting on his degree, letting it go to waste when there were others, like Nina, who would do anything to be in his position.

He had dreamed about it last night, dreamed about Nina and her hopes and dreams, and woke up on a couch, in Griffin's house, where he could have a private shower, all the hot water he could have, all the hot water he could ever want, where he could drink the water right from the tap if he chose.

And still, he wished he was in Mexico, with Nina.

In his dream he'd stood in a rushing stream, somewhere alone in Copper Canyon, surrounded by ancient rock formations and enough wild, open wilderness that he could go forever without seeing another soul if he chose.

But he didn't choose. Even in his dreams he turned to a woman, one woman, with dark, melting brown eyes and a smile that could light his heart.

Nina.

The next morning, he crawled out of bed and picked up the phone. He dialed Hope International, and woke up Sam Logan, a man so dedicated he didn't seem to realize he shouldn't sleep with his business phone right by his head. "Sam, I need the number of Tom Farrell in San Puebla."

"Why, did you forget something?" Sam's voice sounded a little hoarse, and through the receiver, Brody heard the soft murmur of a woman.

He winced, hoping he hadn't caught the guy in the act. "Yeah, I did."

"Why don't I have one of my pilots grab it for you next time they're there?"

"Because to be honest, it's not a thing I forgot at all, but a person. A woman, actually."

"Tom's daughter," Sam said. "Nina."

"How did you—"

"Look, I am not getting involved in this one, not with a ten-foot pole. But here's the number."

Brody scribbled it down, wondering what the hell Sam meant, and then dialed the number for Rio Vista Inn as fast as he could.

Tom answered. "Nina?"

"No, but I'm looking to talk to her. It's Brody Moore. Griffin's brother—"

"I know who the hell you are," Tom growled.

"Where's Nina?"

There was a long silence. "I take it by the question that she's not with you. I can't decide if that's a good or bad thing."

Brody's heart took off. "Why would she be with me? Are you telling me she's—"

"Gone," Tom said flatly." And has been ever since Lyndie's plane left."

Brody sank onto a chair as his thoughts raced. She'd told him she wanted to go to the States, and he hadn't taken her seriously enough. "Has she called?"

"She left me a note telling me not to worry. A goddamn note."

Guilt swamped Brody. If he'd only—

"You paying attention, boy?"

He hadn't been, a lifelong problem. "I am now."

"Good, because I just decided I'm going to count on you to help me find her. You filled her head with thoughts of all she could do there, and now you're going to fix this."

No, he hadn't filled her head with hopes and dreams, she'd already had those all on her own. He'd simply enjoyed her, assuming she'd never really act on those dreams, because how many people really did that?

He should have known Nina was different from most; that

she'd said what she'd meant, and now she'd found a way to make them happen.

He closed his eyes, tormented by that. He hadn't taken her seriously enough, and as a result, she'd turned to someone else for help. Lyndie?

Maybe, maybe not. Pride ran through Nina like blood. She might think she could do this on her own, which meant she was out there, looking for a place to stay, a way to make a living, all on her own.

Anything could happen to her, anything. "I'll fix this," he promised rashly.

"See that you do."

25

Sam called Lyndie every day after her return from San Puebla, wanting her to fly for him, but she said no, claiming exhaustion.

What she really had were two pains in her ass—the cat and Nina. She couldn't just leave either of them and fly for days on end.

But she wanted to. And this morning, the third morning, was the day. She had a flight to Baja, and she was going. She showered, then stood in front of her closet with a towel wrapped around her, wishing she'd done laundry at some point since she'd been back.

Nina had offered, but Lyndie didn't need a keeper. And neither, it turned out, did Nina. She'd spent her time researching her college options and looking for a job, being surprisingly self-sufficient.

"Mew."

She glanced at the cat sitting on her bare, wet feet. "What do you want?"

Lucifer dropped and rolled to his back, exposing his belly.

"Yeah, yeah." But she sighed and bent down to scratch the thing. "And how is Dead Kitty Walking today?"

"Mew."

"Uh huh." Surging to her feet, she dropped the towel and pulled on a bra and panties. "Problem is, you're always hungry. And anyway, tell me this. How does a woman all by herself end up with two extra mouths to feed?"

"I told you," Nina said, coming into the one and only small bedroom of Lyndie's house, looking perfectly put together as always in a crisp, bright Mexican sundress and fancy sandals. "I have my own money. Some, anyway." Silhouetted in front of the bedroom window, with the ocean behind her, she lifted a stack of papers. "And I have college applications right here. Soon I will be getting my teaching credentials, thank you very much."

On the pile closest to her bed, Lyndie found a pair of pants, but had no such luck finding a clean blouse. Turning around in a circle, she searched the room. "There's got to be...ah." She headed toward a pile of clothes on the chair by her window. "A college degree is going to take you years."

"Yes, maybe, but in the meantime, I've got a lead on a job at a senior center—"

"Doing what, cleaning? No."

Nina looked regal when she lifted a brow. "No?"

"It's not good enough, not for you. You cleaned in Mexico, you might as well have stayed—" She broke off when the phone on the nightstand rang. "I'm nearly ready, Sam," she promised in lieu of a greeting. "I just—"

"It's Griffin."

As if she hadn't already registered the low, husky, unbearably familiar voice by the sudden leap in her pulse rate and her weakened knees. "Oh."

"We need to talk."

She let out a low laugh. "Conversations that start with those four words never turn out good in my experience."

"What's not good is how we left things."

She sank to her bed because she was shaking. *Shaking.* "I think we left things just fine."

"Because you like to stick your head in the sand. That doesn't work for me."

She sputtered. "I do not stick my head in the sand."

"Yes, you do," said Nina helpfully, lifting a shoulder when Lyndie glared at her.

"I want to see you," Griffin said in that same voice he'd used at the fire, when his natural leader instincts had kicked in and he was in control of everyone and everything around him.

Too bad he wasn't in control of her. With Nina looking at her, her hands on her hips, Lyndie closed her eyes. "Now's a bad time to discuss this."

Nina sighed. "Give up, Griffin," she called out.

Lyndie turned her back on her. "A really bad time."

Griffin was silent for a moment. Going over his options, no doubt. Making a plan. "Then tell me when," he finally said.

When? When she could look at him without wanting to melt in a boneless heap. When she could tell herself it had been just lust and believe it. "Later."

"Lyndie—"

"I've got to go, Griffin."

"Wait. Please, wait."

At the unexpected *please,* she hesitated.

"Look," he said softly. "I'm scaring you. I know—"

"Nothing scares me."

"Stop it. Stop with the Supergirl act. Yeah, you're strong as hell, and tougher than just about anyone I know, but when it comes to you and me, you're running scared."

"As *you* should be. You're not interested in just sex, remember? And yet you don't want more."

"Says who?"

"Says the woman who knows you're still not ready for any of this."

He was silent for a single beat. "I'm coming over. Now."

"You can't. I have a flight. Bye, Griffin." Heart inexplicably pounding, she disconnected, then stared at the phone for a long moment, wondering what the hell she was supposed to do with all the emotion and drama and anticipation racing through her.

Why did he have to call?

Why did he have to sound so absolutely fierce—and so unbearably sexy?

"Well, done, Lyndie," Nina said, clapping. "Once again you've cleared yourself of any…what did we call it? *Attachments.*" She stood there so smug. "Oh, and I won't be cleaning at the senior center, as you were worried about. I will be reading and teaching the seniors to speak Spanish. It's a job to be proud of."

Lyndie could hardly follow the conversation for remembering how Griffin's voice had sounded in her ear. "It must be some rich senior center."

"It is. They said they were looking to add 'culture' to their list of activities." Nina watched Lyndie pull out a wrinkled blouse from the bottom of the pile and shake it out. "Tell me you're not going to wear that today."

"Okay, I won't tell you." She slipped it on and started buttoning it up. What would Griffin do now? Would he back off?

Would he ever call her again?

"*Dios Mio,* at least iron it. Let *me* iron it."

Lyndie frowned and looked the clothing over. "And what in our history together suggests to you that I even own an iron? So tell me, what did Tom say when you called him?"

"Didn't you say you were late for a flight?"

Lyndie went very still. "Nina. Tell me you called him when I told you to two days ago."

"Sure, I could tell you that."

"But it would be a lie?" Lyndie let out a noise of disgust when Nina just lifted a cool brow. "Damn it. *Damn it,* he's probably worried sick." Stalking back over to her telephone, she yanked up the receiver and started punching numbers.

"If he's worried sick, it's because he didn't read my note," said Nina with a derisive sniff. "But I doubt you will find him surprised."

Lyndie glared at her while she waited for Tom to pick up his phone.

He didn't.

"Damn it all to hell," she muttered while his machine clicked on.

Tsking at Lyndie's use of the language, Nina started folding the clothes she'd just tossed aside, and came up with a blouse slightly cleaner than the one Lyndie had on. "Switch," she demanded.

"This one is fine."

"You have a stain on your breast, you look like a slob. Switch."

Lyndie started unbuttoning and leaving a message for Tom at the same time. "Tom, look, your errant daughter took it upon herself to stowaway on my plane. I thought she'd have called you by now, but I should have known better, as the girl—"

"Woman," Nina corrected.

Lyndie glared at her. "As she does whatever the hell she wants. Call me."

Just as she hung up the phone, someone knocked on her door. "Grand Frigging Central Station." Lyndie stalked to the door. "I'm five little minutes late and the man can't give me a break. "Look," she called back to Nina, "I'm going to be gone until late, late tonight, it can't be helped. Stay out of trouble."

"Are you talking to me or the cat?" Nina asked.

"Both of you."

"I will be out of your hair by this afternoon." Nina turned her back, her thin shoulders stiff and distant.

And Lyndie felt like slime. "Come on, don't get like that."

"I know how inconvenient it is, having me here."

"I never said—"

"And I know how much of a loner you are—"

"Well, I'm not—"

"I am very sorry I bothered you."

"Nina, damn it, would you listen—"

The knock at the door came again, louder and more impatient this time. Lyndie pointed at Nina. "Don't move."

Nina crossed her arms. Lyndie recognized the stance all too well. "I mean it." She hauled open the door. "Jeez, Sam, I have my hands full here, and—"

"Let me guess how you have your hands full." Brody Moore, gorgeous as ever and looking quite tense, stepped over the threshold. "Where is she?"

Lyndie blinked. "How did you know where I live?" She tried to see the street from her porch—Had Griffin come with him?—but couldn't see anything past Sam's huge mansion.

"Just tell me you've got her," Brody said. "I talked to Tom, and he said I'd probably locate her here—"

"Her who?" Nina moved into the room and eyed Brody with a cool smile. "Her me?"

"Thank God." He reached her in less than two strides, hauling her against him, burying his face in the crook of her neck. "*Jesus, you give me gray hair.*"

Nina rumpled his already rumpled hair with her long fingers. "Stop it. There's not a gray in the mix. *Men.* Always exaggerating."

But she encircled him with her arms and hugged him back, closing her eyes, inhaling him in, a look of such rapture on her face that Lyndie found herself staring.

It took her back—the sigh factor she hadn't expected, the dreamy sense of something going so right between two people she cared about. It took her back, and also left her just a little unsettled because, once again, here she stood on the outside looking in. Always slightly detached.

Her own fault, but she didn't know how to change it. She seemed to be missing the get-attached gene. "I have a flight," she said.

But they were kissing now, and not just a how-do-you-do kiss either, but a holding each other's faces, eyes open, I'm-going-to-gobble-you-up kiss that did something funny to her knees. "So, uh, I guess we'll talk later."

No answer, just more sucky-face noises. "Really," she said, fingers tapping on the opened front door. "I have to go."

Behind Brody's back, Nina waved a hand at her. *Go.*

Lyndie started to walk out, then stopped. "Don't let Dummy Kitty out, okay? I don't want the coyotes to get him." Why she was worried about such a thing happening, when it would only save her from buying cat food, she had no idea.

But Brody and Nina were really getting into it now, complete with sounds that made her wish for ear plugs. She wondered if Griffin looked like that when he kissed her, with his entire heart in his eyes, if it showed in every touch and whisper.

She'd never looked at him while he'd kissed her, but now she wished she had.

And yet wishes were for someone who harbored regrets, something Lyndie never did. She lived her life for the here and now, forget the past, don't think about the future.

With that in mind, she slammed the door behind her and headed toward her day.

26

Lyndie ended up staying over in Cabo to get some maintenance done on her plane, and no matter how often she tried to call her place, Nina didn't pick up the phone.

She had no way of calling Brody—hell she didn't even have a way to contact Griffin—but she did try Tom again.

And had to leave another message. Odd since it was eight at night now, and typically Tom's bedtime, as he got up with the sun.

On the beach in Cabo, stuck waiting for her plane, watching a bunch of half-naked kids dodge the waves in the dusk, she called Rosa.

"You coming back to me?" Rosa asked, Tallulah yipping at something in the background. "Because I just make some fresh corn tortilla—"

"Have you seen or talked to Tom?"

"He is right here, *querida.* Want me to tell him something for you?"

Lyndie glanced at her watch again. Still eight. "What's he doing there?"

"Now do I ask you such a thing when you have that gorgeous firefighter in *your* bedroom?"

"I—" She broke off, unsure of which had her more baffled, that Rosa had known she and Griffin had slept together, or that Rosa and Tom were possibly doing the same. She pinched the bridge of her nose and took a deep breath. "You know what? Never mind. Just tell him Nina's at my place. Or she was. Tell him not to worry, she's fine, but she has no plans on coming back anytime soon."

"That is what he suspected." Rosa sighed and passed the news to Tom before saying to Lyndie, "Well, the girl deserves a shot at her own dreams. I've been trying to tell him that for years."

She heard Tom grumble at that, and then he must have grabbed the phone because then he was in her ear demanding, "Is she driving you crazy?"

"Nothing I can't handle."

"Look, I know I have no right to ask, but…" He blew out a frustrated breath. "Keep an eye on her, okay?"

Lyndie thought of how she'd left Nina, in the arms of a man who looked as if maybe he wasn't going to ever let her go. "Well—"

"I just worry about her falling for the first man who smiles at her."

Lyndie thought more than likely it would be the other way around, as Brody had seemed pretty smitten himself.

"Because really, for all her bravado, she's naive as hell," Tom said.

Naive wasn't exactly the word Lyndie would have used for the savvy, streetwise Nina, but she kept her tongue. And her head. "Tom, I'm gone more than half the time, and the other half I'm lucky I manage to feed myself—"

"I'll send money."

"I'm not talking about money. I'm talking about responsibility—"

"You're kidding me. Honey, you're the most responsible woman I know."

"Tom—"

"Please." His voice was soft, devastated. "I can't make her come back, this is the best I can do. Just watch out for her."

She let out a breath. "I'll do what I can." She hung up, calling herself every kind of fool for even caring in the first place.

* * *

That caring thing went a whole lot deeper than Lyndie ever intended. When she finally got back to San Diego the next day, she found her place empty except for one little kitty sleeping on the floor, who lifted his head and glared at her when she came in the front door.

"Nina?" She tossed down her keys and glanced at Lucifer. "Well, what's your problem? You have a kitty box. A huge bowl of food. I was only gone overnight—" She broke off because he looked quite different. Instead of his usual dirty white, he looked like he'd just been through a washer with bleach. Upon closer inspection, he had a white powder all over him. "What the hell—"

It took only one glance in the kitchen. "Bingo." Her tin canisters were sprawled out on the counter. The biggest one, which had been filled with flour, now sat sideways and open on the kitchen floor, along with the entire five pounds of white flour she'd never used because she had no idea how to cook. "You just had to play hockey with the canisters. You couldn't lie around the house and be lazy like all the other cats in the universe."

He came toward her, the usually careless little thing very

meticulously not using his front left paw. "Mew." He sat there, with his one little paw lifted, looking beyond pathetic. She picked him up—generating a cloud of flour in the process—and he carefully held his paw out. When she touched it, he hissed, then licked her hand in a gesture that broke her heart. "Oh, you poor little idiot."

She set him down and waited for him to walk correctly, maybe even smirking at her over his shoulder to prove he'd gotten her and gotten her good.

Instead, he limped a few feet away from her and sat.

Another cloud of flour arose.

Then he very gingerly lifted his paw and looked at her.

"*Shit.*" The pain and suffering in those light blue eyes slayed her. "Let me look." But when she sat on the floor next to him and pulled him onto her lap to see, he pulled the paw free and hissed at her again.

"Fine." Hands on her hips, still on the floor, she watched him walk—limp—away. "Suffer. See if I care."

But she did care. She cared so much it hurt. No question, she needed help with this one. Grabbing her phone, she called Sam.

"You're back," he said before she could say anything but his name. "Great. When do you want to fly next, because I have this entire haul that has to go to Alaska, plus two dentists who are willing to freeze their asses off for the rest of their summer vacation and pay heavily for the pleasure."

"I need Griffin Moore's address."

"What?"

"I need—"

"I heard you." He switched from work to playful mode. "You want the address for the guy you're not admitting you have a thing for. The guy you won't kiss and tell about."

"Do you have it in your records or not?"

"I believe I do. So you're really going back for seconds, huh? That sounds extremely unlike you—"

"Just give me the address," she said through her teeth. She pulled Lucifer closer, getting her blue pants covered in flour for her efforts. The little kitten mewled softly and held his paw up, looking so unexpectedly young and pathetic that her throat tightened. "I'm sorry," she whispered to him. Her fault. He was far too young to have been left alone. She should never have taken him home in the first place, clearly she wasn't cut out to have anything or anyone counting on her—

"Here we go…"

She heard the whir of Sam's fingers over his computer keyboard. "By the way, this isn't exactly professional of me," he said. "Giving out an address like this."

Lucifer whined again, and her heart caved in. "Like you've ever worried about your professionalism. Hurry up, Sam."

"Hey, I worry about *you.*" He gave her the address of a place at Ocean Beach. "Are you going to tell me why you sound like you're an inch away from tears?"

Lucifer began licking his paw, and just the sight of him looking so tiny and defenseless tore at her. "I'm not crying." *Liar, liar.* "It's just that Lucifer has something wrong with his paw, and—"

"Lucifer? Who's Lucifer?"

He'd told her no pets years ago.

"Mew."

"You don't have a pet," he said. "*Lyndie?* Tell me you don't have a pet in my guesthouse."

"Uh…"

"Mew," Lucifer said again.

"A cat? Is that a cat? Named…Lucifer?"

"Lucifer is a figment of our joint imagination—"

"Lyndie—"

"Gotta run, Sam. Thank you—" Disconnecting, she surged to her feet, still holding Lucifer. Grabbing her keys, she headed out the door, and drove to the address she'd gotten off Sam.

Lucifer did not enjoy his drive. He curled up on the passenger seat of her truck, loudly letting her know how much he hated every minute of the adventure. When he wasn't caterwauling, he licked his paw, looking so miserable, Lyndie felt even worse. By the time she pulled up to Griffin's house, she was a wreck.

His place was a small light blue house with white trim, sitting on the bluffs overlooking the beach. The shutters were dark blue and open to the afternoon sun. So was the front door.

It seemed almost overwhelmingly inviting.

Grabbing the kitten, who'd gone silent the moment she turned off the engine, she headed up the walk. "It'll be okay," she promised rashly. "He'll fix you right up."

She hoped. She knocked, and from within, she heard bare feet padding their way toward her.

* * *

Griffin had just gotten back from his interview with Jake Rawlins of the San Diego Fire Department when the knock came. The city work would be a world away from the wildland firefighting in his past, but that was the appeal. He needed a change.

Only the interview hadn't gone as planned, which was his own fault. He'd opened the meeting by admitting he felt he should have been able to prevent the twelve deaths in Idaho. Stupid, but true.

Now he'd planned on stripping down and standing in the

shower until the day was nothing but a distant memory of bad judgment.

What the hell had come over him, thinking he could do it all over again? That he could actually start over at a new place, with a new crew, day in and day out, season after season, putting it all on the line, never knowing if *this* would be the fire that finally destroyed him?

Again.

At least he'd come to his senses and realized it. As he walked to the front door instead of stripping, he glanced at his red bag filled with his gear, shoved in a corner, and a pang of longing welled through him.

So he'd suffered some losses—big ones. He was still here, wasn't he? Here and capable. He'd proven that in Mexico two weeks running. So why did he have to give it all up? He rubbed his eyes, tired of himself, tired of thinking too much, of the indecision...

And now someone had come to his door.

Brody was the only one who knew where to find him, and that worked out just fine, because Griffin was spoiling for a fight and he knew his brother would give it to him.

Only it wasn't his brother standing on his doorstep at all, but Lyndie, cradling Lucifer against her chest. The soft, short layers of her fiery hair were everywhere, and he might have hauled her in close and kissed them both to oblivion, if it hadn't been for the look of pure misery on her face.

"He's hurt, he's limping—" She gulped in some air, and hugged the kitten tighter. "I left him at home all alone."

"Cats are fine alone."

"Not this stupid cat. He took himself for a joy run along my counters and I think he fell off. I think he broke his paw. I think—"

Her voice cracked, and he looked from Lucifer back to Lyndie, shocked to his toes to see her green eyes shimmering with unshed tears. "Oh, baby," he breathed.

"I know. I'm a terrible mom. I—"

"Shh." He took Lucifer from her arms and settled him against his chest. Then he looked the cat over, frowning at the paw, which appeared unusually swollen. "I'm afraid we'll need an X-ray for this."

"An X-ray?"

"Come on." He took her hand and led her back to her truck, opening the passenger side for her. He put Lucifer on her lap.

He'd walked back around, had started the engine and pulled onto the street before he glanced at her. "You're really shaken if you're letting me drive without an argument."

"I never..." She let out a mirthless laugh. "I never even thought about a vet." She stared at him. "I deal with emergencies for a living, and I got so panicked over the damn cat that isn't even mine...I just came to you thinking you could fix it. The stupid cat *likes* you. I just drove straight over here without thinking—"

"I'm glad you came to me."

She let out a sound that managed to perfectly convey her confusion. "I'm glad someone's glad."

The vet clinic was only down the road. When he pulled in and parked, he leaned toward her. "You came because some part of you wanted to see me."

Her eyes never left his. "Maybe."

His fingers stroked her jaw, sank into her wild hair. God, what he'd give for another night with her. "I know how much it costs you to ask for help." He put his mouth to the spot beneath her ear, enjoying her quick and shallow breathing. "So I won't ask you to admit it out loud."

She laughed, but it backed up in her throat when he cupped her face and looked into her eyes. "And when we're done here," he said, "we talk. About what's going on in your head, between us, everything."

"Oh." She tried to pull back. "Well, I don't—"

"It's time," he said. "Past time."

* * *

They went inside the clinic. In the waiting room, Lyndie paced while Griffin held the unhappy Lucifer.

"I should have come alone," she muttered. "You probably had something much more important to do—"

"Nope." He smiled without much mirth. "I'd already blown the interview with the SDFD today, and was pretty much just feeling stupid when you came knocking."

"SDFD? You mean the San Diego Fire Department?" She looked so thrilled for him it hurt to look at her. "You're ready?"

He lifted a shoulder.

"Oh, Griffin. I'm so glad. I didn't think—I mean, you still haven't really opened up about Idaho—"

"And I'm still not."

She was still for a long moment. "I hope it works out for you."

"Yeah." He sighed at both the memory of the interview, and at the surprising compassion and deeply ingrained memories Jake had burning in his eyes as well.

Respecting his silence, which he appreciated more than she could know, Lyndie began pacing again.

"I don't know how I came to this," she muttered to herself a few minutes later. "So many strings: San Puebla, Nina, this damn cat." She stopped and looked at him. *"You."*

"Is this a list of things you're attached to," he wondered, "or pissed at?"

She rolled her eyes and started pacing again.

"Maybe you're just a big softie."

She stopped short. "That's the biggest insult anyone's ever given me."

He tossed his head back and laughed. "I meant that as a compliment. Stop wearing out your shoes and come over here."

"Fine." She plopped down into the seat next to him.

He reached out for her hand, just lifting a brow when she smacked his away. "You know, I just realized something about you. Something quite fascinating, really."

"Yeah? What's that?"

"You really do think you're all alone, that all these so-called strings on your heart are only one way."

"Oh, no, Ace," she said on a laugh. "Don't turn this around. This was about *you*." She tapped him lightly on the nose with her finger.

"It always is when you don't want it to be about *you*." He tapped her back. "This is going to terrify you, I'm sure, but we're all just as attached to you as you are to us."

Her gaze flew to his, and he could see the uncertainty, the heartbreaking need to believe in what he'd just said. Cupping her face again, he leaned in and put his forehead to hers. "What do you think about that?"

"That it's nothing a good pair of scissors wouldn't take care of. Just one snip—" She made the motion of cutting with her hand. "And presto, we're all set free."

"And what would the fun be in that?"

"Fun? *Fun?*" She got to her feet again and tossed her hands in the air. "You think all this yo-yoing on the heartstrings is *fun*? You've been through hell and back, and you can still say that?"

Hell, yes, he opened his mouth to say, but the vet poked her head out and smiled. "Lucifer?"

27

Driving out of San Diego Junior College, Brody reached over and squeezed Nina's hand. The green hills around them were in bloom with flowers of all shapes and hues, bobbing gently in the afternoon ocean breeze, and he felt damn good. "Happy?"

"Beyond." She looked down at the receipt for tuition paid, tuition that was much cheaper than at the university. "Now we just need to find that address they gave me, for the inexpensive housing."

"About that..." He brought her hand to his mouth and kissed her palm, eyeing her over their joined fingers, wondering how she would take this. "I was thinking...

"Ooh, thinking were you?" she teased, and leaning in, kissed him on the throat. "I like it when you do that."

"There's a house for rent right near where my brother—"

"Yes, but you know I cannot afford a house."

"—which is extremely close to the university—"

"—where I am not going yet," Nina pointed out.

"No." He took a deep breath. Smiled. "But I am."

"What?" She stared at him. "Brody—"

"I have my degree, but I need to get certified. For teaching. I could do that at the university. Then I could get a teaching job, too."

"Pull over."

Dread filled him. He'd screwed up, and now she wanted to run away. "Nina—"

"*Pull over*. Please," she added, and when he did, she gripped his face, looking deeply into his eyes. "What is this?"

"I don't like worrying," he said. "About Griffin, about you—"

"I never asked you to worry about me."

"I know that." He kissed her to make sure she would be quiet. "I don't like worrying," he repeated, "and I'm not crazy about the ridiculous yearning I have to get off my ass and teach. But it's there."

"You really want to teach?"

"I always meant to. At first because I thought it would be easy, but later because I liked people. It just turns out I liked being lazy more. But now…my family is looking at me as if I'm all grown up, and you know what?" He shook his head, then grinned. He kissed her again simply because he could. "I like that they're looking at me that way. I like it a lot. I want to be that man everyone thinks I am. I want to be that man you seem to, by some miracle, have fallen for…the man who's fallen for you in return."

Her eyes narrowed. The crystal bracelets on her wrist jangled when she pointed a finger at him. "If you are messing with me, I'll—"

He caught her finger. "You think I'm *messing* with you?"

"Yes. You're…how do you say…*sweet-talking*. So I'll sleep with you." Looking baffled, she shook her head. "But I've slept with you, and I liked it. I know I will want to sleep with you again, so—"

"I am not…*sweet-talking* you," he said, appalled.

"So you've never sweet-talked a woman before?"

"No. *Yes*. But that was before you," he said, more confused than ever. "Look, I know it sounds crazy, but I feel as if I've known you forever. I just want to be with you, Nina."

She was still eyeing him with a little mistrust as traffic whizzed by them. "If that's true, you'd have no problem coming home with me to see my father, to explain to him what I've done about getting set up here to live."

"Yes," he said so quickly she blinked.

"Really? You'll…face Tom?"

"Absolutely." He kissed her, then pulled back. "I'm just so glad you're here, Nina. With me. I'm so sorry I let you come here alone. You'll never have to be alone again."

"That's quite a promise."

"It's one I can keep."

Her smile went soft and dreamy and genuine, and his heart, already snagged, tipped right on its side.

* * *

Two hours after finding Lucifer with a coating of flour all over him, Lyndie was back at her little guest-house in Del Mar, opening the door for the man carrying her kitten with the splinted paw. "Here, I'll take him."

But when she reached out her hands for the sleepy kitten—who'd made a huge pest out of himself at the hospital, requiring drugs before he'd let the doctor wrap his foreleg—Griffin Moore, wildland firefighter, onetime hotshot and all-around shockingly sexy man eyed her with amusement as he shook his head. "No way," he said. "If I give you this cat now, you'll shut the door on me."

"Well, I do have a broken kitten to look after."

"Lucifer is going to sleep." Gently he nudged Lyndie into her own front door, kicked it shut behind them, and set the cat down on her couch.

Then he turned to Lyndie. "So. You asked me about being ready for this."

She stared at him, then let out a little laugh. "You don't seem to ever dance into a subject with subtleness do you?"

"I'm not much of a dancer." He looked into her eyes. "I didn't think I was ready for this, not after losing so much."

An arrow to her heart. "I know. Look…you've loved before. You've *been* loved before."

"Yes."

"Yeah. But…I haven't. I don't know if I even *can*."

"It's not something you think about or decide." He reached for her hand before she could move out of reach, which she most definitely would have done. "You just…do."

Right. But she just didn't seem to have the ability to just…do.

"But…" He let out a long, slow breath. "I'm no longer that person I was."

"Because…you blame yourself for what happened. Even though it wasn't your fault."

"Yeah. Because being alive when they aren't messes with my head."

She lifted a hand to his jaw. "It would mess with anyone's head, Griffin."

"But for how long?" He squeezed her fingers. "Christ, for how long?"

Her heart twisted. "I don't know." They gravitated a little closer, so that their bodies lightly brushed together. "Do you still…miss them so terribly?"

"It's different now…" He rubbed his chest. "The ache is still there, it's just…softer now."

"I'm not good friend material."

"Now there you're flat-out wrong." His eyes smiled. "But it's not a friend I want tonight."

"You still don't want to talk about what happened?"

"No."

"No?" she whispered.

"I want you. More than my next breath."

"For tonight?"

"For tonight."

Good. For tonight was right up her alley.

He put his hands on her. "All night."

"You have quite the habit of doing that. Putting your hands on me."

"Yeah." He slid them from her arms down to her hands, which he squeezed before going even lower. Gripping her hips, he tugged her off balance so that she fell against him, then his hands slid around to cup a cheek in each palm.

She'd wanted this, she'd wanted him for tonight. But suddenly, with the force of a blow, she realized something fairly frightening.

She also wanted him for more. She wanted him to talk to her, to want her to be his friend. "Griffin—"

He stopped whatever she might have said with his mouth, inhaling her soft little moan, his hands sliding into her hair, holding her head against his. Then he pulled back to smile into her eyes. "Love that dreamy look you get on your face when I kiss you."

"Yeah." But she was dreamy with thinking how many nights they could have like this. If he only wanted. "Griffin—"

She broke off with another moan when he began a series of wet hot kisses over her jaw, down her throat, along her collarbone…

Her top fell away from her body, and she let out a strangled laugh. "Honestly, I—"

He cupped her breasts, rasped his thumbs over her already swollen nipples. "Honestly…what?" A sound of pleasure escaped him at the feel of her. "You feel good."

Her own eyes were crossed it felt so good. Then he bent his head, skimming her bra out of his way to suck her into his mouth.

Her knees wobbled but that didn't seem to be a problem since he just used his strength to hold both of them up. "I'm trying to tell you something here, Ace."

The sound of her zipper in the room seemed to echo in her head. Her trousers slid down her legs, leaving her in nothing but a dark blue cotton thong.

"Lyndie, God." His fingers traced the line of cotton down her backside, dallying there, making her very glad he was so incredibly strong that he could hold them both upright.

"You're wet," he murmured with husky delight, dipping into that wetness. "Are you wet for me, Lyndie?"

"I—" She bit her lip to keep from gasping as he found her happy little party spot, leaving her only a whisper away from begging. "Yes." And even before he pressed his body close, then closer, she was lost, and far before he scooped her up and took her into her bedroom, setting her down on the mattress and covering her body with his, taking her to heights only he could, she was found.

Simple and terrifying as that.

* * *

The next morning, Lyndie woke up and found herself tangled up with Griffin's bare, extremely warm, extremely hard body. She was spooned up against his chest, his arms around her. He had one large palm supporting her breast, a thigh between hers and her butt up against a most impressive erection.

The memories of last night filled her, and her insides quivered, which made no sense at all. By now he should have been long gone out of her bed, because no matter what he'd shown her last night, they'd both agreed, this had been a one-night thing.

Even if, secretly, she'd wanted to welsh on that agreement. But in the light of day, she knew the truth. Lyndie Anderson didn't do anything but love 'em and leave 'em.

But she still wanted to stretch and purr like the damn kitten sitting on the floor of her room staring at her right this very minute. "Shh," she whispered, acknowledging Lucifer had actually behaved himself quite nicely last night, leaving Griffin and her alone for the most part—except for that one time when he'd pounced her curling toes at a most inopportune moment.

He didn't seem to be bothered by his broken paw or the wrappings at all, which had been good, because it had allowed her to concentrate on other things.

Such as Griffin's hot bod. She wanted to turn over and devour him one inch at a time. She wanted him to devour her back.

In his sleep, he nuzzled at her neck…oh, yeah, she could get used to that. Damn it, there were those strings again, on the heart she hadn't ever expected to open up and want to share. Uncomfortable, she shifted, and his arms tightened on her slightly, then relaxed with his even breathing in her ear.

Stupid, stupid, she thought, fighting the odd urge to turn over and not just gobble him up, but to hold on tight, to hug him. No. This wasn't happening. She absolutely wasn't going to fall for this man, no matter the bittersweet ache right between her breasts, suspiciously near the organ thumping hard at the thought.

Too much, too fast, and to avoid giving in to temptation, she slipped out of the bed, stalking naked through her living room to her kitchen for sustenance—a walk that took all of three seconds in the small guesthouse.

Last night, the two of them had riffled through her kitchen, starving, having burned all their energy up in her bed. And her shower. And on the floor.

In the hallway on their way to the kitchen.

She nearly dove back into bed with the intent to beg him to start all over again, but thankfully, her pager, left on the counter, went off, vibrating across the tile, reminding her she had a life that didn't include time for a man.

Ridiculously relieved for the reminder, she read Sam's text message to get her "sweet little behind" in gear for a flight to Mexico.

Flight…or Griffin?

Flight, she decided, grabbing up the clothes Griffin had stripped her out of the night before.

Because when push came to shove, flying was much safer than Griffin.

* * *

Griffin rolled over, arms already reaching out for Lyndie, not really surprised to find her side of the bed cold. The woman had probably woken up in his arms in full-blown panic mode and run for the hills, or wherever she took off to in order to be alone. He could understand the sentiment. He felt a little panicked himself.

He got out of bed, wishing he had her back here, warm and

soft and naked, but showered instead. Lucifer was gone, too, so he drove back to his own beach house, wondering why it felt that so much was out of his reach.

There he found one thing that *was* within his reach if he wanted. Jake Rawlins had called. The SDFD appreciated his honesty, they liked his resume. Jake wanted Griffin's experience, all of it.

He wanted him to come to work.

Talk about panic.

28

The walk to Lyndie's plane was punctuated by Lucifer's unhappy mews from the carrier he hated with all his being. The morning was cool and foggy, and her footsteps slapped into the puddles of rain that had fallen the night before as she walked the tarmac.

At her plane, she looked around. Sam had promised to have some rich guy waiting for her with some big cargo of supplies that he'd donated to San Puebla for the ranchers who'd lost everything.

Instead, she found Brody and… "Nina?"

Nina, looking quite American in her hip-hugging cargo pants, tank top, and silver hoops, smiled. "No other."

Brody bent and put his face to Lucifer's. "Hey, kitty." He looked up at Lyndie. "Thanks for giving us a ride back to San Puebla. You're going to come in handy, as apparently you're the only one who can coax Tom out of a bad mood. And believe me, he's in a bad mood."

Lyndie shook her head. "No go. I'm supposed to be picking up some rich kid who's spending his daddy's money. There's some big cargo of supplies for…" She trailed off when Brody gestured behind him, to a pallet of boxes being loaded into her plane by a couple of airport staff.

She blinked. "*You're* the rich kid?"

"'Fraid so. We needed a ride."

"You ever hear of *public* airlines?"

He smiled his charming smile and Lyndie vowed it wouldn't work on her.

"We could have gone that route," he said, waiting while a loud jet zoomed past them before speaking again. "But it'd have taken forever and a day. Travel through Mexico, especially that region as you know, isn't always timely. Plus, you're the best there is." He smiled again.

"The best in buttering up Tom, you mean." But she sighed. All those supplies he'd brought would go a long way…"Wait. You and Griffin are brothers…"

"Yes. Still."

Her frown deepened. "But I didn't know you were…"

"Rich?"

"Well…yeah."

"Just the parentals. Technically, I'm poor as poor can be, though for years I did love to pretend to be wealthy. I went through a good chunk of Dad's money in those years." He sighed in fond memory.

Nina grinned at him, her dark eyes sparkling with affection. "But now…"

"Now I'm reformed. The love of a good woman will do that for a man."

Lyndie divided a shocked glance between them. Another plane buzzed them. "*Love?*" Nina's dreamy smile was answer enough. "Oh, man."

"Love," Brody confirmed, as if it wasn't all over his face. "Now, of course, I'm going to have to earn my money the old-fashioned way."

Lyndie shook her head. "So you really got your parents to donate a bunch of stuff just so I'd fly you guys home?"

"Home." Brody tried the word out on his tongue and nodded. "Yeah, I could happily call Mexico home. But nope, we're just visiting. For now, anyway. I called Sam and tried to buy you as a pilot and he said no go unless I contributed to Hope International in some way…so a quick call to Dad, and voila…here we are."

"Okay." Lyndie moved toward her plane. "Let's just do this."

Nina caught up with her and grabbed her wrist. "Hold up."

"Why?"

"I just wanted to say thanks."

"For…?"

"For everything."

"I didn't do anything but give you shit." But she stopped. "I'd ask you if you're happy but it's all over your face."

"Are you happy for me?"

A million quick glib replies crossed Lyndie's tongue, but she found herself letting out another sigh, and, as she searched Nina's face, a genuine smile as well. "I'll admit to being jealous of that grin you're wearing."

"Really?" Nina looked speculative. "You had one on just like it when you first got here."

Lyndie opened her mouth, then thought about last night, and promptly shut it again.

"Uh huh." Now Nina looked downright amused. "You see any sexy firefighters lately? Maybe sleep with one?"

"This is about you." Lyndie moved away with Lucifer in tow.

"And let's not forget, you want me on your side. At least until I back you up with your father."

"Avoidance…" Nina *tsked*. "Not good for the soul."

What was going to be good for her soul was getting the hell out of here, at least until she could think straight about last night.

And it had been just one night, just more scratching of that itch they always generated in each other.

And if she repeated it to herself often enough, maybe she'd start to believe it.

"Mew."

"Yeah." She looked down at the kitten that had been nothing but a burden and, oddly enough, felt a warmth spread inside her. The damn thing was just so cute. She tried to summon up irritation at all the expense and hassle he'd created, and instead had only that silly warmth she couldn't really explain. "Well, if I have to have someone else in my life other than myself," she murmured. "I suppose it could be you."

She'd have sworn Lucifer smiled at that but then she heard Brody whoop out a hello to someone, and that warmth that had just spread throughout her insides froze up solid.

Griffin. She could hear the low murmur of his voice as he greeted both Nina and Brody.

He'd come. He'd come after her.

She stared at her plane while her thoughts raced. What did that mean? Was it possible he could be having some of these same crazy thoughts she was, that maybe, just maybe, there could be something much more serious going on here than just mind-blowing sex? Since she knew it was all over her face, she kept her back to him as she moved inside her plane to set Lucifer down—

"Hey."

Slowly she turned around and looked into the same eyes she'd looked into while she'd had an earth-shattering orgasm only a few hours before. "Hey yourself." Her heart leapt into her throat, pitifully ready to leap out onto her sleeve with the slightest provocation.

"You left without a word this morning," he said.

"Sam paged me, and you were sleeping so peacefully..."

"Thanks to you," he said with a sexy little smile.

Because all that brilliant wattage made her want to jump his bones again, she looked away. "You didn't have to come all the way out here—"

"Yeah, I did."

"That's awfully sweet, but it's early, and I'll be back—"

"No, you don't understand. I *had* to come out here."

Okay, that had a stupid grin splitting her face. God, it hurt to have fallen for him, but it felt so incredibly good at the same time—

"Brody called me. He said I had to get—and I am quoting here—'my ass in gear and haul on down here' if I wanted a ride to San Puebla."

She went still. What did this have to do with him coming here for her? "Why would you need a ride to San Puebla?"

Griffin shrugged. "He was pretty mum on that, just insisting I be here or else. Said he'd clear it all up for me once we got there."

So he hadn't come for her at all. Which led her to the next, and more powerful realization, one she'd already known but hadn't faced—she'd fallen.

He hadn't.

He still tortured himself over the deaths of his crew and likely always would. Well. She'd wanted to know what love felt like, and now she knew. She just never imagined it would be like this. So...devastating.

He reached for her hand.

Oh, no. He couldn't touch her, not now. "Outta my way, Ace," she said, pulling back. "We're running late." Forcing herself to turn away, she started barking orders. When she had everyone hopping, she stared sightlessly at Lucifer. "I still have you," she whispered. He would be enough. He would.

"Hey." Griffin came up behind her, gently squeezed her waist. "You okay?"

She stiffened. "Why wouldn't I be?"

"I don't know, maybe because you won't look at me."

Oh, that. Pasting an inscrutable look on her face, she turned and looked right at him, giving him a smile, only called such because she bared her teeth.

His gaze held hers for a long, uncomfortable moment during which she had the oddest feeling that he could see everything she thought, everything in her heart, and she began to panic.

"Lyndie," he said softly, with enough regret that she backed up, holding up a hand.

"No, don't," she said. "Don't you dare—"

"Wait." He grabbed her, held her still. "I have to, we have to." He cupped her face with his free hand, looking tortured. "God, Lyndie. I'm an idiot. You thought I came here this morning for you—"

"I didn't think anything."

"Stop it." He touched his forehead to hers. "Christ. I'm so sorry. I'm…I'm a little slow on the uptake when it comes to matters of the heart these days. I'm just taking this land of the living thing one day at a time, and—"

"I know." She closed her eyes. "I *know*—"

"I mean, there's no doubt I *am* living again. And…and enjoying it very much. Last night—"

The guilt and misery on his face killed her. "It's okay, it's okay that you are, Griffin."

"I look at you," he said in a rough voice, "And I see how you forge ahead with life no matter what it hands to you, and it gets to me. You get to me."

"But…?" She took a step back, waiting for the shoe to fall. "Because I definitely hear a big 'but' at the end of that sentence."

"But…" His eyes were sad, so sad she felt her own sting. "I'm not as brave as you—" He smiled at her choked laugh. "I'm not."

"Are you kidding me? You put your life on the line every day on your job and you're not brave?"

"Not when it comes to matters of the heart," he said very seriously, and kissed her so softly, with so much heart, her own cracked. "I thought I could do it, I thought I could give it all, over and over again, but it turns out I can't."

"I understand that about you."

"You shouldn't." He dropped his hands and stepped back from her. "You shouldn't."

"But…" But nothing, because he turned away. She let her voice trail off, because what was she going to do, beg him? Hell, no.

Okay, hell, yes. "So that's it?" she asked his broad shoulders. "We share what, a few laughs. A bed. And maybe I share some of myself, my past, because you coax me to do so, damn it…but you don't have to do the same?"

He went still, then faced her. "I never meant to hurt you."

She knew that, but it wasn't enough. Not anymore.

Brody and Nina got on board then, and in a few minutes they were in the air, flying toward Mexico, toward the village where it had all begun. Fitting, then, Lyndie thought, keeping her chin high, her eyes clear, that this is where it would all end.

Because after this, she was done. With Griffin, she'd put it all out there in a way she never had before. She'd fallen, and fallen hard, and in the process, she'd also gotten burned, but it was done and she couldn't change it.

The day was a glorious one, and she concentrated on that, on the pure joy of the flying, on the unmistakable love flowing between Nina and Brody, and for long moments at a time, it was enough.

They came to the Barranca del Cobre and the Sierra Tarahumara. Such incredible beauty. The canyons, the peaks, the immense, remote wilderness of it all.

And then they came to the burned acreage. The smoke had cleared, and they all pressed close to the window, looking down in somber silence at the loss. Blackened landscape. Ghostlike shadows that once used to be trees. Five destroyed ranches.

And then San Puebla, still intact. Safe, because of their efforts.

That lifted their spirits back up. Brody jokingly carried Nina off the plane. Lyndie sat up front figuring Griffin would follow them, but instead he held back.

Well, she didn't plan to wait for him. She jumped down ahead of him, and would have walked away if he hadn't grabbed her hand.

Her back still to him, she stilled. "I really have to—"

"The fire in Idaho."

She closed her eyes at the rough angst in his voice. She knew, she understood what it cost him to want to talk about it, but damn it, she couldn't help it if she wished things could have been different—

"You've asked me about it, and I've shut you out. I shut you out even when I wouldn't let you do the same—"

"It doesn't matter—"

"It matters," he said grimly. "It matters a lot. I want to tell you about it. I want you to know it all. Please…let me tell you."

"Why?" She made herself look at him. "Why now?"

"Because I need to."

Everything within her softened, and she sighed, reaching for his hand.

"I wasn't the supervisor for the crew that was lost." He stared at their joined hands. "I should have been, I wanted to be, but there was a scheduling mess up, and sometimes, especially within the fire community, there's no arguing with the powers that be."

"I know what happened wasn't your fault."

"Yeah." He rubbed his eyes. "We'd been there for three weeks. Out in the middle of nowhere, with tents and army rations. We were exhausted. Beyond exhausted."

"Sounds like a nightmare."

"It was. I was supervising a crew on the other side of a firebreak from Greg and the others. My gut told me the weather was changing, my weather kit confirmed it. But when I radioed headquarters, they told us to hold our positions. They…demanded it."

She couldn't imagine the conditions he'd faced. "Why?"

"Because we'd been out there too long already. By all reports, we were close to containment and they were feeling federal pressure to wrap it up." He let out a long breath. "So I followed directions like a blind soldier, despite my screaming instincts. And the cold front blew in, the winds whipped through the canyons and caught us with no way out."

Lyndie's heart wrenched at the misery on his face. "You couldn't have done anything differently. Not with the pressures you were all under."

"If the scheduling switch hadn't happened, if the weather report about the cold front had made its way down the line, if I'd listened to myself, if we hadn't all been so exhausted—" He lifted a shoulder. "Lots of what-ifs, but I'm tired of thinking about them, dreaming about them. Mistakes were made, people died. It was…a tragedy, a terrible tragedy. But I'm learning to live with it. Even, apparently, learning to talk about it." He offered her the saddest, most heart-wrenching smile she'd ever seen. "I just wanted you to know."

"Hey! Over here…" Brody, standing near Tom and his waiting Jeep, waved them over. There was no mistaking the tension there, or the desperate plea in his face.

Lyndie looked at Griffin. "He needs you."

"Yeah." He looked so torn, Lyndie decided to make it easy for him. She walked to the Jeep.

And she was fine. She was fine with the fact Griffin had tortured himself when it hadn't been his fault. She was fine with the fact that after this trip, she'd never see him again. She was fine with all of it, and she put the cool, even smile on her face to prove it.

But on the inside, the mourning began.

Tom had grabbed Nina in a big, fat bear hug. When he finally let her go, he turned and nodded to Griffin, who had moved to stand next to his brother. Tom also smiled very kindly at Lyndie, and because she felt so fragile, it had her own frosty smile slipping for a moment. "Thanks for bringing her back to me," he said.

"Actually, I didn't even know that's what I was doing." She put a hand on Brody's shoulder. "Brody arranged for all this; the flight, the supplies, everything, so maybe you should be thanking him."

Tom looked at Brody. "Oh, I'll get to him."

Brody stood up a little straighter and offered a weak smile.

"Papa," Nina warned. "Don't—"

Tom held up his head at his daughter, silencing her, but he never took his eyes off Brody. "I've got a shotgun in my Jeep, boy. And I'm licensed to use it."

A little pale, Brody nodded.

"Tom." Griffin took a step forward, but Tom pointed at him, halting him. "I like you, son. I like you a lot, but don't even think about interrupting me right now when I'm on a roll. I don't get on a roll very often. Hell, I can't even remember the last time I had to muster up a good temper, but I'm mustered up at the moment. Mustered up enough to get us a shotgun wedding, right here, right now."

Despite Tom's standing nearly in his face, Brody reached for Nina's hand. "A shotgun wedding…" He shot her a sweet smile. "Sounds good. Assuming you give me enough time to get my parents here."

"I didn't ask you," Tom said. "I'm telling you."

"Yes, but seeing as we're all adults, I'm pretending you did. In any case, the joke is on you, because nothing, *nothing,* would make my life more complete than to be married to your daughter. I was going to ask her this weekend anyway."

Nina gasped, covering her mouth with her hands, her sparkling eyes on Brody.

He smiled softly at her. "It would put meaning to my life to be a part of yours." He brought her fingers to his mouth, watching her with warm eyes over their joined hands. "Maybe I came here to save my brother, but instead, I saved myself. This place saved me. *You* saved me," he said to her, his eyes brilliant and suspiciously shiny.

"Oh, Brody. *Te quiero.* I love you." Nina threw her arms around his neck. "I love you so much."

"Is that a yes, you'll marry me? You'll be my wife, my friend, my lover...for the rest of our lives?"

Nina's smile was slow and beautiful. "Yes, *querido*. Yes, to all of it." Then she planted a long kiss on him.

After a moment, Brody pulled back, holding her face as if they were all alone. "I love it here," he said. "Your family is here." He never so much as glanced at Tom, who looked as if a good wind could blow him over. "I know you want to get out and see the world. And I look forward to that, too, but I can also see spending time, lots of time, right here."

Nina looked around her, at the magnificent mountains, at the beauty and serenity unrivaled to just about anywhere else in the world, and then at Tom, and slowly nodded. "Maybe we could come here after college, during the summers. Do some extra teaching."

"I'd like that," Brody said.

Tom just kept staring at them as if they'd lost their minds. "You mean...you *want* to get married?"

"Yes," Nina said, her wet eyes still on Brody's. "Oh, most definitely yes. Let's call your parents."

Brody swung her around, while the two of them shared another extremely private kiss.

Tom looked so utterly flabbergasted, Lyndie took pity on him, and slung her arm around his shoulders. "Poor baby. You didn't expect them to *want* to get hitched, did you?"

"Shit."

Smiling, she leaned in and kissed him on the cheek. "Well, you've done it now, Papa. You're going to have to be happy for them."

"*Shit,*" he repeated brilliantly.

Lyndie herself couldn't quite understand why Nina felt she

needed the little scrap of paper that would proclaim her another man's wife, but if Nina wanted it that badly, then she should have it. "It's going to be okay, Tom. They're good together."

Nina danced in a circle and grinned. "We'll do it here, soon as we can get Brody's parents here." She turned to Lyndie, and kissed both her cheeks. "And you, you'll be my maid of honor."

"Now, wait a minute—"

"You'll have to smile, though." Nina cocked a brow. "You do have a smile, right?"

"I don't think—"

"Good," Nina said. "Stick with that. No thinking. Just doing." She clapped her hands. "And we have lots of doing. Let's go get started!"

Lyndie got into the Jeep with Nina, watching Griffin hug Brody before they got in as well, the two of their sun-kissed heads close together, their faces creased in matching smiles. Two brothers so alike, and yet so different. Brody's smile came easily, carefree. His eyes held nothing but love and joy.

Griffin…his smile didn't quite meet his eyes, because swimming there was still so much emotion that it took her breath. She knew this because he turned right then and looked at her, as if maybe he couldn't stop thinking about her.

She knew the feeling. It pissed her off.

They wound their way toward San Puebla, over the railroad tracks, the rickety bridge, down the centuries-old road. Tom drove, with Griffin next to him. Lyndie was in the backseat with the two lovebirds, both of them chomping at the bit.

She had no idea why they had to get married right now, right this very moment. She'd have much preferred to see Tom let his daughter have the life she wanted. Then she'd have given out the cargo of supplies Brody had provided and gone back to the States.

Brody and Nina could live in sinful bliss as long as they wanted, with no promise, or burden, of the actual marriage.

Something she'd hoped to do herself. Instead, she held Lucifer's carrying case, who was extremely unhappy in her lap with the wind whipping around them. Unhappiness she understood, as it had rooted within her as well.

Historically, when she was unhappy, she made sure she was alone to lick her wounds, and she had plenty to lick. But there would be no alone time for her now.

It didn't help that she had a perfect view of the man who'd caused her wounds. Griffin's broad shoulders stretched the material of his T-shirt, his fawn colored hair blowing wild around his head. Then suddenly he stiffened, and when she saw why, she did, too.

A long, narrow plume of smoke rose over the closest peak in front of them.

29

A flare-up. The last thing on earth Griffin wanted to deal with.

Nope, scratch that. The *last* thing he wanted to deal with was the woman standing behind him, arms crossed, face unreadable, eyes filled with misery as she tapped her foot and pretended not to give a shit that he'd broken her heart.

Something he'd never intended to do.

He stood on a rock outcropping, with the river rushing at his feet and the blackened mountainside behind him. About a quarter of a mile below was where they'd left the Jeep, after leaving Tom and Nina off in town to get together whatever crew and tools they could.

Brody had remained at the top of the trail to wait for help to arrive.

Not Lyndie. There was no waiting anywhere for Lyndie. The stubborn woman had insisted on staying with him.

To the bitter end.

They easily found the fire, at the base of the canyon where the blow up had occurred the week before. He figured the embers had been smoldering for days, hidden from view by the rock and fresh vegetation lining the river. The last crew might have called it quits too early, or hadn't checked all the northern perimeters first. Or maybe there'd been lightning.

"Not too bad yet," Lyndie said. "Right?"

He estimated twenty acres. "Not if we get right on it."

"You've got the river as one firebreak," she said. "And the burned hillside behind it as another." She smiled at his raised brow. "I learned a lot in the past few weeks."

"Probably more than you ever wanted to."

Her smile faded, her eyes filled with such sadness. "Yeah."

Ah, hell. "Lyndie—"

"Just…fix this," she said. "Get this fire taken care of once and for all, and we'll go and smile for Brody and Nina, and then we can get the hell out of Dodge. Okay?" Without waiting for an answer, she turned on her heel and walked away, down the river, back toward the direction Brody had gone.

"No, not okay," he said, but no one answered.

* * *

In two hours they had fifteen men along the back side of the flare-up, standing along a trail that they intended to use as a firebreak. They had their backs to a wall of weary, thirsty conifers, ripe for exploding if they didn't stop the fire. Far above them was sheer rock, far below the already burned acreage…but in between was a nightmare playing out that couldn't be stopped.

Griffin wore the same clothes he'd flown here in, which were the jeans and T-shirt he'd pulled on this morning after finding Lyndie had left him alone in her bed. Tom had come up with gloves for him, and a long-sleeve button-up to protect his arms.

It had to be nearly a hundred degrees, with no humidity. The air crackled. As always, the fire created its own weather, and Griffin had never in his life seen a flare-up get so hot so fast. As the afternoon turned to early evening, and then dusk, even the trees and growth with roots in the river were bursting into flame, shooting fire straight up into the sky, where balls of it seemed to leap from treetop to treetop. A crown fire fueled by wind, and now it didn't even need the ground vegetation to spur it on.

Looking around, he knew. This thing had become bigger than them. The narrow, low running river wasn't going to provide protection, not with the flames as hot as they were.

Which left them unexpectedly trapped. They couldn't go down, the vicious walls of flame held them off. The 35 mph gusts shoved the fire ahead of them as well, reducing the angle between the flames and the fuel on the ground, resulting in an overwhelming inferno. It raced ahead of them, up the hill, blocking their road out.

Griffin's mind raced with their options, which were few, when suddenly a two-hundred-foot pine tree fell, crashing down, shuddering the ground around them like an earthquake.

"Griffin?" Lyndie gripped his arm, pale despite the scorching heat.

It was automatic to reach for her. "Scared?"

"Nah." She looked around her, at the trees above them crackling with the dry air and flames, at the way they were becoming circled in. The hot air whipped her hair around her face and she tightened her hand on his.

With an earsplitting crack, a tree just to their right exploded.

Lyndie jerked. "Okay, I'm officially scared now."

The flames were licking at their heels, and he knew it would be only a matter of time before it leapt over the river to where they stood. It'd happened so damn fast he still couldn't believe it. "The burned area to the east," he told Lyndie.

She shouted the directions over the bruising wind and crackling fire. "Let's go. *Vamanos!*"

In a single-file line, they made their way along the river back to the already blackened area that had burned last week. They couldn't go any farther south, or any other direction for that matter, the flames had trapped them in. On a hillside about fifty acres wide, they sat surrounded by flames and watched. There was nothing else to do.

Caught between the rock hillside and the already burned out area, the fire turned on itself, and raged. The sun fell out of the sky, leaving them in the dark except for the fire itself, an eerie, out of body experience for anyone who hadn't experienced such a thing before. Dark, dark sky, leaping flames into the sky, all around them.

Through Lyndie's translation, Griffin did the best he could to ease everyone's mind, and not for the first time, marveled at how she held up. For an hour they sat there, and then another hour, and then finally, the firestorm was over.

They'd lost forty more acres but not a single soul, and Griffin thought maybe he could lie down and sleep for three weeks. They staggered off the mountain and into the village, everyone going their own separate and exhausted ways.

Griffin found himself in the kitchen of the inn, being fed by Rosa, along with several of the men she had also insisted on feeding. Eventually they went off, leaving him alone.

He didn't want to be alone. Hearing a low murmur of voices, he opened the back door and found Brody and Nina in each other's arms beneath the dark, dark night. "Sorry," he said, and went back inside. He headed into the large living room and found Rosa standing behind Tom's chair, massaging the man's shoulders, her mouth teasing his ear as she whispered something that had Tom looking like a mighty happy man.

Turning to head back into the kitchen, Griffin nearly tripped over a sleeping Tallulah and...Lucifer? Curled up together like they'd come from the same litter.

Damn, he'd never felt more alone in his life. It'd been a long time since he'd had someone in his life to kiss, to massage, to sleep with, someone who could just touch him and make his world seem like a better place.

Too long.

He climbed the stairs, then let himself into Lyndie's room, which was dark. Shutting the door, he moved to the bed, which had a very still lump in the center of it. "Lyndie."

The lump didn't move. She was exhausted, and so was he, but this couldn't wait, not even for one more night. "I've got to get this out," he said softly, and sat on the edge of the mattress.

She still didn't move.

"God, I've screwed up," he murmured. "So many, many times." He sighed. "No one knows better than I that life is too damn short, cruel even, but Lyndie, I can't keep living on the outside looking in just because I might get hurt."

Nothing from the lump.

"Yeah, I know you know this. I know you tried to tell me, so many times. I was such a cocky ass, hiding behind fancy words, telling you I could easily risk again, and teach you to do so as well."

She slept on.

He shook his head. "But I know the truth now. It's okay to fail. Just as it's okay to try again. To live, I mean." He wished she would wake up and look at him with those green eyes. "I can't forget what happened in Idaho, but…I can go on." He drew a deep breath. "Somehow, some way, being here, I've learned that at least, and that my heart is still strong and willing. I'm sorry it took me so long to see it, Lyndie, but there's no going back now. I love you."

A soft gasp came not from the lump on the bed, but behind him, and he whipped around. There, at the window, stood the small, petite silhouette of a woman. He turned back to the bed, yanking off the covers to reveal…her pillow. "I thought you were sleeping."

The silhouette straightened. "I'm not."

He stepped toward her at the exact moment she took one step toward him. They collided, and he used the excuse to slide his arms around her warm, curvy body. "You fit against me like you were made for me," he whispered.

She hesitated for a moment, and then slipped her arms around his neck. "Would you have said those things to me if you'd known I was awake?"

"Yes."

"Could you say them again?"

"How about I finish first?" Cupping her face, he tilted it up to his. He still couldn't see, so he reached out and flipped on a light, looking deeply into her blinking eyes. "I've felt homeless this past year, and I hated that. I'm not meant to be homeless, Lyndie. I want a place where I belong, and I want it with you. So now I figure all I have to do is convince you that you want that too, when you've never yearned for stability before."

She took a shuddering breath. "You might be shocked to know what I've yearned for lately." She lifted her hands to cover his. "I don't enjoy being on my own as much as I thought. I found that I like having someone worry about me, care about me. Want me."

She shot him a wet smile. "The way you do all those things takes my breath, Griffin."

He stared at her. "I love you so much. I didn't think I could, and I sure as hell fought it, but I don't know why. You make me want to be a better man, you make me smile, you make me whole." He held her tight. "I love you with everything I have. I hope to hell that's enough because I don't want to be without you. For the first time in a year, I want stability, I want love. I want a home."

She pulled back enough just to look into his eyes. "I love you, so much it terrifies me. And I want a home, too."

"Where?" he whispered.

"Anywhere. As long as it's with you."

Epilogue

Straighten out, straighten out!" Lyndie yelled.

Griffin grinned and did just that, leveling the Cessna out with a skill that shouldn't have surprised her. Beneath them the majestic canyons and peaks of Mexico took her breath.

And for the first time in her history of flying, her eyes crossed with dizziness, damn him.

"Admit it, I'm a quick learner." He smiled. "Come on, show me the next step. Let's land this baby."

"No 'let's.' *I'm* landing. You, you're crazy."

"Fun-sucker." But he let her take over. On the ground in San Puebla, he got out first, then scooped her off her feet as she went to jump down. His mouth covered hers for a deep, hot, wet kiss that effectively rid her of any lingering annoyance. When he pulled back, he cupped her face. "What are you mad at?"

"You learned to fly so quickly."

"Because you're a good teacher."

"No," she said. "I yelled at you the whole time. You learned because you're good at stuff. At everything." She looked over his shoulder at her beloved Cessna. "And that's all I'm good at." She hated the admission.

Hating it even more when he laughed.

"I'm sorry," he said when she glared at him. "But baby, that's the stupidest thing I've ever heard." Leaning in, he kissed her again.

Not willing to be sidetracked, no matter how gorgeous he was or how he melted her bones every time he put his mouth to hers, she slapped a hand on his chest, holding him off.

He looked at her with those seductive, sexy eyes. "You can't really think that flying is the only thing you do well—" He wrapped her close in his arms, putting them nose-to-nose. "My God, you do. Lyndie, do you know what I first loved about you?"

"No." Even after all this time, she could hardly believe he loved her at all.

"Your strength, your passion."

"Sam calls it stubborn and hotheaded."

"You're also giving," he said, smiling. "And incredibly sweet."

She scoffed.

"Do you know what else I love about you, Lyndie?" he asked, cupping her face until she melted. "How much you love me. You do that pretty damn well. So much so that it still takes my breath away."

She stared up into his eyes. "I am pretty good at loving you, aren't I?"

"Yeah, and you know what *else* you're good at?" He put his mouth to her ear but before he could say anything, Brody got out of the Jeep parked on the tarmac.

"Oh, jeez," he called out. "Get a room."

Nina hopped out of the passenger seat of the Jeep. "Don't you listen to him, he's just grumpy because he didn't get so lucky this morning." She grinned. "I was on the Internet planning our trip to Spain next summer. We're going to go and teach English to a group of village kids." She practically glowed. "Exciting, huh?"

"Very." Though personally, Lyndie preferred something a little closer to home these days.

Now that she had one, that is—with Griffin. They'd made his little place on the California coast their own; traveling often, to South Carolina to see his family and friends, to Mexico, to wherever she needed to fly, always accommodating his own work schedule with the SDFD.

"I plan to reward his patience tonight," Nina said, arching her eyebrows up and down suggestively, making Brody smile like a hopeful fool.

"Did you bring the computers?" Brody came in close to inspect the cargo load he'd had donated to San Puebla's library and school with his stateside contacts.

"Got 'em." Griffin smiled at Lyndie, and again, as it had all year now, her heart skipped a beat. "We're ready for your party."

"Oh, that." Nina feigned nonchalance for exactly two seconds before dancing in a circle. "We have everything ready, the food, the music, the beautiful setting off the inn terrace all decorated with so many flowers you won't believe it. I'm so excited, my one year anniversary! I can't wait to see your dress!" She dropped midtwirl and looked at Lyndie in horror. "Tell me you're wearing a dress to my party."

Lyndie rolled her eyes. "Yeah, yeah. Now get out of the way." She hopped into the Jeep. "*I'm* driving."

"Of course you are." Griffin leaned in to kiss her before hopping over her to the shotgun seat. But when he got a good look at her and her sudden solemnity, his smile faded. "Lyndie? Baby, what's the matter?"

Damn it, did he see everything? "Nothing."

He stopped her from starting the engine with a hand to her wrist. "It's something."

All right, yes it was. A big something. A big, horrifying realization that had her throat burning. "Why don't you want to be married to me?"

Griffin blinked.

In the backseat came Nina's surprised choked breath.

"Is it because you don't want to be married to a crabby, bossy, know-it-all woman?" Lyndie whispered.

"No." Reaching out, Griffin took her hand and looked at her ringless fingers. "I've brought up marriage several times this past year, and every time I did, you laughed at me. You said it was nothing but a silly little piece of paper. I thought I had to work my way up to it, talk you into it, get you used to the idea."

"That took about a week," she admitted softly.

"Lyndie." He looked like one good breeze could have blown him over. "Marriage with you would be the second greatest thing to happen to me. You're the first greatest thing," he pointed out. "In case you didn't realize. I love you, with all my heart."

"Enough to be married to me?"

"Yes. God, yes."

"All right." She offered him a shaky smile. "Then, yes, I'll marry you. If you're asking."

"Oh, I'm asking," he said, and got out of the Jeep. He pulled her out, too. Then, before Brody and Nina, before the remote, dizzy peaks and canyons around them, he went down on his knees and shot her an endearingly shaky smile. "Lyndie Anderson, keeper of my heart, love of my life…will you marry me? Will you be mine forever and ever, and give me that silly little piece of paper that says it's legal, the one I want so badly?"

"Yes," she whispered. "I will." With tears in her eyes, nearly blinding her, she smiled over at Nina. "*Now* I have a reason to wear that dress."

"Here?" Griffin asked incredulous. "Now?"

"As soon as we can get your parents down here. Again. Somehow I don't think they'll mind." Lyndie let off her first real smile of the day. Looking at him took her breath, how could she have ever not been sure? "I'm so lucky to have you, Griffin."

"Oh, no, you've got that backward." He ran his hand down the hair she'd let grow to her shoulders. "I never thought I'd get another chance at happiness, but you've given it to me. I can't imagine my life without you, Lyndie. Without us."

Because she couldn't help it, she leaned in and gave him the public display of affection she usually shunned, giving him a long, wet, sloppy kiss. When she pulled back, she was grinning. "Onward?" She put the Jeep into gear, revving the engine as both Brody and Nina hopped into the backseat.

"Onward," Griffin vowed. "Forever."

About the Author

New York Times bestselling author Jill Shalvis has written over four dozen romance novels, including her acclaimed sexy contemporary series set in Lucky Harbor. The RITA Award–winner and 3-time National Readers Choice Award–winner makes her home in a small town in the Sierras. You can find Jill's award-winning books wherever romances are sold and visit her website for a complete book list and daily blog detailing her city-girl-living-in-the-mountains adventures.

You can learn more at:

JillShalvis.com
Twitter @jillshalvis
Facebook.com/jillshalvis

Look for another Jill Shalvis story featuring a sexy firefighter, coming soon from Forever Yours.

Please see the next page for a preview of

Blue Flame

Prologue

Dangling from a third-story window ledge wasn't a good thing. Dangling from a third-story window ledge by the tips of his fingers, with fire blazing all around him was even worse, and though Jake Rawlins had been in tougher situations, at the moment he couldn't remember one.

"Go away!" cried the young teen, trembling on the very corner of the flaming roof above him. "Go away!"

Jake adjusted his precarious perch, and eyed the kid. "I'm a firefighter, I'm here to help you. Just don't—"

The boy scrambled out of Jake's reach.

"—move." Damn it. Apparently nothing about this call would be easy tonight. So far, he had a mansion of a house on fire in the dead of the night; occupants caught unawares on a rural street, with the fire hydrant just far enough away to create a sea of hoses at his crew's feet, all on hilly, uneven land in the outskirts of San Diego county. Oh, and a terrified teen sitting above the inferno, on a roof, holding one arm against his chest as if he'd injured it.

The winds whipped right at Jake, stirred by the fire itself, trying to tear him from the house. It'd only been two minutes since the ladder engine had malfunctioned, trapping him up there, but it felt like a lifetime. He had at least eight minutes before another ladder engine would arrive. Only problem, the roof wasn't going to last another eight minutes.

"Billy! Somebody get my Billy!" screamed the kid's mother from three stories below. Her terror stabbed at Jake, and fueled him on. Adjusting his grip on the ledge, he reached for the rain gutter, which was thankfully anchored to the house, and began to climb.

The house itself was nothing but a bright ball of flame around him. No one could get through the inferno to get inside, not until they tamed the fire, which his crew was working on from below. Long streams of forced water flew through the air toward the flames, which only seemed to enrage them all the more.

"Mom!" Above Jake, Billy's voice sounded weak and smoke-ravaged.

Jake got high enough to see him again, and his heart nearly stopped. Shaking in terror, Billy sat about three feet back from the ledge, completely surrounded by flames, cradling his arm and screaming. *"Mom!"*

"She can't hear you from there, buddy."

"I didn't mean for this to happen, I didn't!"

Had he started the fire? At the moment it didn't matter. Neither did the fact that as captain of the malfunctioned engine, Jake was usually on the ground, strategizing and organizing the crew, not straddling a rickety rain gutter thirty feet above ground. Christ, he hated heights. "Hang on, now." Jake kept his face averted from the heat and flames blasting toward him, but then the kid shifted to bolt away.

The roof was a goner. A wrong move now, and he could fall through. With no ladder and nothing to brace his foot on, Jake had to use sheer strength to pull himself up, and he felt every one of his hundred and eighty pounds, not to mention the additional sixty-five pounds of gear.

The kid stared at the flames engulfing the roof, flinching as areas began to cave in. *"Mom!"*

"Your mom's safe. Let's do the same for us." With the flames leaping far too close for comfort, Jake reached out for him.

"No!" Whimpering, Billy crawled backward, out of Jake's reach and straight into the danger zone. "I don't wanna go over the edge!"

Jake could hear more sirens coming closer now. He could feel the mist of the spray his crew were frantically sending around them, trying to keep them safe. "Billy, we need to go."

"I want to go through the attic door, the way I came!" Dropping to his knees, Billy scooted away from Jake and the feared edge, and directly toward the flames.

Jake understood the height issue, and sympathized more than the kid could know, but there was no help for that. They had to get off the roof, and fast, and they had to go the way Jake had come—via the ledge.

From far below, new swirling lights joined the others, and he knew the other ladder engine had arrived. Relief was cut short by a thundering crash directly on his left. Whipping around, he watched a good part of the roof cave in, including the attic door and stairs.

Billy stared at the gaping hole in horror. Flames immediately filled it, but unbelievably, the kid took a step toward it.

"No." Jake reached out, and got a hold of Billy's shoe, which promptly came off. *Shit.* With his other hand, he caught the kid's ankle, but lost in his fear, Billy thrashed around.

"It's okay," Jake tried to soothe. "I've got you—" He took a well-placed kick to his chest, which nearly sent them both over the edge of the three-story house.

"I want to get down!"

"Yeah, but not the way the stairs and attic door just went, okay?"

Another crash, and only three feet away this time, and more of the roof vanished. Jake's stomach dropped to his toes. It was now or never. With the hot, unforgiving wind whipping his face and the smoke clogging his lungs, he got a better grip on Billy, trying to be careful with the injured arm. "Hold it tight to you." Jake spread a protective hand over the limb as best he could. "The ladder's here."

"We're going down on a fire engine ladder?"

"Yep." Holding on to Billy, Jake leaned slightly over the edge to take a look. Indeed, the malfunctioned engine had been moved, and the new one was in position, the ladder inching its way up.

It felt like slow motion. Another roaring boom came directly behind them, and Billy cried out, clinging to Jake.

Jake's gaze met Steve's, the firefighter on the end of the ladder. The silent urgency passed between them as more of the roof dissolved around them. They were running out of time.

Steve reached out but was still too far away. It was going to be too damn late. Jake could feel the immense heat beneath him, all around him. He figured he had less than a minute to get them down before there wasn't a square foot to stand on.

The ladder bumped the building, and Steve reached for Billy, whose one good thin arm was wrapped so tightly around Jake's neck that he could hardly breathe. "Billy, Steve's going to take you down."

"I want you to do it!"

Again Jake's gaze met Steve's. They didn't have time to switch positions, not with fire raining down over them, the ladder slick from the hose. Jake pulled free of Billy's grip and shoved him at Steve.

An ominous rumble came from beneath Jake's feet. Steve was still right there with Billy, trying to get out of the way for Jake, but the flames whipped up from below, taking over the ledge, forcing Jake back another step, separating him from Steve and Billy by a wall of fire.

Who would miss him? came the inane thought. His mother? Nope. His brother? Double nope. Cici, the beautiful brunette he'd seen twice and who'd been so hot just last night? Yeah, maybe *she'd* miss him—

The roof gave beneath his feet, and he fell.

And fell.

* * *

Jake opened his eyes to find himself still in the hospital, where he'd been for two days. He lay there and listened to his pretty little nurse kick some serious reporter ass.

"No, you can't talk to him," she said furiously into the telephone by his bed. Candy—or was it Cindy?—was the quintessential California girl—blond, tanned, five foot two tops, with a sweet curvy little bod that Jake watched quiver indignantly.

"I have no idea how you people got this room number but you have to stop calling," she said. "Firefighter Rawlins doesn't want to talk to the *Times,* the *Gazette, People,* or *US Weekly.* Nobody. Got that?" She slammed down the phone, gave an incensed little huff, then shot Jake a smile of pure gold as she blew her too long bangs out of her eyes. "There. That should buy you five minutes of peace. Want me to take the phone out of here?"

"Nah, they'll give up eventually."

"I doubt that." Moving to his IV, she skimmed a consoling hand up his arm before she shot him up with the morphine he'd required since his reconstructive shoulder surgery the day before. Amazingly enough, other than his crushed shoulder, he had only a concussion and a few second-degree burns on his back. Not bad, considering. The euphoria from the drugs kicked in, and he began floating happily. In and out...

He came to sometime later, apparently in the middle of a conversation with his good friend, fire inspector Joe Walker. He was leaning over Jake's hospital bed with a look in his eyes that Jake hadn't seen since they'd lost Danny in that horrific building fire six months ago. "I'm not dead," Jake said quickly, craning his neck to catch the welcome sight of his monitors, and the equally welcome movement on the screen indicating he was indeed breathing.

A shadow of a smile crossed Joe's face. "No. Apparently you have nine lives."

"Well then, stop looking at me like that."

Joe's expression didn't change, and Jake's heart started a heavy drumming. Ah, shit. What was the matter? What hadn't they told him? What had he missed while in la-la land? He could see his toes, could even wriggle them—

"Look, Jake. I know firefighting is everything to you." Joe's eyes looked suspiciously shiny. "Jesus, how can I not know that? I've watched you risk life and limb on this job for years. I saw how you hated being injured last year, having to work on the hiring board instead of fighting fires, but..."

Jake closed his eyes to the torment in Joe's voice. Now all he could hear was the steady bleep bleep of his monitors, no longer assuring because maybe whatever was wrong was something he couldn't see. He wouldn't have a clue, as another extremely cute little nurse had just slipped some more excellent drugs into his IV. "Just tell me what you're dancing around."

"They think you're done firefighting."

No. He wasn't done, he couldn't be. *But what if he was?* Maybe he couldn't feel anything because they'd had to cut off his arm—Flailing out with his left hand he slapped at his right shoulder. White hot pain stabbed at him, and he sagged back, gasping. Nope. Arm still there, just numb from the neck block he'd required on top of the anesthesia. "I'll heal." He grimaced and breathed through the pain. "I'll heal and get back to work."

The sympathy in Joe's gaze was far scarier than a thirty-foot fall through hell had been. "You'll need time," he said. "Lots of it and preferably away from here and the media."

Ah, yes, the media. Turned out little Billy *had* broken his arm. Joe and the other inspector on the case suspected that it'd been broken while Billy had been lighting his own house on fire, but the kid claimed Jake had been rough with him, breaking the limb while grabbing and shaking Billy on the roof.

To add insult to injury, Billy's mother was threatening to file a suit against the city, the fire department, and Jake himself, a situation made worse when Jake had groggily picked up the phone an hour after his surgery, telling some reporter that the kid must be on crack as well as being a pyromaniac if he thought Jake would do that.

The press had had a field day with that comment, and Billy's mother had decided to add a civil suit against Jake for defaming her boy in the press, all of which had warranted Jake more publicity than he'd ever wanted.

Joe was surveying the room, and all the flowers Jake had received. "Fan club?"

"Better than the stack of ugly faxes waiting for me at the nurses' station." His words slurred a little, thanks to the drugs. "There's a whole bunch of people who actually believe I hurt that kid, and want to kick my ass."

"And there's a whole bunch of women who just want to kiss it." He flicked a note attached to a basket of roses: *Roses are red, violets are blue, call me when you're better, and our last rendezvous we'll redo.* "Call her," he suggested. "Let her be a slave to your every whim and need for a while."

It was a running joke at the station that Jake could date a different woman every night for a year and not have to repeat unless he chose to. But none of them would be interested in him at the moment, not a one. Sad to admit, but for all the years that he'd been there for others, most of them complete strangers, he had few true connections. So here he was now, needing a little help to disappear, maybe a little TLC to go with that help, and he couldn't think of anyone to call.

Not a single soul.

* * *

Three weeks later Jake stared up at the weights he was trying to pull down to his chest at the orders of his physical therapist, feeling one hundred and two instead of thirty-two. Both mentally and physically exhausted, he'd begun to despair over his shoulder, and how he hadn't bounced back as he'd thought. They'd warned him after the surgery that a reconstructed shoulder wouldn't be a walk in the park, but he hadn't believed it.

He couldn't believe a number of things, including how hard it was dodging the curious reporters at his house on the Del Mar bluffs, or how antsy he felt not working, not doing anything but getting tired of daytime TV.

"Take a cruise," Joe suggested from his perch on the next bench over. He came to Jake's physical therapy as often as he could, offering support and dirty jokes as needed.

But a cruise wasn't feasible. Firefighters weren't exactly rolling in dough, and Jake sank every last penny he had into a down payment on his house last year, and was now the proud owner of a mortgage up to his eyeballs.

"Family reunion?" Joe suggested.

"Nah." Jake's mother was currently enjoying conning her sixth or seventh husband out of his retirement, and wouldn't welcome him. Jake's father—husband number two—had died two years ago. Richard Rawlins had left Jake his guest ranch, the Blue Flame, a place out in the middle of Nowhere, Arizona, where people worked like a dog, camped out on rocky ground, and paid for the pleasure. As a city guy who didn't feel the draw of the great Wild West, Jake had pretty much left it to run itself.

It was thirty acres surrounded by three thousand more of open land in the Dragoon Mountains National Forest, reputedly one of the most beautiful areas in Arizona, which might have been exciting for the value factor, if it had value. But the truth was, the place barely broke even most months, and there'd been several where it hadn't even done that. "Maybe I could go to the Blue Flame."

Joe laughed, then got serious when Jake didn't crack a smile. "But you hate camping."

"Yeah." He also hated that his father, a man who hadn't bothered with Jake in life, had in death tried to tie him to a place that meant nothing except a reminder of a relationship he'd never had. "So how about I just go back to work instead?"

"You know what the doctor said."

He'd said it wasn't looking good for Jake to get his shoulder back to fit condition, at least not fit enough for the heavy demands firefighting would put on it. Jake didn't want to think about that. His cell phone rang so he didn't have to, and since he had his hands on the weights, Joe answered it for him.

His friend listened for a moment, then lifted a brow. "No, I don't think Firefighter Rawlins is interested in doing a spread for *Playgirl*—How much?" His gaze flew to meet Jake's while he let out a whistle, but slowly shook his head. "Sorry. That's...shocking, but no." He disconnected, then shot Jake a speculative look. "I had no idea they paid so much."

Jake didn't respond because it was taking all his energy to lift weights. Actually, he wasn't lifting so much as budging.

Budging while his muscles trembled like a newborn baby and sweat broke out on his brow. And then suddenly a microphone was shoved in his face by a man wearing a *Tribune* badge.

"Jake Rawlins, what will you do if your victim wins his case? Will you be forced to quit?"

Shocked, Jake blinked up at him. Forced to quit the job that was everything to him? For saving a kid's life?

"Have you admitted guilt?" the reporter asked.

Fury filled him so fast his head spun, but Joe's hand settled on his chest, holding him down. "Ignore him," Joe warned quietly, then stood and hauled the reporter up to his toes. "We're busy here."

The reporter, feet swinging above the ground, paled. "Y-yes, I see that."

"Then why are you still here?"

When the reporter had high-tailed it out the door, Jake lay back, one thing suddenly crystal clear. He did need out. He'd go to the only place he could think of, and the last place anyone would look for him. The last place he wanted to be.

The Blue Flame.

1

The rocky wooded canyons stretched to the sharp azure sky, unmarred by so much as a single cloud. Spring had been generous so far, and manzanita, mesquite, and Arizona oak grew in bountiful supply. In the center of all this glory a little piglet pumped its short legs, squealing as it ran from a second little piglet, right across the newly seeded area of the front lawn. A third little piglet chased its tail in circles in the flower bed in front of the big house. Piglet number four sat on its own, happily eating the garden hose.

Piglets five, six, seven, eight, nine, and ten were creating mayhem in the hen pen. Hens screamed and squawked, racing around as if their heads had been cut off, with the pigs in merry pursuit.

Callie Anne Hayes opened the front door of the big house, stepped onto the wraparound porch, and beheld all this in disbelief.

One day away from a highly anticipated spring season of the Blue Flame Guest Ranch, a season she'd carefully orchestrated to be flawless…just one day. Clearly, things had been going too smoothly. Hen feathers flew through the air. Dust and dirt rose in a cloud, and above it all came the incredible sound of pigs in heaven and hens in hell.

Amazingly enough, Shep slept on at the bottom of the stairs, oblivious. Callie nudged the old shepherd's hindquarters, but he just kept snoring.

Callie sighed, and eyeing pigs chasing hens chasing pigs, lifted the walkie-talkie at her hip. "The piglets are on the loose and destroying everything in sight. The latch must have broken. Help pronto, please."

She got nothing back. "Tucker? Stone? Eddie? Marge? A little help?"

Still, no one answered, but at least she knew why. This was her crew's last day off. Tomorrow they had a large group of Japanese businessmen coming in, and directly on their heels, a group of Tucson librarians, and then some professional football cheerleaders on break from the various teams they cheered for. After that, a reunion for a group of nine sisters, and then some frat boys. In fact, for the foreseeable future, the Blue Flame was nicely booked.

Knowing that, everyone had made their last day their own, and if she knew her crew, they'd all escaped at the crack of dawn that morning so she couldn't find something to keep them busy.

Which left her on little piggy detail. She headed down the stairs. The two little guys on the grass first, she decided. They had to be caught before they destroyed the new, tender shoots. She chased them around a large Arizona oak, where the two piglets ran smack into each other, and then sat stunned. Scooping one under each arm, she marched them back to their pen. Brushing herself off, she went to shut the gate, figuring she'd duct tape it for now if she had to, but the latch wasn't broken at all.

Whoever had fed them their slop this morning must have gotten lazy. "Damn it, Tucker." He was one of her youngest employees but the twenty-year-old was usually much more vigilant than this.

Bracing herself, she turned around to go about the next capture, assisted now by Goose, an oversized, bossy female Pilgrim goose they kept around as a sort of mascot who ran the grassy area and front walk like a drill sergeant. Together they corralled the pigs while Shep slept on, and thirty minutes later there was only one stubborn little piglet left to nab. He was currently running from her as fast as his short little legs would carry him, his curlicue tail swinging around madly as he squealed loud enough to wake the dead.

She chased him around the large front yard, gritting her teeth as he led her back over the baby grass, followed by a honking Goose, who hated it when anyone happened onto "her" grass. Around the trees again, and then toward the water pump and hose at the side of the house, which one of the little pigs had already destroyed. Callie pictured a new account in her expenses this month labeled *Ridiculous Costs* and cringed.

To complicate matters, someone had left the hose on, and by the looks of things, water had been leaking all night, turning the entire area to mud.

The little piglet stopped to enjoy the sloppy mess, joyfully rubbing its snout in it. When it saw Callie coming, it prepared to run.

And to think she'd thought today had had perfection written all over it, the beginning of spring, a new time for the ranch, where she'd hopefully prove that the Blue Flame was worth every second of stress it caused the current owner—that is if Jake Rawlins ever even gave this place a second of his thoughts, period. She'd bet her last dollar he didn't, which really ate at her because she'd give her left arm to own the Blue Flame.

But that was a worry for another day. Not today. Today was to be her calm before the storm, and if it hadn't been for the out-of-control pigs, she wouldn't have been able to take her eyes off her surroundings. God, she loved this place, where people could come to relax on a ranch setting, or join in and work it alongside her ranch crew.

The Blue Flame had been the first real home she'd ever had, and it held her heart, her soul, her very inner spirit. She scanned the three hundred and sixty degree vista around her. At an altitude of five thousand feet, the hundred square miles of national forest around her had been unchanged for centuries, probably longer. The Dragoon and Chiricahua Mountains, the Sulphur Springs Valley, the stories of Cochise, of his Chiricahua Apache braves, the legends of Geronimo, the feast of the Buffalo Soldiers…so much history right here.

In fact, the big house behind her had its own history. Once upon a time it'd been a country farmhouse for an early settler and his Indian wife, but now it was where their guests stayed in quaint rooms and shared meals together. The place reflected the air of the Old West, meaning rugged, which was more by necessity than design. It was actually in desperate need of renovation, but they hid that behind all the warm, friendly service they offered.

The house sat on a slight hill, overlooking the rest of the ranch. The large wooden deck housed their hot tub, all cleaned and ready for use. Each bedroom was neat and clean as well, and decorated with individual furnishings, all in poor farmhouse chic. The heart of the house was the living room, where ranch hands and guests alike all gathered. There was a large brick hearth there for long winter evenings, and the place looked hopefully inviting despite the fact they hadn't replaced the scarred hardwood flooring last year because profits hadn't allowed for it.

But this year would be different. As ranch manager, Callie had spent long nights working on their website. She'd scrimped in every way possible to spend more money on advertising, and as a result they were getting more bookings every week.

A surge of excitement went through her, as it did every time she thought about the Blue Flame slowly turning itself around from the dump it'd been two years ago; and she knew she'd had a big hand in that.

She moved up on the wayward piglet. "Stay right there," Callie said softly, coming up on him, hands out. "Just stay right there…" She dove for him, at the exact moment the cell phone at her hip rang.

With a squeal, the pig ran off, and Callie landed in the mud, arms empty. Lifting her head, she wiped her face off on her sleeve and reached back for the phone. "Hello?"

"Hello, Callie. I'd like to book a room."

Sprawled on her stomach, filthy now, Callie went absolutely still. That voice. She hadn't heard it in a good long while, but she hadn't forgotten it.

It belonged to Jake Rawlins, the one man who had the ability to destroy her perfect life, to have her at his mercy with five short words— *"I'm selling the Blue Flame."* He was the only man who could drive her crazy, and the last man to have seen her naked.

She'd rather chase fifty more piglets than talk to him. "You need a room? Why?"

"Why?" He gave off a soft laugh that both grated and thrilled. "Because I thought I'd come stay for a while. Get some pampering."

Pampering. No one knew better than she that Jake had an overabundance of charm and charisma, and thought nothing of using said charm and charisma to get a woman in his bed.…Only a man like Jake would think of coming to a dude ranch to be pampered.

God, she hated to think back to that night of Richard's funeral service. Grief-stricken at the loss of her boss, her mentor, the man who'd once saved her life, she'd contacted his son. She had picked Jake up at the airport, driven him to the church, taken him back to the Blue Flame.

His first time there.

She'd mistaken his low, husky voice for anguish, his quiet, confident movements for ease in his surroundings, and over a bottle of aged whiskey, had thought she'd found a soul mate to grieve with.

She'd really like to blame what had happened next on her sorrow and the whiskey, or on Jake and his amazing voice, his talented mouth, and even more talented fingers. But the truth was, she'd *wanted* to be held that night, to be taken out of herself, to forget.

She'd done exactly that, until she'd realized that what grief she felt, she felt alone, as the only thing Jake had in him for his father was resentment and anger.

Unfortunately she'd been naked and in his arms by then. Kicking him out of her bed had given her great satisfaction...until she was alone again.

She and Jake hadn't talked much since, except to discuss the monthly financials she sent. At least he hadn't uttered those five dreaded words yet. She tried to keep her extremely negative thoughts to herself rather than remind him that he'd like nothing more than to sell this place.

He'd been back to the ranch just twice since Richard's death. Each time had been with a different bimbo—er, woman—at his side and a disinterested smile on his lips as he watched their guests get excited over milking cows and feeding pigs.

Neither time had he indulged in any of the activities available, at least nothing that involved the great outdoors. No, his recreation of choice had been staying in bed with his guest and ringing for room service—which they didn't have.

At least he'd called ahead each time as he was doing now, warning her. She supposed she should be grateful for that consideration. "I'm sorry," she said into her phone. Mud dripped off her nose. "We're booked."

"I didn't tell you when I'm arriving."

"It doesn't matter. We're solid for the month. A group of businessmen is checking in, and we have three more groups booked back to back after they leave."

"I'm sure we can find a spare room," he said easily.

We. That meaning her and the mouse in her pocket, she supposed. "For when?"

"Tonight."

She gripped the cell phone. Mud squished through her fingers. "So soon?"

"Yep." Was that a laugh in his voice? "Why don't you go ahead and finish terrorizing that poor pig first. I'll wait."

Pulling the phone away from her ear, she stared at it, heart hammering in her ears. Another drop of mud dripped from her nose to the receiver.

"I'd offer to help," he said. "But I'm not interested in a mud bath as a part of my pampering."

Lifting her head, she searched her immediate vicinity. Big house at her right, series of small one-room cabins on her left, where the staff lived. One large barn and stables straight ahead, a smaller hay barn beside it, and behind them the open corrals and fields of the ranch. Beyond that, the Dragoon Mountains, where she'd led countless expeditions to abandoned mining camps and old Apache lookout points along mountain precipices and ridges that rolled along as far as the eye could see.

Twisting around, she looked behind her. The new grass, the driveway…and the black truck that hadn't been there before her pig hunt. Leaning against the driver's side stood a man she recognized all too well, despite only seeing him three times in her life.

He looked the same; he always did, which was to say knee-knockingly good. He was just over six feet, with dark hair on the wrong side of his last haircut, thick and unruly to the top of his collar. There was a few days' growth on his lean jaw, and mirrored sunglasses on eyes she knew to be a steely, unsettling shade of gray like his father's had been. He wore a dark blue T-shirt with some emblem she couldn't read over his left pec, probably his firefighter's patch, and nicely fitted Levi's faded in all the stress points. He had running shoes on his feet, not boots, and inwardly she sneered at the thought of him walking in those toward her, in the mud.

Seeming quite unconcerned, his long legs were casually crossed, his broad shoulders relaxed for a man who'd just shown up where he wasn't wanted and knew it.

Or maybe he didn't know it.

In any case, he held his cell phone to his ear, and when he saw her looking at him, he smiled with that mouth that had once nearly made her orgasm from just a kiss, and waved the phone at her.

Gritting her teeth, she pushed herself upright. He looked good and wicked to the bone, which unfortunately she'd learned was a terrible weakness on her part. She had no idea how it was possible to both hate and lust after someone at the same time, but with Jake, she'd always managed it.

Mud dripped off her red tank top, the one she'd put on that morning with a smile and anticipation of the spring ahead. Her fresh, dark blue jeans were now brown. She shoved the phone back onto her belt and put her filthy hands on her equally filthy hips.

To add insult to injury, the last little piglet ran right up to his pen and stood still, waiting to be let in. "I'm feeling hungry for bacon," she hissed at it, then straightened and looked at Jake.

He slid his cell phone into his pocket and shoved his sunglasses to the top of his head, eyeing her with those eyes that made her want to squirm.

She held her breath and waited to hear him say, *"I'm selling the Blue Flame."*

Instead, he smiled a smile of pure sin.

And slowly, slowly, she let out her held breath, trying to remain unmoved. Maybe he really was just here for a visit, just like those other two times since Richard's funeral. Maybe just like then, he'd stay holed up in his room with whatever woman he had with him, appearing only to eat, looking rumpled and sated and far too sexy for his own good.

And then he'd go away, far, far away, until she had enough money saved that she could get herself a big, fat loan and try to buy Blue Flame herself.

That was her dream, and no one could take that from her.

Except him.

Nothing but pure stubborn pride kept her from throwing herself at his feet and begging him to wait to sell until she had enough money to buy. Instead, casual as she could, she opened the pig-pen, let the errant piglet in, then carefully latched it. Then she walked over to him and thrust out her hand.

He stared at it, then smiled. "Formal, given what we've done, don't you think?"

"I was trying to be polite."

"Okay…" Instead of giving her his right hand, he leaned in and kissed her cheek.

She jerked back. "What was that for?"

"A *polite* hello. For two people who've—"

"Don't. Don't you dare say it."

He grinned, and she turned away from the sight because it scraped at her tummy uncomfortably. Like ulcer-inducing uncomfortably. "So you need a room for two?"

"Two?"

She looked back. "Don't you have a woman with you?"

Jake lifted a brow.

"Last time you had a blonde with you," she reminded him. "And the time before that, a different blonde."

"I didn't have a blonde with me the first time I came up here."

No, no he hadn't. He'd had her. A redhead.

His smile spread as he pushed away from the truck and came toward her. "Sweet of you to concern yourself with my social life, but sorry. I'm solo. Unless you're offering—No? Well, then, count me as one."

"So you're here to what? I know it's not to camp, you hate to camp. I know it's not to milk a cow, or to go on a roundup, or hike along ancient Indian trails."

He had his right hand hooked in his front pocket, and lifted his left shoulder. "Like I said, I'm up for some pampering."

"The Blue Flame specializes in camping expeditions, hiking, and ranching activities. Not pampering. You know that."

"You have a hot tub. Food. A massage therapist on call—Macy, if I recall. That'll add up to enough pampering for now." His gaze traveled slowly down her mud-covered body, and then back up again, making every square inch tingle with an awareness that pissed her off. "You're looking a little tense, Callie."

"Oddly enough, I'm feeling a little tense."

"Why?"

"Why?" She let out a disbelieving laugh. "Come on, Jake. You're not that thick."

Uninsulted, his lips curved. "Do you greet all the guests so friendly-like?"

Only the ones who made her world feel like a roller coaster. Damn, she wished she could look at him without remembering what had happened between them on one dark, drunken, foolish night. "I'm sorry." She sounded stiff to her own ear, and lifted her hands to indicate the mud she wore. "Let me take you inside. I'll change, see what accommodations we can find for you, even though I can tell you we really are booked."

"Great."

Great. She told herself she wasn't going to worry. She wasn't going to waste energy thinking about him or what he could do to her life—such as ruin it.

They stepped onto the grass, and with a loud, aggressive honk, Goose waddled toward them, head down, picking up speed as she went.

Jake stopped short.

Goose charged him anyway.

"Goose!"

At Callie's sharp voice, the goose let out one more honk, but slowed. Glared at Jake.

He shook his head. "You haven't eaten that thing yet?"

"She'd be too tough to eat."

His laugh said that he agreed, but he eyed the goose with a healthy mistrust as they walked by her.

Callie tried not to think about why his laugh had somehow softened her, or why his being afraid of a silly goose made her want to hold his hand. Clearly, she had hormonal issues today. Nothing a good hard day of work couldn't cure.

They headed toward the big house, Jake moving with a natural grace that reminded her that she dripped mud with every stiff step she took. She'd never felt more unfeminine or unattractive in her life.

There. Hormonal issue resolved.

"Where is everyone?" he asked.

A safe enough question, and one that didn't surprise her. "Eddie and Stone are most likely in town enjoying their day off." Stone was probably drinking too much, too, she thought with a flicker of worry that she kept to herself.

"Tucson?"

"Tucson's too far for a day run. Three Rocks."

"Three Rocks isn't a town. I blinked on the way in here and nearly missed it."

"Not every place is as big as San Diego."

He lifted a brow in agreement. "Okay, so the Motley Crew is out on the 'town.'"

Callie smiled at the nickname for Stone and Eddie McDermitt. The brothers might have been hell on the myriad of other ranches they'd been fired from because monotony bored them, but the Blue Flame catered to their guests' whims, which always varied, so there was no monotony. She'd known when she'd hired the brothers that she wouldn't be sorry. They had a good work ethic, were fast on their feet, and delighted their guests with their "real cowboy" charm.

In fact, she couldn't have managed without them. That they had some personal problems was another story. "You know Kathy left us last week. I just hired a new cook. Amy Wheeler. I faxed you her employment form? She's probably in town today, too. Marge left yesterday to take a break from cleaning and pre-paring bedrooms, but if I know her, she's at her mother's house doing more of the same, and Lou's looking for work as he just got laid off from his full-time job in town."

"Lou?"

"You remember Marge's husband? He works for us on an as-needed basis doing all our mechanical stuff?"

"Right. But I guess when I said others, I meant Tucker."

Now that did surprise her. "His day is his own today as well."

Jake nodded, and she couldn't tell if he was relieved or disap-pointed.

"So why are *you* here today?" he asked. "Don't you ever take time off from this place?" He looked around as if he couldn't un-derstand why one would choose to spend their free time out here. That insulted her, and since she couldn't come up with something nice to say, she took a lesson from Thumper's mother and said nothing at all.

They stepped onto the porch that might have needed some re-finishing, but did he have to look at it like it wouldn't hold their weight? She kicked off her muddy boots, not wanting to ruin the clean floors inside. Opening the door, she gestured him in ahead, but he stopped in the doorway with her and put his hand on her arm.

She looked down at his fingers on her skin, then up into his face. He was crowding her, darn it. Please, God, don't let him say he was selling. Not yet. She wasn't ready yet—

"I saddled you with him," he said quietly. "Is it working out?"

It took a moment for her brain to shift gears. "You mean Tucker?"

He nodded, and she let out a low laugh. "You 'saddled' me with him nearly two years ago. You're just now asking?" She shook her head. "Tucker is amazing with the horses. This place is better for having him here. You should know that. You *would* know that if you'd looked around at all on your last two visits."

Jake's steely gaze searched hers. "I'm just making sure. He's stubborn as hell, and hard-headed to boot."

"And brooding and moody, too. All traits that run in the family, I'm taking it."

"He's only my half brother."

She knew this, of course. She knew far too much about this man that stood too close. "Look, make yourself at home, okay?" He would anyway. He had every right to do so more often than he did. She needed to remember that, and be grateful this was probably no longer a visit than his others had been. "I'll be back in a few." She turned to go back out, but they were still in the doorway together, too close in her opinion, and she accidentally bumped into him, making him hiss out a breath. "Sorry," she said, a little surprised at his reaction.

His expression shuttered. "No problem."

She looked him over, trying to figure out what she was missing, but he gave off no clue. "When I get back, I'll try to figure out where to put you for a few nights—"

"More than a few."

"So…three or four?"

"Yeah, three or four. *Months.*"

And he turned and walked into the living room.

Please see the next page for a sneak peak at the upcoming novel
in Jill Shalvis's bestselling Lucky Harbor series,

It Had to Be You

Chapter 1

Some things were set in stone: The sun would rise every morning, the tide would come in and out without fail, and a girl needed to check herself out in the mirror before a date no matter the obstacle. To that end, Ali Winters climbed up on the toilet seat to get a full view of herself in the tiny bathroom mirror of the flower shop where she worked. Ducking so that she didn't hit her head on the low ceiling, she took in her reflection. Not bad from the front, she decided, and carefully spun around to catch the hind view of herself in her vintage—aka thrift store—little black dress.

Also not bad.

She'd closed up Lucky Harbor Flowers thirty minutes ago to get ready for the town's big fundraiser tonight, where they were hopefully going to raise the last of the money for the new community center. Earlier, she'd spent several hours delivering and decorating Town Hall with huge floral arrangements from the shop, as well as setting up a display of her pottery for the auction. She was excited about the night ahead, but Teddy was late.

Nothing unusual. Her boyfriend of four months was perpetually late but such a charmer it never seemed to matter. He was the town clerk, and on top of being widely beloved by just about everyone who'd ever met him, he was also a very busy guy. He'd been in charge of the funding for the new community center, a huge undertaking, so most likely, he'd just forgotten that he'd promised to pick her up. Hopefully.

Still precariously balanced, she eyed herself again, just as there was a sudden knock on the bathroom door. Jerking upright in surprise, she hit her head on the ceiling and nearly toppled to the floor. Hissing in a breath, she gripped her head and carefully stepped down. Managing that without killing herself, she opened the door to her boss, Russell, the proprietor of Lucky Harbor Flowers.

Russell was in his mid-thirties and reed thin, with spiked blond hair, bringing him to just above her own almost-but-not-quite, five foot five. He was wearing red skinny pants and a half tucked–in red-and-white checkered polo shirt. These were his favorite golf clothes, though he didn't golf, because he objected to sweating. He was holding a ceramic pot filled with an artful array of flowers in each hand.

Ali took in the two arrangements, both colorful and cheerful, and—if she said so herself—every bit as pretty as the pots, which were hers too.

"What's wrong with this picture?" Russell asked.

She let go of the top of her head. "Um, they're all kinds of awesome?"

"Correct," Russell said with an answering smile. "But they're also all kinds of waste. No one ordered these, Ali."

"Yes, but they'll look fantastic in the window display." An age-old argument. "They'll draw people in," she said, "and *then* someone will order them."

Russell sighed with dramatic flair. The flower shop had been his sister Mindy's until two years ago, when he'd bought it from her so that she could move to Los Angeles with her new boyfriend. "Sweetkins, I pay you to make floral arrangements because no one in Lucky Harbor does it better. I love your ceramic-ware and think you're a creative genius. I also think that genius is completely wasted on the volunteer classes you give at the senior center, but that's another matter entirely. You already know that I think you give too much of yourself to others. Regardless of that big, warm heart of yours, *you* make the arrangements. *I* run the business."

Ali bit her tongue so she wouldn't say what she wanted to. If he would listen to her ideas, they'd increase business. She was sure of it.

"And speaking of the shop," he went on, "we need to talk sometime soon. Um, you might want to fix your hair."

She turned her neck and glanced in the mirror. Eek. Her wildly wavy hair did need some taming. She quickly worked on that. "Better?"

"Some," Russell said with a smile, and put the flowers down to fix her hair himself. "Where's your cutie-pie, live-in boyfriend?"

Two months ago, her apartment building had been scheduled for lengthy renovations, and Ali had needed a place to stay. Teddy had generously offered to share his place. He was like that, open and warm and generous. And fun. There hadn't been a lot of that in her life. And then there was the pride of being in a real, adult relationship.

So she'd happily moved into his beach house rental, and suddenly everything she'd ever dreamed of growing up—safety, security, and stability—was right there. Her three favorite S's. "Teddy's late," she said. "I'll just meet him there."

Russell peered at her over the top of his square, black-rimmed glasses. "Don't tell me that Hot Stuff stood you up again."

"Okay, I won't tell you."

"Dammit." He sighed. "The sexy ones are all such unreliable bitches." He hugged her. "Forgive me for my complaint about the fabulous arrangements?"

"Of course. What did you want to talk about?"

A shadow passed over Russell's face but he quickly plastered on a smile. "It can wait. Come on, I'll take you to the auction myself. I want to get there before all the good appetizers are gone."

"How do you know there'll be good appetizers?"

"Tara's cooking."

Tara Daniels Walker ran the local B&B with her sisters, and she was the best chef in the county. Definitely worth rushing for.

Russell drove them in his Prius. Lucky Harbor was a picturesque little Washington beach town nestled in a rocky cove with the Olympic Mountains at its back and the Pacific Ocean at its front. The town itself was a quirky, eclectic mix of the old and new. The main drag was lined with Victorian buildings painted in bright colors, housing cute shops and a bar and grill called The Love Shack, along with the requisite grocery store, post office, gas station, and hardware store. A long pier jutted out into the water, and lining the beach was a café named Eat Me, an arcade, an ice cream shop, and a huge Ferris wheel.

People came to Lucky Harbor looking for something, some to start over and some for the gorgeous scenery of the Olympic Mountains and the Pacific Ocean. Ali was one of those looking for a new start. The locals were hardy, resilient, and, as a rule, stubborn as hell. She had all three of these characteristics in spades, especially the stubborn as hell part.

They parked at the Town Hall building at the end of the commercial row, and found the place filled to capacity.

"Look at all the finery," Russell said as they walked in, sounding amused. "For that matter, look at us. We're smoking hot, Cookie."

"That we are."

"Not bad for a pair of trailer park kids, huh?"

Ali had grown up in a rough area of White Center, which was west of Seattle. Russell had done the same but in Vegas, though he'd made himself a more-than-decent living in his wild twenties as an Elvis impersonator. About ten years ago, he moved to Lucky Harbor with his sister. Ali actually hadn't ever lived in a trailer park, but in a series of falling down, post–WWII crackerbox houses that were possibly even worse. Lucky Harbor was a sweet little slice of life that neither of them had imagined for themselves. "Not bad at all," she agreed.

They entered the hall to the tune of laughter and music and the clink of glasses. Ali caught a fleeting glimpse of Teddy working the crowd, gorgeous as ever in a suit and good-old-boy smile, which he flashed often. His light brown hair was sun kissed from weekends golfing, fishing, hiking, and whatever other adventures he chose. Extremely active and fit, he'd try anything that was in the vicinity of fun. It was one of the things that had drawn her to him.

He caught sight of her and smiled, and Ali's heart sighed just looking at him. She called it the Teddy Phenomenon, because it wasn't just her—everyone seemed to respond to him that way.

But then she realized he was smiling at the pretty server behind her, who then turned and walked into a wall. Ali shook her head and sipped her champagne. She got it. It was his job, pleasing the public. And he did have a way of making a girl feel like the most beautiful woman in a crowded room.

Mayor Tony Medina took the stage and tapped on the mic to get everyone's attention. A financial advisor, he'd been mayor for coming up on two years now, having taken over when the previous mayor, Jax Cullen, had stepped down from the position to concentrate on his first loves—his family and carpentry.

"Good evening, Lucky Harbor!" Tony called out. "Thanks for coming! Let's all raise our glasses to our very own Ted Marshall, who worked incredibly hard at raising the funds for our new community center."

At that, the crowd whooped and hollered, and Russell nudged Ali. "You worked hard too. Where's your credit?"

"I don't need credit," Ali said, and she didn't. She'd assisted by running car washes and other donation drives to help Teddy behind the scenes, where she was content to stay.

"As you know," Tony went on, "the town council promised to match the funds raised tonight. So without further ado, we're adding a total of *fifty thousand dollars* to the pot tonight."

Everyone cheered.

Teddy hopped up onto the stage with the mayor, hoisting a very large aluminum briefcase. He'd worked damn hard at getting this rec center built for the town, and it was within his sights now. Looking right at home, he smiled. "The build is an official go," he said into the mic. He opened the briefcase and showed off the fifty thousand, neatly stacked and wrapped in bill bands. Obviously it'd come straight from the bank for the reveal, but the crowd ate it up anyway.

After the ceremony, Ali went looking for Teddy. She needed a ride home, not to mention it'd be nice to see her boyfriend. She circled the large room twice to no avail, and then finally headed down the hallway to the offices to check there. She could see the light under Teddy's door, but to her surprise it was locked. Lifting a hand to knock, she went shock still at the low, throaty female moan from within. Wait…that couldn't be…

And then came a deeper, huskier moan.

Teddy.

Ali blinked. No. No, he wouldn't be with someone else…in his office…

"*Oh, babe*, yeah, just like that…"

It was Teddy's sex voice, and Ali got really cold, and then really warm, and she realized she had far bigger problems than finding a ride home.

* * *

Ali woke the next morning, alone. A sympathetic Russell had driven her home. In the dark, she'd paced the big house for a while, steam coming out her ears.

When Teddy hadn't shown up, she'd called her very soon-to-be ex-boyfriend, *twice*, but there hadn't been a return call. She did, however, now have a waiting text:

Babe, this isn't working. It's not you. It's all me. I just need to be alone right now. FYI, our lease ended on 5/31. So no worries, you're free to leave right away.

Ali stared at the words in shock. She hadn't had caffeine yet so her brain wasn't exactly kicking in, but she was pretty sure he'd just broken up with her—by text—and that he'd also rendered her homeless.

Ali pulled up the calendar app on her phone. Yep. Yesterday had been May thirty-first. Flopping back on the bed, she stared up at the ceiling, trying to sort her tumbling emotions.

He'd beaten her to the break up, and after last night, hearing him in the throes and calling someone else "babe," she'd *really* needed to be the dumper not the dumpee. "Damn," she whispered, and sat up.

You're free to leave right away.

Magnanimous of him. And also a vivid reminder. Men came and went. That was the way of it for the Winters women. She'd nearly forgotten that it was a lifetime goal of hers to not perpetuate this pattern, that she needed to be more careful.

She'd remember now. And while she'd like to lie around and plot Teddy's slow, painful death, and maybe wallow with a day in front of the TV and a huge bag of popcorn, she had work to do. She had to get back to Town Hall and take down the floral designs and collect whatever ceramics hadn't sold at the silent auction.

Then she apparently needed to figure out her living situation.

Still stunned, she showered and dressed in jeans and a sweatshirt for loading up boxes and then headed out. The rental house she'd shared with Teddy was high on the cliffs on the far north face of the harbor. It was isolated and not easy to get to, but she didn't mind the narrow road or being off the beaten path. The house itself was old and more than a little creaky, but full of character. Ali loved it and loved the view, and after a childhood of city noises, she loved sleeping to the sound of the waves hitting the rocks.

Normally, early mornings were her favorite part of living in Lucky Harbor. Cool and crisp, the sun was just peeking over the rugged mountains, casting the ocean in a glorious kaleidoscope of light. Beyond the surf, the water was still, a sheet of glass, perfectly reflecting the sky above. A brand new beginning. Every single morning.

Never more so than this morning…

She parked in front of the Town Hall. The place was locked, but Gus the janitor let her in. Mumbling something about getting back to his work, he vanished, and Ali began lugging the heavy floral arrangements out of the building, down the steps, and into her truck by herself. Then she carefully packed up the pottery that hadn't been sold and took that out as well. With every pass she made, she had to walk by Teddy's office, and each time her emotions—mostly anger—coiled tighter and tighter. Her mom and sister had the quick fuses in the family. Ali had always been more of a slow burn, but today she'd gone straight to red-hot ticked off.

When she was finally finished, she searched out Gus again, finding him indeed very busy—kicking back in the staff room watching a ball game on his phone. In his thirties, six feet four and big as a tank, Gus hadn't shaved since sometime last year. He looked like a tough mountain man who belonged on a History Channel show hauling logs—except for the tiny kitten in his big palm.

"Aw," Ali said, softening. "So cute."

At her voice, Gus startled, and with a little girl–like squeal, fell right out of the chair. Still carefully cradling the unharmed kitten, he glared at Ali. "Christ Almighty, woman, make some noise next time. You scared Sweetheart here half to death."

Sweetheart had her eyes half closed in ecstasy. "Yes, I can see that," Ali said wryly, reaching out to pet the adorable gray ball of fluff. "I can also see how very hard the two of you are working back here."

She couldn't tell if Gus blushed behind the thick, black beard, but he did have the good grace to at least look a little bit abashed as he lumbered to his feet. "I wanted to help you," he said, "but I had Sweetheart in my pocket, and the boss told me twice already not to bring her here. But she howls when I leave her home, and my roommate said if I didn't take her with me today, she was going to be his Doberman's afternoon snack."

"Sweetheart's secret is safe with me," Ali said. "I just need to get into Teddy's office for a minute."

Gus scratched his beard. "I'm not supposed to let anyone into the offices."

"I know," Ali said, "and I wouldn't ask, except I left something in there." She'd made Teddy a ceramic pot. It was a knotty pine tree trunk that held pens and pencils, and she'd signed it with her initials. There was no way she was leaving it in his possession. He didn't deserve it. "Please, Gus? I'll only be a minute."

He sighed. "Okay, but only because you guys are always real nice to me. Teddy knows about Sweetheart, and he didn't rat me out." He set the sweet little kitten on his shoulder, where she happily perched, and then led the way to Teddy's office. There he pulled out a key ring that was bigger around than Ali's head, located the correct key by some mysterious system, and opened the office door. "Lock up behind you."

"Will do," Ali said, and as Gus left her, she went straight to Teddy's desk.

No knotty pine pot with the little heart she'd cut into the bottom. She turned in a slow circle. The office was masculine and projected success, and the few times she'd been here, she'd always felt such pride for Teddy.

That's not what she was feeling now. In fact, she sneezed twice in a row at some unseen dust, annoying herself as she looked for the pot. She finally located it in the credenza behind the desk, shoved in the very bottom beneath a bunch of crap. It was the shape of a Silver Pine tree trunk, every last detail lovingly recreated down to the knots and rings around the base. For a minute, Ali stared at the pot she'd been so proud of, shame and embarrassment clogging her throat. Swallowing both, she grabbed it, locked the door as she'd promised, found and thanked Gus, and left.

In her truck, she drew in a deep breath and drove off. It was a Winters's gift, the ability to shove the bad stuff down deep and keep moving. Teddy wasn't even a five on the bad stuff meter, she told herself.

As always in Lucky Harbor, traffic was light. At night, strings of white lights would make the place look like something straight from a postcard, but now, in the early light, each storefront's windows glinted in the bright sunlight.

Things stayed the same here, could be counted on here. She thought maybe it was that—the sense of stability, security, and safety—that drew her the most.

Her three S's.

At least until last night…

She put in her shift at the flower shop, worrying about how light business was. She brought it up to Russell at lunch, gently, that she felt she really had something to offer here, the very least of which was a website. But Russell, equally as gently, rebuked her. Like his sister Mindy before him, he was a technophobe. Hell, even the books were still done by hand, despite their bookkeeper's urging to update their system. Grace Scott, a local bookkeeper, had given up on changing Russell's mind, but Ali was going to bash her head up against his stubbornness, convinced they would make a great partnership.

On her break she used her smartphone to fill out as many online applications for apartments as she could find. By six o'clock, she was back at the beach house, hoping not to run into Teddy. She didn't, which was good for his life expectancy. Even better, the front door key still worked. Bonus. She had a roof over her head for at least one more night.

In the kitchen, she tossed her keys into the little bowl she'd set by the back door to collect Teddy's pocket crap. Out of curiosity, she poked through the stuff there: a button, some change, and…two ticket stubs, dated a week ago for a show in Seattle.

A show she hadn't gone to.

She stared at the stubs, then set them down and walked away. Something else niggled at her as she headed into her bedroom, but she couldn't concentrate on that, because she was realizing that Teddy had been working 24/7 for weeks. And before that, he'd been sick and had slept in a spare bedroom. They hadn't actually slept together in…she couldn't even remember.

Which meant that Ali had been very late to her own break up.

At this, her heart squeezed a little bit. Not in regret. She tried really hard not to do regrets. It wasn't mourning either, not for Teddy, not after hearing him cheat on her. It was the realization that she'd really loved the *idea* of what they'd had more than the actual reality of it.

Sad.

She stripped down to her panties and bra before it occurred to her what the niggling feeling from before was. Reversing her tracks, she ran barefoot back to the large living room.

The house had come fully furnished, but Ted had always made the place his own, thanks to the messy, disorganized way he had of leaving everything spread around. Running shoes hastily kicked off by the front door. Suit jacket slung over the back of the couch. Tie hanging askance from a lamp. His laptop, e-reader, tablet, smartphone, and other toys had always been plugged into electrical outlets, and when they weren't, the cords hung lifeless, waiting to be needed.

Not now. Now it was all gone, even his fancy, highfalutin microbrews from the fridge. Everything was gone, including *her* iPod.

How she'd missed that this morning, she had no idea, but facts were facts—Teddy had moved out on her like a thief in the night.

* * *

Detective Lieutenant Luke Hanover had been away from the San Francisco Police Department for exactly one day of his three-week leave and already he'd lost his edge, walking into his grandma's Lucky Harbor beach house to find a B&E perp standing in the kitchen.

She sure as hell was the prettiest petty thief he'd ever come across—at least from the back, since she was wearing nothing but a white lace bra and a tiny scrap of matching white lace panties.

"You have some nerve you...you *rat fink bastard*," she said furiously into her cell phone, waving her free hand for emphasis, her long, wildly wavy brown hair flying around her head as she moved.

And that wasn't all that moved. She was a bombshell, all of her sweet, womanly curves barely contained in her undies.

"I want you to know," she went on, still not seeing Luke, "there's no way in hell I'm accepting your breakup message. You hear me, Teddy? I'm not accepting it, because *I'm* breaking up with *you*. And while we're at it, who even does that? Who breaks up with someone by text? I'll tell you who, Teddy, a real jerk, that's who— hello? *Dammit!*"

Pulling the phone from her ear, she stared at the screen and then hit a number before whipping it back up to her ear. "Your voice mail cut me off," she snapped. "You having sex in your office while I was in the building? Totally cliché. But not telling me that you weren't planning to re-sign the lease? That's just rotten to the core, Teddy. And don't bother calling me back on this. Oh, wait, that's right, you don't call—you *text*!" Hitting END, she tossed the phone to the counter. Hands on hips, steam coming out her ears, she stood there a moment. Then, with a sigh, she thunked her forehead against the refrigerator a few times before pressing it to the cool, steel door.

Had she knocked herself out?

"It's just one bad day," she whispered while standing in the perfect position for him to pat her down for weapons.

Not that she was carrying—well, except for that lethal bod.

"Just one really rotten, badass day," she repeated softly, and Luke had to disagree.

"Not from where I'm standing," he said.

CPSIA information can be obtained at www.ICGtesting.com
Printed in the USA
BVOW07s1837171013

334038BV00001B/46/P